Fatally Flawed

Thomas Sparrow

VOLUME TWO of the Northwoods *Noir* Trilogy

Bluestone Press

Library of Congress Catalog Card Number - 2002092458

ISBN 0-9672006-2-8

Cover design by Kim McAndrews-Spellerberg

Printed in the United States of America

Bluestone Press
P.O. Box 3196
Duluth MN 55803
218.724-5806
bluestone@duluth.com
www.duluth.com/bluestone

Preface

In his school days, Keith Waverly was like a lot of guys. Smart enough to get by without much effort, good enough to make the team without much work and handsome enough to attract the wrong kind of women.

He always thought of himself as a good boy. Except for a few isolated incidents—labeled "loss of impulse control" by school authorities—he never got in trouble.

Then he turned twenty-two and got married—beautiful blonde with a crazy streak. They had a kid, a little boy. A few years later they were divorced and Keith was back in the bars and back alleys.

Trouble started to find him around 1977. Life seemed to turn black.

"Social Climbing," a short novel in Thomas Sparrow's four-story collection entitled *Northwoods Pulp - Four Tales of Crime & Weirdness*, is part one of the Northwoods *Noir* Trilogy. It finds

Keith in early 1978, trying to change his ways, a recurring theme for him. He is tired of manipulating cards and playing the fool for the guys with the money. He wants to move up from his lousy little jobs and penny-ante deals.

They ask him to deal the cards one more time: a real high roller's game, important people and big money. He agrees: connections are what you need in life.

It doesn't take long for Keith to learn why people say: "Be careful what you wish for." His search for upward movement suddenly turns into a classic downward spiral of drugs, sex and violence, as well as horrible weather.

With four dead bodies, a charred mansion, several angry Greeks in his wake and the mayor's payoff money in the pocket of his old fatigue jacket, Keith has to run and run far.

Where does a Northerner run to when the Ides of March have shredded his soul? Where does he seek solace, prosperity and a new life?

Florida.

Keith finds he's still like a lot of guys, even though he's killed someone. It's 1979 and there are millions like him flocking to the Sun Belt. Like Okies to California, they're all trying to find their place in the sun.

Only things don't work out for Keith. The darkness returns. Loneliness and frustration overtake him. Miserable and desperate, he reaches out for the only emotional anchor he's known since before his mother went off the deep end—his ex-wife. Carole Loraine Stivers Waverly, in all her swirling confusion and beauty.

They get back together and Keith Waverly finds out, once again, that you just can't tell what the hell is going to happen when you're fatally flawed.

Chapter One

The Promised Land

I don't know where I'm going;
I just know where I've been.
–Unknown

"*Make sure you've got the lanterns lit before the sun goes down,*" *Bagley had said, condescension dripping like sour syrup from his puffy lips.* "*You can't just dawdle down there when you feel like it, they have to be shining before dark. If we can't see the lights we may run aground. You'd better stay straight while you're there, we can't afford to have this messed up.*"

Yeah right— like I'd be waiting for a boatload of contraband and taking it lightly—like self-preservation isn't enough motivation to do things right, for Christ sake....

The boys are way late; bastards are at least eight hours behind schedule. After all the crap I've been through, they should at least be on time. Where the hell are they?

Out there, somewhere, on the green-green ocean.... Actually, it's black at the moment and changing to gray as the light begins to rise over the horizon.

You really become aware of horizons by the ocean, especially if you've been up all night waiting for a boat that's hauling your future inside its fuel tank.

It's clearly an either-or situation for me: Either I get caught and go to jail for a good piece of time, or I get away with it and buy myself some freedom for more than likely a lesser period of time. But what the hell, there aren't any better offers in the wind and at least I'm not slaving in the hot sun for peanuts like so many others around here.

They call Florida a "right to work" state. I believe that means that the owners are always RIGHT and that somebody else does the work for them. I studied labor laws in college; I know those kinds of things.

The higher the sun rises above the gently breaking surf, the more I worry. Without some sort of marker, it might be difficult to find this relatively small spot on a long hunk of featureless beach, even in bright daylight. The sand goes on for miles and miles and miles.

I clearly need to rig something up. I try to think but the hot sun is scrambling my brain.

How much warning will the boys need to keep the keel out of the sand? Should I rig a gaudy signal flag? What if the wrong people see it? Will everyone involved in this scam go to burning hell?

I wonder if the cops know about the van.

Maybe they've already gotten to Carole... maybe there's already an A.P.B. on the wire for a white VW bus with Colorado license plates and little black eyelashes painted above the head-lights.... Maybe the highway patrol is going through it now, as I sit here, helplessly waiting, only a mile down the beach....

Then the Big Question hits me like a Portuguese Man of War to the groin. How in the hell did I ever end up here, alone on a des-olate strip of sand, with chaos chasing after me like a pack of rabid hellhounds?

And that's a question that takes one hell of an answer.

First thing, I guess you have to go back to my arrival in the Sunshine State, about eighteen long months ago.

There I was; rolling by the orange juice stands and peanut brittle shops inside a Greyhound bus, gazing out through tinted glass at the verdant finery and thinking that I'd finally made it to the Promised Land. The violence, death and bad weather in my recent past were fading away like a series of bad dreams.

As I stared out at the palm trees and the swamps, I felt a smile coming on for the first time in a long, long while....

Greetings from sunny Florida!

For years I'd wanted to send that message back home to Minnesota, back up to the frozen tundra. Get one of those postcards with water-skiing chicks on the front; you know, two nice-looking girls in bikinis gliding along the water while a third stands on their shoulders waving out at you. A banner flaps behind them proclaiming a welcome from the Sunshine State. The ladies wear big, broad smiles on Miss America faces.

Yep, I always wanted to mail that one up there to someone who hates winter, you know—rub it in a little. The catch always was that I never went anywhere to send it from. Set off for Florida, once, spring break of 1967, but never made it. John Flint's '63 Chevy blew a rod just south of Madison and we were forced to spend three days in Wisconsin drinking cheap liquor, eating cheese and chasing corpulent bar flies. By the time the repairs were finally completed, we didn't have enough money left for Florida, so we stayed two more days in Wisconsin.

Now, eleven years later, I had made it all the way. But as much as I wanted to, I couldn't send the card back home. Couldn't risk it, in case the cops were interested in my whereabouts. Although I was confident that Peter McKay's death had been written off as an accident—which I really believed it had been—I couldn't be totally sure of the district attorney's desires. And if they ever found Johnny Wells in the trunk of his car at the bottom of the Nemadji River...

Second reason I couldn't send that postcard: It was nearly May and the intended sting of the message would be weakened by the promise of spring in the North—however hollow that promise might ring in the land of ten thousand frozen lakes.

That's the kind of crap you think about on a long bus ride. It can get going around in your head and drive you nuts.

I had to keep telling myself to stop thinking about the past, put it behind me like a bad smell. Those kind of thoughts can drive you just as crazy as the guy in front of you who smells like he slept in horse manure and has been stinking up the bus since Atlanta. Or the hillbilly couple in the back who've been drinking Silver Satin and rolling the empty bottles beneath the seats since boarding at a Stuckey's restaurant just inside the Florida state line.

Despite all that, about a half an hour outside of Tampa, I started to get excited. Soon I'd be off the rotten bus and into the Florida sunshine and my suffering would be over.

I closed my eyes and tried to relax. I was too excited to fall asleep. I kept opening my eyes and peering out the window.

The land seemed desolate and lonely in spite of all the vehicles. Maybe it was just me.

My heart was beating fast as we approached the Howard Frankland Bridge, the gray, old-time span crossing the bay from Tampa to St. Petersburg. Water and waves stretched out forever as I stared out and thought to myself that I'd finally gotten lucky. The glistening, glass- and-steel skyline of Tampa confirmed my feelings.

My gut was jumpy as the Greyhound pulled into the terminal. As soon as my boots hit the warm pavement, I stretched and relaxed.

Palm fronds waved hello and a warm wind blew dust. The sun seemed abnormally bright; I couldn't squint enough.

The one-story, faded yellow, forties' era terminal was in a low-ball part of town where the houses and store buildings seemed shabbier and smaller than the ones I had imagined. But it was warm and there were palm trees and that's all that mattered. Southern air was salve for my battered soul.

Put de lime, in de coconut; take it downtown now.

I walked stiffly toward the building, my folded sheet-for-luggage cradled in the crook of my arm. Went through the metal-framed glass door and grabbed a pamphlet off a rack: Glossy pictures of beaches on the front and a lot of chamber of commerce stuff on the inside. Here was Clearwater, Florida—Jewel of the Sunshine State.

Paradise welcomes you, Keith Waverly.

The brochure informed me that Highway 19, or Seminole Boulevard, was the main tourist strip in Clearwater: motels, shopping malls, nightclubs, supermarkets, fruit stands, car dealerships and convenience stores by the peck. To the west were the beaches, where big hotels and high-end, high-rise condos grew together in lockstep, blocking the view of the ocean for tourists and pissants, like me.

That last part wasn't in the brochure; I learned it on my own, later.

I sat for a moment on a wooden bench and retied my satchel, oblivious to the mingling few. Then I picked up my stuff and walked outside.

A Yellow Cab was parked at the curb, running, and it wasn't even cold out. The driver's window was open so I guessed it wasn't for the air conditioning. Driver was a skinny guy in a yellow T-shirt, with brown, stringy hair. He had a leathery face with ameba-shaped patches of thick red skin on the back and sides of his sweaty neck.

I asked him if he could take me to Seminole Boulevard.

"You new in town?" he said, cocking his head and squinting down at my rolled up sheet.

"First time I ever set foot in Florida. I want to stay in a nice motel with a pool and a good restaurant."

One like in the movie "Where the Boys Are," I thought to myself.

"Any particular spot in mind?"

"Just a nice one that won't cost me an arm and a leg. How 'bout something on the beach? Anything available there?"

"You'd be a paraplegic when you left."

"That bad, eh."

"You ain't said shit, brother—even off-season—but I can find you a nice place on the highway. Plenty of restaurants and bars around... everything you might need. I got a couple, in mind. There's one there that has some nice poontang by the pool from time to time, if that's your poison."

"Sounds good," I said and settled back into the dirty brown seat, harboring a slight uneasiness as to what this guy's idea of nice poontang might be.

We pulled out into traffic. I stared out the filmy rear window at some kids mingling around the front of a 7-Eleven store and it came to me that things were starting to look about the same almost everywhere you went in America, even in a filled-up swampland like Florida.

We rolled away from the bus station and soon blasted onto a freeway. For a while, there was nothing along the roadside but foliage and the occasional house trailer sitting in a swath of cleared swamp. Then we cruised by a small airport with lots of expensive-looking planes parked real close together. I couldn't help but wonder how many of them were used in the dope trade....

This was Florida, for Christ sake—home of cheap dope and plenty of it. Or so I had heard... and read about in *High Times* magazine. Even Jimmy Buffet was singing about the dope. I never thought for a minute that it would be hard to get high in Florida.

Although I was trying hard to change my ways after the excesses and tragedies of the past these thoughts still lay in the back of my head like hibernating flies waiting to spring back to life.

Before I could think deeper about my situation, the roadside got commercial again: strip malls and gas stations bracketing foliage-filled residential areas. Something in the surroundings made my chest tighten up and I lost my train of thought.

When we finally got to Seminole Boulevard, I got excited again. Low slung, modern buildings with names like The Blue Marlin and Tropical Bay and Smuggler's Inn put me in a mild Florida frenzy. You know, killer northern boy escapes to the Sunbelt and all that. I was a little giddy. Hadn't felt like that since I don't know when.

A few miles down, the cabby exited onto a frontage road, drove down a block or two and turned into the entrance of the mildly impressive White Sands Motor Lodge.

The sparkling blue-green of the pool peeked out from behind a long, two-tiered stretch of rooms that formed a horseshoe. The Suwanee Restaurant—thatched awning and torches above and on both sides of two red, wooden doors—beckoned from the open end of the loop.

I went into the office. A middle-aged, heavy-set woman in turquoise Capri pants, matching blouse and thick make-up came out of a back room and smiled a plastic smile. She said they had a vacancy. I said I'd take it. I asked her how much and pulled a fold of bills from my pocket. She pursed her lips, sucked in some air and gave me the book to sign. Then she hunted out a room key from the wall behind her and asked me if I had a car to register. I said no and signed the book.

I fetched my bundle from the backseat of the cab, tipped the driver and strolled down to my room like a schoolteacher on vacation. I sincerely hoped that nobody was watching.

When the door of number 132 clicked shut, all the air went out of me. I turned on the TV and lay down on the bed, feeling heavy and exhausted. I no longer felt like the person I used to be, didn't feel like *me* anymore. There was a vague craving inside, growing ever larger. Could I ever go home again?

Maybe I could ask Thomas Wolfe....

The droning of some game show was the last sound I heard before falling into a heavy sleep.

I dreamt that I was floating down a dark river in a wooden johnboat. There were swamps and fires on the river's banks. Alligators rose from the brackish depths with bloody aluminum baseball bats gripped in their toothy jaws. I came upon the body of a vulture with Johnny Wells' battered head where its should have been. It was perched in a tree and bleeding from the chest, leering down at me.

I wanted to say something to him/it but nothing would come out....

Then things turned suddenly sunny and I was lunching at a circular glass table on the veranda of a fine country club. Famous actors Yvette Mimieux and George Hamilton sat across from me, happily munching green leafy salads and gazing out at the plush surroundings. We spoke together cordially of fine and noble things. I was invited to fill out the foursome for an afternoon doubles match on the club's new clay courts. Afterwards, we would adjourn to the yacht for cocktails and dinner and an evening cruise around the bay. The three of us chuckled conspiratorially about my beautiful, blonde and horny tennis partner-to-be.

I knew she would be rich. I ached to see her face....

I woke up sweating, twisted inside the gold, rayon bedspread like a feverish snake charmer—mouth dry, heart racing. I blinked and stretched and finally remembered where I was.

Local news was on the tube: blonde, female head yapping about a robbery in Tampa. I rolled out of bed and headed for the shower, legs heavy. I wasn't as happy as I should've been. Who in the hell was these days, anyway?

I really needed some food and a couple of cold beers. I turned the shower up hot and heavy and let it run. Went back to the bed, opened up my satchel and took out a pair of white linen, flared pants that I had been saving for just this occasion.

The tropics, man—enough to make any Northerner feel good.

I brought the pants into the shower and hung them up on one of those trouser clasp deals that motels provide as a part of their "full customer service." I climbed into the shower, humming little pieces of "Margaritaville" as the steam rose up.

Hot water washed my troubles away.

Dinner at the Suwanee Restaurant was memorable only for the loud, New York-accented complaining of a floppy necked woman whose pathetic, henpecked husband seemed to pay no attention to his wife's grating whine: "The soup is watery... not enough noodles in it." Her potatoes were lumpy, also, as everyone in the restaurant soon found out.

I had a bottle of Heineken as a splurge and ordered the broiled gulf shrimp. They weren't very good but I didn't make a big thing out of it like the New York honey did. I just ate and left a nice tip and walked out of the restaurant like a Minnesota dork that didn't know his ass from page ten of the Shooter's Bible.

When I hit the pavement outside it was dark. Cars whooshed by on the highway. Nice rides: Mercedes, Cadillacs, Lincolns and a load of Datsun 280Zs. Z cars everywhere like swarming hornets. Japan's sports car for the masses had become exactly that.

I didn't see any rust bucket cars, like back home. In Florida, vehicles rusted from the top down—which seemed so quaint to me. And only the real low balls seemed to be driving the rusty ones. Up North, automotive rust jumped across class lines like a prostitute at a Democratic convention.

Everywhere I looked it was bright lights or greenery or glittering cars. I felt a transient sadness as I watched the shiny parade. But the night air was thick and delicious and a couple of deep breaths brought the excitement back. I began to think there might really be something to this Florida as the Promised Land stuff that I'd talked myself into believing.

*   *   *

On the way back to my room, I stopped at the vending machine alcove to pick up a Milky Way for dessert. I popped in my coin, pulled on the red plastic knob and heard the candy bar slide down into the tray.

It looked so damn good that I decided to eat it right there and watch the moths flitting around the pool lights.

I took in about a third of the bar with one bite and was doing my don't-be-a-litter-bug thing, depositing the wrapper in the trashcan, when I came upon the omen that I had been so desperately hoping for.

Lying not more that two inches beyond the rubber reinforced toe of my white canvas tennis shoe, were credit cards: five thin slabs of plastic money spread out on the pavement like a lost poker hand.

I picked up the cards and put them quickly into my trouser pocket, looking slowly around to see if anyone had seen.

There was no one.

I went back to my room smiling, licking the chocolate from my teeth and believing that the gods were once again smiling back at me. This whole Visa and MasterCard world was new to me but now I had a foot in the door.

Wasn't that just like it had always been, little things coming out of the blue to push me one way or another, like there was someone pulling the strings—a Sky Pilot? If I hadn't been meant to use the credit cards, I wouldn't have found them. It was that simple.

But then I started to wonder if it wasn't some sort of a test from above or something. A test of my vow to clean up my act—temptation dangled in front of me to challenge my resolve and mettle.

But it was Florida for the chrissakes. Enough pieces of the pie around for everyone to get a bite: fancy cars, condos, and high-class quiff zipping around in convertibles or sunning topless on the beach.

Why couldn't I have some?

I couldn't see any reason why not. There it was right in front of me: a plastic welcome packet from the Sunshine State.

But something just didn't seem right. Not with me, not with Florida and not with anything.

I sat down on the bed and took a closer look at my find. I discovered sadly, that there were no bankcards, only Schwal's, Seigel's, Montgomery Wards and The Glades: huge department stores that ran full-page ads in the *Tampa Tribune*.

That changed things. The gift from above lost some of its sheen. I could've used some new clothes, for sure, but clothing wasn't worth the risk, I figured. I still had the bulk of my payoff money from Mayor McKay, so why should I risk anything in a new place?

But I had this fear that if I didn't follow the road signs as they were laid out for me, didn't seize the opportunities as they fell; they might stop coming, all together. Thus, if I didn't use the cards, my life would become bland and empty, petty and bourgeois.

I stared at the plastic until the anguish gave me a headache. Getting too far away from my intended desire, which was to relax, I tossed them on top of the tan veneer dresser and looked at myself in the oval mirror.

The white pants were looking good but the rest of me was getting soft.

Decided to go for a walk to the 7-Eleven that I'd spotted earlier, about two blocks away on the frontage road. Maybe the bright florescent lights and the garish colors would give me a lift. I could pick up some tall boys and The *Sporting News*—or a *Penthouse*... maybe another newspaper, like the *St. Petersburg Times*....

To start my new life, I needed a place to live and before that, a car.

I could even peruse the employment section. You know, just to see what was happening around town, what kind of legit opportunities existed for a semi-educated white boy with a noted lack of steady employment on his resume? Cab driver, survey crew, porn clerk, traveling drug salesman, house painter, canvasser for the city directory: not jobs that will move you up the ladder in a hurry.

But in a bustling modern metropolis like this, there had to be something right for me....

Next morning I woke up in the mood for a swim in the pool but it was foggy and cool outside. A nice change actually, but not what I had expected. Curiously, the damp sea air reminded me of Lake Superior and home and made me feel comfortable.

After a decent breakfast at the Suwanee, I got a cab and went in search of a used car. My driver was a fat kid in his mid-twenties wearing a checkered short sleeve shirt that fit loosely over his many rolls of flab like a tarp on an elephant. I asked him if he knew a place to buy a good used car. Cabdrivers are supposed to know things like that, right?

What the hell did I know when I drove hack? Too goddamn much.

There was the old part of town the driver said. Place you could get a good car without getting jacked around. Several car dealers in a three-block area and a damn good International House of Pancakes right in between.

He dropped me off by a nice big lot full of glistening automobiles that all looked to be more than I could afford. And they were.

I wandered farther down the boulevard, the mist getting thicker. I came to the House of Pancakes then crossed the street to get a closer look at Clearwater Motors.

It was the kind of used-car lot that my Uncle George used to run: an old trailer for an office sitting next to a concrete four-stall repair garage. Red, white and blue plastic banners circling the lot on a rope like the fence of a corral, were flapping in the breeze. The encircled herd was a large assortment of junkers, cheapos, and the occasional halfway decent Caddy, Lincoln, Ford or GM sled.

Guy that came out of the office seemed nice enough. I mentioned I was from Minnesota and he came back with the fact that he had lived in St. Paul a while back with his second wife the schoolteacher. We struck up some sort of rapport and pretty soon I was test-driving a nice little blue Volvo sedan. Great interior, peppy, good handler and good on gas—which was what Bob, said, anyway, and I believed him.

Before long, Bob and I came to a stop in front of a big drawbridge, one of those where the concrete slab splits open in the middle and rises on both sides to allow boats to pass underneath. On the other side of the channel I could see a long strip of beach road with the ocean stretching out on one side and the bay glistening on the other.

Looming above us on the right, overwhelming in the sheer size and extravagance of its glass and concrete structure, was Schwal's Department Store. On the left and slightly behind us, a giant, black, ultra-modern monstrosity of glass and marble and neon proudly displayed an oversize, flashing, aquamarine sign: SEIGEL'S.

As I watched the bridge slabs slowly drop back down, ideas started clicking in my head.

I bought the Volvo from Bob Highsmith for twelve hundred and fifty bucks. Paid with thirteen one hundred-dollar bills. Bob didn't bat an eye; just pulled two twenties and a ten out of a green, vinyl bank envelope and handed them to me along with the title card. He had the notary stamps in the drawer of his desk.

I left there feeling pretty smart. Drove across the street to the House of Pancakes, went in and bought a *Clearwater Gazette*. Sat there for a half an hour drinking coffee and searching through the want ads. There were so many places to choose from, in neighborhoods and on streets that I had no clue about, it got confusing.

I made a few calls from the payphone and learned something new. I learned that the letters FLS in a rental ad stood for. First month's rent and last month's rent and security deposit—all up front. This meant, of course, that I couldn't get an expensive place on the beach, trash it for a month and then split. You had to throw down big cash, in advance.

The only thing I knew was that my cash was running low. I could only afford to stay at the motel and enjoy the poolside life for a few more days. That was reason enough to break in my new credit cards. I had put them in my back pocket—just in case. And Seigel's was just too goddamn ostentatious to pass up, I'm sorry.

I was beginning to see the signs coming together so I decided to go ahead with the attack.

Drove down by the cantilever bridge and parked in a public lot next to the Clearwater Tennis Club. I got out and walked by the rusty, sea level building and the poorly maintained courts.

I stopped at the curb, took a deep breath and crossed the street.

I was starting to feel some rust myself as I moved up the black marble steps toward what was undoubtedly the largest monument to consumerism that I had ever seen. They really went all out in Florida when trying to sell you something.

Inside of Seigel's, it was vast as the Grand Canyon. So much merchandise that my mind blew. I couldn't decide what to go after first.

One direction I could go, I thought, would be to try for something big-ticket and re-saleable, like a watch or a necklace or a ring, something like that. But that, I figured, would be pushing it too far. Small charges in different departments were the smart way. Chances were they wouldn't even check on them. And if that worked okay, I could come back later and go for something big. I knew I had a good chance of pulling it off.

Again, I questioned my motives: Why I was doing this? What the hell was wrong with me?

A tropical shirt or two and a real good tennis racket would make a person feel better. Maybe some shorts and some nice socks....

My spiritual guide, my Sky Pilot, christened in honor of the Eric Burdon song of the same name, was helping me to understand.

He had always leaned me towards things that weren't seen or

understood by others. I knew that he had helped me find the credit cards. Now he was pushing me to get the tennis racket.

Tennis in Florida, this was a good thing, you see. I could get healthy, back in shape. When I was in high school, I had played hockey in the winter and tennis and baseball in the summer. After injuring my hip my senior year of hockey, I had let sports slide out of my life.

Sky Pilot was telling me that it was time to get back to where I once belonged.

I wondered how my new racket would feel. I wondered if it would help my backhand....

With my attention finally focused, I went directly to sporting goods and picked out a graphite racket made by Head. Nice sporting goods department at Seigel's, they even had skis.

Over in men's wear, I picked up a pair of white shorts at one counter and a green flowered shirt and some shiny socks like the disco dudes were wearing, at another. Bruce Harding's credit was obviously in good standing.

I became emboldened, drunk on the thrill of charging on a stranger's account. It was a hell of a rush and a fitting gift from the heavens for all that I had suffered: my reward for enduring the stones and spears of a world gone wrong.

After thirty minutes I walked outside to the parking lot, bags full of loot in my arms, and took deep pulls of damp sea air. I was beginning to like this place called Florida.

I put my new stuff in the trunk of the Volvo and once again squinted across the boulevard at the mammoth monument to Mammon called Schwal's. The fog had lifted and the heat was coming on.

Let's try across the street, said the Sky Pilot.

The two of us strolled across the lush tropical thoroughfare. Together we marched in sync with the tolling bell that was sounding everywhere, to everyone, the joys of consumption:

All of this you can have. You can have it all and it will make you happy. It will make you happy....

My stride was light and quick and confident as I glided through the green-tinted revolving doors and popped into the perfectly climate controlled, perfectly designed interior. Truly the future of America was right in front of me in all its scented wonder and majesty.

I thought I'd try for a watch this time, no more pussy footing around. Go directly to the watch and camera section and get with the program. A man needs a good-looking watch to make the right impression. Hell with telling time, it's about status.

The girl behind the long glass counter was squeezed nicely into a dark blue, sleeveless dress. She had red circles of makeup on her cheeks, which—contrasted with her dark tan—made her look like a marionette.

When she spoke, the illusion remained intact.

"Can I help you find something, sir?" Sing-song chirp, mechanical tone.

I fought back a grimace. "Yes," I said. "I, ah—I'm looking for a new watch. My other one was lost—or maybe stolen. The band was broken, too." I felt my face heating up.

"Would you be looking to replace the one you lost? Um... the one that's missing—what brand was it?'

"Oh, it was just a Timex... so I guess it wasn't stolen then, eh? I mean, who'd steal a Timex, right? Unless it was John Cameron Swayze and he was going to throw it off a building or something. See if it keeps on ticking after it took a licking, you know what I mean."

Her eyes glazed over: "We have some lovely Citizen watches over here sir, if you would care to have a look. They are very elegant, with a Rolex appeal and a one-year guarantee. With free battery replacement as a bonus—for twenty-four months." She took a breath.

"Yeah, the band broke on my other one. It was leather. Those metal bands always pinch the hairs on my arm. Got any with leather bands?"

"I'm sure these bands will be fine, sir, we've never had any complaints...from any other men. They are the finest, made in Italy." She stiffened, shifting her head from side to side. "They do carry Timex watches over at Eckerd Drugs."

"Oh well, then..." I was getting nervous: starting to blow it. I shut up and shuffled along as the girl led me down the display case.

I ended up with a three-hundred-dollar timepiece. I hoped it would make me look like a bignuts. Babe-bait, if I was lucky. If not, I could always pawn it.

"Cash or charge, sir?"

"Um, charge. I have a Schwal's card." I pulled out my wallet and handed Ramona—the name printed on the little plastic rectangle above her firm left breast—the card.

Perhaps it was just a little narrowing of the skin around her eyes, maybe the slight hesitation when she looked at the name on the card. But when she said: "Just a moment, Mr. Harding, I need to verify this account balance," and then kind of glanced around searching for something or someone—I knew it was time to fly.

That was the thing about my Sky Pilot; he'd lead you into these things and then make you find your own way out....

As Ramona lifted up the phone on the wall behind her, I started moving quickly away. I was almost through a large portal, behind which I could disappear from sight, when a piercing, "Sir! Sir!" cut through me like an icy pickaxe.

"What about your watch, sir?" she yelled. "It will just be a moment." Louder, closer, now: "Mr. Jacobs, he's run in there to men's wear. I saw him."

I made the turn and the wall was between us. Excited voices shouted. Running footsteps clicked behind me on the slick, shiny floor.

I could feel them about to make the corner when I ducked down like a GI hitting a foxhole and burrowed inside a rack of

British Invasion jeans. Inside the circle of denim it was all muf-fled and protected and blue. The smell was raw and good.

The mob clicked, scraped and growled toward me. I held my breath and forced my mind to count: One thousand one, one thou-sand two, one thousand three....

A long three minutes had passed when I slipped quietly out of my denim cubbyhole and moved quickly in the opposite direction of my pursuers. The racket they were causing throughout the store brought all eyes on them and none on me. A mob of shop-pers hid my urgent exit into daylight.

No sirens or bells sounding as I took a deep pull of air and shuddered.

I went immediately down to beach level by way of a little stair-case in the center of the parking lot. Once at the bottom I stayed close to the embankment on my way to the car.

Getting back inside the Volvo and rolling out of the parking lot was the most joy I had experienced for days, weeks, or maybe even years.

It was always the same with the Sky Pilot: torture you and scare you to death and then give you a nice big reward of a kind that you never knew even existed. Then you find yourself happy to just be the same asshole that you had been before the whole thing happened. Maybe later, you'd get back to hating yourself.

Back in the safety of my room, I tried on my new tennis shorts and polo shirts and swung the racket as I looked in the mirror. Man, I was thinking, the change is going to do me good.

I spent the next two days by the pool. My startlingly white skin kept getting burned. There were some nice-looking women out sunning on occasion but their husbands were always sniffing around like sorry-faced lap dogs. I was thinking that I could show those ladies a thing or two.

In my hours away from the pool I continued to look for housing. One day I found a nice—make that fantastic—deal. A condo in Clearwater with a tennis court directly in front of the door and an Olympic-sized pool about fifty yards down the way. The units had foliage around the edges with cute little salamanders running in and out. A really nice off-season rate, too.

Little retired guy owned the place and we got along from the get-go. He seemed more than happy to have me in the place, at least until his high buck seasonal renters came down in January.

I was quick to sign on the bottom line.

Took me over a week before I met anybody.

I was just lying around watching television. Then, at early dusk, I looked out my front window to check out the tennis court.

There was this guy out there practicing his serve. Didn't have much of one. Dark hair and a real college-boy face, he was wearing white tennis shorts and a white UCLA shirt. He was about my height but a little lighter, probably going about one seventy-five to my one-ninety. He had a nice, modern racket and well-worn shoes.

I went outside and asked him if he wanted to hit. He returned that his name was John Carino and yes, he would like to have a hit. We shook hands and I went in and changed into my new shorts and grabbed the Head racket.

We warmed up a little. I thought I was hitting the ball pretty well but my legs felt heavy.

We played a match and he waxed me, 6–1, 6–0.

Afterwards, I felt old and foolish at age thirty-one. My unhealthy past was rising up from the depths of my being like a festering boil.

I came down with a nasty and weird swamp fever that kept me in bed for three days, hallucinating and sweating and struggling through bad dreams.

One particularly troubling and recurring nightmare featured my ex-wife Carole standing in front of me in a see-through baby doll nightgown and whispering sweet nothings. It was the first time she had been in my dreams for years....

I'd try to put my arms around her and she'd start to cry and plead, begging for something that I could never quite make out.

When I woke, a strange, empty feeling lingered.

Once I finally recovered, I vowed to get in shape and return my body to a healthy state. I took up jogging and drinking bottled water.

Every day for two weeks, I ran along the road by the golf course, staring through the six-foot-high wire fence at the fat men riding electric carts and wearing garish clothes.

Carino and I continued to smack it around a few days a week until my game slowly improved.

John had played varsity tennis at Pepperdine University in California. I didn't feel so bad about getting my ass kicked, him being from a high-flying school.

Slowly, I began winning a few more games per set. My confidence increased. Even my skin started to get halfway tan.

After more than a month of hard work, in which I actually took a few sets off John, I believed I was ready for the next step. A job as a tennis instructor at one of those posh high-rise resorts.

I had often cruised by them on my nocturnal excursions, imagining what life would be like down there under all those lights.

It seemed like the proper kind of life for a man like me. Moving up to hang with the wealthy seemed like the only way I could find happiness. Some rich broad with a serve in need of tinkering could be the next step toward my transformation from parochial loser to international winner.

I could picture myself hitting aces against the resident pro as an adoring crowd of rich, bored and horny ladies cheered me on. There I was, in tennis whites, sipping Tanqueray-and-tonics at the club socials, the idol of many.

Those nighttime flights of fancy became the only times that I really relaxed in the Sunshine State. Driving around in the dark, bathed in neon, I could feel almost good.

In the harsh light of day, the gated communities, never-ending traffic and infinite strings of franchise food joints seemed to be closing in on me. This was a rootless, aimless place, this new Florida. Constant reminders of others' wealth and my poverty rolled by me in every Mercedes and loomed behind every vine covered privacy wall.

My longing grew stronger, a hollow, empty feeling my one constant companion. A soul-sucking parasite was boring into my brain like a hungry cockroach.

It's not easy to get a position at one of those swanky resorts if your job history reads like a bad joke and your demeanor isn't as sunny and crisp as a starched shirt. A lousy tan and a bad haircut don't help either.

But one day, an opportunity finally presented itself, in the form of an advertised opening for tennis instructor at The Dunes Tennis Resort and Health Spa. I called and got an appointment. The fog started to lift.

Getting ready for my interview, I was pretty excited. Got all dressed up in some of my new clothes, went out to the car and turned the key, only to find that the battery was dead.

Getting one of my neighbors to give me a jump was like trying to smack Cuban cockroaches with a straw. Several folks ignored me as I stood there, helplessly holding jumper cables.

Someday they'd be sorry.

This guy across the alley finally gave me a boost, but only after I almost had to beg him. I walked over to him and pleaded my case and I swear to God, he tried to say no. He hemmed and he hawed and he squirmed but finally agreed, out of fear, I think, as I was getting a little frayed around the edges.

By the time I got to the Dunes, I was late for my interview. They wouldn't even let me sit down. "If you're late, you've sealed your fate," the heavily made up and hair-sprayed receptionist said with a haughty flip of her head.

I wondered who was teaching her the clever sayings.

*   *   *

That night, Carino and I played under the lights and I beat him 7-5, 6-4. Pent-up anger and frustration had driven me to the best tennis of my life.

After the match we were having a few beers when John came in from the kitchen with a baggie in his hand, flipped it onto the circular wicker coffee table in front of me.

"Here," he said. "Here's your prize for kicking my ass."

Inside the baggie were a white paper bindle and three large white pills bearing the number 714.

"What the hell is this, Johnny, drugs then?"

"This lady at the radio station gave it to me. Said she didn't want the stuff anymore. I thought of you, knowing you were a former druggie and all."

Cocaine from the sky, for the Christ sake...was this Florida or what?

"Is this coke?" I asked, incredulous.

"Yeah. About three-quarters of a gram she said. She didn't want it anymore... said it was pretty good, though. Couple Quaaludes, too."

"Are you shitting me? These are someone's party favors... I can't believe this shit. How much do you want for it?"

"Nothing, it's free. She just gave it to me."

"Free drugs? You sure you don't want any?"

"Nah. I'm playing in a tournament this weekend. You enjoy it, it's yours."

"Goddammit.... Lady must have found the lord," I said.

"A boyfriend," John said.

"Could that be you, John?"

"No," he said smiling. "She's a little old for me. Nice lady though. Station gossip says she was quite a party girl when she first started."

"I guess she was...."

A dark spot in the back of my brain started to come alive. Then my vow to stay clear of the white powder popped up behind my eyes like a day-glow, no-sale sign and my stomach fluttered. Ah, but what the hell, I reasoned: This was Florida—everyone cool does coke down here.... And the way it came to me, out of the blue, like that... a gift from above so to speak... well... I was meant to have it, was the way it seemed.

For the ennui, Watson...

I didn't feel much like staying at John's, anymore, wanted to get back home and do some drug.

I finished my Budweiser, thanked John for the fourth time, put the baggie in the pocket of my shorts and left. John had to go to work later that night, anyway. He had to go on the air and answer stupid questions from a lot of cracker rednecks who got their jollies from harassing the educated California boy on the FM radio.

An hour later, as I sat alone in my apartment with nothing to do, Wired had turned to Agitated.

I went outside and walked slowly down the pavement, muscles tight, drawn by the haunting glow of the swimming pool.

To a northern boy like me, the green-tinted water of a swimming pool in the gleam of underwater lights represented the true value of the South; that which is unattainable in the North—year-round warmth. The lure of that sparkling emerald water had fools like me flocking to these Venus flytrap cities like blue crabs to a dead Manatee.

Pulling a deck chair close to the pool's edge, I sat there for a half an hour staring down at the slow, gentle rolling of the soothing green liquid. The dream seemed so close to me then, I could almost touch it. It seemed like the good life was only a step or two away....

I reached down and swirled my hand through the water. A breeze blew, rattling an aluminum deck chair behind me. I shivered. The air seemed suddenly colder. That didn't seem right.

I wanted a drink. I got up and strolled back toward my apartment.

On my front yard courts, the tennis ball popped sensuously. The girl was tan and fit, with a great two-fisted backhand to go with her nicely filled bathing suit top and blue tennis shorts. She ran; she sweated; she bent over, whipping up on her embarrassed boyfriend. She could play. Best combination of looks and game I had ever seen.

I lingered, watching her, and got as horny as an Italian priest. Not that I'd ever met an Italian priest—but it seems like if any priests were horny the Italians would be the ones.

After a few *Cuba libres*, I started feeling better, but not so good as to totally shake the lingering dread. The TV was on but I couldn't crack the surface; the glowing tube only made me nervous.

A burst of impulse hit me. I swallowed down a Quaalude with a stiff drink and headed for the Volvo. Started her up and pointed her in the direction of Clearwater Beach. I'd heard somewhere that Keith Richards came up with the riff for "Satisfaction" at a motel on Clearwater Beach.

Since I wasn't getting any, satisfaction, that is, I had a feeling there was something waiting for me out there. It was a happening beach area, the kind of place where I should be welcome. There would be rock and roll, booze and girls....

The lights twinkled and cars hissed by as I drove nervously down Gulf Boulevard. I found myself wondering just how far up the social ladder I was going to climb. Which canal would my mansion be on? What kind of boat would I choose? I didn't know how I was going to make it to the big-time, yet—but that didn't matter. Surrounded by that much wealth, I had to score big, somehow, some way.

Any goddamn way...

I swung the Volvo into a metered spot on Clearwater Beach, near a stretch of bars and surf shops. The wind blew; the ocean roared in the dark distance. Ghostly whitecaps crashed against the gray beach.

Tiny piles of sand swirled at my feet as I shuffled down the street, drawn by the lure of the neon. Soon I came upon the aptly named Beach Bar. Went through the red metal door and was thumped in the chest by the thudding of a bass guitar. High-pitched screeching followed close behind:

"PANAMA, PANAMAHAHA. PANAMA…"

The words came careening at me like a cyclone, stopping me in my tracks. Waitresses with curls, great tans and ghoulish faces patrolled the edges of the smoky seating area. Boys in the band had monster hair. They were four old guys like me—over thirty. I figured they must have been scoring big with the hot young things that were bouncing around the club in what seemed to be a constant state of excitement.

"PANAMA!"

The crowd was young, looked to be mostly in their early twenties—the next generation of hipsters.

I worked my way to the bar, ordered a tall Bacardi orange juice and sipped it for thirty minutes. Never could relax so I left.

Back outside in the wind, I walked aimlessly down the block, my hands stuck in my jeans, until the international homing beacon for lonely males flashed before my eyes: GIRLS GIRLS GIRLS.

All I could think about was Mary, my former girl friend, how she now was at the bottom of frigid Lake Superior, preserved for-ever in her youthful beauty.

Could there be another girl like her waiting for me around the next turn, another stripper?

My crotch tingled and an empty feeling crawled inside my chest. Orange and yellow beer signs failed to soothe.

I turned around and walked back to my car, growing edgy from the roaring of the surf.

A few spaces down sat a Datsun 280Z. A young couple leaned against the driver's door, nuzzling. They laughed and talked and touched each other in a way that made me hurt.

Wishing I could feel like them—be like them—I sunk into the Volvo's blue cloth seats and turned the key. Felt so lonely baby, I could cry. If I'd been Elvis I'd have gone for cheeseburgers.

Instead, I had drugs and alcohol.

Soon I was on the road, once again cruising the Florida night.

I cruised through St. Petersburg where the old people came to die and where high roller bars and vacant, rusted buildings stood side by side in lonely unison.

Going across the bay to Tampa was canceled when my vision turned double. With the lude turning my mind and body into worthless jelly, somehow I ended up on Park Boulevard.

In familiar territory and feeling strange, I jerked the car into the parking lot of a porno shop I had noticed on past trips down the boulevard.

I had grown sick of the porn store that I worked in, back in Zenith City. Now, strangely, I was going to be a customer in such a shop. My dick was doing my thinking but it was no Einstein. Boundaries had been erased, the walls torn down in my mind.

I parked in front of the concrete box building and caught a glimpse of the glaring lights through the glass front door. What would be my passion tonight? *Seka does Salinas? Swedish Sluts Parts 1 and 2? Sinbad and the Seven Sisters of Sappho?*

All at once my feet and hands turned cold and my gut churned. I slid back into the car; backed her up and whipped back onto the boulevard. I drove home in a state of minor delirium, my stomach queasy.

I stumbled into the apartment, locking the door behind me. Threw off all my clothes in a rag pile on the bed and weaved my way to the living room. Dropped down on the floral patterned couch and felt the cool night air wash over me.

My pounding chest began to slow; the sopor took back control. I tried to fantasize about that girl—the tennis player—from before.

She was bouncing on the court in front of my window, beauty

incarnate. Then she was in my bed, bouncing on me. Demonstrating all the energy, expertise and enthusiasm she had shown on the tennis court.

Ride mama, ride; watch the snake hide.

Afterwards I just passed out, fell into state of liquidity and began to dream:

Brooding languid scenes of dark blue rivers and steel gray skies. Boatmen going by in dark boats, with push poles, chanting an unknown dirge. Then the scene changed and I was in the backyard of my first childhood home of memory, on a sunny afternoon. A cool breeze blew the wash as my mother pinned it on the clothesline. She looked over at me and smiled. I was down on the sidewalk where it was warm, watching the meandering ants.

My mother went inside. I was alone. Mrs. Olson, the friendly lady who lived in the big brown house next door, came to her back porch and smiled down at me, a wide, crooked smile.

"I've got some fresh ginger snaps, Keith," she said.

She was old and slightly bent over; dark brown hair tied back in a bun. Her voice was warm and inviting, like fresh-baked cookies. I walked over to the steps and she handed me one of the best ginger cookies I ever tasted. Suddenly the day got brighter and warmer.

"Here's a doughnut, honey," she said, then.

And the doughnut was also the best I had ever tasted.

"I've got more upstairs, dear, but you'll have to ask your mother...."

I never asked my mother but all of a sudden I was inside the Olson's kitchen, sitting at the white wood table on a white wood chair, a doughnut in one hand and a warm, soft ginger cookie in the other.

Across from me, gray-haired Mr. Olson hunched over the table in his white undershirt, an eagle tattoo on his upper arm. A white, tin cup of coffee and a brown pint bottle stood in front of him on the blue and white checkered cheesecloth.

I smiled and turned my head as Mrs. Olson came out of her bedroom and stopped at the small white refrigerator.

"Would you like some milk, Keith? How about some warm milk, sweetie? Do you like it that way?" Yes, I tried to say, but the words didn't come out right.

The milk was warm and had a funny sweet, burnt kind of taste to it.

The picture changed: I was fuzzy and warm; lying in the Olson's darkened bedroom on a bare, checkered mattress on a small cot against the wall. Something between my legs felt strange but not unpleasant. Somewhere in the vast distance, doors were opening, while others were slamming shut.

Mrs. Olson sat on the edge of the bed, leaning over me, talking sweetly: "Doesn't that feel good, honey? Do you like that? Later we can have some more cookies and milk."

I closed my eyes and sunk inside the warm water feeling.

"Come in, Carl," she said to Mr. Olson. "See this beautiful boy, Carl. See what he has. Isn't he special? It's so nice and warm and dark in here, isn't it, Keithy. Have some more of your milk, it will make you feel so good."

Things went black; then it was later in the same afternoon and I was down in the coal bin of my own house, sitting on top of a large pile of coal. The sun shone in through the narrow side window and I felt real sorrow for the first time but didn't know what it was.

I woke up and stumbled off the couch and something snapped in my head. When you have nights like that, you know you need a woman. I felt a strange desperation and an overwhelming desire to do something that I had sworn long before I would never do.

After a few minutes to clear my head as best I could, I picked up the receiver and began to push those familiar numbers....

Not my parent's number... hell no, I was calling my ex-wife, my former darling. Carole Loraine Stivers Waverly, to be exact, my little flower child, in all her swirling confusion and beauty.

It had been a long time since I had felt anything for her. But now I had this deep-seated craving for an emotional anchor, which, somewhere in my twisted mind, Carole represented.

In our first go-round, she had made attempts at keeping my feet on the ground, with good intentions and bad results. Still, I felt that a dose of her was what I needed to start feeling right. If only to talk to her and hear her voice. You know how it is....

So there I was, calling back to Zenith City at one-thirty in the morning Eastern Time, to my ex-wife's parents' house, where her father, a Lutheran minister, still lived. Bastard always hated me, too.

As it was buzzing in my ear, good sense took a hold of me for an instant and I started to hang up. A distant, fearful-sounding *Hello* made me change my mind.

"Hello," I said back, struggling to sound bright and sober. "Is Carole there? This is Keith, Mrs. Stivers.... I'm sorry to bother you so late. Would you let me talk to Carole, please? There won't be any fighting, I promise. I just want to talk to her."

"Keith? Where are you calling from dear? Do you know it's after midnight? Are you in a bar?"

"No, Mrs. Stivers, I'm not in a bar. I'm sorry; I know it's late. I apologize for that. I just want to talk to my wife. Is she there? Put her on, would you?"

"She's not here, Keith, she—"

There was a click on the line and the sleepy voice of Carole's father, Wayne, came through: "Who is this? Who's calling at this hour? Is it Carole again? Betty... you on downstairs?"

"Yes, dear. Keith's on the phone, honey. He wants to talk to Carole."

"Waverly? He wants to talk to Carole? Tell him that I threw the lush out of my house?"

"You did what, you son of a bitch?" I snapped. "What about Mikey?"

"She took him with her, Keith," Betty said, her voice breaking.

"This whole mess is all your fault, Waverly, you punk," Wayne

Stivers shouted. "If she had never met you, this whole mess wouldn't be happening. You are the scourge of the earth. You—"

"Oh, kiss my red ass, Wayne."

I hung up and staggered into the bedroom and passed out.

The next morning about ten-thirty, sober and regretful, I called my ex-mother-in-law again, praying that she, and not Wayne, would answer. I needed to find out the whole story. I hoped that the daylight would help us find some common ground.

Without going into much background information, other than to say that her daughter had been "showing signs of stress" and that her husband was a bit "on edge," Betty Stivers, in her kind and hesitant way, let on that Carole and her father had experienced a "falling out." The result: Mike and Carole had moved into an apartment out in the West End of Zenith City.

Betty was very sad and upset. I sympathized. I knew how stubborn Wayne and Carole could both be, from personal experience. I sure did. But I didn't say anything. I only tried to reassure my ex-mother-in-law:

"Everything will work itself out; Carole is a big girl. But what about this lush business? What did Wayne mean by that? Carole never used to drink much back when we were together...."

But she always did get real hammered on New Year's and birthdays.

"Oh, dear. Yes... I'm afraid it does seem like she's been drinking more than is healthy for her. It could be from the constant strain of having no man around."

Betty never passed up a chance for a shot at me.

"How's Mike?" I countered, knowing he was the apple of Betty's eye. "How's he doing?"

"Mikey seems fine, Keith—but he misses his father."

An arrow of pain hit my gut. "That's what I want to talk to them about, Mrs. Stivers. I was thinking maybe they could join me down here."

What the hell was I saying? Who was making this call?

"Is there any way I can reach them? Does she have a phone at her new place yet?"

"Oh, Keith, do you mean that? Have you got a good job?"

"I'm getting into real estate."

"That sounds wonderful, Keith, I'm so excited for you. A family should be together. You kids deserve a second chance. Why that poor boy of yours, he—"

"Mrs. Stivers, I don't mean to be rude, but this is long distance.... Have you got Carole's number?"

"Yes, Keith. It's 774-0351. That would be area code 218, you know.

"Has Carole been working at all, Betty?"

"She's still at the radio station, dear. Oh, I do hope you two can work things out."

"Thank you very much, Betty—goodbye now."

"Good bye, Keith, and good luck. Try to show some patience with Carole, you know how proud she can be at times."

"Yes, ma'am, I do."

I was mind-blown from the call. What in hell had made me do it?

I wrote it off to being too high; plopped down on the couch and fell asleep.

I dreamt I was floating in the ocean, slowly treading water as huge bales of marijuana drifted by. Bearded men wearing rain slickers and standing in wooden rowboats were shouting, "Square groupers—there they blow," as they threw nets and harpoons at the rapidly moving weed. Each time they caught hold of a bail it would tear away and they would have to try again. Always just ripping a little piece off. Never catching up to the bale. I flailed out as a huge golden block drifted by.

My hand slammed into the wicker coffee table, knocking glasses onto the floor. Exhausted and confused, feeling nervous and guilty, I shook my head in disgust.

Then the phone rang.

It was John Carino calling with the opportunity I'd been waiting for. An instructor at his tennis club had taken ill with the swamp fever and John had recommended me as an emergency replacement.

I quickly called and set up an appointment at the Old Bay Tennis Resort. But after I hung up had second thoughts: Look at that pale face in the mirror. Look at those baggy eyes and feel those legs of lead.

But the opportunity was too big to pass up. Drug flu or not, I was going.

I went back to bed and slept until afternoon, then took a long hot shower, finished off by thirty seconds of cold water, or what passes for cold water down South, then into the kitchen for some instant coffee. I slugged down the revolting brew while slipping into white tennis shorts and a yellow polo shirt.

This time the car started (Clearwater Motors had given me a replacement battery) and I arrived at the club at three-thirty, met the manager and went into his office for the paperwork.

I was nervous about the social security number business. I hoped I could get them to pay me in cash; it was only going to be a temporary thing anyway.

I had no such luck on the cash business. And Mr. Higgins— "Call me Ray"—the freckled, red headed, manager, wanted to know more about me than I could remember myself. I had to sit there and lie about my job history. When he left me alone it to fill in the forms, I almost got up and walked out. Something kept me there, though, and I managed to struggle through. For references, I used John Carino and two doctors' names I had pulled from the local phone book.

I'd been finished for no longer than a minute when Higgins came brusquely back into the room. He picked the application off his desk and tossed it into the top drawer without so much as a glance.

"Let's go then, Keith. I'll show you the courts and the rest of the facility. We get fifty dollars for an hour's lesson here. You get thirty-five of that. Not bad, if you put in the time. Carlos, who you're replacing, used to do about five or six a day when it wasn't too hot. Most of our lessons are at night here, this time of year. But some of the young sweeties like to come in after work. The foxy ones all preferred Carlos, so, my friend, you will be inheriting his harem, so to speak. At least those that weren't already snapped up by the other guys." He put his thumb and forefinger to his chin and looked at me with a bemused grin.

"Think you're up for the task? John said you were a gamer."

I tried to answer but my throat was so dry I could barely squeak. Luckily, we were a step away from a water fountain. I bent over to drink and caught sight of a gorgeous brunette in a red bikini stretched out on a chaise by the glistening Olympic-size pool. All of a sudden I started to like the place. I stared like a fool kid at that gorgeous sight and the shrieking of the birds grew louder in my ears.

Ray smirked: "Business first, my man. Follow me."

We took a brief tour of the high-rise and its glittering splendor. We walked a boardwalk down to the shore of Old Tampa Bay and stood there looking out for a while. Ray pointed across the water at some distant spot and said that was where he lived. Said he lived on a bluff. I couldn't see what he was talking about so I just nodded. I got the sense that he didn't have very much to do and was trying to kill time.

After he showed me the barren but clean employees' locker room, he wished me good luck and headed for the bar. The social hour was upon us. I couldn't partake because my first lesson was in an hour and I had to go back home and gather up my gear.

Brandi Winter—blonde and built—slid out of her yellow 280Z and sashayed over to the courts at about 5:29 p.m. for a five-thirty lesson. She was an employee at WPLF, Talk Radio 97; the same station John Carino worked for. WPLF had some kind of trade-off arrangement with the resort: lessons in exchange for advertising. Trade-off lessons were given at a rate of forty bucks an hour. Instructors got twenty-five of that. One look at Brandi in her bright-red, French cut shorts and I decided it was going to be worth it.

Disappointingly, she wasn't much of a tennis player and really kind of a dud, over all. I found myself thinking that my ex-wife was better looking and certainly a lot smarter. Brandi's snorting laugh, like Suzanne Somers' on "Three's Company," made me cringe. But, by the end of our first lesson, she was hitting the ball over the net with some regularity and seemed pleased with the results.

I drove home that night feeling pretty good about myself. I relaxed and had a few beers. My talk with Carole's mother was still on my mind. I was kind of worried about the kid, I guess. Against my better judgment, I dialed the number that she had given me. It was about nine o'clock.

"Hello," distant and tinny, TV blasting away in the background.

"Hello, Carole? This is Keith. I'm calling long distance."

"Keith?" Her voice became warmer, fuller. "My god, Keith. I thought you were dead and gone forever; it's been so long. Your landlord said that you just packed up and left without any notice. I was worried about you."

She paused.

I said nothing.

"I suppose you're finally calling for Mike, Keith," she continued. "It is about time, he misses you, you know. Where have you been all this time? And where are you now?"

She was a little thick of tongue, not really slurring her words, but the R's carried a slight brogue, the Irish in her coming to the surface.

"Of course I want to talk to Mike, Carole." I tried to stay calm. "But I need to say a few things to you, first. Just give me a chance here. You see, I've been thinking about things, about what went wrong with us before, and all that. I know I made some mistakes and I'm sorry for them. That's really all I can do about anything in the past."

"Oh, Keith," crying softly, her voice scratchy. "I've missed you so. Where are you? Please tell me."

"Down South. Florida. Please stop crying, Carole. You know I could never handle that. I only said that I had made some mistakes, nothing else. Why is Mikey awake at this time of night anyway? Doesn't he have school in the morning? He should be in bed by now."

She stopped crying; her voice hardened: "School's out for summer, Keith."

"Oh, yeah. I guess I forgot it was summer, for a second. It's always summer down here, you know. Sounds like you've been drinking Carole…. Is that what you do now, sit home and get drunk by yourself and let Mike watch TV all the goddamn time?"

"No, Keith—I don't sit around drinking alone every night, if that's what you mean. There's usually a man here—usually a different one every night. And all of them are a lot better in bed than you ever were. Tonight I've got myself a football player—"

"That's enough, Carole. Cut out the bullshit. Even your mother said that you were drinking too much."

"Of course she would—the little mouse, always giving in to my dad. You think she doesn't sneak off to the sewing room with the brandy decanter every night? She's the last one who should criticize…. I'm only getting a little more like you now, Keith. Isn't that what you always wanted? A drinking partner, and all that goes with it?"

"Jeeze, Carole, let's not get into that right now. All I know is that I miss you and Mike. I just thought I'd call and say hello. I'm sure you've got your drinking under control. I didn't mean to start lecturing. Listen, I've got a condo down here, and I'm getting a job pretty soon. As soon as I do, I'll call you and we'll see how things are going and everything. Could you put Mike on now, Carole?"

She sniffed and sighed. "Keith?" she said softly. "You have a condo?"

"Yeah. With a tennis court right in front of my door and a pool down the way."

"Is it by the ocean?"

"No. Just a golf course with a fence."

"That sounds nice, Keith... ah—here's Mike."

Kid didn't want to talk to me, but Carole begged and pleaded and he picked up the receiver. He was locked up tight.Tied in a hard knot like the laces on his tennis shoes after a day in the rain.

"Hi Mikey, how ya doin,' buddy? I've sure missed you."

I could hear Carole hissing, "Say something."

"I missed you too, Daddy. When are you coming back to see me?" Quiver in his voice.

"I won't be coming back to Minnesota soon, Mikey. But I was thinking maybe you and your mom could come down here to Florida and live with me. How would you like that?"

I was going too fast and I couldn't stop.

"I guess so," quiet, reserved.

"That is, if certain things work out," I said, reigning myself in. "And if your mother wants to, of course. But I really hope you can come down. You can play baseball all year round down here, you know. Would you like that, Mikey?"

"Yes, Daddy," he said and I about broke down.

"Okay, Mike, I love you. Put your mother on again, will you?"

The phone clicked, then buzzed.

I was relieved.

Higgins put me on as a "Permanent Temporary" at the club. This meant I had regular lessons and got first grab at any fill-ins.

My two favorite students were a mother-daughter duo, both of them drop dead gorgeous: Tall, dark, perfect bodies—but cold as steel beams.

Mom (Julie) would come on the court first. She had a great body with high-riding, impressive breasts and a regal quality about her. This made up, somewhat, for her obvious lack of education.

After she finished, she'd go poolside while daughter had her lesson. Julie always wanted to catch another hour of sunlight while Gina tormented me with her saucy sexiness and Southern-style laziness.

She was a little smaller and lighter in complexion than her mother, and a lot smarter. The little tease could hit a damn good forehand when she didn't have to run for it.

I surmised that the necessary wrist strength for such a shot was the result of copious hand jobs given out in high school.

My fourth pupil was the gay, teenage son of a wealthy local businessman. Father owned car lots all over the Suncoast area.

How did I know Henry was gay? He told me.

First thing he said to me after his old man drove away from the club: "I'm a faggot," staring petulantly and thrusting out a hip. "If that offends you, too bad. If you don't want to teach me, that's all right. I'll just go into the locker room and ogle the men in the showers." Then he pulled at the bangs of his bleached, rooster-cut hair and squinted at me defiantly.

I just chuckled and grinned at the kid. "You are here for a tennis lesson, Henry, and that's what you are going to get."

He looked in my eyes for a second and then shrugged. "Yeah, well, okay," he said.

After that rough start, the rest of the lesson went pretty well. The kid could run down a lot of balls and keep things in play but didn't have much of a serve. As time went by I began to like him. I had doubts about his supposed gayness because occasionally I'd catch him staring at some bodacious poolside babe. Kid had some kind of David Bowie thing going, I guess.

After two weeks, Carlos returned. Brandi went back to his tute-lage, while Gina, Julie and Henry stayed with me. I kept pretty busy, working on my deep burn, as well as my tennis game. My introduction to the life of a tennis instructor had put temporary brakes on my longing for stability.

But after awhile frustration came back. I hadn't gotten any far-ther than lessons with any of the students: Never any invites to the boss's get-togethers, no offers of money for sex—nothing. Not even, a lousy offer of a drink at the club bar. Not even from Henry.

Slowly, that old gray feeling started creeping back into my head. Sometimes I felt like I was breaking apart inside, one little piece at a time. I was always thinking about Carole and Mike. The chance to be a dad again had stirred up some hope in my damaged soul. We had been happy there, in the beginning. You couldn't keep us apart.

Don't you panic, don't you panic; give it one more try.

The Stones were right, of course—no sense in getting all corn-ball sentimental. The thing to do, I figured, was get something to take away the pain, fill the gaping hole. Hell with the clean liv-ing shit, it was time to do some drugs and hit the bars with a vengeance—find some feminine companionship....

I made a beeline for the coke in my drawer—must have been over half a gram left. Hadn't touched it in all that time....

My hands shook as I lifted out the Snow Seal. Something inside me was crying out for release.

The phone rang.

It was Julie, my sexy tennis student. Her partner for mixed doubles had cancelled at the last minute. Could I possibly be a dear and fill in?

I was more than happy to oblige.

I put the coke away and was in the car and driving before I could say no to myself.

We had a halfway decent mixed doubles match. Julie and I went up against another divorcee from the complex and her son. The boy had a fantastic forehand that kept me off balance all night long. Julie and I lost in three fun sets and then retired to Julie's apartment (real nice place, with a wet bar and a screened-in deck with a view) for polite cocktails.

Lisa and Jeff left after one drink and Julie and I were undeniably alone. Daughter Gina was with her father in Dearborn, where he was an auto executive.

We had a couple more drinks and then I'll be goddamned if Julie didn't open her freezer and pull out roughly a quarter ounce of coke in a zip-lock baggie and drop it on the bar.

"Would you take care of this, Keith? Men always seem to do it better. That is if you don't have anything against a little toot. I sure would like a line."

"What... oh... yeah, I mean, no... ah, sure...."

With an impending sense of doom, I got up and did my manly duty, chopping cocaine and laying out lines.

We did a couple lines and another drink or two, all the while engaged in one of those meaningless, high octane conversations that you get into when you're ripped to the tits and believe yourself to be approaching the True Heart of All Things. Our level of artificial sincerity was only exceeded by our desire to get into each other's pants. Oh, the games that people play—nana nana hey.

Julie let me know that she had been fond of me since our first lesson. That's why she and Gina had stayed with me instead of going back to Carlos, she said. She gave me a sly smile and moved closer to me on the couch, her tanned thigh contrasting sharply with my white one.

I thanked her for that and slugged directly from the vodka bottle.

A recent divorcee, Julie had moved to Florida to avoid the unwanted attention of her ex, she said. Whose money, I assumed, was funding the condo that I was currently doing drugs in.

She went on to tell me how the son of a bitch was using his goddamn money to try and lure Gina back to Michigan for the summer. That wouldn't be so bad but after he had threatened her (Julie) once—said he'd break her neck—well... it was just very hard to want to send your baby girl back to someone who could do something like that. Not to mention just talking to him at all, you know....

I tried to act supportive and a funny thing started happening to me: I began to see Julie as a real person, a person that I really wasn't wild about. I came believe that to her, I was only a swinging dick, or maybe just a dick.

I got to thinking that I didn't like that feeling, but then I decided it wasn't that bad. At least I had a dick. And she wasn't bad looking. The way she held her legs open and kept brushing her hand on the inside of her thigh like that...she did have great tits. And sometimes, at certain angles, she did look like Ursula Andress....

Feeling used was better than feeling nothing at all, I decided. We kept on drinking and jawing and snorting. I couldn't stop talking. Neither could she. The conversation bounced around to everything on the face of the earth. Somehow we started talking about seafood, it being Florida and all. Maybe I was just trying to keep the conversation going.

"I think I'm going to try scallops, next time I go out to eat," I said. "I've heard they're pretty good."

"Euww," she said. "I hate scallops. I don't like to even touch them. It's the texture, just like nigger skin. Euww." She scrunched up her mouth.

"Nigger skin?"

"Yeah, you know—nigger skin... feels like the skin on the head of your cock," she said, nodding down at my crotch and grinning. "Kind of slippery. You don't want to rub against it in the wrong direction."

"No shit? Jesus... is that right? Should we have one more line?"

"I'm fine, honey," she said, "But if you want to, help yourself, and then get your cute butt back to this couch."

I snorted a line the size of a small night-crawler and returned to the couch.

Julie was leaning forward, expectantly, hands rubbing her thighs. Her face was tinged in blue and my heart was beating like a snare drum at a military funeral.

That's when I realized that I was playing a part in Julie's Favorite Florida Fantasy: *Young Tennis Instructor Screws Her.* I was sure of it, and by god, I didn't mind.

She moved her hip until it was touching mine, heat coming through. Then she grabbed the collar of my polo shirt, pulled me to her and jammed in her tongue.

I still wasn't feeling right and I couldn't figure it out. What in the name of all that is holy was wrong with me? This appeared to go against nature.

I pushed her off; said I wanted another drink.

She brushed down her tennis whites; softly said OK.

I was almost to the bar when she came up behind me and slipped her arm inside mine like we were walking down the aisle to a shotgun wedding. Put her hand in my back pocket and kissed me on the cheek as I threw ice cubes in a glass and tried to drown them with Smirnov.

All of sudden, I only wanted to talk.

"Why don't we go into the bedroom—where we can be alone?" she said. "You don't need another drink. Think about what alcohol can do to you... you know." Her eyes dipped down at my crotch again.

I grabbed her pack of Salems off the counter and shook one out. I was so wired my teeth were rattling.

"You put that back, now, you naughty boy. You don't need that. I've got a great big bed; why don't we go and enjoy it?"

Then she was all over me, her hand on my dick and her tongue in my mouth. I got hard and bold.

I can't say that it was torture; in fact I convinced myself that it wasn't such a bad idea after all. It had been such a long time since I'd been with a woman. Mary had been the last one, that night we went off the road and into the freezing water....

Poor girl is dead now and I'm going down slow.

Julie swung open the door to the bedroom. The bedspread was red with black swirls. I was tight as a drum.

I looked at her and figured what the hell?

We started kissing. I stood up and took off my shirt and shorts and threw them on the floor.

"Why don't you do the same," I said.

She did, throwing her clothes on the floor next to mine and slipping beneath the covers.

I got back into bed and we started kissing again.

"You remind me of my ex-husband," she said.

That was a real smart thing for her to say.

"Oh yeah?" I said, pulling back.

I looked at her face; it had lost its beauty. If only she would blow me, I thought. If only she would just go down....

Then a real funny thing happened, I started thinking about Carole. She was thousands of miles away but her face was stuck in my head. Or at least, how I remembered her, smiling, bright and sunny. It seemed I couldn't escape her, and now I was limp as a dishrag.

That said; I was aware that I had crossed a certain line with Julie. There was a degree of responsibility involved—obligations to fulfill, as it were. A man can't just get right up and walk out on a woman who's been so kind as to drop her pants. This should not be done.

It was time to apply Rule Three of the Womanizer's Code: If your dick don't work, give them the tongue.

It seemed realistic at the time. I mean, how could a chick resist a good tongue lashing? And if she got hot enough, it might spark something in me....

If I would have thought longer about it; if I had been capable of such thought at that moment—I might have seen that someone who doesn't give head probably never got head, either. And thus would be prone to lying there motionless, like a beached seal, until the eater got a stiff neck like he'd been carrying a concrete yolk on his shoulders for a month. And believe me, it wasn't my fault.

The pain made me pull away. I sat up on the edge of the bed for a moment, trying to think.

We gave each other narrow-eyed looks before I rolled off the bed and picked my clothes off the floor.

I stood up and got dressed, facing her. She covered up with the bedspread and lit a cigarette, smoking out of the side of her mouth and biting her lip.

"Sorry," I said. "See you at the club."

I walked out of the place.

I turned my ignition key and suddenly the Fears hit me, the spiky, paranoid, lame-dick blues.

The next morning I felt like death warmed over. It was my day off and all I could do was lie around in the dark suffering and feeling guilty.

It was around nine o'clock at night when a fit of anxiety took over.

I picked up the phone and dialed the number. It buzzed a few times; my heart was beating fast. I was going through hell inside, wondering and worrying.

"Hullo..."

First thing that came to mind when I heard her voice: She's been drinking—and crying.

"Carole... this is Keith. Is everything all right? You sound sad."

"Oh, sure, Keith... everything's just fine. Just dandy. Just fucking dandy. And I suppose now you're calling to get on my case. Did my Dad call you? Keith? He did, didn't he? I did the right thing, Keith, I swear to god. Mikey did good too, you know...."

He got us both across the High Bridge without hitting anything. You should be proud of your son, Keith... he can drive. That's good, isn't it?"

"Pardon me? Slow down, here. What are you talking about?"

"I just had too much to drink, that's all. It was the tequila. Tekillya, you know." She forced a laugh. "And I had too much, that's all. And there was this guy in the bar... he gave me a red. Just this little red capsule...I didn't know it would hit me like that, I swear to God. I'm just lucky I had Mike along to help me; I mean it. I could hardly walk to the car, let alone drive across the bridge..." she giggled nervously, relaxing a little.

I felt my heart yearning. "You had Mike in the bar with you?"

"Yes... It was the afternoon, Keith. And Mike plays with the owner's kid when I'm there."

"This a regular thing for you now, Carole? You and Mike hanging out in the bars together a lot?"

"No, silly, just every so often. A girl has got to get out once in a while, doesn't she—and I don't have a good, steady babysitter always available. You wouldn't want me to leave Mike with just anybody, would you? I mean, there's no telling what could happen to a cute boy like him, if—"

"That's right Carole, I wouldn't want that. So, the little tough guy drove you all the way across the bridge and home, huh? What a guy, my son...."

"Not exactly all the way home.... Someone called the cops on us, Keith, and they pulled us over on Garfield Avenue. Poor Mike's head barely made it over the steering wheel and someone spotted him in Hammond on our way to the bridge. It was in the papers, Keith.... And now I've lost my job at the station, because of it. I got fired. They said the publicity was bad for business.... And they're disputing my unemployment claim, now, too. I don't know what I'm going to do, Keith. It seems like everyone's against me, even my Dad."

"Calm down, calm down. Your mother will always help you, Carole."

"And what does she have? Nothing but what my father gives her. I don't know which one I can't stand the most."

She paused. I heard a sigh and a whimper.

"Keith—can Mike and I come down there—to Florida? That would solve everything. My Dad says he won't pay my fine and I might have to go to jail. You wouldn't want me to go to a dirty smelly jail cell, do you?" She cooed.

"No. No more than I want your parents to get custody of Mike and twist his mind in knots with all of their bullshit. Jesus Christ... How much is the fine? Wait—don't tell me. Just find out the cost of two plane tickets to Tampa and add it up together with the fine. I'll pay the whole thing. Shit... I'll call you tomorrow night at the same time to find out the cost. I might need some time to gather it together."

"Keith...."

"Yes...."

"They want the fine paid by next week." There was a pause and another whimper. "Mikey can always go to a foster home," she said, fighting back tears. "I won't be locked inside there too long...."

"Oh, bullshit. That's not going to happen. I'll send the fucking money. Just be home when I call."

"I will, but don't you think I should have your number? In case of an emergency?"

I knew they'd never throw a single mother in jail on a first offense but I didn't bother to give my opinion. I couldn't remember Carole ever being this compliant and needy. Not since before we were married, anyway, and I was going to take full advantage of it.

A warm feeling was circulating in my stomach.

I gave her the number and suddenly wondered if I had just opened the door and let madness walk in. Hell, it felt like I had served it a drink and sat down with it for a while. When a man spends the last of his cash to bring something back into his life that never worked in the first place... well... you've just got to wonder. You've got to think the guy is grasping for the invisible with a butterfly net.

I tried to shake off the feelings but couldn't. I began to wonder who was in charge of the situation, Carole or me? It seemed like old times were coming back again—neither one of us knowing whether we were going or coming. Would I have to go through it all twice?

I swallowed those thoughts and tried to prepare my mind for family life.

"Tell Mikey I love him, Carole. Tell him I'll see him soon. Tell him to be sure and bring his baseball mitt down with him. And Carole... I just got to say that I'm glad you guys are coming. It's warm down here... things will be different, you'll see."

I shivered inside.

"I know they will, Keith. I know we'll get it right this time. I can't wait to feel you squeezed up against me again, honey."

Jesus! She was getting to me, long distance.

"Just call me tomorrow, when you find out the prices. Bye."

Worms wiggled in my gut.

Chapter Two

Memories Are Made of This

The waiting is tearing me up. The more I worry about the boat, the more I start to think about Carole and Mike: how much I miss them.

The thought makes me hurt: a sad, sick sort of pain.

On the run from the law and not fit to be a father anymore.... If only I'd been smarter or tougher or richer, maybe I never would've brought them to Florida. Could've kept them out of this mess, if only I'd been strong enough to make it alone....

I guess I was trying to bring back the past. Carole and I had been quite the couple. I don't think we spent one night apart for the first three years, like John and Yoko or something. We even had their album cover on our bedroom wall.

Two Virgins, that was us.

But when it fell apart, it was gone in a hurry. Seemingly happy at Christmas, separated by the Fourth of July. We went from lovers to haters in one hell of a hurry. I guess it was my fault, but sometimes I'm not so sure.

I was so nervous on the way to the Tampa airport that the ridiculous traffic didn't even bother me. My head was flooded with memories, both bad and good. My stomach danced and churned like a teenager at a sock hop.

The reunion at the airport gait was tense but we got through it. Carole looked beautiful and seeing Mike made me want to cry.

The ride home in the car was nervous. They were blown away by the change in scenery. I was just plain blown away.

Joyously, for me, Mike fell in love with the condo as soon as his feet hit the parking lot. I could see his mom in him when he got excited. Seemed like he had my face and her hair. Damn, it was good to see him.

He spied a little gray salamander in the bushes and immediately thought this was the coolest place in the world. Neat pool. Neat tennis courts. Super color TV. Don't think I'd ever seen him that happy.

Carole seemed pretty impressed too. She was her version of happy as far as I could tell. Her round blue eyes showed fatigue but still had some sparkle. Her skin was as soft and white as ever. Boy, how good she smelled. She had on this lightweight, dark blue polka-dot dress that fit tight in all the right places. Her shoulder-length hair was yellow and shiny.

I couldn't make myself tell them that we only had the rental unit until the end of December. I was afraid how Carole would react. I really wanted us to get started on the right foot. I thought I could break the news later, after we were together for a while.

That first night we took the boy down to the pool for an evening swim and he met a couple of kids. It started to feel like a family, again, if only just a little.

After swimming, we got him set up in his new, nicely furnished

bedroom. All the stuff in there was in good shape: fine wood furniture like your parents might've had if you were lucky. It was
nicer stuff than he'd had back in Zenith City, I was pretty sure.
We got him settled into bed and he conked off in nothing flat.
Carole unpacked and we had a couple of cans of Busch. We
talked evasive small talk. After a few beers, Carole asked if we
could get some rum to celebrate our reunion.
I drove to the mall.

We downed a pint of Bacardi with Coca-Cola and fresh limes.
I had told myself that I wasn't going to rush into things but I'd
been waiting for too long. We'd been talking and laughing a little bit and I started coming on, sitting next to her on the couch
and kissing her deep.
She all of a sudden kind of dragged me into the bedroom.
Strangely, I got apprehensive. A vague uneasiness kept scratching
at my brain.
Then we got going and it was just like old times. She had a little more meat on her now but that only made her warmer and,
seemingly, more enthusiastic. Her moaning and writhing drove
my apprehension right out the open window. I'd forgotten how
noisy she could be....
Afterwards, it was awkward but we tried to talk a little. I
hugged her and smiled. It felt good.
We lay there for five or ten minutes before I started to fall asleep.
She rolled out of bed, slipped a T-shirt over her delicate shoulders,
went into the living room and flipped on the television.
I stayed in bed and thought deep thoughts as I drifted away.
The two of us now had legal problems as a common thread but I
knew I could never tell her about the things that had happened to
me back home. Best that some things are never discussed with
the spouse. No sense in spilling your guts, like some jerk on the
Donahue Show; marriages work better that way.

The next ten days we had a real American vacation. We visited Busch Gardens, the beaches, the waterslides and the Botanical Gardens. If there was a tourist trap, we went there. We had lunches at Steak and Shake or brought picnics to the beach or a park.

On three of those nights, we had dinner at a seafood place in St. Pete called Neptune's Kitchen. I didn't order scallops. Mike enjoyed the live fish in the aquariums but would only eat cheeseburgers and fries.

Other nights, Carole and I would drink rum and cokes by the pool while Mike swam and our steaks or chicken sizzled on the grill. Even our trips to the supermarkets were fun. We laughed a lot. I was feeling like a man should feel.

We got Mikey into a nice new school in Clearwater, located in a nice residential neighborhood. He seemed happy, if a little anxious. I didn't think that I would have handled it as well at his age.

The reunited family settled into a rhythm: Mike to school in the morning, back to bed for his parents.

If I didn't have to go into the club until late in the day, we'd stay in bed until noon. Some days we had breakfast and then played tennis or hung by the pool. I picked up a cheap racket at the club for Carole and she enjoyed playing if it wasn't too hot.

The main focus of our days, it soon became obvious, was the cocktail hour. I found no fault with this; in fact it seemed like a wonderful new Carole had emerged from how I remembered her. She had been transformed in the warm southern sun, before my very eyes, into a colorful social butterfly. Witty repartee, laughter and enthusiastic sex were my rewards. The reticence she had once demonstrated to my desires seemed a thing of the past.

Slowly, we were growing closer together. It was beginning to feel like we were confidants again—the two of us against the world—like it had been in the beginning. That chip-on-our-shoulders determination seemed to be returning.

It was because of this good feeling that I continued to avoid telling her about the upcoming end of our lease. I wanted to maintain the illusion of prosperity that I had created for as long as possible so I kept putting it off. After she'd gotten used to the relative luxury, I just didn't have the nerve to break the news. This place was relative luxury compared to what we'd be able to afford come tourist season. With my sporadic pay from the tennis club and the three of us having to eat and drink so much, I knew it was going to be a struggle. We had to be out of the condo before January 5th. Seasonal renters were coming in for the winter months—at three times the rent that we were paying.

I prayed that the months we already had together would ease the pain and make the changes seem worthwhile to her. Most of all I wanted her—them—to know that the situation was only temporary and things would get better.

But I had a feeling that they might get worse before they got better. Now that the days were shorter and the nights longer, I felt like I was sinking into a vast darkness. The human swamp was calling to me as it swirled around on the freeways, the canals and the hotels....

Wasn't that what I wanted, after all, the high life? Was my family just a security blanket, a pacifier?

I wasn't so sure anymore.

One thing that I was sure of: the family needed more money. All those security deposits and the first month, last month, stuff made the nicer places a difficult acquisition for struggling young families like us. There were places that didn't allow children....

Everywhere you looked it was shitty complexes and developments. Artificial neighborhoods with cul-de-sacs and parking lots and manmade ponds for the alligators all jammed together in the same end of town. Some people will tell you that they're financed by mob money pilfered from union retirement funds.

The only way out of Complex Town was a good chunk of cash and that was something I no longer had.

*   *   *

I dropped the bomb on December 7th, in recognition of Pearl Harbor.

Carole about fainted. Started shaking a little and I didn't know if it was anger or fear or what. Smoked a cigarette and her jaw got tight. She didn't say anything out of hand, though, and we discussed it in a reasonably controlled manner. After a while, she acted like everything was all right.

I wasn't so sure she was sincere but I was impressed that we handled it so well, just like adults. We had definitely progressed. Nobody had gotten angry or hurt; she only got sad. She must have understood that I was trying my best to keep her happy....

"The thought of a Southern Christmas is bad enough," she said to me. "No snow and being away from home... and now this. Now we have to look for an apartment at the same time...."

"You knew you'd be away from home at Christmas when you came down here," I said and immediately wished that I'd kept my mouth shut.

Her face collapsed. She rose slowly and slumped dramatically into the bedroom. Darkness took over.

I took a deep breath and went in the living room and sat down on the couch next to Mike. I couldn't bring myself to tell him that he had to change schools.

We stared at the TV. I don't remember what was on because I had this *loser* feeling that wouldn't leave me alone.

Right then I made up my mind that we would have a great Christmas—one to remember.

To accomplish this, I believed the surest route would be to spend our money like there was no tomorrow, thus enjoying what we had, to the hilt. Celebrate long and often in order to forget everything bad that had happened in the past and then pray that the future worked itself out.

Carole and I got drunk on Tom and Jerry's every night for a week. We shopped for gifts and looked for bargains. I don't remember finding any. Then, on the night after Mike's last day of school, we threw a tree-decorating party and invited John Carino. We strung lights on a six-foot rubber plant for our Christmas tree. Earlier in the week, we had received a package from Carole's parents with presents and cards and candy. We put the presents under the plant, along with a few that Carole and I picked up for Mike.

There was a wood baseball bat under there (Louisville Slugger), and Mike, of course, knew right away what it was, so we let him tear the paper off for an early present. I figured it was the least we could do for the poor kid. He was a trooper to put up with parents like us.

We were all smiles and togetherness when John snapped our picture in front of that skinny, lit-up, rubber Christmas tree.

After John left and Mike was asleep, Carole and I went into the bedroom. We were both pretty lit up ourselves. We fell into bed with our tongues intertwined and stayed there.

I woke in the middle of the night with that old familiar feeling creeping up my spine. I knew it wasn't going away and that I wasn't getting back to sleep.

I rolled silently out of bed and left the room. Closed the door behind me and walked softly on the gold shag carpet into the living room. I slid open the curtains and looked out through the screen at the empty tennis courts bathed in florescent glow. The silhouettes of pine trees swayed in the dim light. A lawn spotlight shined against the husked bark of a large palm, whose fronds were swaying slowly in the cool night breeze.

Sighing reflexively, I turned and looked behind me at the cluttered brown coffee table. Carole's pack of Kools, lit up by neon streaks, glowed like a discovered treasure.

I chose that moment to start smoking again. Plucked one from the pack and lit it up with a flourish. Sucked in the first drag and blew it out slowly.

Not bad... stupid, but not too bad.

I sat there on the couch and smoked, once in a while leaning over and flicking the ash into a coral blue ceramic ashtray in the shape of a mollusk.

Something about that first Kool got me to thinking—and remembering. Recalling the origin of the familiar feeling that was now returning to its old home in my solar plexus.

I flashed back to the ride to Zenith City from the Minneapolis airport, after our Las Vegas wedding. I felt like it was 1969 again and I was right back inside that '52 Chevy, frightened about my first days of married life. It seemed like the gnawing feeling in my gut never left after that; I had just gotten used to it.

I stubbed out my cig and stared across at the white, empty walls of our "second chance" home.

Vegas? Florida? Minnesota? Would it make any difference where we were?

Chapter Three

Reality Comes Slipping In

Approaching nightfall on day two and still no sign of the boat. Worry has turned to abject fear, overcome only by the need to ease the boredom. I've turned the portable radio on; as the grapefruit sun gets sliced by the edge of the world.

Hendrix is playing "Manic Depression" and things are, indeed, a frustrating mess.

And to think that beaches were one of the reasons why I came to Florida....

My only escape from this lonely prison is to go back in my mind and try and see where it all went wrong. Drift back to the edge of disaster and see where I slipped off.

Things were going okay there, in the beginning. Then I had one bad break. A real bad break...

Carole, poor girl, really ceased being happy shortly after we moved out of the condo.

Our new digs, an unfurnished apartment in the huge Twin Lakes complex, turned her sour from the start. The only furniture we owned were a tartan plaid sleeper couch that the owner of the condo had let us keep. You should have seen the look on John's face when we tried to lift that goddamn thing.

John's seasonal condo deal had run out, along with ours, and he had recommended Twin Lakes, saying that other guys from the station lived in the neighborhood. He got a place at the serpentine, two-tiered complex, in the singles section.

I'm not sure of the reason for Twin Lakes' popularity except that it was cheap, relatively speaking, with none of that first and last month down crap.

We bought a table and chairs, kitchen utensils and two beds, at a thrift store in old St. Pete, and moved into the family section.

Directly above us in apartment 227, was an airforce couple: Korean wife had a penchant for staying up all night crying with the windows open. Next door was a divorced woman—husband in jail for some unspecified sex crime. At least according to her sixteen-year-old-high-school-drop-out daughter and ten-year-old son, who told Mike about their dad's troubles, as we were moving in.

I began to wonder about the place.

Mike seemed okay with it, mostly because of the pool and the fact that we could see it from our living room. There were two tennis courts and some good players around, so I was consoled. Greasy brown cockroaches, so thick you could hear them scurrying as you reached for the kitchen light switch, put Carole on edge. She became tense as a rule, immediately after our first night at Twin Lakes, and began to develop a screwy, twisted up facial expression.

I didn't like the roaches, either. They were especially bad when they crawled across your bare chest in the middle of the night and you woke up slapping yourself. It's enough to give me the willies, just thinking about it.

Carole couldn't or wouldn't laugh it off, choosing instead, to drink it off. Seagram's or Bacardi if we could afford it, wine or beer if there was nothing else. If somebody else was providing, it didn't matter what the beverage, as long as it contained alcohol. I started drinking more, myself. But I was always sweating it off on the tennis courts and didn't notice any ill effects.

It was just one more sunny day when John Carino called me up with a proposition: He needed a doubles partner for a big match—a money match at the private courts of a famous entertainer he said.

He filled me in.

This famous Italian singer kept a mansion in the Clearwater area and his son, let's call him Beano, was in town staying at his father's pad. Beano was also an entertainer of some note, although, of lesser status than his father, and also was quite a tennis player. Even played a pro in a movie once.

Beano had been the guest on one of John's talk shows—and, evidently, one thing had led to another. The boys' dueling egos had risen to the boiling point when the subject of tennis came up. John challenged Beano to a singles match. Beano begged off the mano-a-mano battle, explaining that he was entered in a celebrity doubles tournament in Sarasota with his younger cousin and needed to practice.

John didn't miss a beat in extending the challenge to doubles. Beano couldn't say no on the air—and lose face—so he reluctantly agreed.

So one day John and I drove out to this estate with a big vine covered wall around it. The place was full of foliage and birds and gurgling fountains. There was even a fake bayou, for the Christ sake.

We warmed up on the brand-spanking-new, green and red courts. The gamblers put the stakes—Beano's three crisp C-notes, my wrinkled twenty and John's check for two hundred and eighty—underneath a cocktail glass on a circular white metal table next to the courts.

In the middle of the first set, John and I got hot, started hitting the lines and we blew them out 6-2. Beano threw his racket twice and swore. John ate it up with a spoon.

Second set, our opponents were edgy and irritable, biting at each other softly but visibly. John and I were sweating and smiling and went up 4-2. The important seventh game was upon us and it was my serve.

It was a battle, one of those games were you're going deuce-add, deuce-add, back and forth forever. Then, on one particular break point against me, I was out chasing a cross-court shot. I anticipated well, made full speed and gave it the bolo forehand. The ball burned down the alley and skidded off the baseline and I went into a celebratory dance.

Beano held up his index finger, signaling that the ball was out. I jerked my head, screamed, "BULLSHIT" and set my foot to stop.

One sneaker slipped on a dried leaf while the other one stuck to the asphalt. My left leg bent back on itself. I heard a cracking sound and felt fire as I collapsed to the ground.

"FUCK! AAAHHH! GODDAMN IT! WHAT KIND OF FUCKING CALL WAS THAT?"

Tears rolled out; ripping pain seared my left shin.

John came over and knelt down beside me as I writhed in agony, his face gray. He looked down at me. "Partner, partner," he said. "You gonna make it?"

"Yeah, man," I groaned

Cousin was leaning towards us with his hands resting on the net, looking somewhat concerned. Beano stood by the net post with his water bottle; sweat dripping down from those famous blonde locks. I watched in agony as he lifted the plastic bottle and took a long drink, squirting a stream into his mouth from a distance like it was a goddamn wineskin and this was a party. Then he stood there looking down on me, squinting in the sun, droplets falling from his chin onto the red asphalt.

"Sorry, man, I guess it *was* a bad call," Beano said. "Just caught the back of the line, I guess. Sorry, tough break. But, John... if he can't play anymore, we win by default—in spite of that great shot." Then, as cold as the top of a mountain: "The money's ours, I'm afraid, gentlemen. Sorry John. Better luck next time," averting his eyes.

He sniffed a couple times, grabbed his gear from the court and walked away, lifting his winnings off the table without breaking stride.

As he disappeared up the hill, leaving us to fend for ourselves, I couldn't believe what was happening.

Cousin looked over at me apologetically, for a short moment, and then followed Beano up the path like a good little boy.

With John's help and using my racket for a cane, we struggled to the car. Any weight at all on the ankle and it seared with pain. Without any weight on it, there was a dull throb.

John opened the passenger door and I sat down sideways with my feet on the pavement, sweat streaming from every pore. I lifted my legs into the cramped front seat of the VW and we drove away.

"I know where there's a hospital near here," John said. "I saw it on the way over. Hold on, pal, it won't be long."

It was three minutes to a small brick building located on the edge of Beano's high-class neighborhood. John knew right where to go.

I had to put my arm around John's shoulders to make it down the walk and through the glass door of Portman Memorial Hospital. I struggled into the large, bright waiting room and crumpled into a chair.

John gestured to a woman sitting at a desk behind a glass partition.

She stood up and looked at me, curled up her nose and sat back down, motioning John to come over. Couldn't she see that I was a tennis player, not some bum?

After a brief discussion, John was able to procure some admission forms.

"Keith," he said gravely, "Are you going to be all right?"

I nodded to the affirmative.

"I hate to do this to you," he said, "but I have to leave…. I'm filling in for Steve O'Neill today and I'm on the air in less then an hour. It's going to take me thirty minutes just to get there, the way the traffic is. Jesus, I'm sorry, Keith. That fucking prick Beano… we were kicking his ass and this had to happen. What a prick that guy is… walking away like that. What a fucking asshole! Man, we were kicking their ass. I'm going to stop payment on that check. Fuck that son of a bitch."

"That's right, Johnny, fuck him," I said, grimacing. "We did kick their ass and they know it. Did you see the look on his face when I blew that forehand by him? Then he waves it out and look what happened…. Jesus, this fucking thing hurts. I'll be all right, though. Just call Carole for me Johnny, before you leave. They better give me some good pain pills for this one. It'll be shame to waste 'em on pain, though."

I gave him my best brave soldier look.

"Of course I'll call Carole. And I'll be sure and check in on you tomorrow. I'll bring over a couple of tall Buds."

"I'm not giving you any of my pain pills."

"That's cool, You're going to need them, I think."

John made the call from a payphone on the wall and then smiled and waved back at me as he walked out the front door.

I sat there filling out the forms, waiting for Carole to show up.

I was sweating harder after I read the bottom of the form:

ALL FEES MUST BE PAID IMMEDIATELY
UPON RECEIPT OF SERVICES.

I took this to mean that you had to pay on the spot—at the time of service. I hoped that maybe they'd take one of our checks when my wife arrived. There wasn't anything in the account but I'd catch up to them later… that was the way it had to be.

I could feel Sky Pilot grinning at what he had created. Another fine mess he'd gotten me into....

By the time Carole got there, I was in the examining room lying on a long steel table being looked at by the intern. He was just about to wheel me over to X-ray when the lady from the front desk came in and informed us that the hospital couldn't accept our check. Unless we had some credit cards, they would have to stop treatment.

We didn't have any credit cards—in our name.

She suggested I try the public hospital over in Tampa.

"They'll take care of you there without any verification of credit," she said.

"They just won't let you leave the hospital until you come up with the cash," the young intern added.

"Are you serious?" I whined. "Back where we came from, in Minnesota, they give you thirty days to make arrangements."

"Hospital policy," the woman said and left without further comment.

"They would probably take your check over in Tampa," the intern said. "To set your leg, anyway. Then you can plead indigence and file a claim with the welfare people. They have to treat you at Tampa; they get federal money because that's where most of the blacks live. This is high roller territory here. We do more heart attacks and strokes per visit than anywhere else, but downtown St. Pete. But we get more sleeping pill overdoses than they do.... I'm afraid you picked the wrong hospital to break your leg near, my friend. The folks that run this little unit don't even believe you exist unless you're pulling down a hundred grand or more."

Carole was paging through a magazine, and looking nervous, when I hobbled back into the lobby, propped up by the shoulder of the young intern. She looked up at me, worry on her young face. It made me feel good to see her worried about me.

"Keith, what's the matter?" she said. "What are you doing? Why aren't you getting taken care of?"

"The donors of mercy are in short supply today, Carole. They're not going to treat me here. They won't take our check without a credit card. Didn't the bitch tell you that?"

"I told her to ask you, I didn't know if you had any, you know..."

"Let's get the hell out of here," I said, loud enough for the other waiting patients to hear.

An old woman with leathery brown skin and peroxide hair stared at us, clucking like a laying hen. I thanked the intern and put my arm around Carole's shoulder. Her body language now spoke more of frustration than concern. We shuffled out to the parking lot and I got flat on my back in the rear seat of the Volvo.

"Where are we going to go, Keith? You need some work on that leg, honey. John said that you broke it."

"Fuck this shit, Carole. Just take me home. This thing will heal by itself. I'm becoming a firm believer in self-healing. I don't think it's that bad, anyway. It'll get better. Just go to a liquor store and get me some Bacardi, some Coke and some ice. I'll put the leg up. It doesn't seem so bad anymore."

The pain had lessened to a deep dull ache that I knew I could stand if I had enough aspirin and booze in my belly. Screw the goddamn hospitals and the rich-ass doctors; I would become a Christian Scientist.

After we got the liquor, Carole went into an Eckerd Drug and bought some adhesive tape and one of those Ace Bandages.

At home, I plopped down on the hide-a-bed couch and Carole put some pillows under my ankle. Then she fixed me up a pillowcase full of ice and a nice strong drink.

I swallowed four aspirin and asked Carole for one of her cigarettes.

"You're smoking now?" she said.

"I started again," I said.

"What kind of tennis pro smokes?"

"A lot of them, honey. And, in case you hadn't thought of it yet, I'll point out that I probably won't be playing much tennis for awhile—given the circumstances and all."

"What are we going to live on, then?"

"I don't know, darlin'. I don't know."

"I need a drink now, too," she said, tinny.

"No surprise there."

"Fuck you, Keith."

She stomped into the kitchen. I took a long pull on my drink, maybe half the glass.

"You're going to have to get a job, Carole."

"What kind of a job can I get down here?" she said, opening the freezer door.

"Just about any job you can get anywhere else, except down here there are more of them. …There are radio stations down here where you could get a job, I'm sure."

"After what happened back home? I can't use KQBC as a reference, you know."

She sat down near me with her glass in hand, grabbed a cig, fired up, then leaned forward and looked downward.

"Why not? You were a good worker, weren't you? It wasn't job performance that got you shit canned, was it? Maybe they won't say anything bad. Who knows? But hey, John works for a radio station…maybe he can get you a job at WPLF. According to John, these big-time dudes from LA bought the station and are totally re-staffing it. Used to be a rock station and now it's a talk station. That's something you're good at, talking."

"I'm not going on the air down here. I hate it."

"Why not, you'd be good."

"Well… maybe… I'd rather be a receptionist and do voice work."

"Can you fix me another drink, honey?" I said. "They seem to be really working on this pain. The ice, too. When you're done, maybe you should call John out at the station and tell him to stop over after he gets off. I think I'll have him set my leg."

"You'll what?"

"Have him set my leg. He went to college in California... watched trainers work and stuff. Played big-time tennis there at Pepperdine... that's right in LA, I think. He's a smart guy; he'll be able to tape it up and it will heal, no problem."

"You should see a doctor."

"And how are we going to pay for that? Give blood? Shoplift? Answer me that. This town doesn't hand out credit to people like us."

"People like you, you mean, Keith. You're the one who brought us down here. I thought you had money... a good job... now what? You've got one leg and no job and a pregnant wife."

My throat squeezed shut and heartburn came on like a volcanic eruption.

"Pregnant? Are you fucking serious? How do you know?"

"Well... I'm late. There was just spotting—when my period should have been. And we have been doing it a lot, lately...."

"Oh my lord." I said, swallowing back bile. My leg throbbed harder. I chugged my drink. "It's probably just some reaction to the change in climate...different drinking water, or something like that. Could you fix me another drink and then call John? I want to get this thing wrapped up. We can ask him about a job for you at the same time. You've got to look ahead in this world, you know. And I'm going to be down for a while. We are back together, though, Carole—you and me and Mikey. That's what's important. We can make it. We just have to fight. Where the hell is Mikey, anyway?"

"He's over at his friend Carl's apartment. Over at Pleasant Knolls, across the alligator pond."

"Oh, yeah."

She looked at me warily and stubbed out her cigarette. Didn't say anything, just hissed out smoke. Took our glasses and went into the kitchen where the booze was. Turned on the light.

I heard her curse as the slimy critters scurried away.

She came back with the drinks and set mine on the coffee table perfectly within the center of an already existing moisture ring. Then she stepped back to kitchen and lifted the receiver off the wall phone.

"Do you know the number at the station?" she half-whined, half-snarled.

"No," I said, "You'll have to look it up. Pinellas Park."

She got the phone book out of the drawer and began rummaging through. After a few minutes, I could feel her frustration rising, in spite of the alcohol.

"I can't find it in here," she said. There's no WPLF in this book. Are you sure those are the right call letters?"

"Yes, I'm sure. Oh yeah, wait, a minute…. Now I remember… the deal is that they changed the name of the station after they bought it. That phone book must go all the way back to before the L. A. boys came to town."

"That doesn't help me much."

"I'll tell you what, turn on the radio to the station, maybe John is still on the air. They always give out the number on the air."

"Do you know the frequency numbers?"

"Hell no… to a talk station? Are you kidding me? Just turn the dial until you get to the boring-ass shit and then stop.That'll be it."

Carole slowly turned the dial on our plastic radio shaped like an orange until she came upon the gravelly voice of a southern cracker:

"Some of those Negroes on the Bucs just don't play hard enough, that's all there is to it. They take their giant salaries and buy dope—that's what they do. That's why the Bucs are losing all the time, I'll tell you, John McKay just lets 'em carry on like that because he's from California and everybody knows what those

California people are like. They're all crazy out there—and you oughta know, Johnny boy."

John's mellow and bemused voice came through: "I'll comment on that in a second, Andy, being from California. But first I have to tell everybody out there who we are and why we're here. "This is WPLF, Talk Radio 97. We're here doing Sports Talk. Tonight's subject: Why the Bucs suck. We welcome your calls at 555-6161 or 555-1616.

"There you go, Carole," I said. "Write that down. 555-6161. I wonder why John's doing Sports Talk tonight... he was supposed to be on the air this afternoon—for someone else."

"Now back at you, Andy," John intoned. "Don't you think the white guys are doing drugs, too, pal?"

"Hell, no. Just look at the way the team's been playin'. Only good plays that happen... it's the white boys been makin'em. Can't you see what I'm sayin'?"

"No I can't, Andy. What about Leroy Selmon? You trying to tell me that he hasn't been playing well?"

"Hell, no, he's good... but that boy's got religion. That's the only thing 'at saves them boys. Look what happened to his brother and you can see what I mean."

"I'm afraid I do see what you mean, Andy. But I never will believe it. Now why don't you pop another can of warm Dixie and jump back into bed with your sister—maybe watch a little Sanford and Son for educational purposes. G'night, now."

The phone clicked and buzzed; Andy was eighty-sixed. I laughed. I had never heard John like that before. Usually the guy was polite and laid back, even respectful of the most ignorant callers.

Next caller wanted to change the subject: "Hey John, how you doin' tonight?"

"Fine, thank you. Thanks for calling WPLF. Who's calling and what is your comment?"

"This is Bill from Sarasota. I'd just like to say that I hate the

Bucs and that the Lions are going to stomp them next week. But that's not why I called. I was wondering if you were ever going to have Larry Holmes on the show again. I tuned in last week just to listen to him and then he wasn't even on the show, after you'd been advertising it all week."

"I'm sorry, Bill, we're not going to have him on again."

Another voice cracked through the airways. A throaty, rough sounding voice with the hint of intoxication: "Wait a minute, sir, he's not really sorry about that, because all of us at the station know that Larry Holmes is a first class jerk who couldn't punch his way out of Mohammed Ali's jockstrap. I was expecting him to show up for that show, and then at the last minute he calls up and says he's sick. You could hear the sounds of a restaurant or bar on the phone. He was sick all right—because he'd stuffed his fat gut full of ribs and potatoes and couldn't move his sorry butt off the barstool. We will never allow him on the air again at WPLF. But thanks for calling, Bill. Just don't ever mention Larry Holmes again."

"That, ladies and gentlemen was Ted Friday, Sports Talk's regular host, who just walked into the studio," John said, the hint of a chuckle in his voice. "Ted, my friend, glad you could make it in. I heard that your mother had a medical emergency, I hope everything is all right."

"Yeah, it turned out pretty good, man. She can only see out of one eye and talk out of one side of her mouth, but she's doing good."

"That doesn't sound to good to me, Ted, are you sure she's getting better?"

"She's already improving, man. When I brought her in she was totally blind and couldn't talk at all—so she's one hell of a lot better. Oh, oh—I violated FCC rules again. There goes another buck in the kitty. I'm—"

John cut in: "The clock on the wall is telling me it's time for a commercial break. I'm all done for the evening, next up is

Howard Bales with Real Estate Tips and Tales. I don't know what Ted is going to do now, but I'm assuming he'll be back in here tomorrow for the next installment of Sports Talk, right here on WPLF Talk 97. This is John McQuade wishing everybody a good night."

"Jesus, Carole, that doesn't sound like our John boy,' I said. "Our little doubles match must have had an effect on him. Or maybe he and that Ted guy have been getting high. They sounded fucked up to me. Call him up, quick, before he leaves. He'll probably still be there."

I was drunk. The leg pain seemed a great distance away but ready to come back.

"Then you better go get Mike at his friend's house. He should come home now," I said.

"He can stay for a little while longer," Carole said before lifting up the receiver.

John arrived about ten-thirty with a friend: Ted Friday, five-foot-nine Cuban American, with a fuzzy, Afro and a big black mustache.

Mike was home, quizzing me about the match.

"There's the guy you want to ask about tennis, Mike," I said, pointing to John as he sat down across from us. "I'm just out there hacking. This dude can play."

John, without missing a beat: "Your dad was awesome today, Mikey. He hit some serves that Connors couldn't have touched. Hit a few forehands like Ilie Nastase. He was doing great until he slipped on that leaf."

"But you didn't win," Mikey said. "How come you didn't win when you were so far ahead?"

"You got to finish the match, Mike," I said, slightly slurred. "Just like life, son, if you don't finish, you don't win."

"What the hell does that mean, Keith?" Carole said, also slightly slurred. "If you finish life, aren't you dead? How can you win if you're dead?"

"You just don't understand sports, Carole. Ted here is a sports show host...I bet he knows what I'm saying."

"No lie, man, no lie. You gotta finish. That's no bullshit. Is it all right to say bullshit in front of your kid, man?"

"No problem, man," I said. "Make yourself a drink if you want, man. Stuff's in the kitchen."

"Great, I think I will. I got an edge, if you know what I mean."

"I got an edge of pain, man. And these drinks are keeping it away. John, buddy... how would you like to set my broken bone for me? The prick doctors at that rich man's hospital wouldn't treat me. I need you to tape up my ankle. I bet if you wrapped it just like an ankle wrap, she'd heal up nice and straight."

"Are you serious, man? I'm no doctor."

"You are the closest thing we have, buddy. I know you can do it, you're from California."

"You're right. Sometimes I forget that, living down here in this godforsaken swampland. First thing we need is pineapple. Fresh if you can get it, canned if you can't."

"Pineapple?"

"Yeah, pineapple. It speeds the healing process, takes away the inflammation. Our trainer at Pepperdine taught me that. We always had it around at practice in case you got an owee."

"Are you shitting me?" I said. "Pineapple helps you heal, eh?"

"It really works," John said. "So lets go get some." He rubbed his palms together and looked around the room.

Carole took Mike off to his bedroom with his radio and a few books.

"You know, Keith," John said as he watched them walk away, "studies show that kids who live in large apartment complexes like this one, get into sex and drugs, like, years ahead of the mean."

"That's comforting news," I said, before yelling: "Carole, run over to the Safeco and pick up some pineapple, will you please? And some pineapple juice for the rum. And get some more rum, too. We have company."

She came into the room in a hurry.

"You got any money, Keith?"

"Write a check," I said.

"It'll bounce," she said.

"So what," I said.

"If you say so," she said, reaching for the car keys on the kitchen counter.

"I'll drive," John said. "Let's go." Then he gave me a funny look. "Ted can keep Keith entertained with his sports knowledge, Carole. He knows a lot of the Bucs personally. Don't you, Ted boy?"

"Yeah I do, man. That's a fact," Ted said.

"You guys get along now, the longer you wait the worse this leg is gonna get," I said.

"You should take the ice off that leg until we get back," John said. Let it swell up a bit. If I wrap it and then it swells up afterward, it'll get too tight and you'll either have to cut off the tape, or wait a little while and cut off your leg at the knee."

"An amputation situation? That's cool," I said.

"I got just the thing for you, man," Ted said.

He reached back into his shirt pocket and came out with a glossy paper bindle, plopped it down on the worn coffee table.

"This stuff here will do your pain some good, *compadre*. It'll make you nice and numb. Compliments of my man Dracula."

"Jesus, I don't know if I should,' I said. "Give John my share. I'll take some Percodan if you got it, though."

"No snort for me, gentleman," John said. "I don't want to be all geeked out in the supermarket... too damn bright in those stores."

"Ah hell," I said to Ted. "Now you've talked me into it. But you better put it away until Carole leaves."

"Oh, sure, man. Your old lady don't dig blow?"

"No she doesn't, hates the sight of it."

Carole came out all shiny and clean in a blue denim shirt and tight white jeans, bopped into the living room in time to observe Ted's hand as it scooped the bindle off the table. Her eyes widened.

"Is that coke, you guys?"

"No," Ted said. "Just some lousy old crystal I was trying to get rid of."

"Oh, pooh," Carole said. "I've been hoping to do some of that cocaine that Florida is so famous for. Speed might be okay, though, too... anything that keeps the pounds off, y'know.... Save me some, won't you," winking. "Ready, John?" She said with a flourish.

"Sure," he said. "Let's go," sharing a quizzical look with Ted and I.

As soon as the door shut behind them, Ted was over at the cardboard boxes of records on my floor, sifting through the album covers.

"You were shitting me about your old lady, eh, man. Chicks dig blow, man. I know that... I know that much, for sure. Now we gonna have to give her some of the shit...but that's all right. Chicks dig blow.... Wow, man, you've got all these Stones records... you dig the Stones, eh, man." He laid out the lines on top of Mick Jagger's elongated face. "You got any straws, man? Your kid must have straws for his chocolate milk...."

"Yeah, in the kitchen, in the silverware drawer. Second one in. I'd get it for you, but...."

"No problem, man."

We sniffed up the powder. Guilt hit me before my teeth went numb. We didn't say a word for a couple of minutes.

"You mind if I turn on the tube, man?" Ted said. "I did an interview with Doug Williams today over at the stadium, and I think KBLS is going to use it on the ten o'clock sports."

"The news is already over, Ted. Sports, too. It's past ten-thirty, already."

"God damn, man. I wonder if they used it. Maybe they'll play it tomorrow on the morning newsbreak. You got a player for these records, man?"

"Uh, well, no. Ah yes, really. I mean it's just my son Mike's little player that we use. But it's in his room with him. We had a real nice stereo back home, but we didn't bring it down here. Carole didn't. We can play the radio, though. I like some of the stations down here."

"K96 ain't bad, Classic Rock and no fucking disco. Everyone else is playing too much of that goddamn disco shit. I can't wait until that shit goes away. I just don't dig these groups we got today. Fucking Van Halen, man... that's teeny bop shit... but at least it ain't fucking disco. But that fucking David Lee Roth—squealing and shit.The fucking Stones, though...."

"The Police, man...."

"Where?" His face went stiff. "What are you saying, dude?"

"I'm talking about the rock group from England named the Police. Singer named fucking Sting."

"You mean Fucking Sting is his goddamn name?"

"No. I mean, the guy's name is Sting, just plain Sting. They're a three-piece group that really rocks—the Police. You must have heard them. Reggae kinda stuff. You must have heard *Roxanne...* I'd hum a few bars but I don't want to cause any more pain."

"*Roxanne...* yeah, I like that tune."

"Check them out, man, they're good. Even though the fucking guy calls himself fucking Sting."

"Fucking Sting, man. That's cool. How about another line, man? I think I'm going to have another. How about you?"

"Yeah, what the hell... it's not every day you break your goddamn leg. That shit ain't bad. What's that thing about Dracula that you said? You got this from Dracula, you said. Who the hell is that?"

"Dracula is my dealer, man. We call him Dracula because he only comes out at night. That, and he's got some front teeth missing so it kind of looks like he's got vampire teeth when he smiles."

I pinched my nose, held in the line and my stomach flip-flopped. Another part of the country, another toothless drug dealer...what the hell are you gonna do?

Then the glass door slid open and Carole bounced in. A strange light shined from the corner of her eyes. The top half of her shirt was unbuttoned, revealing a good portion of her unencumbered breasts. I couldn't recall her looking like that when she left, but then I didn't remember looking at her when she left, either.

I stared over at John to see if I could catch some kind of a read. He had a look on his face that told me he had just gotten fucked. Not a genital fuck—a mind fuck. The famous Carole Waverly mind fuck.

I had seen that look before. Guys drawn in by her cute face and bubbly ways only to find that somewhere along the line their brains have broken like the worn out spring in a wind-up toy. Yes sir, I had seen that look before.

John rubbed his hand against his forehead and then back through his short brown hair and shook his head like a dog repelling water. Then he went to the kitchen to help Carole unload the grocery bags. The roaches were going to get drunk....

"You should have warned me about your wife, Keith," John said sheepishly as he stepped around the corner. "We walk into the Safeco and she starts spouting this phony Spanish like she really knows what the hell she's talking about. Had me fooled for a minute, too. And I'm from Southern California."

"Lontina que esta la seienta bel sona, por favor," Carole said, sing/song.

"So we get our stuff and we come up to the check-out and she's still spewing out this Chiquita stuff. I thought for sure the clerk would know it was phony—he looked Latin—but I swear to God; she had him fooled, too. I had all I could do to keep from running out of there, screaming."

"Oh, go on, John," Carole said. "You were loving it. *Maltusa paria amore fandango san cou,"* she said as she walked in with drinks for everyone on a metal Coca-Cola tray, with hunks of fresh pineapple in a green plastic bowl.

"Now where did you put that speed, Teddy?" she said, "I've done my work and now I want to perk up."

She set down the tray and went back into the kitchen, grabbed one of our old wooden chairs and brought it back with her to tableside. I frowned at her. She had never expressed anything but contempt for hard drugs when we were married. What the hell was going on?

Ted pulled out the bindle and shook some more powder onto Jagger's lips.

"It's not speed, darlin', it's coke," he said. "You was correct the first time. We was lyin' to you, because your husband had previously informed me that you carried a strong disapproval of said substance. I guess he was mistaken."

"I guess he was," Carole said, smiling at me victoriously, her blue eyes getting wider and brighter.

Ted drew out four lines, using the edge of his driver's license to chop and divide the powder. She put the album cover on top of her thighs and leaned forward, sniffing the powder up her nose like she knew what she was doing. Then she passed the stuff in my direction.

I waved it off, saying: "No thanks, I'm feeling a little shaky."

"Can I have yours?" she asked, her voice lilting, throaty.

"I don't care," I said. "Ask Ted, it's his shit."

"Have at it, *senorita, por favor*," Ted said.

"*Gracias, amigo,*" she said and then popped her head to the drug like a hummingbird to a sunflower.

"You know Spanish, Ted?" I asked, trying to change the mood.

"Yeah, man, I know lots of Spanish. Taco, burrito, enchilada, Cerveza, hacienda del sol, marijuana, la cucaracha... all those words."

I wasn't sure if those words were Spanish or Mexican or if it made any difference. All I knew was that the name on Ted

Friday's driver's license, laying on the table in front of me, was Jimmy Ruiz. Not James, but Jimmy. When it came to Spanish, I figured he must know what he was talking about, except he forgot to mention one very important word.

Puta.

John sniffed a line and was ready to play doctor.

He washed his hands and instructed the other two to get me sitting up on the couch with my foot on the floor. He crouched down on one knee in front of me and began pulling and tugging on my foot. Ted and Carole stood and watched, oohing and wincing. He tortured me like that for a while before wrapping the tape around it in a x-pattern.

It hurt pretty bad but I was too blown away to care.

That was about the highlight of the night for everyone.

I said thank you to John for his Good Samaritan work and the party went downhill after that. John and Ted left and I got the feeling that the whole thing had gotten to John, in some way. Who in the hell could blame him? He'd seen more of us than he had wanted to. These new things he had seen, or thought he'd seen, he didn't like very much.

So there I was, laying on the couch in a semi-stupor, staring out at my wife's tits as they swayed invitingly behind the blue denim.

She was strutting around the room like it was marching band practice, a drink in one hand and a cigarette hanging below a girlishly cocked wrist on the other. She smoked and she sipped and occasionally she'd glide over and turn the radio up or down, depending on the song. Every time she moved in front of me, I marveled at the way her hips and butt rode high in the saddle and elegant. Barefoot, and it seemed like she was wearing high heels.

Those open buttons on her shirt were still bothering me, the questions they posed alternately heightening and dampening my erotic mood.

"Carole," I finally said, staring. "Do you know that your tits are

about to fall out of your shirt? You've been walking around like
that all night long, for Christ sake. You trying to impress someone or some goddamn thing?"

She looked quickly down at her shirt buttons and then to me.
Her cheeks turned red and her fingers went immediately to the
lowest unfastened button.

"Jesus," she said, face turning ever redder.   "I didn't know,
Keith. How long have they been like that?"

"At least since you and John came back. You sure he wasn't
helping you with something?"

"Shut up. What do you mean?"

She looked confused as she began again to button her shirt.

"Nothing," I smiled. "Wait, don't button that up. I didn't say
that *I* didn't like it. Come over here. Bring yourself over here."

She came over, with mock cautiousness, and sat down on the
edge of the couch, facing me. I reached in and gently lifted her
breasts out of the shirt, one by one. With my left hand I pulled her
toward me, firmly cupping a breast and bringing it to my anxious
lips. My tongue caressed and tantalized; she moaned softly. I
struggled with the zipper on her jeans as she rubbed furiously
against my hand.

Then, without any warning, she grabbed the hair on the back of
my head and pulled me away, staring into my eyes, a fire in hers.
Then,without a word said between us, she shoved her mouth back
against mine, lashing her tongue like a hot, wet serpent.

Kisses brought us to a fever pitch. She climbed on top, pushed
down her jeans, and began to grind....

I think she was about to go off when we heard Mikey's door
open. She rolled off onto the floor like she'd been shot, her leg
catching my wrapped ankle on the way down. A rocket of pain
shot all the way to my groin.

Carole pretended she was cleaning off the coffee table as Mike
came out of his room, rubbing his eyes. He went into the bathroom and shut the door and I started to laugh softly.   I had to

adjust my dick inside my shorts. Caught a whiff of my pits and realized how bad I stunk. Hadn't had a shower yet. There was no way I was going to have one on this night. It would be hard enough getting into the bed to pass out.

"Carole," I said. "I'm really fucking sorry, I've gotta hit it. I'm burnt." I struggled to a sitting position, swinging my leg stiffly to the floor. The blood rushed down there and everything throbbed.

"Stay... he'll go back to sleep."

"My leg is killing me."

"I'll make it feel better."

"I wish."

"Okay then, gimpy," Carole said, "let me help you."

"I can make it," I said, struggling to my feet, or more correctly, to my foot.

I need a crutch, I thought, as I half-hopped, half-limped toward the bathroom. Mike came out the door as I put my hand against the wall for support.

"You okay, Mikey?" I asked

"Yeah," he said groggily. "Had to pee."

"Drink too much pop over at your friend's house?"

"Yeah," he grinned.

"I hope it wasn't caffeine pop, Mike. I want you to go to sleep now," Carole said from the living room, lighting a cigarette.

"Goodnight, Mike," I said.

"Goodnight, Dad," he said.

My heart was warm as I stumbled into the bathroom, flipped on the light and watched a greasy brown cockroach scurry into the tub drain and disappear.

I got into bed and the leg was pounding pretty badly but I thought I could fall asleep. Got my clothes off, adjusted the ice bag and towel and then watched as Carole came creeping into the bedroom.

She knelt down beside me and slid her hand between my legs; I was hard in an instant. She pulled down the sheets and brought her tongue to the shaft of my cock, licking it up and down until it glistened in the gray light seeping through the window screen.

I stared, fascinated, as it got nice and slippery. Then she went down like Linda Lovelace at undress rehearsal and I blew like a twenty-cent bottle rocket.

She smiled like a fallen angel and went to the bathroom, returning with a warm washcloth.

"There now darlin', a little something to help you sleep," she said, devilishly, a hint of Southern accent creeping in.

She cleaned me up then left the bedroom and shut the door behind her.

I woke up later when she stumbled into the room. Clock radio on the floor read: 4:13 A.M. I mumbled goodnight. She answered with a garbled, unrecognizable slur, the smell of alcohol seeping from her pores.

Next morning I woke up and rubbed my aching eyes. Everything ached, the ankle serving as the epicenter of my universe of pain.

Mike was standing over me, mumbling something about his friend Stephen's house and the pool. My brain kept switching back and forth between Mike and the various, throbbing areas that were drumming counterpoint to the burning in my stomach. Carole hardly even stirred, except to pull the worn bedspread over her head and turn toward the wall.

I asked Mike what was wrong with the pool out front of our apartment. He quickly informed me that Steven's complex had a separate pool just for kids, and, it was way cooler than our pool. I was too fatigued to argue so I said, yes, but that he had to get something to eat before leaving. I was whispering until I got to the word "eat." Then I raised my voice, good and loud—"EAT".

Carole jerked and rolled her head out from under the covers, licking her lips and struggling to open her eyes.

"Mikey needs to get some food in him before he goes swimming, Carole. I'd get up—like I usually do—but the leg, you know."

Carole rubbed her forehead vigorously with her palm. Her eyes crept open. "He can have some cereal and toast. Mike knows how to make that, for God's sake. Why is everybody being so loud? God, he's not helpless."

Mike turned and went into the kitchen.

I limped to the bathroom and, after, to the kitchen. Mike was in there with his elbows on the green vinyl placemat, straddling a bowl of corn flakes and a shiny piece of white toast slathered in butter. He wiped his mouth with a crumpled paper napkin.

"Well, I'm gonna go to Stephen's now," he said, looking at me with his mother's eyes and my nose and mouth.

"You got your suit and everything?"

He nodded.

"How long you going to be?"

"I got everything taken care of, Dad," he said. "His parents might take us to the water slide. I'll call you."

"Okay, Mike. Have fun. Be careful."

"Bye, Dad," he said.

He grabbed his paper sack of clothes and walked out through the sliding glass doors.

I watched him go away. My eyes burned; there was a pang in my stomach. I wondered how he was adjusting to his new school. Poor kid had already changed schools twice in one year. Now they were busing him way across town. Kid had to ride on the bus so goddamn long; it was a crime.

Carole and I had both believed that busing would be good for Mike, exposing him to racial diversity. That was before I found out it was a fifty-minute ride—if traffic was light—in an old, smoking rattletrap of a bus.

It was at least an hour before Carole dragged her ass out of bed.

I had just finished the last of the pineapple, after a bowl of corn flakes and some shiny white bread toast.

She mumbled hello on her way into the living room; lit up a cigarette and stepped over to the screen doors, blowing out a narrow stream of smoke. A long blue T-shirt covered her ass by only a couple of inches. The flesh on the back of her thighs looked inviting. Her blonde hair was getting lighter from the Florida sun.

"How's your leg?" She asked, walking into the kitchen inside a cloud of smoke.

"It's getting better," I said, lying.

She got the bottled water out of the fridge and poured some into the shiny teapot.

"How much money do we have?" she asked, rustling through the cupboard.

"Nothing, really," I said. "We got enough food to last us a few more days and we can always bounce a few checks if things get bad. You can go in and apply for food stamps; that'll help. I could always pawn my grandfather's gold watch."

"That would be a shame if you had to do that," Carole said, putting a teabag in a cup. "Is it worth a lot?"

"A couple of grand, I've been told, maybe more. It supposedly belonged to Wild Bill Cody, according to my father. W. Cody is engraved inside the cover plate. It's a real fancy watch. I doubt these bastards down here would give me very much for it, though. I don't know; it could be a fake. I always dragged it around with me wherever I went, in case I needed some quick cash. So if we have to, we have to. No big fucking deal. And then, of course, you could get a job...."

"You said that before," she said, pouring bubbling water into her cup.

She returned the kettle to the stove and extracted two pieces of bread from the orange plastic bag I had left open. I was thinking that before too goddamn long the roaches would be attacking stuff as big as that loaf—in broad daylight.

Later that day, actually it was night, John came over bearing gifts: a set of crutches and a few Empirins with codeine in a brown plastic bottle. The crutches were from a knee sprain that he'd received in college he said. He'd hung on to them for some reason. I guess you just never know when you're going to need a crutch.

Carole saw the pill bottle and slid up to me, real cozy. Purred, could she have a couple of pills? There were only six but I gave her two just to keep her off my back. John seemed anxious to leave after a few minutes but stayed around anyway, in a state of polite reprehension. We started talking about the tennis club and how I was out of work. Seemed like he was waiting for me to ask him for a loan or something, judging by the look on his face. Carole came in from the kitchen and sat down next to him on the couch, a drink in each hand—one for John, one for her.

"Where's mine?" I whined.

"It's in the kitchen, Keith. Don't worry, I was going to get it for you," she said. "You wouldn't want me to forget about our guest, would you, sweetie? I was raised to be polite to company, darlin'."

"Well, I'll take your drink, then," I said "Were you raised to treat your husband like shit?"

I smiled and turned to John and laughed like it was all a big joke. This little routine that Carole and I like to put on to entertain our guests.

John tried to beg off the drink. "I better go and let you guys rest," he said. "You're looking kind of rough, Keith. How's the leg doing? Pretty bad, I suppose. I told you I wasn't a doctor."

"I'm doing okay, John, don't you worry about me. I've bounced back from worse than this in the past."

"Yes, John," Carole said. "You did such a good job, you must stay and have a drink with us—just one."

"Speaking of jobs," I said. "By any chance are there any job opportunities at that there radio station of yours for an experienced voice-over person and ace, not to mention beautiful and perky, receptionist."

"You?" John said.

"No, my wife. She's experienced."

Carole made a comic grimace and nodded her head. John got a disbelieving look, on his face.

"I do believe the current receptionist is leaving in two weeks," he said, struggling with an internal demon. "Strange as it may sound, she happens to be moving to Miami, to get married."

"Are you serious?" Carole said, taking a pull on her cig.

"Why is it strange she's getting married?" I said. "Is she ugly or something?"

"I think he means that it's strange that she's leaving right now, and someone is asking about a job," Carole said.

"No duh, really, Carole? Gosh you're smart. I'm glad I have you around to explain things for me."

"You are lucky," she said.

"They've interviewed a couple of women already," John said, wincing slightly. "But I don't think they're excited about either one of them. They want someone who can do traffic for a while, to break in, and then take over when Cynthia leaves."

"I've even got my tapes of all the commercials I did with me. An air check, too."

"You were on the air?" John said, interested.

"Yes sir. Country radio, nine till noon for six whole months. I really don't want to do that again, though."

"Oh yeah, don't want to be a big talk jock?" John said, smiling.

"No."

"Stage fright?"

"No, not really. Just the weirdos who want to get your phone number or write you letters. I used to get a lot of those... no thank you."

"Too bad. That's where the real money is, kiddies, talk jocks. They're paying some unreal salaries to these guys they're bringing in. The bigwigs are throwing a lot of money around; that's for sure. I'm doing pretty well and I had only three months of on-air experience before coming here. Carole could have her own show if she played her cards right...something for the ladies."

"You know," I said, "I think you should start considering that idea of your own talk show. You could have, say... *Norwegian Cooking for Snowbirds*, or something. Maybe—*Getting By On a Shoestring*...or *Books for the Homebound*...."

"Fuck you, Keith," she said, flipping me off and grinning.

The glass doors slid open and Mike walked into the room with dirt all over him. I had forgotten about him. Carole must have too because she hadn't said anything to me, like *Where the hell is my son?*

"Where have you been, Mike, it's after ten o'clock?" I said.
John got up again to leave.

"How did you get so dirty, Michael?" Carole asked.

"Yeah, I thought you were going swimming."

We did go swimming, Dad. Twice. After that, we were playing back in the woods behind Stephen's place."

"I don't know if I like that," I said. "What can you do back in that dried-up swamp?"

"Oh, we play games."

"What kind of games? Hide the salami?"

John snickered nervously.

"Shut up, Keith," Carole said.

"Red light, green light and hide and go seek," Mike said, seemingly oblivious to my tasteless comment.

"Go in and take a shower, Mike," Carole said. "You're filthy."

He went directly to the refrigerator.

"You're not touching anything in that kitchen until you clean up, young man," Carole said. "Now march into that bathroom."

John stood up and gave us a knowing look: "Did you know that studies show that kids in apartment complexes get into sex and drugs much earlier than normal?"

"You already told me that, John. What the fuck, you think I forgot?"

He smiled blankly and backed slowly out the sliding doors, promising Carole he'd check on that job.

Ten minutes later Mike came out of the bathroom and went to his bedroom. He got into his PJs and joined us on the couch. The three of us watched James Bond on the tube while Carole and I finished off the rum.

My leg felt pretty good sometimes; then would start to throb again as soon as I noticed that it felt better. I wasn't sure if the booze was helping or hurting but I kept on drinking until the last drop.

Then we did it again the next night and the next night after that and a few more days after that.

One of those days, I'm not sure which one, John called up with good news: Carole had an interview at WPLF, if she wanted one.

Chapter Four

It's a Small World After All

It's dark again, and still no sign of the boys. I've about given up; I can't take much more. The signal fire is my only solace. I need to make a decision real soon but the only thing I can do is stare at the fire and hope that I pass out.

My memories are like ghosts dancing in the flames, tormenting me and making me sweat. I can see now where our life began to change, how I let certain things push me in the wrong direction.... I'd been craving an emotional anchor and what I got was something else again. I still am not sure what, exactly.

Hell, I'll let you decide.

The big wheels at WPLF, the LA hotshots, were so impressed with Carole's resume and tapes that they hired her on the spot. Wanted her to start the following Monday, they said.

This was great news but with new responsibility I have found, comes new expense. I think it was Thoreau who said, "Beware of all enterprises that require new clothes."

My baby needed a new pair of shoes and a dress or two. Having the proper wardrobe is a woman's constant torment, I think. Or a constant addiction, if properly indulged.

Expensively clad women, the chattel of rich men, were everywhere around me: the tennis club, the supermarket, the malls, the country clubs and the marinas. They were everywhere the money was, like hornets crawling in sugar.

I needed to pawn Buffalo Bill's gold watch.

Drove over to the north end of Seminole Boulevard and found a squat, pink, cinder-block building with a big metal sign on top: STOYANOFF LOANS: WATCHES GUNS CASH LOANS.

Two little bald guys, who looked like brothers, ran the place. They gave me two hundred bucks after I spent fifteen minutes trying to convince them of Buffalo Bill's verifiable status as an American legend. They didn't know Bill Cody from Bill Russell but they spoke decent English, with only a slight accent, and that helped our discussion.

I guess I was lucky to get what I did. But the more I think about it, the more it seems possible that they cheated the hell out of me, played me for a rube. They sure were congenial about the whole thing. Had me believing I'd gotten a good deal.

I gave the money to Carole as a surprise.

"Did you pawn your watch?" she asked.

"Yep, to a couple of goofy little guys over in Clearwater."

"How much did you get?"

"You're looking at it."

Did she think I was holding out?

"How much can I spend?"

"Well, all of it, if you have to. But, it would be nice to have some left over."

She seemed happy, or maybe just relieved.

The three of us got in the car and fought the traffic to the huge Clearwater Mall, in hopes of finding the appropriate wardrobe for the new receptionist at Talk Radio 97, WPLF.

Carole got what she needed with seventy-five bucks to spare. In a piece of logic, that only a party animal can appreciate, we decided to blow some of the remaining cash on a night on the town, or, more precisely, a night in the bars. We'd take one last shot at the famous Florida nightlife before settling down like good, normal people.

We arranged for Mike stay over at his friend's place and headed for the clubs, where we drank and danced till the sweat ran down our faces. Everywhere you went, people were wired on coke; you could hear them sniffling, watch them grinding their teeth and listen to them chatter on about nothing.

We came home and screwed like we were possessed and then stayed up all night long finishing off the coke from my drawer. Walked around miserable, like light fearing zombies, the next day. When poor Mike got home, I could barely move and Carole was spinning around in circles like a wind-up doll with a limp.

The following day was Monday and Carole's first day on the job.

She started with a hangover. It wasn't really much of a hangover, considering the way things got later, but still, somehow, it seemed fitting.

By Thursday of her first week, our food supply was running low and the car was about out of gas. Carole pleaded at work and got a draw on her paycheck. The draw almost got us through another bare bones week.

Then management informed her that the first check wouldn't be coming around for at least another week, maybe longer, because of accounting procedures.

My theory was that they wanted to stay one pay period behind so they could stiff you, if you left without notice.

After another five days of eating cereal for dinner, Carole took another draw.

I knew we couldn't continue like that much longer. I carefully broached the subject. Carole was one step ahead of me she said. The big boss in charge of funding—Paul Gulzeimer—had felt sympathy for the plight of his new employee and agreed to cosign for a Visa card, in her name. Thing had a five hundred dollar limit. It was maxed out in about forty days.

Carole started working longer hours and all the while we were accumulating more debt, just like old times. And ever since her overtime started, our sex life had slowed to the occasional drunken grind. Drunken would be inaccurate, though, because it was more of a sleazy, tired feeling like you got from a six-pack of Busch and a half-pack of Kools.

My life had definitely changed. Carole and Mike were gone during the day. My bad leg kept my activities limited. And we all know that an idle mind is the devil's workshop.

I'd get up in the morning and grab a paper from the rack by the vending area. The air was usually cool and fresh and the complex grounds quiet. Most of the time, the pool area was empty. I could work on my tan and call it rehab.

After a few weeks of saunas, sun and underwater exercise; it seemed like my leg had pretty much healed; although still tender directly above the ankle. I kept it wrapped, replacing the tape when it got too funky. I had a slight limp that I told myself would go away.

Life had become only a matter of passing time, for no meaning and no gain. If you're bored, you must be boring, Carole would always say. I guess she was right.

Boredom and other signs of our disintegrating family life were easily visible to anyone who chose to look, I guess.

But then, that one afternoon, that one bright Friday, Carole came home from work with a surprise that washed all our troubles away.

She had been given passes to Disney World, compliments of the radio station.

At that one sweet moment, I honestly felt like we were going to make it. Not just to Disney World, but all the way to the end of the line. Our union would only get better, like aged molasses.

As if to confirm my feelings of upswing, the perceived bounty we had been long waiting for—Carole's tax refund check—arrived in the mail the very next day.

I was overwhelmed with joy and reassurance. I truly believed that good things *do* come to those who wait.

We had some cash. We were going to Disney World. This was the stuff of the American Dream. This was the joy that I had seen on the people in television shows. Now we were going to have some of our own.

It didn't take us long to decide that we would go the following weekend. I don't think Mike could have waited any longer than that. Coincidentally, it was also the day after Carole's payday.

I called an old college pal of ours, who was now living in Orlando, name of Barry Eastman. He said he was doing pretty well, selling dental equipment and supplies. Said it would be great to see us again. Invited us to join him, as he had plenty of room.

Once the arrangements were set, Carole decided we should have some coke for the trip. Not fighting the idea, I called Ted. He said he'd do it for me but I had to come along with him and meet Dracula. I agreed, at first, but later had a vague premonition and called him back and cancelled.

Something didn't seem right about bringing cocaine to Disney World, I don't know....

At the time of departure for Orlando—Mike liked to call it our "launch time"—we climbed into the Volvo like Ozzie and Harriet from a parallel universe and hit the freeway just before dark on a Friday night.

Both lanes were full of cars. The sun sank quickly. I couldn't enjoy the set for the whizzing traffic. Got black so fast I never saw the countryside, bumper to bumper the whole goddamn way. On the outskirts of Orlando, life was moving even faster. Colored lights streaked by. Neon flashed and autos hissed; headlights stung my eyes. Horns honked; street lights blurred and billboards drew us in. Well-dressed people whizzed along in world-class automobiles, perfect smiles on perfect faces.

It was past dinnertime and Mike was hungry so we stopped at a Denny's. I got a roast beef sandwich. It tasted like cardboard. I gave the rest to Mike and he liked it. Carole had three bites of a BLT and gave that to Mike. The kid chowed everything we gave him, plus his own cheeseburger, fries and a coke. Kid had a bottomless pit.

I rang Barry from the payphone and he rattled off directions to his place. It sounded like he'd been drinking, not surprising for Friday night. My ankle started to hurt as we left Denny's.

We drove through the frantic night, across freeways and boulevards and strip mall-lined streets. Every time we slowed down I smelled burning oil. The oil pressure gauge was reading next to zero.

I figured we were about two blocks from Barry's place when I really took notice of my exhaust. The Volvo was blowing fumes like a wood-stoked steam engine in a mountain climb.

Nervously I approached a four-way stop in a nice residential neighborhood: low brick fences in front of sprawling, one-story homes.

Billowing clouds of oily blue smoke floated from my tailpipe and enveloped us in a greasy fog. Sensing impending disaster, I made a right turn and drove down two blocks to Laverne Place and hung another right.

We cruised slowly down the block, checking out the house numbers, settling smoke behind us.

Rolled up to 3414 Laverne, a medium-size, aluminum-sided, ranch style home with a small pool and a decent yard behind a chain-link fence. A white Plymouth Duster was parked in the up-sloping driveway.

I made the turn into the driveway and suddenly, seemingly from out of nowhere, flashing lights lit up my windows and sent my heart into overdrive.

Cops.

Did I forget to signal or something?

Sure enough, the Orlando Police were on my ass: Trooper hats and glistening badges pulsing beneath the red and yellow waves of roof cherries. If it had been daylight, they would have been wearing aviator sunglasses, for sure. I was wishing I had a pair.

With a tight feeling in the pit of my stomach, I got out of the car to greet the officer as he walked up the driveway. I made sure to move slowly and act real nice.

Behind me the porch light came on, and, all of a sudden Barry popped out the front door. Dressed in a bright orange tropical shirt and white jeans, swaggering and grinning, his nose red, he approached the car like a pissed-off fighting toucan.

"Keith, you made it," Barry said, rapid fire. "And you've brought friends along. I'm not sure we have enough liquor for everyone, though." He smiled at the officer.

Barry's eyes were red, like his hair. The patrolman studied him closely. Then he turned his attention back to me.

"Having engine trouble, sir?" he said, looking down his large, angular nose at me. "We noticed an inordinate amount of smoke coming from your exhaust at the intersection. I think the clouds are still lingering."

He bent over and peered in the window of the Volvo.

"Yeah, I think something broke in the engine, officer. It just got bad all of a sudden like that. Just after we hit town. Something must have happened out on the freeway."

The cop straightened back up. "Where are you from, sir? Is that your family in the car?"

"They're from Clearwater, officer," Barry butted in, leaning casually against the trunk of his Duster, staring at the cop. Barry was only about five foot six, but his mouth had always been over six feet—especially when he'd had a few. "My old college chum and his family come to visit... they're here on my property... and you decide to hassle them.... Now isn't that something? If they haven't done anything wrong, officer, I wish you would please leave us the hell alone so we can begin to relive old times. Consider these people my guests that you're bothering."

The cop stared at Barry and frowned. The other patrolman got out of the cruiser and started up the driveway. The two of them met halfway and had a small discussion. I assumed that cop number two had run my plates.

As the first cop turned and walked back toward us, Barry started up again: "I know lots of lawyers in this town who would love to drag your butts into court for harassing tourists, officer. Think how that one would go over with the Chamber of Commerce. Everyone knows what those bastards are like. You want to have those pompous windbags on your ass, officer?"

"No need for hostility, sir," said the cop in his best polite lie. More than likely, he would rather have played Dixie on Barry's forehead with his nightstick.

Instead: "Your friend's vehicle is a pollution hazard, sir. All that smoke from the exhaust is a violation. That same Chamber of Commerce wants us to have clean air in our city. This vehicle either needs to stay off the road or get a mosquito spraying license."

Turning to me: "Promise to keep it parked and I won't write you up."

He was standing next to me and my heart was pounding out the base line from *In-a-godda-davida* .

"May I see your driver's license please, sir."

I began to stammer and Barry jumped to my rescue: "Now officer, there you go again. I gave you specific instructions to vacate my property. Must I remind you that I'm a landowner and taxpayer? Unless this man has committed some genuine crime, which so far, you haven't mentioned, please leave immediately.

Consider this is a formal request from a taxpayer of your community. The horrible polluting vehicle has been shut down. I'm sure you boys can find some real action in some other part of town, now cantcha? Hell, betcha somebody's taking down a 7-11 store somewhere, right now. Maybe some niggers are hitting Zak's Liquor—for the third time this month.... I do think you boys have got better things to do."

The cop thought for a moment, staring at Barry the citizen, then nodded politely—if forced—and peered back into the car at Carole and Mike. Seemingly reassured of something, he turned and walked silently back down the driveway to where the other cop was standing. Cop number two frowned up at us.

"Have a nice evening, folks," said cop number one, strained.

They got in the squad, talked for a moment then slowly drove off. The minute they disappeared from sight, Barry and I started laughing. Man, if it wasn't just like putting the buffalo on some of those Zenith City cops back when they'd raid one of Barry's famous "purple passion" parties.

Carole and Mike stepped nervously out of the car and onto the driveway, Carole looking all the worse for wear. Barry gave her a big hug—and a kiss on the lips.

"Hey there, kid," he said unclasping, "Good to see you. I can't believe it. I'd heard that you guys split up; I guess that was bad information...."

Carole and I looked at each other; color returning to her face.

"We were apart for a while," I said, "but we're back together now."

"I can see that," Barry said. "And who's this handsome young man?"

"That's Mike," Carole and I said in unison.

Clasping his hands in front of him and looking at Mike: "I remember Mike when he was just a weasel in the woods. I bet he's a good baseball player. He looks like he is. Just like his dad, I bet. Your dad could really swing the bat, you know, Mike."

Mike beamed, "Really?"

I winced and smiled weakly, trying to push back the memory of what I'd done to Johnny Wells, back in my old life in the frozen North.

"No lie, kid," Barry said, grinning wildly and spinning on his heel. "We won the intramural championship at UMZ when we were just freshmen. The old boy here was pretty damn good. Played a pretty good centerfield, too. But hey, enough nostalgia, what do you say we go inside and get ourselves some refreshment. Mike could use a Coke after a long drive, I bet. I bet all you guys are dry.... Jesus, Waverly, it's really good to see you, you and your little family.... Come on into my house. I've got a friend over who's thinking about becoming my roommate, you'll love him."

"So Margaret's not living with you anymore, Barry?" I asked. "I didn't even think of asking you, on the phone."

"Nah, she split two years ago, went back to Minnesota. Nicky was getting older and she wanted him to go to school in Minnesota, so she split. That was it. I still talk to her on the phone now and then. We're still close. She didn't like it down here... and I love it. So that was about it with that. Just couldn't make it work. Jesus. Now it really is time for a drink."

The next morning, everyone was moving kind of slow.

Barry had decided to come to see Disney with us, to save us from having to drive the smoking Volvo, so we jumped into the Duster, joyful and expectant. The sun was shining. The air was perfect. The sky was blue.

We were to pick up our entry passes for Disney World at the ticket window. Carole assured us that the arrangements had been made: in advance, by Paul Gulzheimer, on account of her good work performance. The station's show of gratitude for all the overtime she'd been putting in, she said.

The parking lot was only about half full when we got there. Mike couldn't sit still. We walked to the ticket windows and he jumped up and down by the fence, trying to see in.

"Hi," Carole said to the smiling girl behind the counter. "I'd like to pick up the tickets for Waverly."

There was a long silence as the girl searched. Too much time went by and I started to get nervous. I was pacing and kicking at the ground when I heard Carole say:

"But Paul Gulzheimer and Lance Stevens from WPLF had all this arranged a week ago," calmly, her elbows on the counter. "WPLF radio, Pinnellas Park," she continued, anxiety creeping in. "Can you check again? This is my son's birthday present. They told me last week that it was all arranged. Paul arranged this himself."

She stepped back from the window and gave us a nervous look. Barry and I stared at the powder blue sky. Mike chewed on his fingernails.

I was thinking Hell—the Epcot Center isn't even finished yet.

"I can always write a check to get us in," Barry said.

A minute went by slowly, then another. Then I heard Carole say, "Thank you very much," and tickets slid out of the window into her hand. Throwing her head and shoulders back, she waved four tickets—and there was only supposed to be three.

"They didn't have a record of anything from WPLF," Carole said. "The girl called her supervisor and he gave us the tickets, anyway."

"I told you those L.A. boys were liars," I said.

"I'm sure it was a simple mistake," Carole said. "Somebody must have forgotten to call."

"I thought you said that Paul told you he called and set everything up."

"I must have misunderstood him. We've got the tickets now, so let's forget it, okay?"

"Those fuckers are liars and cheats."

"Relax, Keith, we're in."

*   *   *

Things we discovered about Disney World: (1) there was no alcohol in the park. (2) There is one dark ride where you travel around the imaginary world in a boat and they play the song: "It's a Small World after All". It sticks in your head and drives you crazy. (3) Kids don't care; they still love that ride. (4) There was no alcohol.

We had a great time but tired quickly. We used all the ride tickets provided with our entry passes and I don't think Mike ever loved us more. Driving back to Barry's house, we were bathed in a Walt Disney glow.

Barry got a wicked grin on his face. "An old friend of yours is in town, Keith," he said. "I meant to tell you last night, but all that tequila and the doober kind of got me crispy."

"Someone I know—is in Orlando—right now?"

"Yep, from back in Zenith City."

"Who the hell is that?"

"Dan Bagley."

"You're shitting me...."

"Nope, it's true. He called me the other day from Daytona Beach, said he was going to be in town in a few days. He's got some other dude with him."

"*It's a small world after all...*" I sang.

"Don't start in on that shit. I was just thinking how glad I was not to have gone on that ride with you guys."

"*It's a small, small world....*"

"Fuck, please, that's enough. He wants to have dinner tonight, or breakfast tomorrow. You should join us."

"Yeah, I suppose. But I'm not sure that I want to. It's been six or seven years since I last saw him, maybe longer. I can't remember exactly.... It was just before he moved out West, I think. Ran into him in a bar over in Hammond, he was selling shitty coke. What the hell is he doing in Florida?"

"He didn't say. But if what I've heard on the grapevine is true, he's probably down here shopping in our state's fastest-growing export market."

"Dope?"

"Dope, yes. I heard he's going big time."

I got nervous and turned around to see if Mike was listening. He was asleep, his head on Carole's lap. He looked so beautiful and peaceful. She had a dreamy look herself.

Barry's house was bigger and more comfortable and inside than you might guess by looking at it from the street. Coming in the door, there was a hallway with an exotic, dark blue stained wood floor that lead to a kitchen of chrome and black: kind of disco but nice. To the right of the kitchen was a large living room with a bright hardwood floor and a blue oval rug in the middle. Beyond that, was a larger room, with a couch and some plants and a sliding door to the pool area. There was a fallout shelter in the backyard.

Barry pulled out the blender, saying, "This thing gets a lot of use around here," and proceeded to whirl up a batch of margaritas.

We were into our second one a piece. Mikes pizza was in the oven. We were mellow. The phone rang.

Barry picked up and after a few seconds mouthed the word "Bagley," his eyes looking down at the phone.

After some discussion, Carole agreed to stay home with Mike while Barry and I went to Fisherman's Bounty Seafood Restaurant and Oyster Bar to meet my old pal.

Chapter Five

Here We Go Again

Now it's somewhere before dawn and I'm up from a restless sleep to revive the fire and stare out at the blackness. I also light two of the lanterns in case I fall back asleep.

Regret fills me as I look back on that time in Orlando. If only I had stayed with my family instead of going to the restaurant, there might be someone else on this beach instead of me and I might still have a chance at a life.

Bagley and Schmidt seemed so confident and free; I guess I was taken in. I guess I let Bagley lead me down the wrong path, much like the first time I had met him, way back when we were kids.

He got me to sneak out of Sunday school to go and smoke Lucky Strikes in the alley.

Sometimes you're a little slow to learn, I guess.

I was a little apprehensive on the way to dinner. The minute that I heard his name, I knew there would be drugs and money floating somewhere around the situation.

Dan Bagley was arrogant and capable of being a first-class ass-hole, but I was willing to overlook his flaws if he could help fill the vacuum in my monetary fund. Yeah, go ahead and think it, you're entitled—the lure of easy money got to me.

Barry and I approached the hostess and inquired of the Bagley party. She didn't need to answer, because at that moment the unmistakable sound of gusto and released inhibition that was Dan Bagley's laugh came bouncing out at us from the interior of the restaurant. A practiced sound, much like his faux New England accent, I found it both irritating and stimulating at the same time. The man could be entertaining at times.

Barry's head turned sideways. "Shall we go, Keith," he said. "I think I hear Bagger.... We'll show ourselves back, ma'am."

"Follow me," she said, raising her dark eyebrows.

Barry shrugged an oh-well kind of shrug; then followed the hostess through a short narrow hallway to a darkened dining room, staring at her ass the whole way.

"Weird shit always happens to me when Bagley's around," I said, as we moved along the soft, sea-blue carpet with silhouettes of fish on it. "We go back a long time. I remember when he used to steal rental skis from the local hills and sell them to the guys in high school. Another time, he went out soliciting for a phony charity, first one in town to try that scam, I think. Then one time, he was going to—"

"There they are," Barry said, grinning and waving.

I sucked in my gut.

Bagley's blonde curls and suntanned head were bobbing above a dark green polo shirt, by the far wall. A tall, wiry, redheaded dude wearing white jeans, an ocean blue T-shirt and boat shoes with no socks, sat across from him.

Bagley's baby blues fluttered with surprise. "Keith Waverly... Keith... I can't believe you're here. I never thought you'd ever get out of Zenith City. Ah ha ha. Come on, then, sit down. Where did you find this guy, Barry? Out trolling the bars for shoeshine work? Haw haw. He and I go back all the way to Sunday school class." He looked at me and winked. "Waverly was the only one who had worse attendance than me. That's why I liked him."

"Yeah," I said. "We were the only ones who didn't have a pound of attendance medals on our lapels. Those other assholes looked like fucking Brigadier Generals."

Bagley guffawed and then introduced his pal Steve Schmidt. He seemed like a straightforward guy: angular face with sharp eyes that studied you. I figured he must have had money because Dan always seemed to cultivate friendships with those that had wealth in their background, keeping with his belief that if you stand close to the fire; you're gonna get warm.

It must have been something else that he saw in me....

"What are you guys drinking?" Bagley asked, cheeks red and puffy. "Steve and I have been enjoying a few cocktails and taking in the ambiance of old Florida."

"And Dan has been enjoying the ambiance of a fat cracker whoor," Schmidt said. "Only a few hours ago. I can still smell the cheap perfume. It's about to make me gag."

Bagley: "She wasn't a whore, Schmidty, just an abundant Dixie farm girl. A true Southern belle."

"Yeah, I forgot," Steve said, bringing his glass to his mouth and swilling heavily.

"Dan has always shown a fondness for corpulent bar flies, at least as long as I've known him," I said.

Bagley clicked his lips and fidgeted in his chair. "What do you mean by that, Keith?" Trying to act innocent.

"Well, man, I can remember more than once—at the tail end of a drunk—you dry humping some old, fat broad against the side of a building somewhere....You're famous for that shit back home. You're known as the fucking Midnight Rambler, for the Christ sake...."

"Me? Come on now, Keith... where do you come up with these things? Your hold on reality is getting a little tenuous, I'm afraid."

He looked around at the others, searching for approval, his face now crimson.

"How about that chick you used to drive around naked with in your camouflaged Ford, Dan?" I said, leaning forward. "Wasn't she just a tad on the portly side?"

"No, she was a beauty, I swear to god. She really was...."

Barry and Steve were shaking with laughter.

Dan screwed up his face for an instant, guffawed and took a swill from his frosted glass. Steve coughed and fidgeted in his chair.

"What are you doing for work now, Keith?" Bagley asked, suddenly.

I felt my stomach tightening and my neck getting hot. "Well, I was a tennis pro, at least until I broke my leg. I was making good money at a big resort, but I had to give it up."

"Really... how about that... that's too bad," Bagley said, lowering his eyes. "But doesn't bad luck seem to follow you around, Keith? Maybe you should consider looking for a real job and start think about controlling your own destiny."

"You should talk," Schmidt said. "The last job you had; was at Black Valley Lodge, a couple of years ago."

"You're wrong Schmidty, I was ski patrol after that."

"Yeah, like that's working," Schmidt said.

"So Jesus, Dan," Barry interjected. "What brings you to Florida? Vacation?"

"Yeah, kind of. This friend of ours owns a sailboat that's getting some work done to it down on Longboat Key. Steve and I are going down to check on the work and then do some test sailing out of Key West."

"That sounds like my kind of fun," Barry said.

Dan waved his hand in the air. "Waitress: another round here, for everyone. And then we'll order dinner."

"I haven't even looked at a menu yet," Barry said.

"Take your time," Schmidt said.

Bagley got up from the table and started toward the oyster bar. "Anybody else want some sliders?"

Barry followed him. Steve and I stayed.

"Don't let Bagley get to you," Schmidt said to me as the other two disappeared around the corner.

"I won't," I said, lowering my eyes. "How do you get along with him?"

"It's not easy. He's going to be leaving soon, after we get the boat in the water, so I don't have to put up with him too much longer." He took a drink, shrugged his shoulders and glanced briefly around the room. "You and your family should come down to the boat for a visit when we're in Key West. Go for a sail."

"I'd like that. Just like Jimmy Buffet," I said. "That's the stuff that got me down here, you know. Listening to his songs in the middle of winter and wishing that I was somewhere warm. I just needed the right impetus, I guess. I've never been on a sailboat before. That would be great, though. First Disney World and then Key West, what more could a person ask for?"

Schmidt looked at me and smiled slightly. "A million dollars, for a start," he said, quietly.

Barry and Dan returned carrying little white bowls filled with raw and fried oysters. Steve ate two fried and I had one fried and Barry and Dan sucked down the rest. If you wash them down quickly they're not too bad.

"You've got to do the raw oysters with beer, Keith," Bagley said. "They're better than the fried."

"Say listen, Barry," Bagley went on, ignoring me. "Why don't you come down to Key West and spend some time on the boat?"

"I'd love to, but I'm afraid I'm all booked up for the next month and a half. I got a golf tournament next weekend, a dentist convention in Gainesville the weekend after that. Then I go—"

"I didn't know you were a dentist," Bagley interrupted.

"I'm not. But I sell dental supplies and tools and shit. Conventions are where I can really make hay. Dentists are mostly a bunch of drunks, anyway—partying all weekend. It's easier to sell them shit if you're drinking with them—and it's not a bad time."

"You sure you want to pass up the chance to sail on the big blue waters?"

"I'd really love to, but the timing isn't right. Maybe next time you come through...."

"That's a shame, Barry, I was hoping I could leave my van with you, and then you could pick me up at the airport when I come back through, in about a month. Then we could go down to the boat."

"You can leave your van in my driveway if you want, Dan, but there's no guarantee I'll be available when you get back. You can always take a cab from the airport....Anyway, I thought you were going sailing."

"Well, I'm ah, ah, ah, going to be flying back out West and then coming back d-d-down, again."

There was the stutter that Bagley got when caught stepping in his own bullshit.

"Why don't you leave the van with Keith in Tampa?" Schmidt said. "Tampa's closer to the Keys and the airport is nicer."

"Well, I, ah, ah, s-s suppose that's okay," Bagley said.

"Yeah," I said, "I could do that if you want. There are plenty of spots in the parking lot at my place. Turns out my own car is blowing oil like crazy... maybe I could use your van to look for another car."

"If you're vehicle is broken down, Keith, of course I'll leave the van with you. How else would you get around?" Bagley frowned. "Your family needs some kind of transportation. If I leave the van with you, do you think you can get something fixed on it, for me?"

"No problem," I said.

"You promise you won't space it out...."

I grimaced, my face heating up again.

"I'll give you some dope you can sell to pay for the repairs," Bagley said, looking down at me.

"What kind of dope?"

"Some hash. Got a little bit of that... got some coke, too—if you want it...."

"I don't know... I'm not so sure about that. This is a weird fucking state."

"You turning religious, Keith? Carole got you turned around?"

"No, it's not that. I just don't want to get stuck with anymore of your lousy ass shit."

"This stuff is good," Schmidt said, raising his eyebrows. "You can take my word for it. Surprising—I know, coming from our man Dan."

"I shouldn't think you were in any position to refuse my offer, Keith," Bagley said, cocking his head back. "It's not like you're pulling down the big bucks."

The waitress showed up with the appetizer tray before I had time to respond, except to shake my head and turn my eyes to the table, thinking, next remark he makes, I'm going to jump across the table and rip out his Adam's apple.

We lit into the tray of food like frenzied sharks, quickly tearing the peel-and-eats into shreds. The calimari was tangy and salty; the scallops flaky and sweet—hell with the oysters.

The main course followed quickly. More drinks arrived. Laughter pealed and rose. In a wall aquarium, a black and white striped fish with a forked tail glided effortlessly through sky blue water.

Bagley, now quite loose, his face red, inquired about my "lovely wife Carole."

Then: "How interesting that she's still working in radio, Keith."

I wasn't sure what he meant.

"She's doing fine," I said. "You can come see her later if you want, when you bring the van over to Barry's. She and Mike are there. You guys can relive old times."

Dan nodded, then looked away and signaled the passing waitress.

The rest of the dinner conversation was light, mostly small talk and braggadocio about skiing in the mountains, or sailing. When the cigarettes were lit and the coffee was steaming inside white china cups, Barry wrote the directions to his place on the back of a napkin. Schmidt grabbed the napkin off the table and stared at it for a few seconds.

"There," he said. "Now you can have it, Dan. I know you'll need it."

"You can follow me over if you want," Barry said.

Barry and I got into the Duster and led the caravan out of the parking lot. We were blowing down the always-busy freeway when Barry said, "You know that Bagley's up to something with that shit about the van.... You know that, don't you, Keith? I wouldn't trust him as far as I could throw him. Everybody knows he's a scam artist."

"No, man, you're right. I don't trust him. I know him as well as anyone. But I don't mind being used a little, if I get paid enough for it. If he thinks he's fooling someone—well, it ain't me. Problem is that he never *does* pay enough and then he still tries to make you feel guilty about the deal, even while you're doing it for him. I could never understand it. Fucking asshole would cheat his own goddamn mother, I think, and not care a lick about it. But still, I have to admit, he's got balls and he does have some good dope, from time to time."

"I'd stay away from him if I were you," Barry said, lighting a cigarette with the car lighter.

"Can I have one of those?"

He put the lighter back in the hole in the dash and handed over the pack of Viceroys. I shook one out.

"I thought they were both traveling in Bagley's van...." I said. "I wonder where that gold boat came from."

"It's Steve's mother's car," Barry said as I punched in the lighter. "She's got a condo here in Orlando. She flew back home to Pennsylvania, I guess. Steve is driving the car back up North for her, sometime later."

"How'd I miss all that?"

"You must have been in the can. Bagley was trying to sell me on driving the bus down for him. What's he got against you, anyway? He was really laying on the shit there for awhile."

"I don't know… he's just a fucking asshole. He made a move on Carole once, and he's probably embarrassed or something. Maybe it's genetics… it's probably his father's fault. Schmidt invited us down to the Keys, so we're going anyway. Fuck Bagley."

"He made a move on Carole? You're shitting me."

"Nothing serious, it was a long time ago. He was partying at our house one night, a few years back; Mike was still a toddler. The three of us were drinking and smoking quite a bit and Dan starts up on this weird sell-job speech for "open marriage." It was really hard to believe at first. Seemed that some of his friends from out West had been reading a book on the practice. Dan kept saying how he thought that all modern couples should 'explore.' I thought it was an idea worth considering, but Carole just winced. Then, at one point in the evening, I'm in the kitchen getting a beer or something when I hear this yelp—an I-just-saw-a-mouse type yelp. I run into the living room in time to see Bagley on top of Carole on the couch, pawing at her tits. Then she shoves him off onto the floor and he comes bouncing up like a run-over cat and stumbles out of the house, stammering something about 'exploring.' He stopped coming around after that, as you might expect."

"No lie," Barry said, and then we were turning into the driveway. There was a black 280Z parked by the house.

"Jack Kline is here," Barry said, pulling up next to the Z car.

Alone with my wife and kid.

"Don't worry, he's harmless," Barry said. "He's a dipstick, but he's harmless. He owns a bar in Cocoa Beach."

"Jesus, I'm sure," I shrugged, beginning to accept the inevitable. "I'm also sure that Carole is keeping him entertained."

Barry and I were opening his front door when Schmidt rolled up in a gold Chrysler convertible with a yellow canvas top.

Bagley was right behind him, gripping the leather-covered steering wheel of a white VW bus. The thing had sheepskin seat covers on the front seats and someone had gotten cute and painted eyelashes above the headlights.

The guys got out of their rides and walked up to the porch. Bagley didn't want to go inside, said he didn't have time, so we loitered in the driveway for a few minutes, exchanging pertinent information and drunken bullshit. Schmidt and Bagley seemed anxious to get rolling, as they were driving nonstop to the Keys, they said. Dan would be back to pick up the van in approximately a month's time.

As Bagley moved his gear from the van to the massive Chrysler, Schmidt reiterated his invitation to me. Come down in two weeks time, he said. And then with a wink, as Barry and Dan discussed Florida real estate: "Dan will be gone then—if we're lucky."

From out of the van, Bagley fetched a zippered leather case about the size of a book. Inside was a half-pound of fragrant blonde hash and two and a half grams of cocaine.

My bone had been tossed.

Barry and I waved goodbye as they wallowed off down the palm-lined streets in the golden whale. Then we went inside and the wind was out of our sails.

Carole and Jack Kline were playing backgammon in the front room. I took one look at Carole and knew instantly that she was drunk, as well as ripped on coke. Jack turned as we entered the room. He had a gold chain dangling between the open collar of his white linen shirt. He was tall, thin and sharp featured, had a great tan.

"Hey there, guys," Carole said.

There was a half-full glass of brandy on the table in front of her. She gripped a cigarette loosely between her delicate fingers. Her hand and head bobbed to the same drunken rhythm.

"I see you and Jack found something to do," Barry said, grinning oddly.

"We've been playing backgammon. The big shot has beaten me out of sixty dollars. I owe him sixty dollars, Keith...have you got it?"

"Pardon me?" I said, getting rankled. "You always gamble with drunken women, Jack?"

I glowered down at him.

"She's a grown up," Jack said, avoiding my eyes as he lit a cigarette with a gold Zippo.

"Would you like to play someone who isn't drunk?" I said slowly. "Give me a chance to get even?"

"Let's get it on," Jack said, tightening his rodent-like features into a challenge.

"I've had enough, that's for sure," Carole slurred as she stood up, stumbled over to the couch and collapsed down.

Barry, standing next to me, rubbed his palms together and smiled a toothy, manic smile. "I'm going to roll a doober," he said.

We played for an hour and I won back the sixty, plus fifty more. After the last game Jack accused me of cheating and refused to pay. I got pissed and grabbed him by the sleeves of his leather jacket and dragged him out of the room. We struggled to the slippery hallway where I flung him toward the door. He caught his balance but kept on going, gave me the finger and slammed the screen behind him.

I thought Barry would never stop laughing. Carole was unconscious through the whole thing. I made a drink and started to laugh, myself. I was very tired. Barry felt the same. We finished our drinks quietly then he shut down the lights, leaving the TV on in case Carole woke up and needed some light.

I went into the bedroom and stepped over Mike and an empty Doritos Bag by his outstretched hand. I got between the sheets and all of a sudden realized that I felt genuinely glad to be exactly where I was.

Going down to the Keys, baby—Margaritaville—that was what it was all about. Living on sponge cake, shrimp beginning to boil. Pop tops, ragtops and pink crustaceans. Christmas in the Caribbean, a few months late.

With dreams of the Gulf Stream in my head, I set the alarm for four a.m. and closed my eyes.

Chapter Six

Ripping Down the Road to Ruin

Who woulda thunk it, eh? First you go to Disney World, then you run into a couple of smugglers in a seafood restaurant and before you know it you're being treated to a full plate of lunacy and a side order of paranoia—maybe incarceration for dessert.

It's dawn now and starting to look like a desert around here. I expect a dying-of-thirst guy to come crawling by on his hands and knees, any minute.

My mind drifts back to the dawn of the day we left Orlando.

My idea was to get an early start and hopefully, avoid the cops. It was a bad beginning and things got worse as the day grew older; the wheels started falling off.

The alarm went off at four a.m., hitting me like a phone call from the IRS. I was dreaming that I was squashing a giant, buzzing palmetto bug as my hand slammed down on the plastic drugstore clock. My head was heavy and my eyes burned.

I wanted to get out of town before any cops would see the Incredible Smoking Volvo. Carole was going to have to drive it. I would've preferred her behind the wheel of the VW but it was a four-speed and she had never mastered the art of shifting.

My brain throbbed out a message: SLEEP.

My head fell back down and I closed my eyes. Just a little more sleep was all I needed....

The next thing I remember was Barry coughing in the bathroom. I still felt like shit. Tried to wake Carole but she wouldn't respond. Pushing on her was like trying to move a roll of linoleum up a hill.

She screwed up her face and slashed out at me with her hands, snarling: "Leave me alone, I didn't do anything to you."

Mike was awake and I asked him to get me a glass of water from the kitchen. By that time Carole was semi-coherent, propping her self up on one elbow.

Mike came in the room with the water and I told him it was for his mother.

"Don't you dare spill that on me, Michael Waverly," she snapped. "I'm getting up, I don't need any water, thank you."

She slowly began to move. It took her fifteen minutes to put three things in her bag. She was in the bathroom for at least a half hour, came out looking the same way she went in—disheveled and blown away, the corners of her mouth sagging.

"What the hell is the matter with you, Carole?" I asked. "You look like death warmed over."

"Feel like it, too," she croaked. "Why didn't you tell me you had blow?"

"What?"

"I woke up on the couch and I was looking around for a cigarette and found that little pouch of yours with the stuff in it."

"So you were snorting it? I was supposed to sell that shit. How much did you do?"

"I don't know… few lines… it's good stuff… had to drink myself back to sleep."

"Seems like you did a good job, goddamn it—Jesus fucking Christ."

I went into the kitchen and sat down on a stool. Carole limped after me, laid her head on top of the shiny black counter and promptly fell back asleep.

I was beginning to worry. I figured that Mike didn't know what to think, probably never seen his mother that way before.

Then I remembered. Hadn't Mike driven an intoxicated Carole over the Haavik Bridge? Wasn't he Mike the Driver?

Maybe he could drive one of our vehicles, I thought. What would the State of Florida do to me if we got caught?

"She could use some coffee, it looks like to me," Barry said, grinning widely. "I'm going to make some instant, if you'd care to join me. Maxim." He held up the squat jar of brown crystals.

"I don't drink coffee," came the slow, drawn out response as the pretty blonde head rose up slowly and grinned crookedly at us. "I drink tea," she said, steadying her head with the upturned palms of her hands.

"I'm afraid tea is just not going to cut the mustard today," I said. "How about some antifreeze…maybe a cup of Lysol Spray…."

"How about a black beauty?" Barry beamed, triumphantly. "I've got one—if you want it. It'll get you percolating; I swear to god."

"No doubt," I said. I had to admit that it was the perfect chemical solution for this particular problem. A black dex would have her ready to pass military inspection in about forty-five minutes' time.

It was six-thirty before we got rolling but we managed to get out of Orlando seeing only one cop, and he was going by in the opposite direction. I still got a nice adrenaline rush out of it.

As we drove along, I could see Carole in the rearview mirror, chewing gum and chain smoking, bopping her head to tunes I couldn't hear—oblivious to danger and just about everything else.

Things went smoothly, for about an hour, until I looked behind me and saw her coming around for a pass. Couldn't believe my eyes.

Clouds of smoke billowed across my windshield as she chugged steadily by. I put the VW pedal to the floor but couldn't close the gap. She passed me by and then pulled into my lane. The smoke was so thick I had to swerve out into the passing lane just to see.

After a long period of slow momentum building, I finally caught up. I signaled for her to pull over with a violent wave of my right arm.

She slowed and turned onto the shoulder, a wide-eyed angry look crossing her tightened features. I turned in front of her, stopped and backed up until our bumpers were almost touching. I stepped out, told Mike to stay put and slammed the door behind me. Beer cans and candy wrappers lay ugly in the ditch.

I needed to check the oil on the Volvo. The way it was blowing, the engine could've been nearly dry.

Nothing showed on the stick.

That seemed to me to be an apt description of my life. Lucky for us, there was a half-full case of Valvoline in the back of the van. Bagley was so prepared that he must have been a Boy Scout.

"Carole, you can't be passing me up like that," I said, searching through the Volvo's glove compartment for a can opener.

"Why not?" she bubbled, eyes as wide as saucers, pinholes for pupils, sucking rapid-fire on a Kool. "The way I see it is, if you're behind me, the smoke will bounce off the bus and not seem so bad to anyone else on the road who happens to be driving by or sitting along the shoulder watching cars go by and seeing if there's anything wrong or something. You know, like a cop or something... like those two troopers back in Orlando, you remember, Keith. If you're behind me, they won't notice how bad it is and then they won't come after me and pull me over."

"Carole... back in Orlando, it was calm, nighttime, and in the city. Out here it's windy, and nobody gives a shit about a little exhaust smoke. They got smokestacks and stuff out here."

"I don't see any. And I still think that I should be in front of you in case I do get stopped, so you can see what's going on and explain the situation to the patrolman. If you were in front of me you might not be looking back at the time and be gone too far down the road before you saw what was happening. Then, if you had to back up all the way to where he had me stopped, you might get a ticket, too."

I couldn't have that happen now, could I, folks.

"Believe, me, Carole, if you get pulled over, I'll know about it. But the longer we stand here on the side of the road, the longer it is before we get home. As soon as I get this oil in here, we have to git and git quickly. Can't be standing out here very long... no telling what might be coming along... we haven't got time to fuck around."

"You drive behind me," she said, one hand cocked on her hip, "or I'm not driving anymore."

"Then what the fuck am I supposed to do, for Christ sake, drive both cars? Oh, sure... that's cool... I can drive one car a block and a half and then run back and get the other one and drive that one three blocks and then run back... keep doing that all the way home.... That makes a lot of goddamn sense, doesn't it? I'm surprised you haven't suggested that Mike drive."

"I'll do it," said the voice from the van. The side door slid open and two, tennis shoe clad feet popped out.

"You stay right where you are, Michael. You are not going to be driving, so don't even think about it," I said. The feet slid back in. "All right, Carole, I'll follow you. Whatever you say. Just let's get the hell out of here, I'm getting nervous."

Mike and I followed just close enough behind her that the oil cloud was breaking up by the time it got to us. Even with that distance between us, I still got a headache. Mike just stared nervously ahead and asked why our car was smoking. I told him it was broken.

About twenty miles outside of Tampa, Carole signaled for me to get in front of her. I pulled in front and led the caravan all the way to the Courtney Campbell Causeway. In among the city traffic, drivers held their noses and honked their horns in protest of our oily residue. Embarrassed but not yet beaten down, we eventually limped happily into the asphalt oasis of the Twin Lakes parking lot.

We had made it all the way without seeing a single cop.

In the Sunshine State, it is indeed a rare occurrence to go that long without observing the presence of law enforcement. I often mused upon the possibility that half of the rednecks in Florida were criminals and the other half were cops. That way, some sort of socio-economic balance was maintained for eternity.

Watching my wife and my kid carrying their bags into our apartment, I felt warm and fuzzy. It seemed like the right time for a celebration, kind of a two-wrongs-make-a-party type deal.

Carole threw her bags onto the bed and Mike did the same. After making sure that Mike put his dirty clothes in the hamper, she went into the kitchen and took up scrubbing the counters and the sink, smoking constantly.

I helped Mike get his room straightened up. Then we went out to play ball. Carole was vacuuming when we left. I didn't see any reason to stand in her way.

We took the VW to the park and Mike smiled at me from the passenger seat; he said he liked riding in the little bus with eyelashes.

Mike and I returned home after a couple hours. Carole was on the couch doing a crossword puzzle. A cigarette sent up spirals of blue smoke from a plastic ashtray beside her.

She was coming down, like a brick falling from a building. She could barely speak and her eyelids were fluttering. The Black Beauty was losing its electric grip.

I could see that if I wanted any action that night, I would have to break out the powder. I knew she wouldn't argue. I knew she'd be real happy.

We started off with a little line around six o'clock. I remember going to the glass doors and watching the sun fall behind the rooftops and feeling sad. Carole put a Swanson's TV dinner (chicken) in the oven for Mike. We adults decided to skip food and go for the gusto—right to the liquor store.

All the shit was gone before eleven p.m. and my insides were doing summersaults. Carole's eyes were wide and empty.

I called up Ted. He said he didn't have time to help me out. Snickered that he had a date. I was ready to spend the last of our cash on dope and he was playing hard to get.

I pleaded.

He reiterated.

I kept on him and finally he realized that I wasn't going to let him off the hook. Being a polite guy, he didn't even tell me to fuck off. He said he knew where the man Dracula was and would call him for me, if I so chose. Said that all I had to do was drive over to a little bar in one of the old sections of town and Dracula would be there.

It was about a ten-minute drive on the freeway and five minutes on local streets to a low-down residential neighborhood with a little box-shaped dive as the centerpiece. Jay's Diamond Lounge, it said on a cheaply made, hand-painted sign mounted on two wooden posts. There were two spotlights shining up at it from the dirt. The building had faded red siding and a long, rectangular window about shoulder height from the ground.

I could see some pretty hard faces moving around in the yellow, smoky light. For a moment, I thought I was back in East Hammond, Wisconsin. Make it a little colder and it would've felt the same.

I took a deep breath and got out of the car. Old pickups and ratty muscle cars were parked erratically to avoid the many ruts and puddles.

Inside of Jay's there was a low ceiling and slowly turning, rusty overhead fans. To my left, people lingered around two pool tables. To my right was a long and dark wooden bar, behind which an ancient jar of pig's knuckles glowed beneath a red Dixie Beer sign. The warped, gray floor was filled with Formica tables and metal-framed chairs of various sizes, shapes and colors. Rough hewn, blue-collar white folks filled about half of them. An aging photo of Robert E. Lee on a big, white horse rested against the cloudy bar mirror.

The bartender was in his forties: big man with heavy, red veins showing on his cheeks and a crooked, gin-blossomed nose. The amber glow of tiny Christmas lights, strung along the wall behind him, bathed his wide shoulders.

He kept an eye on me as I moved slowly and nervously towards him. I was jonesing. I wondered if he could tell....

Dracula, the object of my desire, was down the bar a ways, leaning over the bar and spinning a bottle of Miller High Life between his fingers while a small group of scruffs lingered nearby.

Too nervous to walk over, I ordered a Bud and sat down. My throat could barely function.

I swallowed hard and drank down some of the swill. I would have pulled out a cig but I forgot to bring them. I was trying to quit anyway. I looked around cautiously and nobody seemed ready to attack.

After choking down half the beer, I walked up to Dracula and slid into the stool beside him, trying to act confident and friendly. He looked at me with tired eyes and grinned, a toothless grin. Then he quickly looked back at his beer.

His eyes told me that I shouldn't be there and I felt a chill crawl up my back.

When I sat down, the pack of hangers-on got restless, shuffling their feet and dispersing. I knew that that was the way with drug people. Hadn't I been through this many times before, only the places being different? The harder the drug, the more paranoid the crowd, especially in Florida, where they could put you away for less coke than it takes to jack up a cockroach.

Ever been in a low-down saloon drinking away your time—but minding your own business—when suddenly you discover that some weird stranger has homed in on you, locked in on you like a laser sight?

You catch this guy staring at you with a gleam in his eye, a sinister gleam. You know that it isn't romance; it's a different kind of thing. Every time you sneak a look at him, he's staring back at you. You turn away, but you know he's still staring at you because you can feel his eyes burning in.

You have become the center of his warped attention. For some odd reason, be it your looks or your clothes or your haircut or just about anything else, this dude wants to kick your ass. You've never met the son of a bitch before but all of a sudden he hates the ground you're standing on and your mother, too.

Most of the time, you can just ignore the guy. After a while he'll get loaded and either leave or forget about you. Unfortunately, some of the time, the squid is going to get aggressive and lay one of his tentacles on you. Maybe go as far as coming over to find out how tough you look, close up. Might say something obviously meant to annoy. And then, if he senses weakness, he might strike.

This dude was different   than most, I thought—he really looked dangerous. Or maybe it was me who was different, this time. I sure as hell didn't feel right. Too much drug had my nerves raw and my spirit weak. I was beginning another ride on the greasy road to the bottom and I wanted nothing to do with the guy staring at me with those wild, piercing eyes.

He was Charley Manson with short hair: a five-foot, ten-inch, cracker ball-of-hate. Faded, blue flannel shirt half open and showing a grease-stained yellow T-shirt over a muscular chest.

And I knew, without a goddamn doubt, that I was his target for the night. *Oh lucky day*....

Serious doubts rose up like boils, as I studied Drac's disheveled body and prematurely wrinkled face. It dawned on me that these Southern fried dudes had probably been expecting him to bring a narc into the place someday. And I was the proof of his incompetence that they'd been waiting for. Shit, they were probably hoping that I really *was* the heat so they'd get their first opportunity to torture a narc. Good sport between gator hunts and tractor pulls, I suppose.

"Hey man," Drac finally croaked with a smoke-cured hoarseness, reaching out a bony, slightly trembling hand in my direction, "I see you made it okay. Ted said you were coming over, man. Forgive me if I'm a little spacey—I've been up for fifty-six hours straight, man...."

"You sure it's all right I came over, man? Some of your friends don't look so happy to see me."

"Don't worry about those assholes. It's okay, man; take my word for it. Ted said you were coming. I told him to send you over here."

Turning slowly away from Dracula, I locked on to the wild, dark-circled peepers of my night stalker. He was staring right at me.

"You know that guy over at the pool table, man?"

Psycho was sneering directly at my reflection in the bar mirror.

"That's Jimmy Stewart, believe it or not," Dracula said out of the side of his mouth, hand and cigarette in front of his face. "His old lady's been giving him a lot of trouble lately; he's all twisted up. She's been fucking some tennis player, some stud she went to high school with—or some shit like that."

I finished my beer and ordered a Heineken from the bartender, a cold, hollow feeling growing inside me.

Barman raised his eyebrows, mumbled: "I think we might have one somewhere."

I made a desperate scan of the room and couldn't find anyone who might even possibly have the slightest inclination to come to my aid. It seemed like they all would've enjoyed kicking my ass, or, at the very least, watching it get kicked. And Jimmy Stewart was at the top of the list of tonight's Hate Parade.

The bartender returned with a bottle of Heineken so skunky I smelled it even before he set it down. I took a deep breath, sat up straight, flexed my shoulders and started talking business with Dracula.

While I was in a goddamn hurry to get out of there, Drac was in no hurry, whatsoever. There wasn't much hurry left in him.

We talked while he smoked three cigarettes, and all the time Jimmy was staring at me from various parts of the room. I kept my head turned toward Drac, trying to avoid the piercing, fluorescent stare.

After Dracula finished his beer and one more cigarette, he decided to do the deal. I felt somewhat relieved. Maybe Jimmy was just a starer....

I took a big slug of skunk juice and saw Jimmy's face in the mirror, right behind me, leering down. My heart skipped a beat.

"Who's your friend here, Gaptooth?" Jimmy said. "Ain't seen him here before. Sure is a clean looking one, ain't he. Looks like a goddamn tennis player...or some shit...."

"Ease off, Jimmy. He's a good guy," Drac said. "He's a friend of Ted Friday's, from Minnesota. He's a hockey player, not tennis."

Stewart backed off a bit and his expression changed a little. Now he was studying me.

"What you doin' in Florida?" Jimmy snarled. "Come down here for a job?"

"Ah, no. Came down for the weather. I'm still looking for work."

"Another one of those guys, huh.... I s'pose yer collectin' unemployment and shit. Its people like you that's draggin' this country down."

"No unemployment, just living off my wife," I said. "And I gamble a little."

"Some kind of card shark?"

"Nah, dog tracks, Jai Lai, backgammon, horses...you name it." And I bullshit a lot, too, I forgot to add.

"No shit," Jimmy said. "You some kinda shark, coming down here to fleece all the Southern boys or something?" He leaned closer, eyes almost glowing. "You ever play pool?"

"I play, but I'm not very good. Not good enough to gamble, anyway."

"Now yer not talkin' so big, are ya? Whattsa matter, 'fraid of losin'?"

"Jimmy, we're trying to conduct some business, here," Dracula said, still staring at his beer bottle. "Do you suppose you could give us some privacy? It looks like it's your shot over there. Bill is waiting for you."

"Yeah, I know that, toothless Joe. Why don't you get your fucking teeth fixed, anyway, you fucking geek?" Jimmy reached over a greasy paw and pinched Dracula's nose. "I need some shit, Dracula, or should I call you Kevin? How bout a gram—on account...."

"You still owe me for a gram and a half."

"So give me another one and I'll owe you for two and a half."

"I can't do that, Jimmy, give me a break."

From the pool tables: "C'mon goddammit, Jimmy, we're waiting."

Jimmy turned in the direction of the sound, flipped the bird and turned back to us.

"I gotta go," he said, "but I'm not going very far. I need that gram, gapper." He tilted his head sideways, chuckling dryly, and walked away.

"That guy is a friend of yours?" I said, weakly.

"Jimmy's not as bad as he seems," Dracula said. "But when he sets his mind to it, he can be a real asshole. One of those guys that's always trying to prove how tough he is. If I buy him a beer he'll probably leave us alone. Steve, get Jimmy another one. And a couple more here." He pointed his tobacco-stained fingers at his empty bottle.

"No, man, I, ah—I have to get going."

Bartender bent over and grabbed another Heineken from the cooler. "Ah—sure, thanks, man—yeah… that's okay… I guess I will have another one. No problem."

"Shall we do our business, man?" Dracula said.

"Fine with me," I whispered.

"Let's go into my office," he said, gesturing in the direction of the men's room. A large rendition of a white-gloved hand, with GENTS painted on it, pointed toward a green partition.

I went in first and Drac followed a minute later. I assumed it was a familiar drill. We took care of business inside a stall, urine and camphor providing the proper ambiance.

On the way out of the bathroom, I was staring at the lurid pictures on the condom machine and almost banged my head on the towel dispenser. I snapped my head back to avoid it and Dracula started laughing so hard he had a coughing fit. Thought his lungs would end up on the floor.

Upon our return to our stools, two fresh bottles of beer sat waiting for us, glistening and sweating. Looking horrible. That made two full bottles apiece, untouched.

"We didn't order these, Steve," Dracula said.

"Jimmy got'em for you."

We looked toward the pool tables and Jimmy was waving his cue stick at us, grinning like the last speaker at a convention of lunatics.

Wasn't halfway through the beer when Jimmy was again standing at my back. I flinched a little and he sat down on the stool next to me.

"What's your name," he said, looking at me like he knew something that I didn't. "I'm Jimmy," extending his thick hand.

I took it. He squeezed; I squeezed harder.

"Keith Waverly," I said, thinking that I didn't want any trouble. What I wanted was to be back inside my shitty, roach emporium of an apartment, *snorting whisky and drinking cocaine.*

"Since Dracula is pulling prick on me," Jimmy said, moving even closer to my face. "Do you suppose I could get some of your blow from you?"

"Pardon me?" I said.

"What the fuck are you pulling, Jimmy?" Dracula said.

"Stay the fuck out of this, snaggletooth; I'm talking. All I need is a little, for the rest of the night. I can't go home cause my old lady'll call the cops if she even sees me in the neighborhood."

I thought it best to try an appease him. "I'll give you a line if you want to walk out to my car with me," I said.

He grinned again, with an edge to it. "A whole line? Gee ain't that generous.... You come into my part of town fer yer dope—and that's all the thanks ya show?"

"Thanks for what?"

"Thanks fer not kickin' yer Yankee ass."

"I'm leaving," I said, turning to Dracula. "See you later, I have to get back to my wife."

"Yeah," Drac said, like a dead man talking.

I got up and started for the door.

"Pussy gotta run ta his mommy?" Jimmy said, catching up to me and staying alongside as I moved toward the door.

"Changed your mind about that line, eh?" I said, smiling weakly.

His mouth fell into a grin. His head moved closer to my shoulder—almost touching it—like he was a hockey player, going to ride me into the boards.

I looked behind us and noticed some of the bar patrons paying close attention. Dracula gazed on woodenly for a moment then turned back to his bonanza of beer.

Jimmy followed me through the door and into the parking lot.

A charge of fear hit my gut. Adrenaline started me shivering inside but I held it tight.

We moved towards the car like a two-headed man, me wondering if I should say anything or not, and him grinning crazily back at me, head cocked like a rabid dog getting ready to bite. We got close to the van and I put my hand in my pants pocket, searching for my keys. Jimmy eyes bored in and he started to chuckle: "Ya got a goddamn hippie bus, Yankee boy.... You a draft dodgin' fuckin' peacenik?"

"It's not my car. Belongs to a friend of mine from Colorado. See the license plates.... My car's a Chevy. It's broken down. If you want a line, Jimmy, I'll get in and draw one out. I've gotta get going, people are waiting for their drug."

"MMMHHH, look at those furry fancy seats, fer god sakes. You kill those animals, for 'em?"

"I already told you it wasn't my van."

"I never sat on anything like that before, why don't you let me in the other side so I can enjoy them seat covers."

"You're not getting in this van, Jimmy"

"What in hell ya mean by that?"

"Just what I said. I said I'd give you a line, I will. A big one, too. But you ain't getting in, because it's not my car."

"Well that's a fine howdaya do," he said and launched a bolo punch at my head.

I saw it coming and ducked. The heavy blow glanced off the side of my head, just above the ear. I saw stars.

Lowering my shoulder, I rammed it into his chest, knocking him backwards a step.

Stumbling, he threw a weak left that hit the back of my head as I scrambled to open the car door. I jerked on the handle and he was back on me, slamming the door shut with his shoulder and punching me in the back of my neck.

Exhausted, bad leg killing me, I turned and tried to grab him.

He spun out of my grasp, landed a solid uppercut to my gut and came down with a roundhouse left on my upper cheekbone.

That was all she wrote for me. I staggered against the van, my back sagging against the door.

"Go ahead, hit me," I screamed, hands at my sides. "Beat the shit out of me." I didn't recognize my voice. "Kill me if you want." Tears rolled down my face, mixing with blood and snot. "I deserve it. Hit me again, you fuck! Hit me goddamn it!"

He paused for a second, confused, looking into my eyes, a sick grin on his lips. Then he let fly with a haymaker. I turned my head at the last instant and it caught me on the cheekbone.

I crumpled to the ground in a heap.

A crowd had gathered and a thousand angry bees were buzzing in my brain.

I started gagging. My head was throbbing all the way back to my past lives.

Shouts of "Kill him, Jimmy... kill the fucker..." punched holes in the night.

My head was cockeyed against the van while my spastic hands scratched in the dirt. Blackness filled me up as Jimmy paraded around, flexing his muscles and grinning. Strutting.

He stopped in front my face and grabbed his crotch, making like an ape. Harsh, tinny laughter came from the crowd.

Things were getting clearer inside my head. With one eye I watched as his boot drew back for a kick.

I didn't care. "Come on fucker, get it over with," I said.

A voice in the crowd: "He's had enough, Jimmy, leave him alone why don'tcha...."

Dracula, I thought. I lifted my head but couldn't see right.

The boot didn't come.

"I guess I don't want to get my clothes all bloody," Jimmy said, playing to the crowd. Then he crouched down and slid his hand inside my pants pocket.

I tried to focus.

Another voice in the crowd: "You feeling him up, Jimmy?"

"Fuck you," Jimmy said, shooting out the bird with his free hand. "I'm looking for his shit."

While his fingers were in my shirt pocket, my right hand was digging out a rock the size of a jumbo egg from the oily dirt beneath the van. Something, or someone, wouldn't let me give up.

I squeezed the rock, slowly dragging my hand into position, all the while moaning and drooling.

His fingers were inside my other pocket when I came up hard and caught him in the temple, full force. There was a dull, crunching thud and he collapsed down on my legs like a headshot deer. I shoved him off and stood shakily up, some mysterious force pushing me on. I got into the van and turned the key before the stunned crowd knew what was happening.

Threw it in reverse and backed up without looking. Bodies scattered.

Turned so hard, I near tipped over, the weather it was dry. *Sun so hot I nearly froze to death; Suzanna, don't you cry.*

I headed for the exit as fast as those four cylinders could take me, forgetting about the huge hole at the edge of the lot. I hit the dip at about ten-mph and the front tires smacked the ground and rebounded up like a circus stunt.

The springs slammed; my neck snapped. I flew off the seat and hit the top of my head on the ceiling.

A drum machine in my head pounded out a manic rhythm while a hundred bongos of pain throbbed with the backbeat. Throw in the Fever Singers and the red and yellow flashes and you had one hell of a crazy midnight orchestra:

Oh Suzanna, don't you cry for me;
For I come from Minnesota with a heartache on my knee.
Sun's so hot I'm almost froze to death and I cannot figure why
Wish I was back in Minnesota and I still knew how to cry.

I had to hand it to the Sky Pilot; he had risen back to his previous heights. I hadn't thought about him in so long, except for wondering when he might return. This was his way of showing me that he still cared. He was now truly worthy of being called a "higher power."

I couldn't wait to get home and show Carole my new face. I could ask her to fix it for me. Mike would sure be proud, I thought....

What happened, Dad? Oh, nothing, Mike. I was just fighting with a redneck that was trying to steal your mother's and my cocaine. Me and this other guy were only trying to kill each other, in the parking lot of a sleazy bar—nothing to worry about. And you know what, son? I'm going to let you in on a little secret. I think I enjoyed getting beaten up. Funny thing, don't you think? It's like there was some satisfaction in getting punched silly.... All the questions inside my head went away for a while... What do you think about that, Mikey? Aren't ya proud of your old man?

Mike was sure lucky to have an old man like me. And Carole...what about her? Wasn't I bringing home the dope? Wouldn't she try to coax more out of me—and get what she wanted? What more could she ask for, for the Christ sake. Like having your cake and eating it for breakfast, having a guy like me around.

Wasn't I the guy who just put down Jimmy Stewart?

Reality gnawed its way back into my gut with sharp rodent teeth. A tangled mess of torment came tumbling from my mind's closet:

I should have saved the money instead of buying dope. We need a car and I'm blowing money on dope...Mike needs some new clothes.... My leg is still hurting... my teeth need fixing....

I had stepped onto the same old merry-go-round and wasn't sure how to get off. Not only did we need a car and all that other stuff; but I also had to pay for the Key West trip. I could not have Bagley see any more of my failures. It was easy to imagine him lording over me, rubbing it in.

Perhaps if you had a decent job you might be able to afford things, Keith.... But I suppose if you're maxed out, you're maxed out.... I imagine I'll have to bail you out again... maybe someday you'll learn.

Things were moving steadily backwards, towards a very familiar place: A place where everyone was out for themselves. Wasn't that the way of the world? Weren't they all grabbing what they could, not thinking about anything else?

My mind reeled as I struggled to drive straight.

Carole would have to get some more pineapple... Jesus, that son of a bitch Jimmy sure dropped hard... how lucky to find a rock in the ground.... Was I already crazy or just getting there? Getting higher every day, that's for sure.... What goes up must come down.... It's going to get worse before it gets better....

I managed to make it to the safety of Twin Lakes but barely had the strength to pull the key out of the ignition. I sat there, slack-jawed, staring out past the dumpsters at the flat nothingness, God forsaken piece of land that it was.

I dug into my right pants pocket and fumbled out the coke, my bloody fingers stiff and thick. I couldn't have spoken if I had to. I struggled to unfold the sharply creased photo of a large naked breast and wondered if any of the blood was Jimmy Stewart's? *Jimmy, Jimmy Stewart—where for art thou, Jimmy?*

I lifted the packet to my hungry nostrils and wedged a corner of the paper right in, snorting and rooting it in through the mucus and the blood.

Stuff got me going and I climbed out. I even remembered to lock the van. I don't remember remembering.

Carole's face was amazing when I walked through the door: how it went from strung out, to elated, to shocked, to concerned and then to freaked out, in such a short time.

"My god!" she screamed "What happened to you—oh my god."

"Mr. Hobbs took a vacation on my face," I said, collapsing on the couch.

"What the hell does that mean?"

"Some asshole fucking burnout at the bar took a dislike to me and we got in a little tussle in the parking lot. Seems as he was trying to extract a toll."

"What?" She chewed savagely at the cuticle on her fingers, her eyes bulging.

"He wanted some of the coke as payment for using his neighborhood. Kind of a Mr. Rogers type thing."

"Did you give him any?"

"I offered to give him a line, but that wasn't enough for the prick. Fucker's name was Jimmy Stewart, can you believe that?"

"Yeah, right," she said moving toward the bathroom. "Was there a big white bunny with him?"

"No, just a little white rabbit."

Carole returned with a warm, wet towel, some band-aids and some hydrogen peroxide—household necessities when you've got a nine-year old kid and a loser for a husband.

She fussed over me for twenty minutes. It seemed like she was lacking in gentleness; I sure was stinging when she got through.

"Where's Mike at, Carole?" I asked, through the pain and the fog.

"He's at Pete's. He was so excited to tell him about Disney World.... I said he could spend the night." She made a cute sort of frown: "I had something special planned for you and I." Then her face went blank and her eyes got round: "Can I have a toot?"

"Sure, the stuff is in my pants pocket here. Can you get it? I'm a little sore. It only hurts when I move."

Her hand felt good in my pocket.

"At least that part of you still works," she said smiling coyly.

"That's for sure," I said.

Assessed damage to my face seemed to be moderate: split lip, a couple loose teeth, swollen ear, some abrasions, a black eye and one hell of a headache. I figured I could tell Mike I'd been mugged or something.

"Keith, if you promise not to get mad at me, I think I've got something that will make you feel better."

"Now why would I get mad about feeling better? Am I some kind of backwards fuck?"

"Well, 'cause I took a bunch of pills from Barry Eastman's medicine cabinet. Some pain pills and some downers."

"You fucking stole pills from Barry's medicine chest? Jesus fucking Christ! ......What kind are they?"

"Empirin number three. There was one Percodan, but I already took that—when you were gone. I was all jangly...."

"I'll take two Empirin, please. With a rum pineapple for a wash."

"Care for a Seconal?"

"Sure, why not. Unconscious is better than no conscious."

"Uh huh."

Carole went into our bedroom and returned quickly with the little white tablets and the little red capsules.

I took two Empirin; she had a line. I had a red; she had a red. I had a line; she had a line. I drank a drink; she drank a drink. We both had a drink and a line. I had another red; she had another red. We both had another line.

Drink / line / line. Drink / pill / line. Line / line / drink. Drink/ line / drink. Pill / drink / line.

To say I felt better after all this would be a lie. To say I felt worse was less distant from the truth but still not quite right. What I had created, with all this reckless ingestion of toxic substances, was a war, a war inside my body with skirmishes going on at various areas.

For a while, I'd feel painless and relaxed only to give way to anxiety, fear and tension as the coke got a leg up. It would get real uncomfortable until the reds dragged me down to their nauseous, liquid delirium.

It was at one of the high, edgy points when I decided to take a shower. The reds kicked in as I turned the handles on the faucets so I settled into the tub instead—because I couldn't stand up.

I couldn't help but think of Jim Morrison. I wasn't as fat yet, but

I could see the start of middle age creeping in. My gut stuck out above the waterline. I didn't want to die in the bathtub. *It would suck to die in a shitty, shallow tub like this one. No one would build a shrine.*

After soaking for a good long time, I toweled off and stumbled into the bedroom and dropped down onto the mattress.

Everything was shutting down; my head getting heavy.

Carole came into the room. I watched as she got her pink flannel nightgown from the drawer and pulled it over her shoulders. I remembered the garment from back when we first got married.

Clock read 12:40 A.M. when my eyes popped open. Every movement hurt as I felt around in the bed. Carole wasn't there and I needed another pain pill in a bad way. I struggled to my feet and went into the hall. The living room light glared painfully against the white walls, accentuating the cheapness like never before. Scurrying roaches in the kitchen sounded like a distant army on the retreat.

Carole was cross-legged on the couch, crusts of white powder circling her nostrils, pink nightgown covering her knees—cowboy boots below them. The boots that I'd bought her for Christmas, so many years before. She didn't notice me until I was almost upon her.

Her head jerked up. "Oh hi, Keith," she slurred, "how are you feeling?" Empty Cutty Sark bottle leaning against her thigh.

"You coming to bed pretty soon, Carole? Don't you have to work tomorrow?"

"Paul said I could have the day off because of his mistake at Disney World. He said I could come in on Tuesday."

"Yeah? You call him? Where'd you get the Cutty from?"

"I brought it from work. It was left over from Mariana's going-away party."

"Oh, yeah. Got any more of those pain pills? My head is really throbbing. Jesus, I could use some fucking Pepto."

"All that's left is in the medicine cabinet."

"You coming to bed?"

"Pretty soon."

"Okay. G'night, again."

I got two Empirins and bent over to get water from the bathroom sink. My head pounded and nausea made my ears ring.

The opiates brought me sleep and dreams. But not the sweet dreams your mother wished for you....

Something dark was biting at my heels, chasing me through strange houses and unknown neighborhoods. Through constant vigilance, cleverness and unending fear, I stayed one step ahead. Sometimes I outwitted a pursuer altogether only to find a new chaser waiting on the horizon.

I maneuvered and manipulated myself through every obstacle with expertise, until, I came upon this huge, red—and very locked—double door.

I was trapped. Blood-lusting citizenry were closing in rapidly from behind shouting angrily about decency and obedience. I pounded and kicked furiously on the solid door. Its red color changed suddenly to green but it still wouldn't open. I tried to shout but had no voice. I pounded and pounded.

I woke up and I could still hear the pounding—only this time it wasn't in my head. I rolled off the mattress and pushed myself upright. Clock read 4:44 A.M.

The pounding stopped as I stepped into the hallway.

I was almost to the door when it flew open and Carole came falling through, landing on her knees in front of me.

To my shock, standing behind her was a paunchy, forty-something guy in a green Hawaiian shirt and a wrinkled, green sport coat above tan, creased slacks.

The clothes looked dirty without having any dirt on them. His

thinning brown hair was combed back to cover the emerging bald
spot and his eyes were inquisitive above red cheeks.

He looked down at Carole apologetically as she lay crumpled
on the linoleum.

"What the... what the hell is going on, Carole? Who is this
guy? Where have you been?"

I crouched down by her; she was mumbling incoherently. I
looked up at the guy; he was showing me a badge.

I stood up, shaken.

"What's the trouble, officer?"

His eyes narrowed as he checked me out, up and down and then
back up to my damaged face. "Run into a door tonight, son?" he
said, squinting.

"No. I mean what the hell is going on? What are you doing
with my wife? Last time I saw her she was doing a crossword
puzzle on our couch."

I could barely stand up. I struggled for composure.

"Lieutenant Douglas of the St. Petersburg Police. Seems your
wife must've had a hankering for more liquor sometime during
the night, and made a run down Fourth Street to find some.
Must've stopped somewhere on the strip for a while, judging by
her condition—though I don't know how she was when she
started out. Must've been on her way back home, I 'magine,
when she sideswiped a car. That was about a mile down from
here. I saw the whole darn thing and pulled over to have a look.
Well, this young couple that she hit—they say they don't want to
press any charges. Felt sorry for your wife, they said. Must've
been religious folk. Well, I told them the charges would be at the
option of the arresting officer—in this case, me. Now it's kinda
against the rules, you understand, but I think I can cut her some
slack. Think I see something redeeming in your wife.... Although
it don't seem like that at this particular moment, now does it?"

He looked down. Her cheek was pressed against the floor, drool running from her gaping mouth. "As I was saying, that couple got me to see the helping side of things, ya might say. Sweet little thing here reminded me of my daughter, in some way, I s'pose. So anyway, the husband drove your car home and your wife here, she rode with me. The three of us helped her down the walk and then they said goodnight while she was fetching her keys. Seemed like she might fall and hurt herself, so I stayed—but I didn't think she was going to fall through the goddamn doorway...."

He stepped inside and surveyed the interior of the kitchen. "You know, a lot of people make that same mistake. They leave the bar feeling okay, and then the last two that they slammed down before closing catch up to them and bam, they go comatose. You ever have that happen to you, son?"

"Yeah, a couple times," I said, squirming. "Not the comatose part, though."

"Jesus, you oughta get that car of yours fixed too, she's blowing a lotta oil. You know, son, your wife has quite a temper on her. She showed a little, tonight. But I like that in a woman, y'know. She was pretty adamant, at first, about how she was okay to drive and everything, ya see. Then I ask to see her driver's license and she falls out the door on her knees and dumps her whole damn purse out on the road. I'm tellin' ya, there was stuff every which way. Which the good couple is kind enough to pick up for her, I might add. Now that was a sight to see... I wasn't so sure it was an accident, her dumping her purse, if you know what I mean. She's a feisty one, all right. Now if a patrol car had spotted her instead of me, she would most surely be in jail right now, you understand what I'm saying?"

I nodded slightly, beginning to feel something funny, happening in my gut, like I was going to puke.

"You see, son, I figured it would be a damn shame to have a pretty thing like her get locked up, just because she had some problems at home and got a little too soused. And I'm truly sorry that she fell down, but when she finally got the key to work in the door—which she wouldn't let me do for her without fighting— she collapsed too fast for me to catch her."

As he spoke, Carole rose up to her hands and knees and began to crawl along the kitchen floor. At least she had put some blue jeans on under the flannel nightgown. Put on her denim shirt, too.

The cop and I both stared at her as she made her turtle-like progress into the living room and out of our sight.

"Jesus," I yelled after her. "What the hell is wrong with you, Carole? You could've killed somebody or wrecked the car."

"I think it's best that you just let her crawl into the corner and lick her wounds, son. Ain't no use yellin' at a whipped filly." He shifted his gaze back to me. "Carole do that to your face, son? Looks like someone did a toe dance on you."

"My wife and I don't engage in physical violence, officer. We only call each other filthy names and try to destroy each other's soul."

"I'm a lieutenant, son. Lieutenant Robert Douglas. And that's some funny kind of talk yer spoutin'." He put the crook of his hand to his chin and paused for another round of studying my countertops and my face ."Well, son, I'll leave you and your wife to settle this problem on your own. You make sure there's no rough stuff, okay. I don't want to hear about any of that. Cute girl like Carole shouldn't have to get shit-faced like that... a damn shame is what it is.... By the way, Keith—that is your name, isn't it?"

I nodded.

"She said you were her ex-husband."

"Yeah, technically, I am. But we're trying to make a new start. We've been back together six months or so, now."

"That's good, Keith. You treat that girl of yours real nice, now, you hear. If you ever need to talk to me about anything, give me a call." He handed me a card from his coat pocket. He turned to

leave, took two steps and then turned back, just like goddamn
Columbo.

"She kept mentioning a Paul," he said. "Know anyone name of
Paul?"

"That's her boss at the radio station."

"What radio station would that be?"

"WPLF in Pinellas Park."

"The hell you say. I listen to that Ted Friday all the goddamn
time. Ain't that something." Fake smile: "You folks behave your-
selves, now. It's time for me to go home."

He smirked at the sounds of retching coming from the bathroom, and moved slowly out of sight. I frowned as I shut the door
and locked both locks. That's all I needed, a fat Florida cop
snooping around.

And it seemed, like he'd taken a liking to my wife, formed
some kind of twisted alliance in his balding head.

I could thank him for that, as long as things ended right there.
I put his card on the kitchen table and went into check on Carole.

She was crawling out of the bathroom, hair wet and stringy, her
face sagging like a bloodhound on scent.

"What the fuck is going on, Carole? How could you be so
fucking stupid to go out in the car like that? What the fuck is the
matter with you, for Christ sake?"

"I was jis lonely—missin' Minnesota," she said, struggling to
her feet and trying to regain some dignity. "I jes wanned to have
sommore drinks, thas all. Mussa bin thoss reds I took. Jeeze, I
dinn know y'could get thiss fucktup."

She giggled weakly and stumbled into the bedroom, collapsed
face down on the mattress and passed out.

I had to shove her dead weight over on the bed so I could lie
down next to her.

I closed my eyes and hoped that she wouldn't wake up for a
long, long time.

The light was still on in the kitchen but I didn't care.

It was 10:30 the next morning when my eyes finally focused. Carole was gone from the bed and, for a second, my heart jumped. But then I smelled the bacon frying and the coffee steaming and a warm feeling swirled through me.

The radio was playing just loud enough for me to hear: *I believe in miracles—you sexy thing.*

"You awake yet, honey?" Her voice was like a sweet angel's song riding in on waves of heavenly aroma.

Only trouble was, my stomach was in no shape to eat. Carole had probably been eating bacon as she cooked, I figured. She could always eat, no matter what.

"I've made your favorite breakfast," she said, a lilt in her voice like a country chanteuse.

Jeeze, she seemed so sweet. Her voice seemed to beg forgiveness and promise future rewards, all at the same time.

I felt a stirring between my legs that got me up and out of the bed.

I went into the bathroom and puked into the toilet. Cleaned up a little and walked on rubber legs to the table. Every wound on my body seemed to sing Jimmy Stewart. Carole had the newspaper and the napkins and the whole shooting match, all set up and ready.

We were quiet at the table, neither one of us wanting to bring up the horror of the previous night.

Without ever saying that we were sorry, we managed to get through breakfast without any fighting. I managed to struggle down some food and got a gut ache like a giant crab was nesting in my gallbladder. Goddamn fried breakfast after a binge... Carole's good intentions were putting me on the road to gastrointestinal hell....

I helped clean off the table and the tension started to lessen. Both of us were too burned out for more battling, I guess. Fatigue in a marriage can be a good thing....

With the kitchen cleaned, we had to face the reality of being alone with each other.

Dread took up residence in my chest like a deadly virus. There was a new thing nesting there, too, hand-delivered by that fat fucking cop. I could feel it lingering, dark and toothy. I hoped that if I ignored it, it would go away.

I went in to the living room and turned on the tube and collapsed on the couch. Carole took a chair, smoking a cigarette. TV was the only thing I had the energy for. Life's cheapest high: the cathode ray.

Mike walked in carrying his gym bag and saved us from our self-made abyss. Carole and I gravitated toward him like he was our one saving grace, the only thing in our lives that we could be proud of. He was such a damn good kid, always smiling and giving things a go. I admired him for his attitude in the face of all our craziness. How could you not like Mike?

We were both in a giving mood that gray, empty Sunday but we didn't have anything left to give. We had already pissed it down the drain; turned ourselves into open wounds instead. The regret made me feel old.

Old wounds and past sins came back for another go-round.

Chapter Seven

Backsliding

I was feeling desperate, you know what I mean? I'm desperate now and hungry, but it's an immediate thing—right here, right now. Back then it was a steady, gnawing feeling, sometimes imperceptible but always growing.

The next morning, Carole went to work. Mike went off to school and I had the chance to sit around the apartment and let my wounds heal. It was two weeks before the Key West trip and already the coke was gone. Fortunately, I still had the hash.

I needed to stir up some business right away. Ted or maybe Dracula were my only options, besides setting up a little stand by the pool.

What I needed was a local boy with a lot of friends. That's where Ted Friday came in. Dude had his hand in all sorts of shit.

He was also a native Tampa Bayan? Tampanian? Tampaxian? Guy new all of the cool little spots and tricky people. Used to be a wrestling promoter before he became a radio jock, had a large collection of bizzarro friends and homeboys. Some of the Bucs were even known to drop by on occasion. I set up a rendezvous with Ted for the following evening.

I always enjoyed going to Ted's house; a small, typical cinderblock home in old Tampa: Foliage growing around the outside, and a fruit bearing orange tree standing in the back yard.

As I pushed open the chain link gate and stepped onto the circular walking stones, I couldn't shake Lieutenant Douglas from my mind. I'd known a few like him in the past. He reminded me of those pit bulls that you see for sale all over Florida.

There was definitely a fascination with pit bulls in the Sunshine State. I think they were the role models for the cops. Douglas came from that mold, even had a slight overbite. Ever got his teeth into you, he'd be hard to shake.

Despite my fears, I still thought it would be relatively easy to move some quality hash in the land of cheap Colombian. What the hell did Robert Douglas know about me, anyway? Jack shit, it seemed.

I knocked on Ted's door and he came grinning, his wife smiling behind him. She was bigger than he was. Name was Ann.

The house smelled faintly of mildew and air freshener. Fading floral-patterned slipcovers were draped on the furniture to absorb the humidity. Requisite sea blue, shag carpeting in the living and dining rooms and a small Florida room with a few plants and a cracked tile floor.

Ted had this pipe made from a conch shell. Had cold beer in the fridge. This was the kind of thing that I had come to Florida expecting: good friends and high times.

"Let the good times roll," I said

"Certainly, certainly," Ted said, handing me the burning hash.

The conch shell in my hands made me think of Key West—and the future.

The next week flew by in a hurry. Ted moved some of the hash and I was able to get the repairs done on the VW that Bagley had requested. The wounds on my face had turned to fading scabs but I still had a limp. Carole was working longer hours and some nights she rode home with John. Often, they'd sit out in the parking lot, talking. I'd ask her what they had been discussing and she'd come up with these stories about this co-worker or that co-worker, their marital difficulties and personal problems and shit like that. After a while, I started wondering if she and John were having an affair.

Mike was spending a lot of time hanging out with these kids from another complex down the street whose parents made Carole and I look like god's gift to children. The kids were always playing back in the dried-up swamps or going to the movies with somebody's sister or swimming in somebody's pool—anything to be out of the house.

A week prior to our scheduled departure for Key West, WPLF was throwing a big party on a large tour boat. Being scabby of face, I had a built-in excuse for not going. That and I wanted to play some ball with Mike.

When I informed Carole of my desire to stay home, she smiled agreeably, said it was fine; she could ride with John. I was surprised and suspicious. One of the big causes of disharmony in our past had always been her wanting me to go places that I didn't want to. Her acquiescence threw me for a loop.

The ironic thing about that night was that Mike didn't want to stay home with me, either. My desire for old fashioned, familial togetherness was dashed.

He had plans to go to the waterslide park with Jimmy Lund and his older brother. And did I have ten bucks for snacks? Well of course I had. I gave it to him and cautioned against eating too much junk food, as befits a good parent—what I so wanted to be.

After the both of them had gone, I stoked up a big bowl of hash and turned on the tube. At some point I dozed off, eventually waking to a knock on the door. Jerked me right out of a Key West-inspired dream of topless twenty-year-old girls frolicking in the surf.

I opened the door and my stomach clanged like I'd swallowed the sinker from a deep-sea rig. There in front of me, in garish living color, was Lieutenant Douglas; toothpick sticking out of his mouth and bright red Hawaiian shirt hanging over his snakeskin belt.

"Evening Keith, how y'all doin'?"

"Ah, I'm doing fine. What brings you here tonight, Lieutenant Douglas?"

"That pretty missy of yours home this evening, Keith?"

Jesus, now she was "Missy".

"Carole? No she's not. She's at a company party. Out in a boat on the Gulf. Won't be back till late."

"That's a shame, son, a real shame."

"Anything I can do for you?"

"Well, Keith, you could start by telling me where it is I know you from, I swear we've met someplace before."

"I doubt that Lieutenant, I haven't been down here that long."

"Right, right. Minnesota, isn't that right?"

"That's right. Land of ten thousand lakes and ten billion mosquitoes."

He chuckled dryly. "Looks like your face is healing up pretty good, son. Must be a fast healer."

"Maybe, I don't know. I'm feeling better, I guess."

"You worried that the guy is going to come back on you?"

"No. It was just some drunk in a bar. He won't remember me."

"It wasn't at a bar up on Clearwater Beach, was it? Kid got stabbed up there the other night. Witnesses said it was a guy name

Tex: about five-feet-nine or ten, hundred and sixty pounds, black hair and a mustache. How tall are you, Keith. About five-ten?"

"Six-foot-one. And I don't have a mustache."

"Bet you got a razor... you must go about one-sixty...."

"One ninety. Do I look—or sound—like a Tex, Lieutenant? Come on, that's not me. My deal happened down in St. Pete somewhere—I don't even think I could find the place again."

"What were you doing there—in a strange bar, then?"

"I was just driving around, wandering, seeing the sights. I saw this bar and decided to stop in for a beer. I'm new around here. I didn't know that people in Florida liked to pick fights with strangers for no reason."

"They don't do that up in Minnesota?"

"No." I lied.

"Let me get this straight, son: You were driving around sightseeing—at night—and you walk into a bar in a strange neighborhood. Some guy picks a fight and you kick the shit out of him and leave."

"I didn't say I kicked the shit out of anybody. The guy got wore out from hitting me, was what happened. Somebody pulled him off me and I ran out of there. Didn't stop until I got home."

"Mm, huh. And you couldn't find your way back to that place if you tried, Keith?"

I nodded.

"I don't want you to try, Keith. Let's leave this situation lie, okay?"

"I was planning to."

"Now, the other reason I dropped by was to see how you and the missus was gettin' along after that little incident the other night. You folks seem to be consuming a lot of alcohol and I was worried about you two. I'm sorry that I missed Carole, because that means I'll have to come back again to make sure she's not drinking and driving anymore. She's kind of my responsibility now, after I let her slide and all, you understand…. I'm concerned about the public safety."

"I understand Lieutenant, and you're doing a fine job of it. Is there, anything else?"

"I'd swear we'd met before, Keith. But I can't recall—you sure we haven't met?"

I shook my head.

He turned to leave and then did the Columbo bit again: "I s'pose Paul's going to be out on that boat tonight, huh. Boss of a big radio station would have to be there showing off all his money to the staff, huh, Keith?"

"I guess so."

"I'd be nervous about guys like that, if my wife was as cute as yours…. This town is filling up with sharks like him. They all got them pearly white teeth, if ya know what I mean."

He nodded his head like he was telling me a great truth. Little ticks of electricity shot through my gut and up under my arms and the bottom of my stomach shrunk up tight.

The voice started in: *Run, Keith, run. And don't look back. You've got to run and not look back.*

"Evenin', then, Keith," Douglas said, a puzzled look now sitting on his sweaty ham face. "Be seein' ya. Drive safely now, you hear."

"Good night, Lieutenant."

I watched him strut away, locked the door and put up the chain. Closed the sliding doors, pulled the curtain and turned on the air conditioning. Drank a couple beers and smoked some more hash.

I couldn't believe the way my head was swirling. I wanted to hightail it but I couldn't.

Determined not to quit on the family, I swallowed hard and resolved to wait it out.

Then the phone rang and my heart jumped into my throat.

I turned on the kitchen light and watched those greasy little bastards scurry for the cracks. "Hello," I said, my voice scratchy.

"Keith, Keith... is this Keith?"

"Yes."

"This is Steve, Steve Schmidt. I'm down on the Keys with the sailboat."

"Oh hey, Steve, of course I remember...."

"You guys still planning on coming down?"

"Yep, we're planning on it, trying to get it together...."

"Well, listen, Keith, sorry to spring this on you at the last minute, but you need to bring the van down. Bagley's plans have changed. Now he wants you to drive the van down here. I hope that doesn't present a problem."

"Ah, no... but... I mean—how are we going to get back?"

"You'll have to bring another vehicle down, I suppose. I'll pay you for the added expense, don't worry about that."

"My car won't make it. We're hoping to ride down with someone else, if there's room for one more on the boat... if that's alright."

"No problem at all. That'll work for you then?"

"Maybe, if the guy decides to go. He might have to work on Sunday or something...."

"Hell, if worse come to worse I'll rent you a car to drive home in. But try and work something out and I'll see you when you get here.... One more thing... think you could bring down some vitamin C?"

"I can try."

"Great, great. So long, then."

"Yeah, goodbye, Steve. See ya down there."

Seemed like everyone wanted the powder. From the megabucks banking scammers to the lowly working guy and the partying college student, Vitamin C was in high demand; everywhere you looked.

Key West and cocaine together was too much like the songs and the stories to pass up. The more I thought about it however; I just couldn't bring myself to call Dracula.

Carole arrived home from the party about midnight, earlier than expected, but just as drunk as expected. John neglected to come in, once again. I was looking forward to telling her about Steve's call but as soon as I saw her, I turned sour.

"You're looking loose," I said.

"Thank you," she said, sneering.

"Have a good time?"

"No. Bastards were laughing at me for singing along with the music."

"No shit, too bad."

"Thanks for the sympathy."

"You forgot the taste."

"Cute," Carole said. The scorn of a thousand angry shrews dripped from her tongue. Her eyes turned to marbles. "John said he could drive to the Keys with us, by the way," she continued. "If that makes you happy.... I knew we couldn't take the Volvo that far, so I thought I'd ask him."

"Better, anyway. But I already asked him, before... you and John will be happy now that he's going...."

"What's that supposed to mean?"

"Nothing. Forget it."

She stormed into Mike's room and came back out with his record player under her arm: a little suitcase thing with stereo speakers attached to the sides. She set the thing up on the dining table.

She kneeled down to the cardboard box full of records on the floor in front of the TV, began flipping through them at high speed.

"Your new friend the cop came by tonight looking for you. You know, I really don't need that kind of shit around here."

"What did he want?"

"Just to check on you and accuse me of murder."

"Murder? What the fuck are you talking about?"

"Nothing. Just some deal in Clearwater that had nothing to do with me. Let's just fucking forget about it. I'm sure it's nothing. The guy has got a thing for you, I think."

"That's weird," she snickered and pulled an album out of the box.

Knowing it was going to be a night of off-key Linda Ronstadt songs until the wee hours, I went out to the 7-11 for a twelve-pack of Busch. I could escape to the mountains. I had to get to the store before one a.m. because the pricks wouldn't sell after that. You'd think somebody with a shit job like that would cut you some goddamn slack once in a while, but no—they always had to lay the power trip on your ass. Just like everyone else, I guess.

Seemed like I was only gone for twenty minutes but when I walked in Carole was splayed out on the living room carpet, unconscious, "Heart Like a Wheel" moaning in the background.

In a state of bemused concern, I checked her for wounds and vital functions. I tried to shake her awake but gave up after about ten seconds.

I concluded that she had passed out.

I stood up and watched her for a while, wondering if it was real. Started thinking about guys I knew who had naked pictures of their girlfriends in their wallets or stuck on their bedroom mirrors.

I was thinking maybe I should strip her down and take a few snaps, just for the fun of it. For a joke, you understand. Show them to her later and see what she thought. We could both get a kick out of it.

Instead, I just left her there where she was quiet and popped myself a can of beer. Watched a little tube and then went to bed. She was still lying on the floor when I hit the rack. Never heard her come to bed. She made plenty of noise the next morning, though. I enjoyed her pained movements.

The next week we leveled out a little bit, trying to get our act together for the trip. We both wanted to put our best faces on parade in Key West.

Staying clean would be good for us, I thought. Maybe we could find that old magic again. Maybe she would finally see my true value and worth and finally realize how indispensable I was to her life. She will worship me, then, I told myself. Hadn't I seen it in her eyes at the airport that first day? Or was that because she was thinking I had money?

I'd been worrying about John but now it seemed there was a possibility that my wife was having an affair with the boss. Hell's bells, maybe she was banging the whole goddamn station....

The image of that fat-ass cop was still itching at me. What the hell was he trying to pull anyway? What was this—I know you from somewhere—bullshit? Why was he trying to get in my head?

I couldn't stop my head.

Morning of our scheduled departure for the Keys, I was in the shower and I heard pounding at the front door.

I knew it was Douglas—I could feel it. The guy was trouble with a capitol goddamn T.

My heart skipped a beat as the pounding moved around to the poolside doors. I ignored it and stayed in the shower.

Finally it stopped.

Five minutes went by. Fear's frozen talons gripped my balls as I toweled off.

Three loud thuds hit the front door. Bastard was back.

Had he pulled the old summons server's trick, pretending he'd left, only to come back when you think he's gone?

I sat down on the stool and waited.

Time went by real slowly and my legs were numb before I mustered the courage to get up and leave the bathroom. I tiptoed into the bedroom, lay down and tried to slow my raging heart. The apartment was quiet.

I was drifting off when the phone rang. My body jerked like a snake on a hot wire: Should I answer it? Could the cop be calling me? What if it's Carole? Or something happened to Mike and the school is calling?

There was so much shit to worry about all of a sudden.

I ran into the kitchen, took a deep breath and picked up the receiver: "Hello..."

"Keith... you're there...I was just there pounding on your door...."

"Who is this?"

"John. Who'd you think it was? Weren't we supposed to head to Key West today?"

"Oh yeah, right... I must have been in the shower when you were knocking. But ah... there's been a change of plans. I have to take the VW bus down now."

"But I still want to go," John said, "I got Steve O'Neill to work for me on Sunday, so now I can stay the whole weekend. Don't have to be back until Tuesday. I don't want to miss the opportunity, after all this trouble."

"That'd be fucking great, John, whatever you say, buddy. Just come over after work and we'll go. I'll follow you."

"What?"

"You have to take your car."

"What about the van? There's room for everybody...."

"I have to leave it in the Keys. The boys need it down there...."

"I guess I'll follow you, then. No problem."

I got dressed and made a cheese sandwich on white bread. I made two more for Mike and put them in a paper bag. I packed my suitcase and went back to bed.

Carole came home with John around four-thirty. Paul let her leave early, she said. I had everything packed, including a sleeping bag for Mike.

Chapter Eight

Key West is the Best

Cocaine is bad. Why couldn't I have seen that? It's like borrowing energy from the future that you have to pay back with interest.

I read that somewhere. But it's true. And let me tell you, the APR is steep. Someday everybody has to pay.

The only reason I agreed to go along with Bagley and Schmidt's little enterprise—besides the fee—was that they were running ganja, not coke. Goddamn cocaine was driving me crazy.

Of course those assholes had needed my help. Who the hell else but me would be a big enough sucker to wait for them on a lonely hunk of beach in the middle of Florida's western coastline? A beach—I'm now thinking—that more than likely has video cameras hidden in the eucalyptus with a direct link to the local sheriff's office.

The Man is probably sitting back in his chair and taking it all in, waiting until we have the shit unloaded. Then he'll come, ripping down through the vines in force, machine guns blasting,

*vicious dogs barking and enough TV cameras to make even
Geraldo proud.*

*I try to fight back the feelings of foolishness as I face the real-
ity that my future depends on Dan Bagley's ability to work a half-
million dollar deal. A deal, that, unfortunately, I'm on the hot end
of. If I didn't know that Schmidt was along to do the thinking, I
believe I'd step into the ocean and keep on walking.*

I start to shiver, even though the temperature is in the eighties.

*I decide to walk the mile-and-a-half back to the van and get
more food. Just in case the boat comes in when I'm gone, I tie my
yellow T-shirt to a stick in the sand. The way things are going; the
boys will come into view as soon as I step off the beach.*

*As I trudge along the shimmering sand, I start thinking about
Key West. It seemed like the doorway to the big time was opening
up just wide enough for me to slide in sideways.*

The two Volkswagens turned out of Twin Lakes and headed
down Fourth Street, rolling along on their way to the fabulous
Florida Keys. I assumed that everyone else but me was too pre-
occupied to notice the big green Ford with the whip antenna that
rolled by in the opposite direction and turned into Twin Lakes.

As I looked back in the mirror and felt my stomach tighten, a
strange picture began to form in the back of my mind: a picture
of my mother.

My mother in her chair in the living room, sitting there, drinking Rob Roys and smoking menthol cigarettes like they were
candy. She was always worried about something and scared
about most everything else. Later, at night, she'd get into the
Valium and the codeine.

And all the old man would ever do when she got going on one
of her fear jags was wave the back of his hand at her and growl:
"J-e-e-s-u-u-s Priest, I tell you."

Then I'd be laughing and he'd threaten to kick my ass.

I was feeling like the both of them at the same time. It was scary. I started to worry about the gasoline shortage.

It was 1979 and the first great oil crisis was in full swing. We had heard stories of long waiting lines, skyrocketing prices and closed down stations. President Carter was taking it up the ass, all the way from the Persian Gulf. Dudes with the turbans were flexing their muscles and making the American motorist do the suffering. The moral equivalency of war, some people said.

Across the bridge in Sarasota, at the first Chevron station we came to, prices had jumped way up. John asked the attendant if he knew how it was, further south, and the slow-talking kid answered that he thought we might have some trouble on Sunday.

Outside of Sarasota was farm country, gentle countryside with cows and horses. We rolled on bucolic blacktop until sundown. Then it was freeways and tollbooths and smooth sailing all the way to Miami.

South of Miami, around Key Biscayne or maybe Key Largo, I was sipping a beer, thinking that the trip was almost over. In the next several hours, I discovered slowly and painfully, that it had just begun.

We continued to roll along, over bridges and dark, empty land, for what seemed like forever. Lights on the bridges glowed. Signs whizzed by. I bounced and drifted, soothed by the hum of the tires. Chewed gum and smoked cigarettes to stay awake.

It must have been well after midnight when we finally arrived. Carole and I were excited. Mike was tired and bored, also irritable.

I sniffed the air and stared, wide-eyed, at the lushness and the gay crowds. The fern bars glittered as I searched for the parking lot of the Harbor House Hotel. I was excited for our high-rent rendezvous with Steve Schmidt.

"Let's go in the bar and have a drink," Carole said as she stretched her arms to the stars and soaked in the shimmering night
.

"They won't let Mike in the bar this late," I said.

"He's sleeping in the back," she said. "Just stretch him out in the sleeping bag and we can lock him in. We won't be gone long, he'll be okay."

She lit a cigarette and yawned. John, waiting patiently, didn't say anything, just looked around.

"Well, okay," I said. "But just one drink. If Schmidt hasn't shown up by then, I'll come back here and wait."

I fixed Mike up and told him we were going out for a few minutes. He mumbled something. Sounded like *all right*. I kissed him on the forehead.

Carole smoothed out the sleeping bag. It was a brown bag with little rocking horses on the red flannel lining.

We locked the doors, sauntered off in the direction of a neon mollusk shell at the far end of the walk. It was shining above a red, wooden door with a porthole.

Palm fronds swayed and whispered in the devilishly warm breeze. Boat horns tooted. Bugs buzzed and dive-bombed. Aqua blue was the color of my vision.

Money was how they made it shine.

We sat down on wood and leather barstools inside the Hemingway-styled lounge. Saw the harbor lights and the gently bobbing sailboats tethered offshore.

Schmidt showed up fifteen minutes later.

"Glad you people made it," he said, rubbing the palms of his hands on his marlin blue polo shirt. He looked fit and relaxed; his freckled, sun reddened skin glowing like an orange.

"It was a long haul," I said.

"No doubt," Schmidt said.

"Oh—it wasn't that bad, Keith," Carole said, suddenly miss cross-country traveler.

"The van perform okay?" Schmidt asked, smiling.

"It ran fine. We didn't have any problems," I said. "Oh, by the way, let me introduce you to John Carino."

We got the introductions out of the way and sipped our ten-dollar drinks. John bought Steve a margarita that cost $7.50. Steve asked about the vitamin C. I put on a blank look and mumbled something about how I couldn't find any. Steve squinted for a second and then shrugged. Carole shot me a sidelong glance.

After one drink we said goodbye to the hotel and made our way back along the sea rope-and-driftwood walkway to the van.

Approaching quietly, I sneaked a peak inside through a crack in the yellow curtains. Mike's eyes were open. He got scared at first; then he recognized me.

We grabbed our luggage and made a dark pilgrimage to where the dinghy was pulled up on the pale, heavily traveled beach. The water was black; colored lights reflecting made the surface a jellified Christmas tree.

"I'll take the Waverly's out first and then come back for John," Steve said. "Wouldn't want to sink this thing on your first night here."

"I hope not," Mike said.

"It's not going to sink, Mike," I said. "I bet it's Coast Guard approved—eh, Steve."

"Your Dad's right, Mike—Mexican Coast Guard." Steve looked at Mike and grinned sheepishly.

"How about if I row, Steve?" I said. "I could use the exercise, after that car ride. I used to row a lot when I was a kid, at my uncle's cabin…."

It was about forty yards to the sailboat. Steve sat in the bow and pointed the way. Long deep waves made the going tough. I was surprised the waves were that high at that time of night.

The rowing felt good; got my blood moving. Schmidt was glad to have me do it and found humor in my struggle.

I was sweating when we finally pulled alongside the *Larson E,* a name I found hard to fathom.

Steve grabbed a hold of the keel to steady us. Carole stood up and the rubber raft tipped a little. She yelped like a stepped-on cat.

With some effort, we all got on board and went quickly below to survey our surroundings. Steve showed us around then hopped back up top for the return trip to shore.

Carole and I got the captain's quarters: a wood-hued room with a king-sized waterbed and a narrow, curtained window running above the curve of the hull, at eye level.

We moved a thick rug to the side of the bed for Mike and dove into the waterbed.

I remember thinking that a waterbed on a sailboat was overkill but as soon as I got flat, I was gone.

Woke up the next morning feeling not too bad—for about five minutes. It took me that long to realize how hot it was in the cabin. And we were rocking like a bad ride at the fair. Last night's alcohol was not sitting well.

I pulled on my shorts and went up top, squinted out at the piercing blue sky. The wind was up hard from the Northwest. Whitecaps broke endlessly on the green, rolling sea.

"Waves on the ocean are a lot different than the ones on freshwater lakes." Steve said. "You don't get this rolling effect on Lake Superior, do you Keith?"

"Don't say rolling," I said, as a wave of nausea wracked through me. I stuck my head overboard just as Carole came on deck.

"What's the matter?" she said, giving me an icy stare.

"I'm not feeling too good. This wave action is a little rough on me. I slept good—but now—Jesus.... I've always had a weak stomach. Ever since I was a kid. I could never keep medicine down or anything."

"We can go in and get some breakfast and some coffee in town," Steve said. "That will get you right. You just need some grease in your stomach."

John came up, rubbing his head and looking pretty green. Seeing the pain in his face made me feel a little better.

"Morning," he said, staring mournfully out at the infinite sea. Looking to Steve: "Is this considered rough weather by the sailors down here?"

"Yeah, I guess," Steve said. "I doubt if many boats will be going out today. Maybe we'll try it later this afternoon. Maybe we can have a few beers, maybe get some nice cheese—and do a little trolling. You'd be surprised at the fish you can catch just dragging a Rapala behind the boat."

"How big is this boat?" John said.

"Thirty-seven feet," Steve said.

"Is that a big enough boat for waves like this? Back in San Francisco, where I'm from, I don't know if they'd be going out in this kind of weather."

"This boat will make it," Steve said. "I sailed her across the ocean from Spain, last fall."

"Alone?" I asked.

"There was two of us. I had a Frenchman for a mate. We got caught in a storm so bad the second night out, that the only thing we could do was throw out the anchor and hope. Hope you don't hit anything until it blows over. All we could do was lie down and wait for it to blow on by. As you can see, she held up pretty well."

"No shit," I said.

"That's so cool," Carole said.

"I guess I'm a landlubber," John said.

"I can relate to that," I said.

"I love sailing," Carole said. "The wind, the water, the sky… I think it's so beautiful."

"Where's Bagley?" I said. "I thought he was going to be here. Isn't that why you wanted the van?"

"Oh Christ, don't get me started about Bagley," Steve said, grimacing. "Let's just say he's up to his usual tricks. Which means it usually turns out lousy for me. He was supposed to be here two days ago, but he ran into a little trouble in Denver, the fucking idiot. Now I think he's due in on Sunday night. He'll expect me to pick him up at the airport, but I'm going to be unavailable."

John smiled weakly, continued to look somewhat green around the gills.

"Why the delay?" I asked.

"I can't even talk about it I'm so pissed off." Steve said. "I'll tell you later, after I've had a few drinks to deaden the pain."

"Poor Dan," Carole said. "He must be uncomfortable in his own skin."

"Since when are you defending Dan Bagley?" I said. "I thought you were always down on his case."

"He's harmless," she said.

"I'm not so sure," Steve said.

We all grew silent and stared at the distance.

We floated in on the raft for breakfast. Steve rowed. It was crowded with all of us in there, our knees up around our ears. The sound of the raft hitting the beach was reassuring. Sand felt good beneath my bare feet.

Key West was everything that I had dreamed about and more. Even the sun shone brighter. Bohemian, colorful, seemingly filled with dope and money, it was the stuff of my American Dream.

I saw an avenue to the stars, an entryway to the gold paved streets of heaven-on-earth. Every little piece of the dream was here. You could see it in the shining sailboats, the glistening Mercedes and the sexy women in tiny bikinis on the decks of million dollar yachts.

I could feel myself getting closer to a window of opportunity. It felt as if my destiny was finally coming to fruition. I could smell the money.

Bagley and Schmidt were tapping into it somehow. Somewhere

here was some carrion and I was duty bound to find it. If I played my cards right I, too, could be riding the *dinero* breezes: hundred-dollar sunglasses and ten-dollar cigars, all the right places and all the right faces.

The boys could do a lot worse than bringing me into their game. And they could fall, a long way down, by underestimating me.

A short drive in the van, Steve behind the wheel, got us to a worn, white, beachfront building that looked like it was made out of pressed sand. Faded wood boardwalk in front of a u-shaped, open-air entranceway, with an artistic *CAFÉ* sign stuck on the wall above it.

After a large breakfast, we drove back to the hotel lot. I got out and went on ahead, walking out on one of the large docks. Numerous boats bounced heavily on the green water. Nobody was going out today, it seemed.

I leaned on the railing and let my gaze fall down to the water. Bits of rope, cigarette filters and a crushed plastic cup floated, stuck inside a dark scum.

Carole caught up to me: Steve, John and Mike at her side. She was breathless and excited to go sailing.

Mike had already informed us of his desire to stay on shore, in no uncertain terms. Steve said that he had some women friends on the island that he thought would baby-sit.

I wasn't too enthusiastic about the sailing thing, either.

"You look like you could use a drink," Carole said to me.

"Maybe two, " Steve said.

"Maybe I could," I said.

Mike picked up a shell from the dock and flung it out at nothing. It blipped the water and we headed for the bar.

After a couple of drinks and an hour or so of shelling and sightseeing, Steve and Carole took Mike to the babysitters for the afternoon. When they returned, we rowed out to the boat.

The swells showed no sign of lessening. It was warm, about eighty-five degrees, and humid. There was no escape from the heat, even in the infernal wind.

I hoped Mike was doing okay. I swore I'd make it up to him, somehow.

We got out to the boat and Schmidt put on his swim gear and hit the water; he had to do a little repair job before we sailed. John took his shirt off, popped a beer and pulled a lawn chair up next to the cabin. Carole fixed a gin and tonic.

It seemed to me like she was flirting with both of them.

After the repairs were completed, we were ready for sailing. *Chip chip* and *hey hey* and all that.

Carole was enthusiastic. John had second thoughts and begged off, saying he would take the dinghy to shore and look for us around sunset. I was determined to make the sail, even though I would have preferred a powerboat to the *Larson E.*

Carole's enthusiasm was indeed admirable but what you must understand is that it would have been possible for her to be enthusiastic about her own drowning, given enough liquor and the proper audience.

I sat and watched, fascinated, as she badgered John, trying to make him change his mind. She didn't let up. Eventually he stormed off when she called him "chicken". His face was red as he climbed down the ladder.

"We need another round," Carole said. "To wash the poop stain away," she giggled.

"One more, and then we hit it," Steve said.

"Aye aye, Captain," she said.

I tried a rum and coke and started feeling better. All the pastoral beauty was nice. What I really wanted was to know where the money was.

I drained my glass, stared out at the rolling surf, took a deep breath and leaned back in my deck chair.

"Come on, Steve, tell me that story about Bagley that you promised," I said.

"All right, I'm numb enough now... but it's a painful story... fuck." He paused and bent over, lowering his head between his knees and sighing with fatigue worthy of a much put upon soul.

"Bagley was supposed to be bringing a load of coke down to some people he knows in Minneapolis. Going to make a quick sale to raise funds for a bigger situation that he and I are trying to get together. I mean... we don't even need the extra cash—I told him that. But he insisted that he had to do it anyway. 'It'll be easy, don't worry' he tells me. And really it should've been. Unless you're a fucking idiot."

"What the hell did he do, man? The suspense is killing me."

"The dumb shit stops in Denver for the overnight—before his plane to Minneapolis—and rents a top-shelf hotel room. He goes down to the bar after dinner, and as fate would have it, runs into a high-class hooker. Can you see where this is heading?"

He chuckled, ruefully.

"Turns out she's a real professional gal, who gets him up to his room and manages to slip him a Mickey. When he wakes up, the whore, the dope and all the money are gone."

Schmidt took a chest-heaving breath and stared out at the water, pain creasing his red, bushy eyebrows. Then he turned his head slowly, caught my eyes and we both burst out laughing.

"So that's what our buddy Dan has been up to," Schmidt said, coughing. "I'm so glad that I kept most of my money out of the deal, I can't fucking express it. At least, if everything else falls through, I still have that. Otherwise, I might have had to murder Daniel. Which wouldn't necessarily be so bad, except that I might get caught."

"No lie," I said.

"You are effected by this, too," Steve said, "because there's going to be a change in plans. I'm not quite sure yet, but I think we're going to need your help with a few things, Keith. That is, if you want to be a part of this ragtag deal. You'll certainly be amply compensated. I'll have to fill you in on more, later, after Dan boy comes rolling in. I'll need to assess the situation better at that time."

He swallowed the last of his Mount Gay rum. "What do you say we give fishing a try."

"It's about time," Carole said.

"Do you guys like Brie?" Steve inquired, smiling.

"I love it," Carole said.

I groaned.

We weren't out for even thirty minutes before Carole was prancing around on the edges of the deck with no safety rope, a bottle of Becks in one hand and a cigarette in the other. And she never liked beer.

I was thinking it would be okay if she fell off, if she had a rope. She'd only be dragged for a while, not killed. Being dragged alongside a thirty-seven-footer for a few moments might wash some sense into her.

I pointed out the lack of a rope to Steve, after which he fixed one up.

I learned a lot about sailing that afternoon.

Learned that you shouldn't try it when it's really rough and someone opens up a package of cheese that triggers your gag reflex like a punch to the solar plexus. If that happens, you should go inside the cabin and lay face down on a bunk for the whole goddamn trip.

Then you get up just before your back into port and stand on deck like you're a real pro sailor and wave to all the people on shore, celebrating the sunset.

After dinner, we walked around the town. We were broke.

I made the decision to sleep in the van; I couldn't take any more wave action.

It was pretty early when Steve bade us goodnight and returned to the boat.

John found a motel room. Had enough waves, also, I guess.

The Waverly family got settled into the back of the VW at a small parking spot by the beach. We fell asleep quickly.

That was our Saturday night.

Sunday was our last day of vacation and Bagley was due at the airport in the late afternoon.

Schmidt had refused the task of picking him up, saying, "Let the asshole take a cab."

Carole couldn't drive a stick shift so that left me as the likely candidate for chauffeur.

Yep, I was the only one left. I saw it as my chance to get close to the deal.   Bagley would never know that my friendly act wasn't for real. Sure, I'd play like his buddy... but this time, the compensation was going to be up to my standards....

I could tell he was drunk when he got off the plane. He was weaving down the tarmac in khaki L.L Bean hiking shorts, boat shoes with no socks and a light blue polo shirt that matched his eyes.

I watched him wobble—a picture from a twisted catalog. I wondered which one of his two personalities would be on display: the overly polite, schmoozing guy, or the obnoxious, pushy guy.

"Keith," he said, upon seeing me. "What are you—how did... where's Schmidt?"

"He was busy."

"Oh, I see...." He shrugged his shoulders and blinked rapidly, staying surprisingly amicable. Having me there was obviously better than dealing with Schmidt.

I had a feeling that it was going to be a long and eventful night, a night that I would benefit from, because I would be sober. I would no longer pollute my body like the others. They would soon find out about the new me....

We waited for the baggage to come off. Dan was muttering something about Schmidt that I couldn't quite make out because of the sound of a taxiing airplane. I didn't want to get into it with him, the discussion, I mean, so I just nodded my head and stared vacantly.

The cart pulled up and I slung one, of Dan's two canvas military duffels, on my shoulder and we walked to the van. It was another beautiful evening. My ankle throbbed slightly.

I asked Dan if he wanted to drive, it being his vehicle and all.

"Nah," he said, his lower lip going a little loose. "I'm too gassed. I like the idea of a driver. But I gotta tell you, old buddy, I'm getting burned out, Keitho—burned out." His head swayed from side to side. "You drive, that'll be fine. You drive. You're a good driver. You always used to end up driving home from those keggers back in high school, too—remember? You're good at driving."

"I s'pose. Are you staying out on the boat tonight?"

"Don't know. Arrogant Schmidt thinks he knows everything. I'm not sure if I can tolerate being out there with him. Maybe I'll sleep in the van…. That's the way they are when they come from the East, Keith—know-it-alls. I've met a lot of those guys… Schmidt thinks he knows it all…."

"Yeah, no shit. You know, ah, Dan… Carole and Mike and I slept in the van last night. It works for the three of us."

"You did, huh. What's the matter, Schmidt wouldn't give you the big bed?"

"No, he did, the first night. But I got kind of seasick. Too much rocking in that bed."

Really? Huh…you can't take it? Well—maybe I'll get a hotel room and you guys can have the bus. If there are any rooms in town… but let's get a drink. We need to stop at a bar. I'm buying."

"I'm laying off the sauce."

"Uh, huh, I knew it. I knew your wife would get to you, even-tally. Carole has got you turning religious, hasn't she? Don't let your woman push you around, Keith. They'll try to dominate you."

"She doesn't, man."

"It's a pity, you turning straight, like that. I've got some toot that's pretty fine, pretty fine."

"I thought you lost all of that. Ah, uhm—I mean ah... Steve told us about your bad luck out in Colorado. An unfortunate incident, for sure. What a drag."

"Huh, he told you about that? Hmmfh, huh... bad luck, that's all... just this goddamn cunt. God, she looked so nice...." Then all of a sudden he started banging the tip of his finger on the window and shouting with an aged, metallic voice: "Right there, right there. Pull over, pull over—you'll love this place."

Suddenly his hand shot over and grabbed the wheel, giving it a jerk toward the sparkling Sloppy Joe's sign.

I chopped down at his arm and hit the brakes.

"Don't ever grab the goddamn wheel again when I'm driving, Dan. Never do that shit to me, you understand?"

He kind of cringed and his Adam's apple did a double dip. I wanted to bloody his lips like Marty Clark had done, back in high school, but I knew that the best path was the sugarcoated one.

I took a deep breath, turned the corner and parked. We got out of the van and went into the tavern, Bagley muttering that I should lighten up.

I followed him through the open door. He sauntered up to the bar and ordered a Papa Hemingway Jumbo Margarita from a tanned, young bartender wearing shorts and a green Sloppy Joe's T-shirt.

I ordered a draught beer.

My mind had quickly done an about face. After fifteen minutes with Bagley, drinking was the only way to get through. I could start sobriety *manana*.

"Changed your tune, I see," Bagley said, know-it-all.

"Yeah, but I can't stay too long, Dan. I have to get back to Carole and Mike before too long."

"Yeah, I suppose. Otherwise your old lady will get in a snit, I suppose. But uh, well ah... anyway... did you take care of that little business deal we had?"

"I got the front-end fixed, if that's what you mean. I still have to finish up the hash."

"But Keith... you knew that I wanted it done by the time you came down here."

"Yeah, well it didn't work out that way."

He frowned and took a blast of his drink. "Oh well, I suppose you can money order it to me when it's taken care of. It wasn't very much, anyway, I guess. Drink up now, and I'll get us another."

"Ah man... okay, one more. Mike wanted to go down to the beach for while and look for some more shells."

"Lousy shelling around here, you have to go out to some of the little islands for the good shells. Too many scab heads around Key West."

"Scab heads?"

"Yeah, you know, bald guys from up North who get the top of their heads sunburned and it scabs up."

"Oh, yeah."

The beer tasted good.

"Looks like you've gotten your thirst back," Bagley said, raising his empty glass toward the bartender.

"I guess so," I said.

"What's the matter, Keith? You're not your usual happy self. Whatever happened to that skinny kid we used to see on the hockey rink, laughing and having fun?"

"I'm not that fat, for Christ sake—whattaya mean? And I still have fun. Life changes, man, things happen. You can't always control what happens to you, you know."

"Maybe you're just not trying hard enough. You can't get very far lying on your back on the couch," he said laughing, turning his eyes downward. "You can't take care of much business if you're asleep or stoned out."

"Fucking Christ, Dan, ease off... Schmidt was right about you, I guess."

"Huh? What did he say? C'mon—you know I was just kidding. C'mon... we're old buddies.... Schmidt turning you against me now because he didn't get his way?"

"Never mind. Forget it," I said. "I have to get going."

"You have to finish your beer first. And I'm going to have one more. You need another one, too, my good man."

"All right, just one," I said, and got up and walked to the men's room.

My crankcase wasn't even half way drained when Bagley sidled up to the urinal next to me and stuck his fist under my nose, a small pile of white powder sparkling in the hollow between his thumb and forefinger.

I stopped reading the graffiti on the wall and looked around the room nervously, then hurriedly sniffed up the cocaine, more out of fear of being seen, than anything else.

While zipping up my fly, I had an epiphany. Suddenly I realized how mistaken I had been about the drug. Coke wasn't really the tool of the devil as I had previously suspected. No, much more than that, it was both a tool and a reward, for the rich.

You do the coke and do the deals, play the right games and tell the right fibs and pretty soon you're parking a cigarette boat next to your canal-side mansion and pissing Dom Perignon into the channel. Toot, blow, snow, girl, snort: It goes real well with the thousand dollar watches and the three-hundred-dollar shirts. Just like sugar in your Cuban coffee and lemon in your Lipton's.

I felt truly beatific. How I had misjudged the drug. And, the more I thought about it, Bagley.

Now I could see that he was, indeed, a rare old boy—and, as totally unaware of himself as he was, he was still pretty darn fun. You had to give him credit for balls and good dope, if nothing else. Maybe I said that before.

I started thinking that I might join him in a jumbo, Hemingway

margarita. Fucking Hemingway, man... fucking Papa....
Catching big fish and drinking margaritas until he went insane. In
this day and age, they'd have him on anti-depressants and his
dick would still go limp.

If only he'd had cocaine, he might have been around long
enough to write *The Sun Also Sets* and *A Farewell to Heads*.
They might not have been great books but they would have
played well on the tube. Or maybe he would have died of a heart
attack and avoided all those messy suicide attempts. The nervous
system shutting down, had to be better than walking into airplane
propellers or eating shotguns, don't you think? Anyways, a
coked-up Ernie would have been one nasty son of a bitch.

Dan and I walked out of the men's room with a new spring in
our step. We returned to the bar and a pitcher of Papa-ritas came
sliding up, as if on cue. We took to the translucent liquid like trout
rising to mayflies on a dark, gently flowing stream.

We drank up and surveyed our good fortune. All I needed in
life, it seemed, was right in front of me—right here in this fine
room, ready for the taking.

"Y'know, Keith," Bagley said. "I think we ought to tie one on
like we used to back in high school. I'm going on a little trip
pretty soon and I might not come back. This could be my last
opportunity to party for a while."

"I think we're doing a pretty good job, already." I fought back
a smirk. "Come on, man, what's this about not coming back?
What's that all about?"

"It'll probably be okay... but you never know on these kinds of
deals. High-risk stuff. International intrigue. That's the way it is
in this game. I don't even like to talk about it." He shook his head
slowly from side to side, looking solemn. "Let's have another
toot," he said.

For a moment, my mind turned dark. The lights seemed to
dim. I was wishing that I were somewhere else, sober. Then it
passed.

"I have got to go—this time for fucking sure," I said, tearing the wrapper off a fresh pack of Kools.

"Awwright. Awwright, then. You go on and I'll stay here. You can come back and get me. I don't feel up to dealing with Schmidt tonight. I'll be seeing enough of him, only too soon. Right now I'm going to stay here and work on those honeys over there." He waved his fingers in the general direction of the far wall.

I looked over there and it seemed like all the women were old and worn out.

"I'll be back in an hour at the most," I said. "Then you're gonna have to leave with me or take a cab."

He looked at me like he was going to say something but stopped himself. He took a long gulp of margarita, put the glass down, wiped the back of his hand across his mouth and sighed.

"It must be time to toot," he said, grinning crookedly and spinning off his barstool.

The clock on the wall read quarter to eleven. I had been there for three goddamn hours and the sun had long since set. I felt sure that Carole was furious. Schmidt was probably a little miffed, also. I didn't know how Mike might react. And John would probably just cringe a little on the inside and become even more distant than he already was.

I drove four blocks before I said *fuck it*, turned around and headed back towards my friend Dan and his magic powder. I wasn't going to let this opportunity slide through my fingers like so much sand.

I walked through the bar with renewed confidence and resolve only to discover that Bagley had wormed his way into the company of two women. What I saw at first was mostly hair. Blonde one was thin, with angular shoulders. The brunette was on the heavy side.

I heard the brunette laughing from all the way across the room:

a nightmarish sound that sent stinging memories of too many feverish nights in lowdown saloons ringing through my head.

Bagley was sitting between the two of them in a scarred wooden booth: an almost empty pitcher on the black table, as well as three different packs of smokes, two ashtrays, one purse and four long-stemmed margarita glasses.

Bagley had the heavy girl in a headlock as I approached. He was using the old charm. The girl's thickly painted eyes caught sight of me as I came alongside. She pulled out of Bagley's clutches and smiled up at me. Her large, red lips and long, wide teeth were glowing like a ghoul.

I sat down across from them, not wanting to smile but doing so anyway. The other girl was a cute little blonde thing. What a shock to my system, that was.

"Wavers... Wavers... you're back," Bagley said, his head bobbing. "Jesus, doesn't seem like long since you left... I knew we were having fun, but not that much fun—eh, girls."

"Nah, nobody was around. They must have gone out to the boat when I didn't get back," I said. "I didn't see anyone so I came back. And now I'm bummed out and need a drink."

"Poor honey, get yourself a glass and I'll pour you a margarita," said the cute doe-eyed thing.

She had little strawberry blonde ringlets cascading down the sides of her tiny head. A head so small it seemed out of place on her very grown up body. She looked over at me as I sat down and made a sweet, puckering sort of smile. Her lips were full and red. There was something about the girl.

Three in the morning:
Bagley is passed out in the passenger seat of the van, cheekbone resting crookedly on the frame of the open window, mouth agape and drooling.

It was really all his fault that we were late, as anyone could see—especially those that knew him. And besides, we were only late for Christ sake, nothing more.

I parked in the Harbor House lot, crawled into the back of the van and lay down on the big blue blanket that smelled a lot like drunken bar fly. My stomach was churning my head was racing and all I could think about was getting back home and starting up as a better father and husband.

I hoped I still had time to make it work. I could get a regular job during the day and come home and play catch with my son at night.... We could go to big league exhibition games in the spring and eat hotdogs.... How sweet was the sound of wooden bat against baseball.... I could taste the beer and feel the sun. Life would be safe, secure...

My god, it was going to be great, I kept telling myself, over and over and over again....

Then I remembered Schmidt's words: what he had said about needing me for the next gig. Sounded like a big one. Maybe there was good money to be had, after all.

Maybe I could look for a steady job *after* the deal was done.

I finally drifted off.

I dreamt I was behind the wheel of a large sailing ship, a fierce storm raging, angry waves washing over the boat. My muscles rippled out from beneath the rolled-up sleeves of my red shirt as I firmly gripped the nautical wheel. Standing behind me, his comforting hand resting on my shoulder, was Jesus.

With confusion and fear, I struggled against the wind and water.

Was Jesus my Sky Pilot? Or was he my *new* savior?

The waves grew ever higher.

Why had Jesus chosen me, if not to show my superiority? Couldn't they all see that the lord had chosen me? Doesn't it say in the good book to follow him and you shall be rewarded? And hadn't I been getting a preview of my future rewards?

A deep voice rang out: *"The lord sees in you what others don't.*

The lord knows of your superiority, the value of your future.
He'll get you through to the other side of the storm. The streets of
heaven are paved with gold."

My dream was shattered by the sound of the side door opening;
Bagley's thick, edgy laugh following behind the dragging of
metal.

The sun was barely up. I didn't feel as bad as I thought I would.
I had kept my pants on the night before.

Dan and I walked down to the beach. It was already hot. He
wanted to get to the boat. I figured I'd better go along and say
hello to my wife.

The dinghy was, of course, dangling off the stern of the *Larson
E,* seventy-five yards from shore.

Dan's proposed solution for this problem was to "borrow" one
of several other dinghies on the beach and row out to the boat.

"Let's go get some breakfast at this place that Steve took us," I
said, lighting up a Kool with a match from a book that I'd just
peeled off my back. "I'm fucking starved. I haven't been eating
right lately."

"Too much stress from the wife, I bet. You're probably getting
an ulcer."

"No. That's not it."

"I'm amazed you get away with it, Waverly."

"Get away with what?"

"Heh, heh. Ha ha. That's funny. I've got to give you credit."

"Credit for what?"

Just then, Steve Schmidt surfaced on the deck of the boat,
stretching and scratching the back of his head. Bagley put his two
pinky fingers in his mouth and blew. Out came a loud whistle,
almost like a shriek. Then he yelled and waved his arms:
"SCHMIDT! SCHMIDTY! IN HERE! STEVE!!!"

He whistled again; my ears rang.

I thought I detected Schmidt's body slumping a little when he saw whom it was doing the shrieking. He took his time about it but got into the raft and came ashore. Hit the sand and gave us the once-over.

"What a sorry pair you two are. Waverly leaves his family alone—doesn't tell them where he's going—and then he shows up with the king of the fuck-ups, himself, Colorado Dan Bagley—mountain man and destroyer of deals."

"Oh, come on, Schmidty, give it a rest," Bagley protested with a grimace. "I-I've got everything all figured out. I know h-how, we can do the same deal without having to cut back on anything, so get off my back. Well... only one cut back.... It will have to be a slightly more h-hands-on operation, that's all. We can still do the same weight."

"And how are we going to pull that one off, Professor Corey?"

"We cancel out Marsha. Tell her we don't need her, or her boat, because of a major emergency. Send her on her way with a thank you and an apology. We'll just have to sail it ourselves."

"On the *Larson E*? You forget that the compartment here is for hash, not pot. We won't be able to get enough pot in there to make it worth our while."

"Don't worry about that. These Jamaicans got their own trash compacters. Press it flat like hash. Flat, stringy, reddish bud."

"The suppliers were Marsha's people. How you gonna get by that one?"

"I've made some new arrangements: This guy that I know from Aspen. He's big-time—real big-time—and he's flying down to the island this week."

"Do I know him?" Schmidt asked.

"I don't think so."

"Ever done anything with him before?"

"Not directly. But he's well known in the right circles in Aspen. I've had pieces of his loads in the past and it's always been an A-1 situation. He's looking at this as his swan song. Getting out of the game, he says."

"Yeah, but isn't that going to cost us?"

"All he's doing is tacking on his own personal load on top of ours." Stuttering now: "Ah-ah-ah, he ah, h-he's paying for it himself—and that will r-r-run our price down. H-h-he gets it free of delivery charge, at our v-v-volume rate, and everybody's h-happy."

"How in the hell are we going to handle all that extra weight?" Schmidt said, frowning and pinching the bridge of his nose.

"I've got it all figured out. We can d-discuss the details l-l-later."

My legs were turning to rubber and I felt about as lively as an eviscerated Billy goat. I stumbled back into a shady spot of sand by the pier, sat down and leaned against some pilings.

"I've got to eat," I said, shakily.

"And eat we will," Bagley said. "And I'll buy your breakfast and that of your family. We're going to need you, on this deal, now, Keith. The old plan had me waiting for the boat with the van. Now it's going to have to be you and the van and a u-haul trailer. I-I'll make it w-worth your while, I assure you. That is, if you think your wife will let you do it."

"I'll be able to do it, don't worry. She doesn't have to know anything that I don't want her to know. I'm going to need a good chunk of bread, though. I've got family to consider, you understand."

He gave me a sideways look and started back toward the van. Schmidt squinted at me with a crooked grin on his face and turned toward the raft. I got up and walked into the water up to my waist and splashed some briny on my neck.

Hey guys, I was thinking, we're partners now.

That is, if the offer is good enough.

We rowed out to the boat. Carole was waiting on top.

"You're a little late," she frowned as I climbed on.

"Yeah, I'm sorry," I said. "I had to baby-sit Dan. I tried to get back downtown to you guys but you were gone when I got there.

Then I had to go back and get Dan, and one thing led to another. I was wishing I was with you the whole time."

I moved in and gave her a light hug. She looked up at me, sadness in her eyes. I hadn't seen that before.

Bagley clucked as he approached us. "Hey, lovebirds, break it up," he said, smirking. "Greetings, Carole."

Carole's face turned a little crimson. She managed a smile and a hello. She looked at me and then at him. Then back at me like she was studying.

"You guys have fun last night?" she said, indifferent. "You look like you did."

"Yes, my dear," Dan said. "We definitely got the pipes cleaned out. I thought your husband was going to boot on me on a couple of instances, but he managed to hold himself together. He must be out of drinking shape... now that he's such a good husband, I mean."

"Oh, far from that," she said. "I'm sorry I missed all the fun."

"You didn't miss anything," I said.

Mike and John came up top. Carole and I squinted out at the ocean. Bright sun and soft white clouds like cotton balls. The wind was down for the first time in a while. I felt strangely confident and healthy.

John said he wanted to get out of Key West early and head for home. Didn't want to be late getting back to Clearwater because the next day was a workday. Carole reluctantly agreed. I think Mike wanted to stay. He was getting used to rhythm of the waves and his shell collection was growing nicely. At least he wasn't pissed at me. He didn't seem like he was, anyway.

We decided to leave before noon. It was a long drive and there were tales circulating of long stretches of road where all the gas stations were closed.

We packed our stuff went in for breakfast and at twelve-thirty we said our goodbyes. Dan assured me several times that he would call me enough time in advance of their arrival for me to prepare. I was already in possession of detailed instructions and a marked map.

We stopped for lunch north of Miami. John bought. The Waverlys were now officially broke enough to beg.

But I had a secret: My ship was coming in.

Chapter Nine

Bang Your Head

The sun is laying out flat in the West. A light mist is rising up from the water. I don't know whether to light the lamps and put together another bonfire or haul ass out of here. Losing a chance to score big is really hard to accept.

I elect for a compromise: Get the hell out of here for a time, go for a walk with the intent of gathering some fire wood, then come back later.

Burnable wood is not easily found along the beaches. Occasionally there's some driftwood that's workable, once you get the blaze going, but you need some starter material. Something with some substance to get the flames leaping up to the stars.

On the way in, I had noticed an abandoned shack that reminded me of my childhood attempt at making a fort from an old piano box. Upon closer inspection, I could tell it had been the firewood stash for other enterprising campers before me.

The shack proves to be as convenient a find for me as that lone, open gas station was on our trip back from Key West. It felt so good just to find one that was open, I'll never forget....

It was dark as pitch and the gauge was reading E. We had seen no open stations for the last four hours.

Joy was ours when we rolled into a small town and discovered the cheery lights and the friendly sight of a line of cars waiting at a functioning gasoline pump. Big, yellow letters flashed: Cold Beer.

My mind shifted as Mike asked for Cheetos and chocolate bars, undisguised glee pushing up a grin on his sweet, young face.

We stood outside eating junk food and watching the moths commit suicide against the lights. I felt a tinge of excitement for my future. At the same time, a tugging in my gut kept reminding me of the ultimate despair that waits for those who stumble.

Getting back home was a relief.

We returned to routine. I began to realize that one had to work at things like marriage.

I got off the coke and the hard liquor and tried to get back to living healthy. I couldn't play tennis anymore—I still had a limp—so I tried to stay in shape by hitting baseballs to Mike, at the park. Some nights we stayed until we could barely see the balls in the grass.

Those were good nights.

Some other nights, we'd be waiting for Carole to come home for dinner and we would play catch on a strip of grass in front of the laundry room. Many of those nights she didn't show up and we had to eat without her. The kid would go to bed without seeing his mother.

She'd come in late, always with liquor on her breath and always sniffling. Talking fast and gesturing erratically, she'd tell me she'd been recording spots for new projects. She wanted me to know that she was taking much time and effort to help both the station and her family. It was only natural that "they" went out for a few drinks after working so hard.

I held in the frustration, suspicion and anger because deep inside I believed I was on the path to glory. It was only a matter of waiting for the mail or the phone call from the Jamaican Sweepstakes Committee.

Just when it seemed my life was getting better it was really turning to shit behind my back.

Ten days had gone by without any word from the smugglers and I was starting to get a little anxious.

Maybe I overreacted that night. All I know is that I'd been waiting a long goddamn time for her to come home. I was strung out on anger and frustration and worry, nervous about the future and the past at the same time.

She had been at a party, at the station, allegedly being thrown in celebration of a ratings increase. I was suspicious but didn't have the energy to be constantly vigilant. That stuff will wear you down in a hurry.

Mike and I had stayed up watching TV and then gone to bed. I woke up at two. Carole wasn't there. I tried to go back to sleep but the worms crawled into my gut. I got the feeling I might lose control. I rolled out of bed, slipped on a pair of shorts and went outside with the intent of checking the parking lot.

I walked down the sidewalk past door after door and curtained window after curtained window. Voices and laughter floated out of screens. The air was warm. I saw nobody. The lot was quiet.

Where in the fucking hell was Carole?

I went back and tried to sleep. Kept my shorts on this time. Tossed and turned for a long while but still no Carole. Got up and went into the living room. Smoked a cigarette and dragged my fingers through wiry strands of oily hair. Went to the sliding doors and pulled open the curtain, put my nose against the screen and stared out at the pool.

Nothing moving but the green water. A light breeze was feathering the surface, blowing the scent of chlorine my way. Then the flash of a headlight bounced off the buildings, swung quickly by and disappeared.

I got a funny feeling in my gut; my heart started to pound. Slipping on my shoes, I slid open the screen. It was time to check the lot again. I was thinking about bringing the baseball bat but didn't want to scare any neighbors.

Got to the end of the complex and saw headlights burning. Heard that fabled, rumbling exhaust.

A red and black Porsche was idling in the parking lot about thirty yards away. What looked to be Carole's blonde head, bobbed and jerked behind the tinted passenger side window.

I stopped and squinted. What were they doing in there? Did I want to go any further?

Kill the fucker. He's diddlin' your woman.

Man, it looked they were kissing. I rubbed my eyes. I was afraid to go closer, for what I might see.

Stomp the slimy son of a bitch; he's fucking your wife.

There—I saw it again. What the hell was going on?

Cut off his fucking nuts, man, you're cuckold.

Clouded with rage, I started toward the car but then I stopped. The inside light was blinking on. Carole was climbing out.

Then she sat back down inside the car. I screamed HEY. She jerked upright and I started running towards her. Ready to rip open that door and grab her by the arms; make her feel as bad as me.

I got close enough to see her eyes—like a deer in the headlights. I stopped.

Paul Gulzheimer jumped out of the driver's door and stared across the black canvas top at me.

"Behave yourself," he said, striking a pose of authority. "It's later than you think."

"What the fuck are you talking about, and what are you doing with my wife?" I said, confused.

"I can assure you that this was work oriented. I only meant

that it was late and your neighbors will wake up if you cause a disturbance."

"Yeah, Keith," Carole said, slightly slurred; her eyes like pretty, blue marbles, and her face like a porcelain doll. "We were just discussing the details to the next proposal."

"And did Paul have those details printed on his tonsils, Carole? Because it sure fucking seemed like you were exploring that area with your goddamn tongue."

She stumbled out of the seat toward me and took a swing, a looping overhand left. I caught it and spun her around by her arm, held her around the waist for a moment, squeezing, then let her go free. She stumbled to a startled halt, her head hanging loosely.

"Get the fuck out of here, Paul, before I rip out your Adam's apple and stomp it on the fucking sidewalk," I said, enraged, but feeling helpless.

He didn't move, just stared at Carole.

I faked like I was going for him, taking a couple of aggressive steps. He jumped back into the Porsche and threw it into reverse as fast as his scaly appendages could move.

I bent down and picked up a loose chunk of concrete about the size of a baseball that was lying by the parking barrier.

"Don't Keith, please," Carole cried hysterically. "Please don't…. Don't throw it. I'm sorry. Please don't do it…."

I heaved it just as he was popping the clutch. Chunk caught the top of his trunk on a nice downward spiral, put a good-sized crater on the shiny red finish then bounced through the unzipped rear window and slammed into the dash.

Dude hit the brakes. I didn't move, just braced up. He hesitated for a second, turning his head and looking back, but then squealed down the road.

She was crying, her body kind of collapsing in.

"Look what you've done," she sobbed. "I hope you feel proud of yourself. I'm going to lose my job now…. What are we going to do?"

"What are you talking about, with this *we,* shit. What makes you think I'm going to stay around after this?"

"Because I didn't do anything."

"I saw you fucking kissing him."

"I was kissing him goodbye, saying I was sorry. He's been trying to get me in the rack for a month, for God sakes.... Buying me drinks, giving me toot...I was just along for the party but he had a whole different idea. Look, the guy pays my salary—our support. I was only trying to keep him from firing me, smoothing things over."

"Fucking sure."

I grabbed her by the wrist and pulled her in the direction of our apartment. Her body jerked suddenly forward but her legs never caught up. She tripped and fell onto her knees, the momentum driving her face down into the blacktop.

She wasn't moving, only moaning softly. I knelt down beside her; her eyes were closed.

"Get up, Carole, get up," I pleaded. "You can't stay here. Someone will call the cops."

I grabbed her by the arms and tried to lift her but my knee buckled.

"Get up Carole, goddamn it. Come on, you've got to get up. Help me for once in your fucking life, goddamn it."

I lifted her up to her knees. She held her hand against her forehead, sobbing staccato.

"Leave me alone,"she snarled. "Look what you've done to me."

"Look, honey, I'm sorry. It was an accident. I was just trying to get you out of here. I didn't mean for you to fall. Come on, let's go inside and talk about it. I'm really sorry, I swear."

Somewhere above us a glass door scraped along a rusty track.

"What the hell is the matter out there?" boomed a concerned voice. "Is everybody all right?"

Carole looked around fearfully, hunching her shoulders. She stood up, took a step forward and staggered. I caught her before she fell and we made our unsteady way back around the building. I think I squeezed her arm a little too hard when we went through our apartment door.

"I want this relationship to work, too, you know," she cried, stumbling into the kitchen.

I stood across from her and leaned back against the counter. "What makes you think that I do?"

"Cause you love me? And even if you don't, you're the one who dragged me down here to Florida. Mike and I became your responsibility once we got down here. And you've been doing a real great job of looking after us, from the looks of things."

"Wait just a fucking minute. You weren't exactly in a perfect situation back in Zenith City, now, were you? Weren't you going to jail, or something like that?"

"You're still the one who asked us to come down here. Poor Mike has had to change schools three times now in the last year."

"Two."

"No, three. Two down here and one back in Zenith City when I moved out of my parents' house."

"Couldn't you keep him in the same school?"

"Well, there was that incident at his school. I thought it was better if—"

"What is this, now? I can't believe this shit."

"This other boy at school told Mike that his father was a smut peddler—that you were a smut peddler. And Mikey got in a fight with the kid…and got suspended."

"Did he win?"

"I don't know, Keith, try and be serious," she said, her eyes flashing a millisecond of mirth.

"How did this kid get that kind of information, anyway—you tell him?"

"Oh, fuck you. How should I know how the kid found out."

"His father was probably a customer." I said. "Probably the air-force major that used to shit in the movie booths."

"Oh gross, I don't like that stuff."

"Hey, the pay was good: three dollars an hour and all you could steal… and they let me off to play softball. How could I complain about that? I did get sick of it after awhile, though. Working in a place like that can get you in trouble."

"It would be nice if you were working anywhere, right now."

"We're back to that again, are we? You know what would be fucking NICE. It would be FUCKING NICE IF YOU WEREN'T FUCKING YOUR GODDAMN BOSS."

"STOP IT. STOP IT. I told you, I didn't do anything wrong."

She shrieked like a banshee and dragged her fingernails down her cheeks.

"Shut the fuck up, you'll wake up Mike," I said. "You want to explain to him what you were doing in your boss's sports car at four in the morning? Maybe I'll tell him…how would you like that? Or maybe better, maybe you can explain to him what it was you were doing in the preceding hours. Maybe you could start by telling him where you got drunk. And then where it was that you FUCKED YOUR BOSS."

Out came a primal yowl as she slammed her fists into my chest, growling like Mathusala's mother.

"That's good, Carole. Mike needs to hear this. Keep it up."

She sobbed hysterically. "Look," she said, sniffling. "We went to the Don CeSar. A whole bunch of us were at the piano bar. We were all partying."

"Was John there?"

"For a little while. He left after a couple of drinks. You know how he is sometimes about drinking, with his tennis and everything."

Her eyes pleaded, mascara ran down in streaks.

"Well you didn't stay at the Don fucking CeSar all goddamn night till four in the fucking morning for Christ sake. What about those two hours after the bar closes? Is that when you fucked him?"

"Shut up, Keith, now who's making noise?"

"Yeah, I'm making FUCKING noise. Because you're a GOD-DAMN FUCKING WHORE, THAT'S WHAT YOU ARE."

"I'm not a whore, Keith," she said softly, her face, now gray like mottled steel.

"Then what are you, some kind of—"

Then a tiny voice: "Mommy... Mom... I want Mommy...."

My throat constricted. Horror and sorrow struck me like an arrow to the heart.

"Just a second, honey," Carole said, turning ashen white and suddenly looking in control. "I'll be right there."

Her back stiffened; her shoulders picked up as she walked by. She wiped her face with the sleeve of her dark blue dress.

I backed up slowly and sat down hard on the couch. Time to rethink things.

A few minutes later she emerged from Mike's room, a serious look in her face.

"Is he all right? Do you think he heard us?"

"Of course he heard us. He wanted to know what was wrong, how I got these cuts."

"I suppose you told him that I did it."

"No I didn't. I said it was an accident. You're in the clear; you don't have to worry about what Mike thinks about you."

"You know, Carole, I almost cheated on you, too. Down in the Keys that night I was out with Bagley—a really cute girl, too."

"Why didn't you?"

"Because I had this sense of responsibility inside me you know, unlike you."

Her eyeballs tilted back in their sockets and a look of terror crossed her features. "I'm just no good," she said. "You must hate me. How can you stand me?"

"You aren't that bad, honey."

"Gee, thanks a lot."

"I wanted to tell you the other reason I didn't fuck that girl."

"All right, go ahead. I guess I've got it coming to me."

"Bagley drove off and left the two of them at a bar out in the boonies. Just drove off and fucking left them in this goddamn redneck bar."

"You assholes," she said. "She must have been pretty."

"She was, in a sad sort of way. She liked country music."

"You must have gotten to know her pretty well... I'm jealous."

"She probably reminded me of you, back when we first got married. All I really wanted was you, I guess."

"You didn't even know about Paul when we were in the Keys. You were running around before you even knew about Paul.... That's the way you've always been. Maybe I'm just taking after you...."

"Oh fucking please. A man knows when there's something going on with his wife, for Christ sake. I'm not deaf, dumb or fucking blind."

"Please just let this drop, I can't take anymore. I'm sorry I ever encouraged him. I got him off my back by appealing to the one thing I knew would get to him."

"What was that?"

"I told him that he'd stand to lose a pile of cash if his wife found out about me."

"A pile of some other people's cash, no doubt. You know, he fires you, or files a complaint against me, his wife is going to want to know why it was me threw that rock, and what the pretty little receptionist had to do with it. I think you drew the wild card, dear, and now we're stuck together in the same old swirl."

Women are always going to fuck you over, someway or another.

Suddenly I was worn out, limp and stinky like a dishrag.

"I'm going to bed," I said, defeated.

She stood up. I looked in her eyes. They were empty.

I went into the bedroom and flopped on the bed. Closed my eyes and pictures of Carole and Paul, fucking, came floating through my head like a cheap 8mm porn loop.

*   *   *

After a couple days of treading on eggshells, things started to thaw out.

According to Carole, Paul had handled the situation at the station very smoothly; showing no indication that anything untoward or unreasonable had taken place. It was truly as if nothing had happened, she said.

With that worry out of the way, we started to loosen up. It was like a door had been opened and the light was getting in. And then one day she came home with the news that Paul was revoking her credit card and expecting immediate payment for the remaining balance. This, of course, would be extracted from her paycheck if we didn't pay up in full—about three hundred and fifty bucks.

There went the money I had received from Ted.

Next, Carole's on-air opportunity was cancelled. This did not make her feel bad. The money squeeze, however, had us both pissed off.

Then, a strange thing happened. We seemed to bounce back. Because of this mutual enemy, our reliance in each other began to grow. We even smiled at each other sometimes.

Another weekend rolled around without any word from the boys. When Carole meekly suggested that we go out someplace, alone together, for dinner and a few drinks; I jumped at the chance like a sea trout to a live shrimp. We'd been so good, hadn't we?

We found a nice little restaurant down in St. Pete with a dark wood interior, moody blue lighting and big tables. The refrigeration was on too high but I managed to enjoy our meal.

After dinner we got in the car and drove across Central Avenue, chasing the sun, ending up at St. Pete Beach. We cruised down Gulf Boulevard and came to a stop beneath two blinking, neon cocktail glasses.

Dirty Phil's Beach Club was a low, white building looking out on the water. I could see the thatched roof of a Tiki bar, on the beach side.

It was a beautiful evening. We took a table by a big window, overlooking the Gulf. We had drinks and dug the sunset; the days were getting longer.

Part way through the third cocktail, a different tone came into Carole's voice and a dark and previously unseen look filled her eyes.

She hadn't had a drink for a few days so I thought maybe, the change was to be expected. But I could sense a new edge, ever closer to hysteria. Or maybe I was just seeing for the first time what had always been there....

Her glass bone dry, she began searching anxiously for the wait-ress. With no help in sight, she stood abruptly and clucked: "Do you want another one?"

I shook my head to the negative. She threw back her hair with a snap of her elegant neck and high-stepped it up to the bar, shoulders squared.

I turned my chair and looked out at the water as two beautiful, teenage girls walked by, their nubile flesh barely contained in skimpy bikinis. Up North, it would have been a scandal.

It seemed like I watched those girls for an awful long time— until my glass was empty—but Carole still hadn't returned. I craned my neck around and found her sitting at the bar, sur-rounded by three seemingly enthralled guys. Everybody was laughing, having a grand old time.

It seemed to me like the gentlemen were arguing among them-selves for the right to buy her another drink. These guys didn't look like anyone you could bluff; they were all big.

Carole was so impervious to anything but her immediate sur-roundings that it was like I had gotten so small she couldn't see me anymore. Ten minutes went by before she returned to our table and my gut was doing the Mexican hat dance.

She sat down across from me, lit a cigarette, cocked her wrist elegantly and leaned back in her chair. There was some kind of alien life in her eyes, way in the back.

"Made some new friends, I see," I said.

"Yeah, those guys were pretty friendly. Nice guys...One of them was a little pushy, maybe...cute, but scary, I guess. But they were nice guys... They bought me a jumbo, see."

She held the glass aloft, foam sticking to her upper lip, a lip that with the sun setting on it just right was one of the world's masterpieces.

I was almost relaxing when the fat bastard walked into the club. Only he wasn't as fat as I remembered. Seemed like his gut didn't hang over his belt quite so far. This time, he was wearing a different colored Hawaiian shirt and a pair of new blue jeans instead of those shiny, creased trousers. Some kind of gel on his hair made him look sleazy, like a gambler in a B movie. The black cowboy boots kept up the image.

Lieutenant goddamn Douglas was strutting like a rooster in a hen house. And he was striding up to the bar like my wife's new buddies were his old friends.

They all exchanged greetings and then I knew what it was that I'd been feeling. Dudes were cops. We were in a cop bar.

A shiver ran through me. Even if I was clean, the Man always gave me a shiver. Ain't nothing better for the world than a good cop. Ain't nothing worse than a bad cop.

I kind of shrunk up my neck, like a turtle trying to get back into his shell, but unfortunately, I had no shell. Suddenly I missed the North and its heavy jackets. I turned my chair slowly until my back was facing the bar.

"Jesus, Carole," I said. "That cop that brought you home that night you smacked into those people just walked in. Don't look."

She looked.

Ten seconds later she was waving and smiling.

My balls shrank up.

"Please don't tell me that the fucker is coming over here," I whispered. "Don't encourage him, for god sakes."

She smiled, hissing through her teeth: "It's too late, he's coming over. You'd better sit up straight."

"Jesus."

Goddamn if I didn't smell the fucking Right Guard from ten feet away.

"Well, son of a gun if it isn't the Waverly's, out painting the town red. How y'all doing?"

I turned and feigned surprise as he extended his large, meaty hand. I stood up and took it. A dead fish would have felt more alive.

He jerked his hand back like I had a disease: "And my, my, if you aren't a vision of loveliness tonight, Mrs. Waverly. Carole, isn't it?"

Starting the cop game.

Carole blushed and smiled: "I'm afraid I can't remember your name, but your face is a friendly and familiar one. Thank you again for what you did for me that night."

"It's Officer Douglas, dear," I said.

"Lieutenant Douglas, ma'am," he shot back. "And I'm always ready to help a sweet young lady in distress. How you folks all doin'? Everything's turning up roses for you two, these days, I hope."

"Real good, Lieutenant," I said, my nerves talking. "How about yourself? Working on any interesting cases lately?"

"I imagine your job is quite interesting," Carole said.

I couldn't for the life of me figure out why the two of us were encouraging the guy.

"Mostly drug cases, folks. Stupid, sleazy people getting in trouble and ratting on their friends, for the most part. Seems like just about everybody's messed up on drugs down here. Y'know, we get a lot of Northerners who come down, thinking they're going to make a killing in the drug scene by buying their stuff down here. They come down from someplace and find out the game is played differently in Florida. You see; we don't screw around here—pardon my French. When we catch up to these people, they're not so sure about life in general, anymore. The prisons around here aren't real nice, ya see... too far away from the beach and the food ain't real good, if you catch my drift."

He smiled and waved his hand at the beach.

"The ocean, the weather... seems like it makes some folks think they can get away with anything, and still enjoy the good life. It's a funny place, this Sunshine State. But the sun don't shine at night, jes' like everywhere else. You got your neon and your jewelry and, of course, the cocaine. Hell's bells, some of them dumb Yankees are lucky we get 'em before the Colombians do. At least that way they stay in one piece... after a fashion, anyway. But say now, folks, I don't mean to gab on you for the whole evening. How 'bout if I buy you two a drink? Hows about it—whattaya say?"

"Ah, we... ah... um..." I stammered.

"That would be awfully kind of you, Lieutenant," Carole said, falling into her Blanche Dubois impression. "Everybody is just so hospitable down South, I do declare."

"Yes, ma'am."

"Yeah, that'd be great," I said, fixating on a giant yacht sailing by, wishing I were on it.

"Won't you have a seat, Lieutenant?" Carole said, fluttering her eyelashes. "Is a lieutenant more important than an officer?"

"Yes ma'am, it is—or I am, anyway..." Douglas said, flashing his cornpone grin and giving me a look of mutually shared conspiracy. "What is everybody drinking?"

He held up his hand and an attractive bleached blonde, her hair tied back in long pigtails, flounced over. Her healthy chest pressed tight against a teal body suit that led down to a pair of satiny white, French-cut shorts. Watching her move brought me back to my days as a tennis instructor, back when I was young.

Douglas stood up and put his arm around the girl's shoulders: "Linda, these are my friends the Waverlys, I want you to get them another round and put it on my tab. While you're there get me another scotch and water—no ice."

I guess I was admiring Linda for a little too long. Disdain swept across Carole's face like a gray cloud passing over the sun.

"Hurry back, now," Douglas said, giving her a fatherly look. She nervously hustled off while he eyeballed her ass. Turning back to us: "She's a good girl, that Linda—but she's got a drug problem and a boyfriend problem—like so many girls that I run into. I guess I try to help girls like Linda get their lives back in order, if I can."

He sat down in the chair across from me, leaned over and touched Carole's forearm, his fingers lingering briefly: "Now you, Carole… I don't recall ever seeing anyone so out of it as you were, the other night and still talking wise. But you were so gall darned sassy and smarty-pants that I had a hell of time to keep from laughing. Them people you hit, I think they fell in love with you, in their own Christian way. You had all three of us grinning, with your little routines. You know—the purse thing on the pavement… If you hadn't been so funny, I don't think I would have let you go. You sure were a kick in the old pants…"

Carole blushed. Time stood still. Linda came back with the drinks.

"Did she speak any Spanish?" I asked, as the booze made me, even more stupid. "She likes to do these fake Spanish routines when she's drunk, you see. She's pretty good at it. She calls me Zorro sometimes."

"Really… that's ah, interesting. Can I hear some?" Douglas said.

"I won't. I can't. Not here… You really want me to?"

"Oh, come on darlin'," Douglas said. "Don't be shy. We're all friends here. That is if you and your husband still get along… Heh—just a little joke."

"Yeah, come on, Carole," I said, feeling the madness grow.

She blushed, reached out for her drink, took a long pull and shook her hair. Then she began chopping at the air with her hands and carrying on in a rhythmic singsong: "*Mi amore don ciesta balluna pontovi marimba el sonta. A caleetcha mon rella bien-solina bahai.*"

She paused, searching for approval.

"I think some Italian slipped into that last one," she said, smiling a beautiful smile, ivory white teeth sparkling.

The cop was enraptured like a moonstruck polecat. Staring at her like she's the greatest thing since televised car races.

"That's ah, mighty fun, Carole," he said. "Pretty hammy, but still fun. No cop'd ever fall for it, but I have to admit there's some ring to it. You two guys are really out of sight, y'know that." He glanced over at me like we were sharing another magic moment.

I slurped at my drink with added speed. Carole, for some unknown reason, had slowed down. Her glass was still almost full. Way too much left to get up and leave—especially for her.

"Why don't we play some pool, Carole, like we planned," I said, allowing the slightest hint of annoyance to creep in. "A table just opened up. If we go now, we can grab it. I'm sure the Lieutenant won't mind. I'm sure he knows how tough it is to get a pool table in a crowded bar."

Carole looked nervous and uncomfortable but she went along with my play. "Thank you so much for the drinks, Lieutenant Douglas," she said, smiling her best midwestern smile. "And thank you again for the other night. I don't know what got into me."

"Just a few too many, I reckon. Never oughtta mix love and whisky, they say."

"Thanks for the drinks, Lieutenant. See you later."

Much later, if I'm lucky.

He stood up.

"You two be careful, now, on your way home," he said, turning away.

He paused and turned back to me: "Say ah, funny thing, but I just recalled a complaint from up in you guys' neighborhood—

came in a little while back: Vandalism, on a brand new Porsche, it was. Guy claims someone threw a brick or something at him, over near Twin Lakes. Now that wouldn't necessarily be interesting, but the Porsche happens to belong to Carole's boss at the radio station—Paul Gulzheimer. So... I'm assuming that you guys have already heard about the incident. If you have, then I don't need to tell you to be careful—at night—around there... sometimes trouble can come a callin'."

Carole's face turned wan, like a wax dummy, while tiny beads of sweat wiggled onto my forehead like inchworms.

We smiled weakly at each other as we stumbled over to the pool tables. Fucking cop put a pall on the night.

Our game started out horrible—and ended up worse. I couldn't knock a ball in the ocean and Carole had trouble even hitting the cue ball with her stick. Once, she dropped the cue on the floor and it clanged around, causing a bunch of heads to turn and stare. My skin was so hot you could have ironed a shirt with my neck. Carole staggered around giggling after every terrible shot—embarrassed, but too drunk to change anything. The game seemed to go on forever but time and the law of averages eventually got us close to a possible ending.

I had two very makeable shots in front of me, and then the eight ball, for the win. Sweet escape was within the realm of possibility.

Preparing to knock the two-ball into a corner pocket, I caught sight of a guy walking toward us. Right in the middle of my stroke, he rushed over and snapped his quarter down on the table.

The two caught a piece of the rail, rattled out, kicked back and double kissed the cue ball into the eight ball, knocking it into the corner pocket.

I lost.

I gave the guy a quick stare: He wasn't very friendly looking, but he was sure quick to grab a stick off the wall. He was a well put together six feet tall, had dark eyes and thick eyebrows, hairy forearms and kinky black hair.

"We were just leaving," I said. "Whattaya say, Carole, shall we go?"

Dude was racking up the balls.

"Oh let me play this one game, Keith," she said. "I'm not going to win, you know that."

"You just beat me...."

"But that was sheer luck and you know it. And if I'm going to get better, I need the practice. Why don't you get yourself another drink and relax?"

"Well, all right."

"Get me another, too, will you?"

"You break, pretty lady," the guy said.

My spirit sank as I weaved my way to the bar. Could everybody see that I was a fool for a drunken woman?

I returned with a pitcher of margaritas and sat down at a small round table near the pool tables. The other cops, including Douglas, had moved to the booths around us, effectively dominating the area. Three more quarters lay on the rail.

Carole lined up her shot, took a quick back swing and stroked fiercely. The cue ball careened wildly into the side cushion, hit two rails and knocked the four-ball into the side pocket.

"Ooh," she screamed. "Would you look at that."

"I didn't hear you call that," the cop said.

"Are we playing that way? I always play slop. A lady must be allowed her luck...."

The cop grinned and looked at her with a hunger dancing on the edge of his eyes.

"That sounds fine to me, honey."

Next shot, she missed everything, drawing laughter and lots of encouragement from the rest of the cops. Even I was beginning to enjoy her embarrassed-little-girl-act; it had been so long since I'd seen it.

The cop sank three balls before he missed. Then Carole made a clean hit on the cue ball but nothing fell. The cop proceeded to run the rest of the table, except for the eight.

Butterflies with steel wings flew into my gut, as I watched him line up for an obvious scratch shot.

Sure enough, the son of a bitch scratched.

I sat up straight in my chair and tried to stretch my neck but the muscles were like steel bands.

Then cop number two, an angular guy with thinning blonde hair and a marine tattoo on his forearm, stepped up and placed his quarter in the slot, shoving in the slide with extreme force.

Carole was grinning from ear to ear, schucking and jiving with the guys like she was the State Fair Queen of Mississippi and they were the judges who just voted her in.

Her pool shooting didn't get any better but she won the next game when her opponent followed the eight ball into the corner pocket on an easy straight-in shot.

A third cop, tall and thin, olive-skinned with a moustache, clean white shirt, rolled up sleeves and a gold chain bracelet, sidled up to the table.

Carole came over and drank heavily from her glass, shook a Kool out of the pack and put it between her lips at an angle. Her hand shook slightly as she brought match to the tobacco.

"Don't you think we should go?" I said softly.

"But I'm winning all these games...this is so much fun..."

"Yeah, lots of fun. These guys are letting you win, you know..."

She snapped her head back: "Huh... don't you say that. I'm shooting a lot better now...and I am lucky, you forget. I've always been lucky.... You know how lucky I can be some-times.... You're always trying to put down everything I do. Now it's I'm not really winning; they're letting me. Why can't you accept the fact that I can do things right, sometimes? Why can't you see that I can be good at something?"

"You're good at a lot of things—pool just doesn't happen to

be one of them. I think you've made about eight shots in three games. I'll give you credit for those...."

Dude: "Break'em, Carole."

They were calling her Carole... Christ.

She gave me one last dirty look before she was off to her game.

The guy began missing easy shots and flirting with her so openly that I finally had to jump up and put my quarter on the table. It looked like I was going to have to win back my wife.

Just about the time my finger lifted off the coin, the cop became a shooter. He ran his last four balls and knocked down a one-railer on the eight. Carole's streak of "luck " was over.

She went over to her drink, sniffing and tossing her head back.

I racked the balls, feeling the storm clouds approaching.

"Play for a fiver?" The guy asked.

What could I say without losing face?

"Yeah, sure," I said. "No problem."

He broke, sinking the twelve-ball. Made his next two shots before missing. I made two balls and then missed. Carole walked over to the booth where Douglas and his two buddies were sitting. Douglas stood up and she slid into the wall seat next to him.

I pretended to shoot pool but I really wanted to flagellate myself. Amazingly, I managed to win the game, getting lucky on my last two shots.

My opponent reached into his pocket and tugged out a five-dollar bill. The jukebox kicked in loud, "Okie from Muskogee." Voices rose. My ears rang.

"I'll get you next time," the cop said, grinning and pointing to the booth full of fuzz. "Jerry here—Ol' One-eye—he'll give you a better game."

A bearded, undercover-type guy with a black eye patch and a sharp nose slid out. Scrawny torso, and wiry arms hanging out of a yellow cut-off sweatshirt. Dirty blonde hair, long and straight.

I downed my drink while Jerry set up the table. Fear was creeping in.

Fight or flight—I never knew which one would emerge. I wasn't about to take on a bunch of cops; that was one thing I knew.

"I'm sorry, I'm afraid I'm done," I said. "I'm getting too loaded. I need to go home."

Jerry gave me the fish-eye. "You look like a big enough guy," he said. "What's the matter, can't take your liquor?"

"I guess not, not tonight, anyway. You wouldn't want me to be out there driving drunk, now would you?"

I looked into his eyes and smirked.

"Cracking wise, are we?" he said, shoulders rising, eyes squinting.

I couldn't help but wonder what was going on behind that patch.

"As a matter of fact," he continued, authoritative, "now that you mention it, I think you probably are too drunk to drive. You need to play another game here with me—and sober up a little."

"I think I'd better get my wife and go home."

"I'm sorry, I'm afraid I can't allow you to endanger the life of you and your pretty wife. Not to mention, the citizens on the roads. You have any children at home?"

"One."

"Little girl?"

"Boy."

"What do you think would happen to your boy, if you and Carole got into an accident? I want you to think about that."

"I don't think I'll have any problem. I can walk a straight line. Watch me." I stepped around him and started towards the booth where Carole was obliviously chatting it up with the rest of the good ol' boys.

He quickly jumped in front of me, puffed up his chest: "How straight are you gonna walk, with my foot up your ass, wise guy?"

I looked down at him; he was only about five-nine. I was more embarrassed than scared... two grown men standing chest to chest in a crowded barroom.... Not a dive, either.

The heat of a thousand eyes poured into the back of my skull and I thought I could take the guy, cop tricks or no.

He kept staring up at me, unbending.

"I'm afraid you'll have to surrender your keys to me until further notice, sir."

Coming with the *sir* crap.

I ignored him, spun away and moved to the side of Carole's booth.

"I think we should go, Carole, are you ready?"

She turned her head slowly, looking right through me.

"Look at all these drinks they've bought me, Keith. I have to finish them; it wouldn't be polite. Bob can give me a ride home if you want to leave."

Fucking Bob, for chrissakes.... That was too much.

All I wanted was to escape. Run—that which truly I did best.

This new pain beneath my chest was another reason to run faster and harder—an excuse to keep on running no matter where it took me. Pain is good, you see, because it gives you something to run *from.*

Running *from* something is a lot simpler than chasing *after* something: like love, happiness or success.

Futility, though, is easy to find. Desolation, regret and self-recrimination—they're easy, too.

One-Eye came up next to me, put his hand around my back and let it rest on my shoulder, real friendly like. Carole looked away for a second and he dug in his fingers, pinching my tendon. I didn't move, just stood there and took it.

"Do you think our buddy here is fit to drive, Bobby? I'm not so sure," One-Eye said.

Douglas looked up at me, quizzical.

I tried to make my face look sober, like he was a teacher and I was the student.

"What are you talking about, Jerry? He's fine. You're the one in bad shape."

Douglas turned his attention back to the story he was telling to his companions. Including, of course, my lovely wife.

I looked at her one more time. Her face was like clay.

One-eyed Jerry dropped his hand from my shoulder.

I turned on my heels and walked out into the night, brushing nervously at the spots where the cop's hand had been. A heaviness of body and soul was on me like barnacles on a shipwreck.

I got in the car and started driving in the direction of home, miserable excuse for a home that it was. I felt like something was going to explode inside me. I wanted to cry—but that would've been stupid. I wanted to kill somebody but that would've been dumber still.

The neon lights... the cars... the swirl of life: it was all too much. I had no taste for anything except to be left alone. I was just another moth bouncing off the glass.

The darkness, the unknown: how I feared it, yet longed to embrace it. And still there were the lights, accusing me.

Who was going to help me now?

Back home, inside the prefab shell, the vibes felt ugly. Mike was spending the night at his friend's house. I fought with the urge to pick him up and send him back to Minnesota on the first flight out, deliver him from this nest of rats and snakes that I'd created. But whom in the hell could I send him to, Carole's parents? No way. Poor kid wouldn't stand a chance of growing up sane. As unbelievable as it seemed, I knew that his best chance was still with Carole and I.

If only we could pull it together....

I fought the urge to think but anguish washed in like a red tide. My gut was churning too much to do anything but lie on the couch and smoke cigarettes and stare at the TV and wait for my wife to come home. Wait to see what condition she was in and what she'd managed to pull off. Wait and wonder how my life ever got this fucked up.

It was after three a.m. when the apartment door opened, pulling me out of a feverish nightmare of fire and prison and chains, whiskey, guns and drugs.

Carole had played a part in the dream. I could never see her face, only hear her voice. She knew what I was all about, she kept saying. Had seen me for what I was: A little kid just like her younger brother Andy—picking his nose and wondering where to put it.

She knew me, she said, superiority in her voice: *I've seen you and I know how bad you suck. I know how weak and scared and dirty you are and I'm going to find someone else who's a real man—with a Porsche and a big house and a huge salary.*

I rubbed my eyes and shuddered as Carole burst into the living room, heavy scent of alcohol following close behind. She whipped on the light and I winced. Her face was pale, big round eyes stared down at me like a ghost.

"Fucking cop Douglas says he remembers where he saw you before," she said, right off. "Says he's got a video tape of you ripping off a department store with some stolen credit cards. He says they have the tape at every precinct in the county. It's like one of the first times they've ever used a video for evidence, or something. Says he's got it at the station and can bust you any-time. You want to tell me about it, Keith?"

Fear rushed through me like a flood of ice water and my heart was squeezed in a vise. We weren't even thirty seconds into my time to bitch at her and she had already turned it back at me. I didn't even get a chance to start up, for Christ sake.

"What the fuck, are you talking about? You're the one who's fucking up here, not me. What the hell did you do that to me for? How could you fucking stay there with those cops and make me look like a fucking asshole?"

"I just stayed and had some drinks, Keith. That's all. No, big thing. And you're goddamn lucky I did, honey child. Lieutenant Douglas promised me that he'd see what he could do to have the charges dropped if you promised to make restitution."

"Fuck Lieutenant goddamn Douglas… he's the one who went to all the trouble finding that tape of me. That little incident happened months ago, when I first got down here. I found these credit cards on the ground…. I thought it was a sign from god or something. I know it was stupid, but how was I to know they had cameras? I'd never done anything like that before."

I got up and went into the living room, grabbed a Kool and lit it. Carole followed.

"You are crazier than I thought," she said.

"Don't call me fucking crazy. How big is Douglas's dick anyway? Did he show you?"

"GODDAMN YOU," she shrieked. "I FUCKING HATE YOU. I HATE YOU; I HATE YOU. YOU COCKSUCKER… YOU ARE WRONG!" She pounded her fists on my chest and scratched hard with her fingernails. Her eyes were red balls; spit flew out of her mouth.

I grabbed her arms and started to swing her around in a circle like a human hammer throw. She tried to scramble away but her boozed-filled legs hit the edge of the sleeper couch. She tumbled down. Her pretty head slammed into the thick metal frame. Her body went slack.

"Carole, I'm sorry," I said, loudly, trying to wake her, not quite believing she was actually unconscious. "I don't want to hurt you, but you're driving me fucking crazy. I'd almost rather be in jail, than here with you. BECAUSE I CAN'T FUCKING TAKE IT ANYMORE!!"

I swung my arm wildly, knocking the lamp off the end table. The shade crumpled as it slammed against the floor.

She came to, moaning and sobbing and rubbing her head, tears and mascara running down her face.

"Oh no, no, no, no. I've done it, haven't I? You hate me now… I've ruined it…you hate me now I know it. I can't blame you…. I deserve it…. Your really so good and I'm so bad…. You hate me, I know. You can't fool me…you both can be happy when I'm gone. I'm gonna leave so I won't be around to cause any more trouble.... I'll go... heh heh..." her eyes tilted back in her head.

"Nobody wants you to go anywhere, Carole. Let's just calm down and think about it, here. What the hell are you gonna do, anyway, run into traffic? The fucking road is three blocks away and it's the middle of the night. You could probably lie on the centerline for an hour and the only thing to come around would be a snake or a gator. If that's what you want, have at it, you fucking crazy bitch."

"YOU BASTARD," she roared, struggling to her feet. "HAAEIEIAUUGGHH!!!"

She loosed a roundhouse left at my head like Joe Frazier's daughter on Quaaludes.

I dodged the blow and the force of the swing carried her fist into the wall. The impact elicited a scream befitting a wildebeest being pierced by a knitting needle. Gripping her hand and squeezing, she collapsed to the floor sobbing.

I figured that the evening's entertainment was over and suddenly felt very sorry. Sorry for every angry word and every smart-ass remark I'd made. I knelt down beside her and put my hand on the back of her neck. "Come on, Carole," I said, stroking gently, "Why don't you come to bed? Here, I'll help you."

I put my hands under her arms; she was mumbling incoherently, a dark metallic chuckle punctuating the rambling. I set my feet and lifted but about halfway up she shrieked and jerked out of my grasp. Her head snapped forward, her knees buckled, her body fell sideways and the side of her face smacked into the textured wall with a sickening thud.

Blood began to seep from her cheek as she scraped slowly down to the floor.

And then she was out cold.

I got a washcloth from the bathroom. I lifted her head and put the cloth on her face. All I could think of was escape.

Our little dance had ended up the same, once again. The madness seemed to be ratcheting up a notch. Strangely, though, I thought I could sleep. It seemed like the storm had run its course, at least until next time.

I lay down in bed with my hands balled up in tight fists. Many were my troubles and Carole was the least. That son of a bitch Douglas had my ass in a sling. It was amazing that I fell asleep. Sky Pilot must have been playing me the Sandman Blues on an opium-filled saxophone.

As is often the way with these domestic explosions, they're never quite over when you think they are.

I woke up about four a.m.; Carole wasn't in the bedroom. I checked her spot on the floor and she was gone. The washcloth, too. I was about ready to head out to the road and check the centerline, when I noticed the light seeping out below the bathroom door.

I slowly turned the knob; the door creaked as I pushed it open.

Blood on the mirror, blood in the tub, sink streaked red. Carole on the floor, head listing against the wall, bleeding wrist dangling lifelessly over the bathtub.

To my horrified surprise, she turned and looked up at me, a lunatic grin creeping across her bloody features: "Look, Keith, I did it. I did it for you." She lifted her arm and stared at it with glazed eyes. "Someone as nice as you shouldn't have to put up with someone like me. I've hurt you so. But don't worry. I've taken care of everything. You and Mike won't have to worry about me anymore."

She held up her wrist, proudly, smiling as the blood dripped down into the shallow tub.

Shock and panic hit me square in the chest. This time she had really done it. Blood was everywhere.

The voice came into my head: *Things are not what they seem. All that bleeds is not red.*

Very serenely, very surreal, I knelt down and grabbed Carole's bloody wrist. I pulled a towel off the wrack and rubbed at the incision.

It was really a series of dull scratches. Most of the blood, as best as I could determine, was coming from her facial scrapes and a cut inside her mouth that she had spread around with her fingers. Mixed with saliva and tears, the volume was increased by at least threefold.

"What did you use to cut yourself, Carole?"

She didn't answer but her eyes dropped down to the tiled floor and a broken piece of a beer bottle; it's semi-sharp edge enough to draw blood but not much else.

I wanted to stand up and shout, FAKER. WHY DIDN'T YOU AT LEAST USE ONE OF MY RAZORS AND DO THE JOB RIGHT? But instead, I soaked a towel in warm water and wiped her off, starting with her face and hair and working down. By the time I was done, it seemed like the scratches were already drying up. She'd have a few scabs but she'd get better. Her only scars would be emotional.

For me, the scar tissue was building up.

She was shaking softly but somewhat composed—resolved, I suppose. I took her in the bedroom and covered her up with the blankets. She tried to say something but her eyes turned back in her head.

I stood at the side of the bed. All I could do was shake my head and think, this is another fine mess you've gotten us into, just because you're so damn cute.

I went into Mike's room, tore off the bedspread and went back to the couch. I didn't bother pulling out the bed.

For hours it seemed like I was lying there and not sleeping but then I'd wake up and realize that I had been sleeping—and only dreaming that I wasn't.

Chapter Ten

Down and Dirty

And then things really got weird.

At first light, I got up and walked stiffly over to the double doors and peeked out the side of the curtain. Wind bounced a cigarette butt across the pavement and I felt cheap and dirty.

I walked over and looked in our bedroom; Carole was still unconscious. The red scratches on her face made me sad.

I started to feel sleepy so I went back to the couch and got flat. Something about the daylight made my anger recede.

I woke up to the pounding on the front door. I thought it was John, at first. I'd been dreaming that he was coming over and we were going to play tennis. I remember thinking that it was strange, as I walked to the door. Why would John want to play with a gimp?

I was reaching for the doorknob when something made me stop in my tracks. A vague realization was slowly forming.

I could smell that cop on the other side of the door, last night's booze oozing from his oversized pores. The stink was mixed in with cheap after-shave and a breath mint, maybe a Tic-Tac, to cover up the onions.

Man, I swear I could hear him breathing.

Three hard knocks rocked the door.

Moving agonizingly slow, I took silent, backward steps. My toes sweated on the shag carpet, every muscle fiber struggling for control. As I crept by the kitchen, the smell of roach poison hit me and a thundering headache took roost above my eyes.

Three more forceful and demanding knocks struck the door.

"Mr. And Mrs. Waverly, This is Lieutenant Douglas of the St. Petersburg police. Open this door, please."

If Carole didn't wake up and blow it, I figured I had a chance. I tiptoed around, grabbed the car keys and all the money I had—$17—and went into Mike's bedroom. I slid open the window and pushed at the edge of the screen. It popped out and fell quietly to the grass below. I peeked out and looked both ways like my mother always taught me to, then jumped out and walked quickly towards the laundry building. Once there, I would be out of the sight of anyone standing at my door. I could walk across through the back of the complex and make my way to the parking lot through the woods.

I got to the brush at the edge of the parking lot feeling pretty good, thanking Sky Pilot. Chuckling to myself, because even though the wolf was at my door, I was still going to make the big score.

The van was about thirty yards away, parked in the middle of a long row, between a Winnebago and a speedboat.

My plan was to move along the sidewalk until I got directly in line with the van and then turn towards it, walking between the cars for cover. The only problem, which I discovered about thirty feet from the bus, was that the keys in my pocket weren't the correct ones. The VW keys were still back on the wall in my kitchen. Big bummer.

I stopped at the back bumper of the van and peered anxiously back at my Volvo. There was a lot of open space between where I was standing and it.

Then I watched, stricken, as Douglas popped out from behind the building and went to a green Ford Crown Victoria parked right next to the Volvo. Fucking cop was dressed in the same clothes as the first time I had seen him.

Son of a bitch looked right at me.

What could I do but keep walking straight towards him like I was glad to see him and had no reason to be afraid? I had lied to cops before; I could do it again.

Douglas cocked his head back and hitched up his belt with both hands as he squinted at my sorry skulking ass. It's funny how cops can be the same height as you, maybe even a little shorter, and make it seem like they're bigger, like they're looking down at you.

I smiled. "Morning," I said. "Ain't seen you in a while.... What brings you by here so bright and early, Lieutenant Douglas? Myself, I've been out making sure that my son wasn't playing in the swamp, where we have forbidden him to go."

"I think you know why I'm here, Waverly. I told Carole last night about a video tape that I have in my possession, which clearly shows you ripping off Schwal's Department Store, in Clearwater. Which connects you with credit card fraud at Seigel's Department Store, also in Clearwater.... Didn't she tell you? I thought you northern boys were smart enough to take advantage of an opportunity when presented... didn't think you'd still be around."

"My wife didn't tell me about any video tape, Lieutenant. I was asleep when she came in. Us northern boys don't have to wait up for their wives. We know we've got nothing to worry about, so we sleep like babies. But I would be interested in seeing that tape you mentioned, because it's not me. You know how cheesy those security cameras can be."

"We can go down to the station and look at it together, Keith—you and me. How do you like that? We can watch it together, you and me—like buddies. It shouldn't take too long. Then, if it's not you, you'll be free to go."

An evil grin creased his porcine lips. He snorted, shook his head and took a toothpick from his coat pocket and jammed it in his teeth. His eyes narrowed: "Know any lawyers 'round here?"

"No. Ah, yeah... one, I think. But he's a good one, I've heard."

"Now we're going back to your place, Waverly, so you can tell Carole what's going on here. She'll want to know."

"My wife is sleeping. I prefer to leave her that way. If you need me at the station, I can call her from there. I do get one phone call, don't I?"

"Look, Waverly, let's go back to your apartment, now, quietly. I'd like to talk to Carole and explain the situation. Police courtesy."

"I don't think so."

"What's to stop me from dragging you back there and twisting your arm until you give me the key?"

"Cause I'll be screaming *police brutality* and *no warrant*—shit like that—as loud as I can yell. What do you think the neighbors will think of that?"

"Around here? This bunch of white trash? Half of 'em are perverts or drug addicts, anyway...they'd think it was just another average day in the life of one more stupid freak. Now let's go back to your place and maybe I'll forget where it was I knew you from, to hell with those fancy Jews at Schwal's. But you see now, Mr. Waverly," louder now, putting his hand on my back and pushing: "we received a call about a disturbance in your apartment and I must check on your wife to see if she is okay. All I need to do is have a look at your wife, sir."

Two young guys carrying golf bags stopped to gawk. Above us, on the second tier, a girl in a white robe leaned on the railing and stared, spooning ice cream out of a carton.

I'm sure there were more eyes prying but I was only seeing stars, by then. I knew that if Douglas got a look at Carole's face he'd kick my ass without stopping to ask questions.

"Okay, Lieutenant," I said. "I'll walk back there... no problem. But I'll tell you what. If you can get Carole to open the door, we can go in without a warrant. If not, you going to have to do what you're going to do to me and get on with it before my kid comes home. I really don't want him to see me getting dragged off to jail."

"What do think this is, dick head," hissing, like a giant snake, "a fucking monopoly game? I'm the one that makes the deals here."

Finally, a weak: "Who is it?"

"Lieutenant Douglas, ma'am, of the St. Petersburg Police Department." Taking on a deeper tone. "Is everything all right in there?"

"Everything's fine," she said, stronger.

"Please open the door, ma'am so I can see that you're okay. I need to make sure." His head was an inch from the door.

"Carole, honey," I said. "If you're not dressed decent you should know that there's people out here watching. You don't need to open the door until you're dressed, honey."

Douglas gave me a cop stare.

"Pig!" someone yelled from behind us. Douglas jerked his head around. Feet scuffled franticly on the loose gravel.

"Leave him alone," was shouted from another direction.

Douglas' face reddened. He turned back to the door. The lock clicked.

"It's unlocked," said the soft voice behind the door.

Douglas turned the handle and slowly pushed.

Carole was standing in the darkened hallway a few steps back from the door, at a slight angle to us, brushing her hair out.

Brushing it out so it dropped gently across her face on the side where the scratches were. The dimness and the angle of her head kept the wounds in the dark. She was wearing nothing but a white T-shirt, blue panties peaking provocatively, out the bottom.

"Lieutenant Douglas..." Carole cooed, "May I still call you Bob? As you can see, I'm doing just fine. But a girl needs her beauty rest, and I can't catch up on it with this door open and everybody staring at me like this." She lifted up one heel; toes arched on the floor.

I was going wild.

"Yeah, right, honey,' I said. "Me and the Lieutenant are going downtown to check on some tapes. It shouldn't very long, he says. But don't wait up. G'bye."

I waved and closed the door and looked square into Douglas' face. He seemed a little flustered. He grabbed my arm hard and squeezed. But then he released his grip and said, "Let's go," jaw muscles working.

He tried to smile as we walked by about a dozen of my gawking neighbors, half of whom I'd never seen before.

By the time we got to the car he was steaming. He pushed me into the backseat but didn't cuff me, then went around to the front seat and started her up. The air conditioning blew like hell.

"You're gonna pay for that, Waverly," he growled, boozy throated. "I was willing to cut you a break because I thought you were a pretty good guy. But after that little bit of grandstanding at your apartment, I have to tell you that I feel inclined to throw you in a cell and see how long I can hold you."

"I was only trying to protect my wife and family's dignity. What would you expect of me? You know those people—white trash, you said. They were like, at a sideshow at the fair, or something. You'd have done the same thing, in my position."

He looked over at me, studying. "Maybe. I sure wouldn't let my woman stand there half-naked like that, very long. I guess that's true. I'd a sure keep better control on my woman than that."

"Yeah, I suppose. You married?"

"None of your goddamn business."

"Sorry."

"I'll tell you one thing: You can't let a woman get the upper hand on you, get to controllin', things. You have to let her know who is boss no matter what it takes."

"So you do have a wife."

"I didn't say that."

Oh, I thought you did. I must have been mistaken."

"What I meant was, if I did have a wife."

"Oh. Have you got a thing for my wife, Lieutenant?"

"What do you mean, a thing? Am I trying to make a pass, is that what you're getting at?"

"Yeah, I guess."

"Listen to me, boy.... My interests in your wife are strictly protective—as a member of the police force. Truth is, she reminds me of my daughter."

"You have a daughter?"

"You ask too many questions, that's *my* job."

"So, if you have a daughter, you must have had a wife—or at least a woman. Chances are the daughter looks like her mother...."

"You're a real smart guy, huh? Fucking Einstein, huh."

"I just meant—"

"She left me after our daughter ran off."

"Your fucking daughter ran off? No shit."

"Don't you use that kind of language in the same sentence with my little girl. Never use those words when referring to any of my family, you follow me? You need to be reminded that this situation here is about you being in trouble—not my personal life, you hear?"

"I'm aware of that—just making conversation."

"I got some conversation for you, smart guy. How would you like to blow me—if I promise to let you go, in return? What do you think of that?"

"Blow you? Jesus Christ, are you serious?"

"Damn straight I'm serious. I'm sayin' if you put those big Yankee lips of yours around my hog and do the dirty work, I'll let you go free."

"Oh man, are we really getting down to this? I can't believe this shit."

I could feel his eyes boring into me. All I could do was stare straight ahead. I guess I was ready to do anything. My face was burning and sweat poured from my armpits. The silence grew thick and oppressive. Seconds seemed like minutes.

"Nah, boy," he said suddenly, throwing his head back to guffaw. "Just testin' you. Seein' if you really were as limp as you look."

My body sunk back into the seat.

"What exactly does that mean?"

"It means you got that curly black hair and those high cheek-bones—those sad doggie eyes—just like the swishes. Except you got shoulders and biceps like a football player. You're a cute one, you are. They're gonna love your white ass up at Raiford. Niggers'll make a damn good French maid out of you, in no time."

"Now look, Lieutenant, there must be something I can do, here. I mean, if you'll really let me go in exchange for a blow job, I suppose I can stomach it."

"Get off of it, cutie pie. I was only testin' you, I said. But, I do have a proposition of sorts. I've been thinking that you might be the right man for a special project of mine. One that's coming up real soon."

"What might that be?" I said, the wrenching in my gut, changing tempo.

"Well, my boy, it seems that some big shot over at the mayor's office got propositioned by a queer down at The Pier the other day. He raised hell about it with his buddy the commish—and these two geniuses came up with a plan: They want us to set up a sting operation down in queer park—Operation Fruit Fly, they're calling it. You like that? Anyway, son, I'm thinkin' that you'd be perfect for an important role in this little operation. I'm thinking that you could be the main man, boy."

"I don't get it. Where do I fit in? What the hell are you talking about?"

"You make good fag bait. Like trolling for 'gators with some nice fresh chicken.... Like throwing out a big golden shiner to catch a bigmouth bass. 'Cept now we'll be using a golden ass to catch a bigmouth cocksucker."

He laughed like a jacked-up pig, obviously enjoying his joke a lot more than I was.

"C'mon man, you have to use cops for that shit," I said, grasping. "They don't allow citizens to do stuff like that. Even I know that. It's not exactly what the courts would consider community service, I don't think."

"Yes it is, boy. You'd be doing the community a real service. Should see some of those sissies down there, preening about in public like that. Working each other over... making a spectacle... it's an eyesore to the good citizens of the Suncoast. We have to keep this town nice for the tourists and visitors, you understand."

"I heard queers spend a lot of money. Look at Key West, for Christ sake. Isn't that good for the city?"

"People around here don't like that kind of carrying on. This is the Bible Belt, son. There's a reason they call it that."

"Real righteous place, all right."

"Listen, son, don't you worry. I ain't gonna waste you on your average, everyday fag. I got a special little private job in mind for you, one that takes a guy like you. Ain't no ordinary queer I got in mind, you understand, there's one special fruit I want to pick. This prick can smell a cop a mile away from so many years of living in Los Angeles. We need a special ol' shiner minnow like you to get this cocksucker to bite."

"Gee, I'm flattered that you hold me in such high regard. But aren't you overlooking the possibility that it's not me in that video tape you say you saw?"

"I never forget a face, Keith. That's why I'm such a goddamn good cop. I got you like a 'coon in the flashlights, and you know it. Only thing between you and jail is me, so you better start thinkin' about things. You see; you take care of business for me and your record will stay clean. I mean if there ain't already some black marks. I hoped to keep this little thing personal, you know. Just between you and me. That way we can all go home at the end of the job and forget we ever knew each other."

"I'd like nothing more."

It was then that it hit me: If Douglas just wanted to arrest me he'd have done it already and not offered this deal. I was indeed something special to the twisted bastard. I decided to work it.

"Tell me, Sergeant, does this queer have a name? And what is this special passion that you mentioned?"

"All in due time, boy, all in due time. First I'm gonna prove to you that I ain't just whistling Dixie."

Then we were pulling into the precinct lot. I had no choice but to play along until I could find a little leverage.

As we walked together through the station doors, I got that claustrophobic feeling. Sweat beaded on my forehead and I began to shake.

Walking down the lousy black linoleum floor, eyes on my shoes, tagging along like Douglas' dog, I was wondering how my life had taken this latest turn into the shit house. Then I swore I heard somebody calling my name and laughing. I looked behind me and there was no one there.

Douglas led me over to his cubicle in the jammed precinct room and had me sit down at his desk on a stiff, plastic chair, behind a stack of papers. It was hot. I felt like a mullet in a school of sharks. A plastic ashtray, filled with butts, smelled stale and disgusting.

Douglas left me there and walked out of the room.

Nausea rising, I stared at the side of his battered, metal desk, not wanting to see anyone. No telling when one of those cops from the bar would walk in. That's the way things seemed to be going. Sometimes you get on a run of bad luck and the momentum just carries you along; you can't stop it.

Douglas came striding confidently back. He had a large, black cassette in his hand. He sat down across from me at his desk, leaned over until his face was on my side of the desk and spoke quietly.

"This tape here is where we're going to find your pretty face, Waverly. I had them dig it out of the files for me, on your behalf."

"Gosh, thanks."

He smiled arrogantly. "We got a little room down the hall with a brand new machine that plays these things. Come on down and watch a little movie with me. I've already seen it, and it's a good one. Catches you with your hands in the cookie jar, boy. By the way Keith, that was sure clever, you hiding in the blue jeans like that." He slapped the cassette down in front of me and swelled up his chest. "What do you think, boy?"

I think you've got me, you fucking asshole.

"I'm not sure what to think."

"What if we were to look in your closet at home, think we might find a T-shirt that says "Mr. Flood's Party" on it? Not many a them around, I bet. Think that'd help, if we found that? Fucking thing, though, it don't really make any difference. Juries down here don't give a rip, son. Don't give a fat fuck. They'll convict you as long as the guy on the screen is the same color as you. They enjoy watchin' trash like you go down; makes 'em feel like they're doin' some good for the world. Besides that, they believe anything that they see on the goddamn TV."

We went down the sweaty hall to another sweaty room where Douglas shoved the tape in the machine and pretty soon we were watching me in action.

I didn't need to see much before I had something to say: "I think I need a lawyer. I want to make my phone call."

"Keith, son...you lawyer-up on me and I'll have to throw you in a cell. We can keep you here for longer than you want to stay, I guarantee. If you just hold on and listen to my offer, this tape might get lost from the file. Shit, anything can happen around here."

"What choice have I got?"

"About as much as you deserve."

"Fair enough. What's this deal you were talking about?"

"Ever hear of Von Rokken, son?"

"The rock band? Of course. What do they have to do with this? I did hear that they were coming to Tampa pretty soon."

"That's right, they are. You're up on this stuff, boy. You like that band, Keith?"

"Not particularly. Some of their stuff is okay, I guess."

"You like that Jew boy singer they got?"

"Danny Lee Neil is a Jew? He's got blonde hair, for Christ sake."

"Ever take a look at the schnoz on that fairy motherfucker."

"I guess not. What do you mean, fairy? He's got women all the time. I mean he's the sexual attraction for the band, isn't he? Look at all the young chicks that—"

"Shut up. That's enough about that. Sure he gets a lot of women." Angry now: "Young girls too young to know any better. They follow his switch-hitting ass around the country and then move out to California so he can turn them into slaves. Son... I don't have to tell you about how it is out in California, now do I? Everybody knows that everybody is dorking everybody, out there. Don't matter who or what you are, just so long as you're wet and warm, to those people. Hell's bells, they got sex clubs and wife swapping and all that stuff as an everyday thing. Course maybe you hippie people are into that sorta thing, even up in Minnesota."

"Unfortunately not," I mumbled.

"What'dya say?"

"Fortunately not. We're clean and forthright up in Minnesota. But let me get this straight. You want me to play fag bait for Danny Lee Neil? How is that going to work? Gonna set us up on a blind date? Do I win a police contest or something—A Night With Danny Lee Neil?"

"Cut out the wise-ass crap. I got it on good reliable information that Mr. Neil frequents The Pier when he's in town as well as a certain public restroom known to be a gathering place for the limp-wristed set. I've got someone on the inside to tell us when he goes out, and then we put a tail on him. Soon as it looks like he's on the prowl, I let you loose—you'll be wearing a wire—and you get him to make a grab for your schlong. That's about it."

"You know, Lieutenant, in the past, strangers in bars have suspected that I'm a cop. I've had it happen to me, many times. This one guy even told me that he thought I was a cop. I swear to god. Chances are Neil will get the same vibe."

"Not on any force I've ever been on do you look like a cop."

"What do you mean by that?"

"Nothing. Never mind. Quit changing the subject. You gonna do this or am I gonna throw you in a cell? I can find a real nice one, if ya want me to, maybe one where some wino puked in the corner and shit his self, besides. Maybe we got a PCP head trying to chew through his straitjacket, or a drag queen. Ever seen a drag queen in the fucking morning, boy? Send shivers down your goddamn spine.... Now what's it gonna be?"

It was already sending shivers down my spine.

"I need to think about it."

"Think about it? You can think about it while I book you for suspicion of robbery and possibly murder. Never have solved that bar murder over in Clearwater Beach...you'd be as good as any suspect 'bout now." He stood up. "Let's go then, Waverly. Let's go sign your name on the dotted line. Sorry it had to be this way. That poor wife of yours and that boy... he's gonna be disappointed in his Daddy, I'm afraid."

"Sit down, Lieutenant, please. I'll do it."

He sat down.

"My son can be proud of me when I tell him, don't ya think, Lieutenant? And maybe then, he'll stop listening to "Running with Satan," over and over. Can't you hear it, man: I seduced Danny Lee Neil, son. Are you proud of me? It's all right, though—I really got him arrested—that make you feel better? What the hell you got against Neil, anyway, Lieutenant?"

"Stop yer whinin'. Name like that makes big headlines, that's all. Makes the department look good."

"Why do I get the feeling that there's more to this? Like there's something personal going on for you?"

"Just trying to improve myself, son. Move up the ladder. That's about it." His neck turned red. "Now suppose I take you back home and we'll discuss the details on the way. I'll just put this here movie in my drawer and lock it up, for now. You like Steak and Shake?"

"Ah, yeah—uh—yeah."

"Whattaya say we go and get ourselves a nice steak-burger-with-cheese and a big chocolate malted—on me? It's almost noon."

"Yeah, my final meal before servitude."

"Quit yer whinin, boy. You don't know how lucky you are that ol' Uncle Bob has taken you under his wing."

I always did like Steak and Shake. And despite Douglas' presence, the steakburgers and fries tasted good. For a second there, I even thought that he could be a likeable guy—if maybe we were in a parallel universe.

The resultant heartburn told me different.

We didn't talk much at Steak and Shake. Douglas just pounded down the food and commented on what a fine woman Carole was. How I should feel real lucky.

That was exactly what I was feeling right then, lucky. Lucky, to be under the thumb of a power-tripping cop with a sadistic streak. Yeah, you bet.

After we ate we got back in the car and Douglas started filling me in on the details. He had this plan all thought out. I could see the excitement on his face when he pictured busting Von Rokken's lead vocalist.

There was someone in the band's entourage that hated the singer and was going to keep us advised of Neil's prowling hours. The arrangement with the roadie had, allegedly, been set up by Douglas' cousin. He had been at the scene of Douglas' daughter's apparent suicide, out in L.A.

I admit I was a little shocked. I don't know what it was that made Douglas open up to me. Maybe he really did like me. Maybe it was the food. Maybe he was one of those guys who gets high on food. He just started blabbing the whole story. Even shed a tear or two. I couldn't believe it.

I found it all pretty hard to swallow. Everything seemed too pat.

But I must admit I could see the pain on his face when he told me about "his lovely daughter" and how she ran off with Danny Lee Neil after a Tampa concert, just two years ago. How those evil bastards in Von Rokken got her into drugs and group sex and all them other filthy things that they do out in California. How the poor, sweet child had finally become so down and out from heroin and abuse that Neil had abandoned her on the street one night; left her there and drove off to his "fag boyfriend's fuck pit." Didn't so much as even bother to call an ambulance for the sick child.

She died alone on that dirty, shabby sidewalk.

"You'd think you'd want to kill him for that," I had said.

"Funny things can happen to a Jew queer when he goes to jail in Florida," Douglas answered back.

That part had me a little shaky. Neil wasn't *that* bad, for Christ sake—not bad enough to be killed, anyway. For all that I knew; the daughter might have been a raving nympho, begging every rock star that came through town to fuck her in the ass and give her drugs.

There sure was enough of that type around. Bitches would walk right by you like you didn't exist if you didn't play rock and roll. A guy didn't even have a chance with those chicks until after the band got sick of them. Who wants that?

Reminds me of the time I was backstage at an Allman Brothers concert. Man, there was this beautiful, coked-up chick back there. She comes up to me and starts asking weird questions, like if I knew how to get out of the country in a hurry and shit. But that's another story.

I imagined that Von Rokken would probably fade away if their singer were caught in such a scandal. They surely couldn't continue with another singer.

I, Keith Waverly, could have an effect on the world of rock and roll. I would be the dude who drove Von Rokken down.

Far out. Far fucking out.

Douglas dropped me off at the entrance to Twin Lakes. "I'll be in touch," he said, severely, looking me in the eyes.

I closed the car door without saying anything and walked in from the road. Went through my door to find Carole's anxious, apologetic face. Also waiting for me was a letter, postmarked Jamaica, with no return address.

I opened it with sweaty fingers and read the hand-printed note inside:

Dear Keith,

Schmidty and I are having a great time, as expected. The weather has turned out fine. We will be arriving back in Florida on the tenth. Anxious to get back. See you at the airport, as we planned. The flight should arrive sometime in the early evening. Please be on time. —Dan

So there it was—the arrival date—exactly two days in the future. In forty-eight hours, I had to be miles up the West Coast of Florida, ready to meet the boat.

To say that I didn't know what to do next would be a vast understatement. Basically, I was fucked.

Fucked in the ass. Isn't that what they always say?

What in the hell was with all these homosexual scenarios that were sticking to me like a fuchsia jockstrap, anyway? First, it was Peter McKay, back in Zenith City. And now, here I was, about to go trolling for celebrity dong in Florida.

What was it about me that brought this stuff on? Karmic retribution from a past life? The Sky Pilot? Jesus? My ass?

I didn't have much time to ponder. The longer I let it spin around the farther I got from the answer. Finally, I said the hell with it.

I was fed up to my eyeballs with drama, psychodrama and psychosis. The whole family reuniting thing had become a nightmarish joke, just another bad idea of mine. The best I had felt in weeks was when Carole sent me out for Tampax and I realized she wasn't pregnant.

The only thing I could do was get ready for the trip, come hell or high rollers.

That afternoon I went out and rented a small, covered trailer to tow behind the VW, as per my instructions. Then I stocked up the van with some food, first-aid supplies, and fuel for the Coleman lanterns.

The Von Rokken concert was scheduled for Saturday night and was sold out. If luck, was with me, I'd be gone by Friday. I wondered when Mr. Neil's alleged proclivity for penis would raise its ugly head, so to speak.

I'd think about what might happen to Carole—and especially Mike—if I split. The whole deal would spin around inside my head like a mixing bowl full of radioactive sludge.

I began to waver. I started to think; maybe I should stay in town and get the legal thing off my back, cooperate with Douglas and his bizarre scenario. Schmidt and Bagley were resourceful guys; they could take care of themselves…they would understand….

But what about all that money, the stuff that makes the world go round, world go round?

If I met the boat, chances were good that I would have the

bread to leave the state. The cops probably wouldn't chase me very far for the credit card scam.

On the other hand, you could never tell what a guy like Douglas might do, what agencies he might contact in trying to run me down. One thing was clear, if I stood up Schmidt and Bagley, I'd never have another shot at that kind of opportunity. I'd be black-balled, for sure.

Eventually, I chose the decision-making process that I was becoming used to: The wait-and-see-what-happens-and-then-do-what-you-have-to-do-to-save-your-ass method.

Friday morning, after a lousy night's sleep, I made my decision. If I left in the afternoon, after Carole and Mike got home, I'd get to the spot in plenty of time.

I went in the bedroom and started to pack a bag. Then I sat down on the bed and lit up a Kool and decided that waiting for Johnny Law to come was a better course of action. I figured if I got Douglas off our back, we could stay together as a family.

So many men were running from their kids; I didn't want to be another one.

I decided to stay the course until I either busted Danny Lee Neil or Von Rokken left town. I paced around the room and smoked and drove myself nuts. Mixed that in with the occasional peek out the glass doors and the random walk to check the van.

It must have been around three o'clock when the phone rang. I picked it up expecting trouble and got it.

"You better get ready, Waverly, you're going to work."

My decision had been made for me.

"Lieutenant, are you kidding me? Jesus, not now, Carole and I are—"

"Listen, Waverly, our man says he's headed for The Pier. You'll have to tell Carole that you're going to be gone for the weekend."

"Are you shitting me, why so long?"

"In case he don't take the bait on the first pass. We got you a nice hotel room on the beach, at the Don CeSar, just in case we have to wait for the cat to come out and play. He'll come out eventually, though, don't you worry. You just be there when I get there, boy. Don't try anything stupid."

"Wouldn't dream of it, Lieutenant, I'll just go and pack a bag."

But I sure was dreaming of a lot of other things. Like bashing in his ignorant goddamn head with my baseball bat when he came through the front door. But man, I couldn't have Mikey seeing things like that, he was too young.

"Just make sure you got clean underwear, boy. Unless you don't want to wear any, for the sake of realism," he chuckled. "We got everything else you'll need. Got some nice duds for you to wear."

"You're picking out my clothes?"

"Me and some of the boys from vice."

"I can hardly wait to see what you've got for me."

"You're gonna be good, son, you wait and see. Pretty soon you'll be able to forget this ever happened, you'll see."

"Sure Lieutenant, sure."

I wrote a note to Carole, explaining the situation as best I could, put the pen in my pocket and waited for Douglas. When he knocked on the door I grabbed my shaving kit and walked out quickly.

"Don't be so goll darn hang-dog, boy, he said, hovering in the doorway like the devil himself. "This'll be over sooner than you can whistle Dixie."

"I wish."

"Our man says Neil is on his way, the pecker is on the prowl, so to speak. Even stopped to buy some KY jelly, he says. We're gonna get you down there in just a few minutes and set you loose."

"Sounds like a great plan, Lieutenant."

Then we were at the side of his Crown Vic and I was getting in the front seat.

"Throw yourself in back, Waverly," Douglas said sternly.

"Can't have anyone seein' ya an' thinkin' that yer part of the force. And while your back there; put these on."

He tossed back a pair of ultra-short, cut-off blue jeans and a white, sleeveless undershirt. The better to show my muscles I assumed.

Driving down Fourth Street, Douglas was humming. Sounded like the Notre Dame fight song.

I saw no escape. I struggled into the clothes and imagined that I looked like Freddy Mercury on steroids.

"You do any fishing back in Minnesota, Waverly?" Douglas said, out of the blue.

"A little. I like to fish."

"Lotta good fishing around here.... You oughtta take your boy fishin' someday."

"I'd like to."

"And you'll be able to with a clean slate, if you pull this deal off."

"What do you mean, *if* I pull this off? You never said I had to be successful—I mean—I can't guarantee that the son of a bitch is going to like me, for Christ sake. I'm not very good at that kind of shit. I mean, with women—you know."

"Well, son, maybe you'll try a little harder knowing that you have to succeed. Besides, fags are less fussy. They'll stick their dick in a hole in the wall, for god's sake. You'll just have to wiggle that booty of yours in the right way. That's what the niggers say, you know—booty."

"For sure."

"Yessir, boy, our Mr. Neil is about to meet his next cornhole."

"Jesus Christ.... Please, Lieutenant, no more of that kind of talk—please? I need to be light and joyful looking, for this dork. Dare I say it—gay? So please stop depressing me or I'm going to have to cry and ruin everything. No one would want me if I'm all puffy-eyed and sorrowful looking."

"Cut the shit."

"And I can't wear these clothes, man. I got a little gut on me now, since I can't play tennis, anymore. I need something to cover it up. Something flowing...."

"I'll find you flowing. You'll be flowing your wise ass up to Raiford—to improve race relations in this state."

"I'm just getting in character."

"You're a natural."

Fuck you, you ugly, fat bastard.

"Well thank you, sweetie."

"You got your hot pants on, Waverly, now put this on." He threw back a loop of elasticized cord with what I assumed was a tiny microphone on it. "The fruit is heading for the loom and we're going to be there, waiting. Be sure you get that wire on right. The thing goes in the back; you snap it in the front."

"You sure you wouldn't like to do it for me, Lieutenant Hunky-pie?"

"Shut up and get ready. I told you, he's hot to trot."

"Man, how do you know where he's going? Maybe he's got a sick aunt in Sarasota or something."

"Our man knows this guy. Says this is the way he operates. Says when he's on the way for some *Jose* The Pier is his spot. We got a man on him, anyway—we'll know."

The singer and I were on a collision course, like two hunks of rock in a meteor shower... like two falling stars....

Oh, Christ.

As we turned into palm-lined parking area my head felt like the top of a volcano ready to erupt.

We rolled to a stop next to a big old palm tree and a strange thing happened: Serenity washed over me. From within or without, I could not tell. I was pumped and excited but strangely calm. Suddenly the sun felt warm and the sparkling blue water made me smile.

Maybe it was because I was working for the St. Pete Chamber

of Commerce: Operation Fishes for Swishes. By god, man, I was determined to do a good job.

Douglas made me go over to a park bench that faced the bay and wait for his signal. Shiny sailboats bounced on the choppy blue water. A pink condo complex on the far shore sparkled in its hugeness, reminding me of the life that I was missing.

It was a busy day at The Pier. That was the official name for the place: The Pier.

Down at the far end of the concrete structure (an actual pier) was a big yellow building, containing an observation deck, shops and concessions. Gulls and other sea birds circled and called while tourists of all ages milled around.

Behind me was a local history museum and to my left about fifty yards was a public toilet; an older brick building that resembled a miniature Gothic church. About fifty yards or so to my right was another public toilet, a faded, green, cinderblock box.

I was to keep any eye out for Neil. Douglas was camped on the northern fringe of the park, close to the gothic toilet.

After minutes of trying to be one with a gliding sea bird, allowing my spirit to fly along, I caught sight of Douglas' thinning pate peeking out from behind a stand of exotic greenery. He was gesturing for me to come over.

I got reluctantly up from the bench and walked slowly along the shoreline in his direction.

"He's in the park," Douglas hissed, as soon as I came within earshot. "He's in the park. His car is in the lot. He's walking down the pier, on the far side. You gotta go over there and flirt."

"I ain't fucking flirting with the son of a bitch."

"Just get your ass over there. He's got a red shirt on."

I turned and walked slowly up the pier. Lots of people with cameras and bright clothes milled around the concession area. A huge yacht and a smaller boat were tied to a wooden dock on the western edge.

I saw that famous blonde mane blowing in the sea breeze, those tanned arms and the red muscle shirt.

He was strolling casually along, looking out at the water from behind large, dark sunglasses, occasionally stopping to check out the passers-by, his head bouncing as he moved.

I headed straight for the entrance to the big yellow building at the tip, knowing he couldn't go in without seeing me. I leaned against the side of the building and gazed across the water at the long strip of land that was Clearwater and St. Petersburg Beach. Speedboats circled and buzzed.

Part of my ass was actually sticking out the bottom of the goddamn cut-offs.

I had no choice but to wait there and let the people gawk. It was a surprise, to me, that I hadn't already been arrested by some rogue vice cop.

No such luck for me, instead, I had to endure the stares of tourists and their children. I could only imagine what those midwesterners were saying to their little ones: *Don't look over there at that man, kids. Why not, Daddy? Because that's a genuine Florida ho-mo-sex-u-al, honey. How can you tell, Daddy? Can't ya see how his patute hangs out of his shorts, boy?*

I looked around to see if I could pick out the other cop, the one that had tailed our man. I thought I had him pegged: muscular six-footer with short, dark hair and a mustache wearing jeans and a yellow polo shirt and hanging back on the edge of the palm trees near the foot of the pier.

Neil was moving slowly, eating something from a multi-colored bag. It might have been sunflower seeds; looked like he was throwing the shells in the ocean.

I would have checked my watch—but I didn't have one.

I walked over to the edge of the wooden docking area and spread my arms across the railings, showing off my biceps. I turned my head slowly and watched the red shirt and the tight white bellbottoms cross the street to the east-side walkway. I didn't know whether I should follow him or wait. I looked down toward the circle of palm trees and saw the cop pointing me in the direction of the flowing blonde hair.

I dutifully crossed over the road, staying near the tip of the pier, in hopes that Neil would come my way.

He got to the other side, stopping to lean on the railing. I did the same, about twenty yards down, thrusting out my hip and staring at him.

Shaking his head from side to side like he was hearing music, he turned in my direction.

The wind blew his hair over the side of his face, covering all but the tip of his nose. I thrust out my hip even further.

He started walking away. At the end of the bridge he turned, shook his blonde mane like a horse and stared back at me.

I knew that was my signal.

I went after him; my white legs and tight clothes a testimony to my strangeness.

My worst fears were once again confirmed: He was loitering around the green, blockhouse toilet.

He pulled a white, silken cap, like the kind jockeys wear, from his pocket and put it on. Then he preened toward me, a cigarette dangling on the end of a bent wrist.

I was really concerned about my white legs. Would they turn on a California guy?

I was about twenty yards away when he decided to play hard-to-get, turning and giving me a lingering stare and another toss of his hair. Then he walked around back of the toilet to the water's edge.

I followed as he sashayed to the other restroom, the gothic one, and went through the door that said "Men" up above it.

I wondered why it was that homosexuals had a fondness for public restrooms and steam baths and such. I mean, you don't see many guys hustling chicks at the women's public toilets.

At least Neil had chosen the building with the best architecture; that was something.

My reverie was interrupted when Douglas stepped out from behind a stand of eucalyptus and waved me toward the toilet, with an angry slashing of his arm.

Like I wasn't already in the toilet....

I walked cautiously through the door. The place looked like a fucking Steak and Shake: black and white tiles on the floor and black and white marble walls. There were three sinks against the wall to my right, three black-painted stalls in front of me and three urinals against the far wall, to my left. Above the sinks was a leaded glass window, spun halfway open. There was a sign on the wall: No Clothes Changing in Men's Room.

I walked toward the urinals. Christ if I didn't catch sight of those bright, white bellbottoms beneath the door of stall number two. Silver, pointy-toed, snakeskin boots sticking out from under.

Barman, bring some liquor, another round of brew. My future lies waiting behind stall number two.

The door was slightly open. I couldn't make myself look in. The air smelled dank and sour. Suddenly I was overwhelmed, turned into a helpless kid. Flashbacks of Mrs. Olson's bedroom came flooding in. Hideous laughter echoed in my head.

I watched in horrible fascination as the boots dragged across the floor, moving wider apart.

I went to a urinal and pretended to take a whiz.

No one came in the building; nothing changed. Those snakeskin boots weren't made for walking.

I could sense Douglas lingering outside like a fat viper. I could sense his impatience. If he could see behind the stall door, he'd be claming his prize, his headline—his revenge. Whatever the hell he was after.

This was not the time to be faint of heart. I walked to the first stall and went inside. I sat on the stool. Next to me, the squeaking toilet seat and thick breathing got louder.

I began to pull toilet paper from the roll. It was one of those rollers where you can only get a few sheets at a time or the stuff rips.

I struggled out about eight sheets of tissue and folded them together, took the pen from my pocket and wrote the word COPS, in big bold letters. Then I climbed up onto the toilet and stood up, leaning over into stall number two.

I didn't want to look but I had to.

Sure enough, the dude was squeezing the snake.

He stared up at me with glazed eyes. I showed him the paper and put my finger against my lips in the signal for quiet, pointing my thumb toward the door.

Panic crossed his face and he dropped his wand.

I was looking hard—at his face.

Something was wrong with the picture: The nose was too big and the hair was thinning and I could see dark roots. This jack-off looked ten years older than Danny Lee Neil, what the hell was going on?

I panicked, jumped down from the toilet, scrambled around and pushed open the door to stall number two. The dude was standing, zipping up. I pulled up my shirt, showed him the wire. Again I put my finger to my lips.

I said, "Hi there," ripping off the wire at the same time. He stared blankly at me, confused, as I looped the tiny microphone over the stall, went in the other room, climbed up on the sinks and pulled myself up to the tall narrow window. Those Goths sure knew how to make a toilet.

I was half way out the window when I heard singing coming from behind me. Damn near jumped out of my skin:

I'm yer candy man, baby, got yer sugar right here... Yes, I'm yer candy man, baby, I stay sweet all night long.

Dude was crooning into the cop wire. What a fuck stick....

I pulled my legs through and jumped to the ground. Brushed myself off and took a look around. No one seemed to have noticed my unusual exit. Maybe escaping from the shithouse was a common thing around there. Douglas, I knew, was in his car, on the other side of the toilet, listening to the wire.

I walked toward the building at the tip of the pier, keeping the restroom between Douglas and I. I hoped that the crooner—whoever he was—was still busy with his vocal renderings. With any luck, he was doing "Running with Satan."

I was halfway up the pier when I heard Douglas screaming from behind the shithouse. I took off running, pain or no pain, as the other cop popped out from behind the palm trees, walkie-talkie in hand.

My only hole, my only window of possibility, was the water.

I could run into the water and start swimming. But I was never much good at that.

I veered right and booked it for the dock on the western edge. The cop was about fifty yards behind and closing fast. Riding high on adrenaline, I was feeling no pain. I dodged a young couple pushing a kid in a stroller and kept running—and looking. Looking for an avenue of escape, another window....

Come on Sky Pilot: SHOW ME THE GODDAMN WAY!

The cop was twenty yards behind and closing fast, when BANG, there it was: A boat gliding slowly up, a twenty-footer with two beautiful black Mercs on the back and one old guy at the helm: One skinny old guy standing up to get a look at the dockage.

I swore I could feel the love coming down from the shining blue sky.

As the old bastard came alongside the dock I sprinted toward him. He must have thought I was some kind of Chamber of Commerce welcoming committee.

Pelicans scattered every which way as I hit the last board like a long jumper going for the gold.

I flew through the air; my feet hit the deck and my shoulder slammed into the old man's chest. He fell backward and we both tumbled down. Trying desperately to break his fall, the old boy grabbed at the wheel and veered us away from the dock.

The cop caught only air and salt water trying to duplicate my leap.

I jumped up and banged down the throttle while the old man struggled to his feet. He grabbed at my shoulders from behind and tried to pull me away from the wheel. I pulled back the throttle, spun around and bum-rushed the poor guy into the briny. Didn't have time to throw a float.

Slamming down the stick and bearing hard a port, there was a whole big ocean surrounding me. Panicking, I did what most fugitives do—headed for home.

I swung north, up into the bay. I knew that the water went all the way up to the Derby Lane Greyhound Track near my home. Many times I had looked down at the water from the road. I knew there was a big, three smokestack, power plant down there.

I took one last look back and saw the cop pulling the old man out of the water. Now I could escape in peace.

Man, how those Mercurys roared. The sun glinted sharply off the swirling azure and indigo and I was flat-out flying, skipping like a stone. Keeping the throttle on full bore, I barreled north along the St. Petersburg shoreline. Off to starboard, the Tampa peninsula stretched out like a giant cigar.

It was an easy run to where I could see the three smokestacks belching out crud. But I couldn't find an opening into Bayou Grande. Then I cruised around the tip of a small island and the shore magically opened up in front of me.

I let the boat drift while I lay down on the floor and changed into the bright green polo shirt and green and white-checkered shorts with the white belt that I'd discovered beneath the bow. After putting the light blue canvas pork pie hat on my head and tossing the fag garb in the drink, I was ready to continue my journey.

Inside the bay, I planed by glistening, glassy homes with massive privacy walls in front and boat docks stretching out from shore. A few moored sailboats seemed frozen on the calm, flat water. A baseball stadium loomed in the distance. Up ahead, on the far shore, the power plant was busily polluting.

I slowed down as I came to a narrow channel, praying that you didn't need a secret password to get through. I drifted along and eventually the canal widened into a small bay. I jammed the throttle back down. No sense in wasting a beautiful day on the water.

Blowing along, throwing out big tails of spray, I wasn't thinking much about tides or tidal banks or anything but my escape. I did, however, notice a clearly defined line between the brilliant blues and greens of the water that I was skimming across and the muddy brown water where I sought to go.

In the brown part, wading birds pecked slowly along on their spindly legs as far out as a hundred yards from shore.

I knew from experience that when the water ahead of you is a different color than the water you're in, there's a reason for it. Either there's something on the surface, like a school of baitfish or a bug slick—or something under the surface—like a sand bar, a reef or a sunken island.

I didn't get three blocks into the brown water before the keel caught sand.

Slammed me to a dead halt. My chest smashed into the steering wheel. The motors kicked up, rudely; the props spun madly, helplessly. Engines roared in disgust.

I switched off the key and the two black beauties gurgled to a silent halt. Cursing myself for being such a stupid asshole, I looked over the side and instantly grasped why there were no other boats around.

Guessed it to be about a foot of water laced with what seemed to be waste from the power plant.

I climbed over the side and slid into the briny. It was warm.

My feet hit the slimy bottom. I sank up to my crotch. I flailed at the boat; my fingers grazed the gunwale. Hot bile rose up my esophagus as the *Luvin' Arms* floated delicately past my outstretched hand.

My legs were stuck in the ooze as if held by a giant magnet. All kinds of imaginary sea creatures swam through my mind and up my shorts.

I pulled and struggled and sweated, ready to scream, until one foot finally popped out of the muck and I moved forward. I was able to lean out over the water slightly and fight the other foot free from its manacle. Each lift of a leg was like pulling tree trunks from cement. Sea lice and tiny leeches attached themselves to my insanely itching skin.

By leaning forward and doing a manic breaststroke/doggie paddle with a frog kick, I kept up enough momentum to stay moving. It took me forever to cover a quarter mile.

I was maybe twenty yards from dry land when the bottom changed color to a deathly concrete gray.

I crawled onto the hard bottom, babbling like a baby.

"I made it," I was saying in disbelief. "Made it made it made it. Huh huh ha ha. Fuckin' A. Goddamn made it—Jesus Jesus Jesus."

Exhausted and breathing hard, I crawled on shore and leaned my torso against a rotting tree trunk. The ground stunk in a sulphurous, sickly way. My nerves were pins and needles; purple leeches stuck to me everywhere.

I couldn't afford to stay and tan very long.

After about five minutes of heavy breathing and feeble attempts at grooming my hair and clothes, I started down the shoreline towards the far end of the bay. I could see some people fishing down where the highway came close to the water. They must not have noticed me struggling. But in this town, you never could tell; people just didn't give a shit.

Between the anglers and I was a stand of actual trees: leafy, deciduous trees. Near as I could figure, behind those trees was a hill that led up to Highway 92: The road that I used to take to the Circle K for donuts and a peek at the girlie magazines.

I imagine the tourists and others driving by me as I emerged from the trees must have figured I was just one more of the many ragged-ass vagabonds limping daily into Florida from all over the map. They probably assumed that I was only another wandering, dirty man looking for something that I'd never find.

Those people in the cars, instead of checking out what the hell a soaking wet guy is doing walking down the road barefoot, couldn't turn their heads away fast enough. They didn't want to see what was in my eyes.

As I walked painfully along, I couldn't help but think that I should've taken the boat up to the Howard Frankland Bridge then beached it and walked back to Twin Lakes through the swamp. But there was no time for regrets or back-tracking.

Limping into the parking lot of the Circle K, water dripping off my sodden outfit, I badly needed a dime for the phone. I decided to panhandle, what the hippies used to call "spare changing."

You know the drill, people are walking by and you smile and ask them if they've got any spare change. I hoped that my country club outfit—soaking wet and mud splattered or not—could be worked to my advantage. Maybe people would think I was a golf pro down on his luck... maybe an insurance salesman whose boat had sprung a leak... perhaps a tourist who'd been mugged on his way to the golf course....

Strolling casually, I slid up and leaned against the yellow front wall of the Circle K. I wasn't there a minute before a tall balding fellow in a white shirt and black dress pants walked out of the store with a paper bag in his hand.

"Spare change, kind sir," I chimed.

He looked at me like I was Death and Disease rolled into one, averted his eyes, climbed into his Volvo station wagon and pushed the lock.

Perhaps it was something in my delivery....

Two more unsuccessful tries and I got to thinking that I needed to try a different line—perhaps "Brother can you spare a dime?" Then the front door opened and a pint-sized, shorthaired brunette in a Circle K smock came stomping out like an angry pit bull.

"No panhandling in our parking lot," she bellowed, sticking out her thin, witchy chin. "You can't be bothering our customers, or I'll call the cops."

"Look, ma'am," I said, softly, letting my body relax and trying to act sane. "I've just had a boating accident, and lost my wallet and my car keys. I don't mean to cause anyone any trouble. All I need is some change for the telephone, so I can call someone to pick me up. I'm sorry if I bothered anyone, really."

I gave her my best smile.

She looked at me up and down, her face softening. She was still puzzled, looking at me sideways, when she growled: "Come in the store, then, and I'll give you three dimes. If that ain't enough, it's just too damn bad; you'll have to start walking because you can't stay around here bumming."

"But ma'am, I'm not bumming. I've had an unfortunate accident; can't you see? I'm really a man of wealth and taste. I don't look like this, usually...."

"Yeah, sure," she said, looking to the sky for guidance. "Just come on in. And hurry up."

"Yes, ma'am."

We went inside the grungy little store and she gave me three dimes from the side of the cash register and told me to go into the restroom and wash my face. I walked in the direction she was pointing her bony finger, went through a yellow door. I turned on the overhead light, looked in the mirror and pulled a leech off my temple. Wiped the rest of my face with paper towels and got to looking pretty good.

I said thank you to the Bulldog Lady and went out into the warm sun. Dropped a dime in the payphone and listened as it clinked its way to the bottom. Something seemed to resonate for me as the dial tone came on loud and full of possibilities.

I called the radio station but got no response. It was past five o'clock, I guess. I dropped the second dime and dialed John's apartment. A semi roared by and made me jump. I turned toward the street and saw a cop car going by. My heart thumped loud; the phone buzzed in my ear.

"Hello." A sleepy-voiced John.

"John? John... this is Keith. What are you doing?"

"Keith, hi... not much. Just woke up from a nap. Gotta go into work tonight. Why? What's up?"

"I need your help, man. I'm in fucking deep shit. I need you to pick me up."

"What's the matter now, Carole finally have enough and kick your ass out?"

"No, man, the fucking cops are after me. They had me working this sting for them, and I ran. Now they're out to get me. Not the whole force, though, just this one cop—and maybe one other one. That's all—I think... it's a long fucking story. But you can save my ass... nothing will happen to you, man, I swear. All you gotta do is go to my apartment and get the keys—"

"Hold it. Hold it right there. Won't the cops be watching your apartment? Wouldn't that be a logical thing for them to do?"

"Yeah, but they don't know who you are. You could be Carole's illicit lover for all they know. Fucking cops think she's banging everybody, anyway. You wouldn't have to stay long, just grab the keys for the VW and drive, man. Then come pick me up down at the Circle K on ninety-two, on the way to the Gandy."

"Whoa, whoa, here. You seem to be pretty deeply involved in something that I know nothing about....Does this, by any chance, have anything to do with our trip to the Keys—and those friends of yours, Steve and Dan? Is the van full of dope or something? If it is, I don't want any part of it."

"No, Johnny, I swear. There's no dope involved. That's where I'm going—up to meet the boat. That's why I need the van; I'm running very late. This deal with the cop was supposed to be over. It wasn't... it didn't... I split. I got away from those fuckers, and now I really have to leave town in a hurry."

"I'm afraid this is a little too much for me, Keith. On one hand, you tell me that you're doing a sting for the cops. Excuse me, only one or two cops—and then you tell me that you're involved in a smuggling ring. Heh, heh... are you sure you're feeling all right, Keith? You haven't been hanging around with Dracula too much, have you?"

"Fuck you, John, this is serious. I'm fucked if I don't get out of town right away. I swear to you, man, the local cops know nothing about that van...they know nothing about you. Just drive it over here, please, that's all you have to do. You can take a cab back or something. Please, John, partner—I need this. It was your fucking doubles match that got me into this mess in the first place."

"Excuse me? What the hell are you talking about?"

"If I hadn't busted my leg trying to save your ass from humiliation, I'd still be working at the tennis club and I wouldn't be involved in these outrageous scenarios."

"Are you kidding me? You really believe that? I mean, I'm sorry about your leg and everything, but I think your problems are self-induced. You and Carole seem to have a knack for being in the wrong place at the wrong time."

"Are you coming or not, John? You need to make up your mind so I can figure something out."

"Jesus, Keith, I don't know. I've got a lot to lose."

"I've got a lot to lose, too, John—like everything. Come on, man. It'll be no sweat, I swear."

"I'll try, Keith, I will. You think Carole is home?"

"No—I don't know...but there's a spare key above the front door, on that little ledge."

"What if someone sees me?"

"Who gives a fuck? People do shit like that all the time. Just come and get me for Christ sake. I can't stand out here all day. And I can't go back into the bay.... Come on, man, please."

He clicked off without saying anything more and I hung up the receiver and sulked away. As soon as I got out of sight of the clerk, I scampered behind the cinderblock building, took a deep breath and tried to stop the fluttering in my chest. Above me, a red squirrel chattered accusingly from a scrawny tree. Squashed cups and empty pop cans were scattered on the thin grass beneath my still damp tennis shoes. Cars hissed by, seemed miles away. I listened for sirens.

What seemed like fifteen minutes went by and still no John. My gut was doing flip-flops. Where was that son of a bitch? Had he abandoned me? Turned me in?

I stood up and stretched; my clothes were almost dry. I was convinced that John was stiffing me. I paced around and wished I were back in Minnesota, no matter what the weather. Even Wisconsin would've been fine.

All this opportunity and I was going to lose it. I wanted to pound my head against the wall. Then I saw, at eye level, in the hollowed out cracks of a crumbling cinderblock, a flattened-out pack of Camels with a book of matches wedged inside the cellophane wrapper. Sometimes you get what you need.

I pulled one of the half-crushed, slightly twisted cigs out of the pack and examined it. Looked like it was okay, smelled like it was okay. I sat back down on the ground and lit up, inhaled deeply and blew the smoke out slowly. My throat burned and made me feel better. I squinted up at the sunlight poking through the leaves. This was better than banging my head into a wall I thought, then leaned back and accidentally banged my head on the wall.

I rubbed the smooth cellophane of the Camel pack between my fingers, holding out hope for John. *Good things come to those who wait,* said the voice.

I stared at the Camel pack; so much symbolism and myth contained therein: The naked woman inside the camel…the pyramids… the palm trees. All of those clues and messages, were they for me? Was this the communication from above that I had been waiting for?

Good things come in small packages.

I searched the pack for more hidden messages and lit up the second of the two lowly Camels. Started to get dizzy from the nicotine overload and stubbed it into the mossy dirt.

Then I saw the VW turning in to the far end of the lot, U-Haul trailer bouncing behind it. The eyelashes above the headlights never looked so good.

I took off running, had fifty yards to cover. Twenty-five yards away, without slowing, the van started rolling towards the exit.

I was praying but I didn't know to whom when the van stopped abruptly, then whined back to me.

I stepped up to the passenger door as the engine putt putted softly, pulled on the handle and swung the door open. Sitting there on that outrageous, sheepskin seat cover, was Ted Friday. Looking to me, at the time, like the Cuban Jesus Christ— Haysuse Christy, himself.

"Hey man, what's happening?" Stoned and grinning like a jackal.

"Ted, you motherfucker. What the hell are you doing here? Before you answer that, drive me someplace where I can piss. I'm about to fucking explode."

"We are gone, *compadre*, out of fucking sight. You don't look so good, man. Nice threads, though…."

"I don't feel that great, Ted, but at least I'm alive. What the hell happened to John?"

Ted clicked the floor shift in gear and slammed out onto the road, turned right and headed toward the Gandy Bridge. The trailer tugged and the VW bounced.

"Nothing happened to him, man. Dude called me and told me you were in need of some assistance, that's all. Said you were having trouble with your car and needed me to pick you up, right away. Said he had to research an interview or he would've done it. I was coming over to your place, anyway, man, with a little scratch, you know? Where is your vehicle, man, stuck in the mud someplace? You been out with some young chicks or something,

man? Getting stuck in the boonies with some jailbait? That's it,
isn't man? I can tell by the way your face is turning red...you
been chasing poontang, haven't you? She got a little sister, man?
If you're a buddy, you'll tell me."

"No, man, no chicks. I wish. Truth is that I'm trying to avoid a
cop that's after me for a credit card scam I pulled when I first got
to town, here. I've gotta split town right fucking now."

"You shitting me, man? Fucking John never said anything
about any cops. I don't like the pigs around here, man.... You
sure they aren't following us."

"Yeah, relax. They don't know this van and it's got Colorado
plates. We're safe—for a while, anyway. I suppose John was
freaked."

"He was a bit tense, I would say. Fidgeting like he'd been sucking down too much java, or something. If he wasn't such a
straight arrow college boy, I'da sworn he was into the blow."

"And he accused me of hanging with Dracula.... How is the
toothless one doing these days, anyway? I might need his help, in
a few days. That is, if I can get out of this little difficulty I'm in
with my nuts intact."

"Hey, man, let me tell you—you don't want anything to do
with our man Dracula. He's goin' down fast, like a two-dollar
whore. Word on the street is that he owes a lot of money to some
very angry people and he's too burned out to save himself. Like
he's just snorting and drinking and making everything worse. I
can't even stand to look at him, man; he's so pathetic. Looks like
a fucking cadaver. Don't ever get like him, man... do anything
for that buzz and shit... all kinds of shit can get you into trouble,
man, and that shit is one of them."

"No lie. How much cash you got for me?"

"I got a yard for you, dude."

"Only a hundred? You had seven hundred worth of shit."

"It's fronted out, man. I fronted to some wrestling people from
Ybor City. I was at the gym trying to collect just the other day, I

swear to god. One of them took a swing at me and the other one threatened to rip my fucking balls off, man. I ran out of there, scared shitless...."

"Are you shitting me?"

"I swear to god on a stack of bibles, my friend. I swear on my mother's grave."

"I thought your mother was still alive...."

"Yeah—but she's not doing that good." His eyes looked to the sky.

"Oh."

I took a deep breath and held it in for a moment before letting it out slowly. A hundred bucks would have to do. It would be enough to get me to the rendezvous. I guess you're a fool to expect satisfaction when you're on the run.

"Here. Stop here. I'm dying," I said.

Ted jerked the VW into the parking lot of a small green lounge, The Bayside Club. Trailer rattled and banged. As soon as we stopped, I jumped out of the van.

"Come on in, Ted. I'll buy you a beer."

"I don't like that drinking in the daytime shit, man. Smoking the reefer is okay but not booze. Makes me fat and slow...."

"Well have a goddamn coke, then. I'm going into piss and have a drink. I need a fucking drink just to tolerate these clothes I'm wearing, for the Christ sake."

"Those *are* some sharp duds, Keith, my boy. You been hanging at the Salvation Army up in Lakeland, or something?"

"Something like that."

We went into the lounge and it was dark enough, quiet enough and empty enough. Behind the bar was a pleasant-looking bleach-blonde woman in her forties. She seemed more interested in the soap operas dripping out of the TV, than the two of us.

I had two tall screwdrivers; Ted had two tall Cokes. I was nervous; he was uncomfortable. He said he knew places that I could hide out if I needed to. I said thanks and maybe I'd take him up on it some day. He kept grilling me about my clothes, why they were damp and mud-soaked. And what was the deal with this cop? Did I want something done to the dude? A little dope in the hands of the right people can get a lot of things done, he said.

I told him I didn't want to talk about it and he didn't ask anymore. I said I had to get out of town and grabbed the keys off the table. Then I walked out of the lounge and back into the hot sun and felt drained. I jumped into the driver's side of the van, adjusted the seat. Ted stepped in the other side.

"Where to, Ted? I have to hit the highway. Gotta go north to Alaska, man, the rush is on."

"Bobby Horton?"

"Maybe...I don't remember. I don't even remember the movie, except the title. I think Bobby Darin was in it....Where should I drop you?"

"Bring me back home, man, my man's Vic's got my wheels. But first, you can drive me by Rudy's Deli—I could use one a them po'boys. Ever had one of Rudy's po'boys? Nice... beef and chilies and onions. Maybe a little guacamole...."

"You'll have to show me where to turn."

In spite of my belief that I was traveling incognito, I had my head on a swivel. Got to the sandwich shop without any trouble and went inside with Ted. He ordered the po'boy of his dreams from a jolly-looking man in a white shirt and butcher's cap.

I bought two—turkey and a beef—for the road, paid the bill with the hundred-dollar bill Ted had given me.

Ted stood behind me and carefully peeled back the butcher paper on his sandwich. He took a giant bite and the pungent odor of spicy meat filled the air. Then he took a deep breath, sighed with appreciation and said he'd walk home. I said *Hasta la vista* and headed for the door. Ted followed me out; he'd changed his mind he said. I gave him a ride the eight blocks to his house while he munched. He seemed nervous when he got out, looking all around.

Ted's directions got me to the freeway. I found the entrance with no problem but there was a traffic jam. Somebody had taken out a whole section of concrete wall with the front of end of a white Buick Rivera. Took me an hour to get through. I ate both sandwiches while I waited. The bread was soft, the beef rare and garlicky. The turkey was some lousy, rolled shit but I still ate it.

I stared out at the houses all surrounded by green and wished I was swinging in a hammock on the front porch of one of them.

When I finally got moving, the whine of the tires on the pavement was comforting. Traffic was heavy, as always. I slid over into the northbound lane and put the hammer down. Van was maxing out around seventy-three mph.

I rolled north to Ocala, turned west on Highway 27 and took that to Bronson. Away from the freeway, the pace slowed down. There were farms and orange groves and two-lane roads and lots of greenery. At Bronson I turned onto State Highway 24 and drove southeast to the coast.

At least I had direction.

Following Bagley's detailed instructions, I drove directly to the prearranged spot and scrambled to get a few things together.

It was a good walk from where the van was parked to the actual landing area. Bagley and Schmidt's research had shown a favorable depth and most importantly, a small, private road nearby— with limited highway access.

As soon as they were anchored, I was to run back for the van. Soon as I rolled up on the frontage road, we'd load up and be gone. Schmidt would sail the boat back around to West Palm and put her in dockage while Bagley and I drove across the state to meet him. Finally, after transferring the dope-filled trailer and a load of furniture to Schmidt's mother's gold whale, we would go our separate, merry ways.

At least that's how it was supposed to work....

Chapter Eleven

My Ship Comes In

It's more than two days, now and I'm still alone and waiting. Waiting for something that I'm not even sure is going to happen. But I have no other place to go. I can't go back to Tampa—and ninety-three bucks won't get me very far in any other direction. I'm stuck with sticking it out.

The adrenaline high has washed out, leaving in its place an unfocused longing and a nagging suspicion that I've really fucked things up this time. I'm aware that I can't wait on this beach forever; food and patience are nearly depleted. In the back of my head, a hyena mocks my every thought.

After much soul searching, I decide to leave by noon tomorrow, boat or no boat. After this much time has gone by, I can't be sure of what, or who, might show up, if anybody.

Will a flotilla of coastguardsmen fresh from drug interception training be hitting the beach like the second assault on

Normandy? Or will Bagley and Schmidt float in, all big-timey, acting like it's no big deal to get stood up on a lonely beach for two days by a couple of assholes.

Just because they're the big-time smugglers and I'm the lousy pick-up guy doesn't mean I haven't run a few risks, myself. If only they knew, for the chrissakes.

I don't know how many times I've gotten up and said to myself that I'm leaving, only to sit back down again, light a cigarette and wait. Stare out at something in the vast distance and wait. The waves just keep breaking slowly and rhythmically against the shore. The sound has become an annoyance, nature's insistence. No longer relaxing, it grates on me like a constantly nagging voice: *Sucker, sucker, sucker....*

You get to a point in a situation like this where you run out of things to think about and your mind starts covering the same old territory, over and over like a broken record. *Round and round she goes, where she stops nobody knows.*

And if you stare long enough at nothing, *something* might finally appear.

If it's far enough away, an object can take the shape of many things. Sheer wishful thinking, if you're tired enough, hungry enough or scared enough, might make you see something that isn't there. Whether you're sitting in a deer stand or a duck blind or against a bank of sand, it's conceivable that a stump could seem to be a deer, a pigeon might look like a duck and a hunk of driftwood on the horizon could become a boat.

There's a dark speck on the horizon that brings this theory to mind. How long has it been there? Could it actually be them, after all this time?

Adrenaline again begins its bubbling drive through my blood-stream and I stand up to look closer at the dark speck. The waves and the wind seem to change, begin to sound like an orchestra. An orchestra that's playing something exhilarating and uplift-ing,like a Sousa march, or a hymn maybe. Not a solemn, weepy hymn; a strong and warlike hymn, like "Onward Christian Soldiers" or "The Battle Hymn of the Republic."

I stand up and squint out at the water.

The object is closer now—and most definitely a sailboat. Possibly approaching my little home away from home.

Clouds start to roll in and a damp breeze kicks up from the North. The sun disappears and the blue and yellow sky slowly fills in with gray and black.

The object seems to have stopped.

I light the lanterns and stretch them out along the beach in a thirty-yard strip, ten paces between each one. I build up the sand around the signal flag and fetch the binoculars from Bagley's pack.

Not enough light, to be sure, but indeed, the object looks to me like the *Larson E.* But something is different; she doesn't look quite right going through the water. But then, what do I know about sailing? What does a northern boy like me know about sailboats? Still, I swear it looks as though the sail is down and the bow is listing.

I start to think about it and my paranoia alarm goes off like the dive signal on a submarine. Suddenly I'm sure it's the feds driving the boat, trying to clean up the loose ends of another failed smuggling attempt.

But then, it could be thieves, redneck thieves....

Could it be that Schmidt and Bagley are drunk and trying to fuck with my head?

I squeeze the field glasses tighter and search for any sign of life. One of them should be on deck, scanning the shoreline. But the deck is empty. There's nobody out there.

I drop the glasses in the sand and look nervously around for some kind of weapon. My eyes lock onto an axe handle's length of wood lying in my pile of scraps. I pick it up and run the smooth, worn surface through my hands.

It's a little thicker than an axe handle, a little hard to grip. It's going to have to do.

The boat keeps moving slowly in my direction and the sky keeps fading to black. It's raining, now, steady. Coming down straight, big drops. I let it pour down on me, pointing my face to the heavens.

A tiny bow light breaks through the dark curtain, glowing both red and yellow, like the glass cover is broken. Then a beam, like a flashlight, sweeps the cabin's interior and goes dark.

I pick up the driftwood and step back into the dunes, watching silently as the light moves ever so slowly toward shore. I hear the murmur of the diesel engine for a moment and then it's gone, swallowed up by the rain. I hear something moving behind me, in the brush. I hold up my club and yell, "Who's there?"

Nobody, answers the rain.

Then I think I hear a splash over the water and a weakly shouted: "Keith."

I stand there frozen in the warm rain. The bow light is gone; the sea is dark. If Schmidt was on board there would be something more than a muffled shout, that much I know. Was it drowned out by the waves and wind and steady rain?

I'm hoping that they're just being cautious…. My gut churns at the possibility that Bagley and Schmidt have doubted my reliability.

Another brief cry of pain reaches my ears. A shaky flashlight beam points down at the water, then goes dark.

Five eternal minutes go by. The only sounds the hammering of the rain and the pounding of my heart. I don't move.

Squinting in the dim light of the lanterns, I can see the dinghy coming ashore, landing rope dangling in the water. The bow lifts as it hits the sand and a bent-over figure struggles out. Slowly he makes his way towards the lantern light.

Looks like Bagley to me. And just like the *Larson E,* he's listing to one side. Dark splotches on his torn safari shirt.

Schmidt is nowhere to be seen.

I drop my club and start running down the soggy sand.

"Keith," he says weakly, "Where are you? Keith, can't you see I need help?"

"I'm coming, Dan. What the hell's going on? Where's Steve?" I get to him and discover that the blotches appear to be blood. He has a bandana tied around his right bicep.

"He's dead. We were attacked by goddamn pirates... had to fight them off. Schmidty got shot. He's dead, Keith. Those bastards killed him. I got lucky or I'd be dead, too. It was terrible. I'm just so goddamn lucky... they were trying to board us when Schmidty shot a flare into their fuel tank. I guess he saved my life—and now he's gone."

I stop dead in my tracks; my heart sinks. Blackness descends over me like a tight-fitting skullcap and my knees buckle.

"He was good man," I say, weakly, struggling for composure.

I help Dan to my camping spot. We sit down on the sand and the rain lightens. He has blood on his face and hands and what looks to be shallow stab wounds around his neck and right shoulder. He's pale, like maybe he's lost quite a bit of blood.

"Jesus, Dan, I can't fucking believe this is happening. Schmidt is dead... this is horrible... fucking awful, man. What the hell should we do, goddamn it? You don't look so good. We've got to get out of here."

"I'll make it," Bagley says weakly, but resolved. "I've got too much money and too much time involved in this to give up now. Schmidt would want us to keep going, Keith. You've got to hold it together. If we can just get this job done, I think everything will turn out all right."

I'm shaking convulsively, the last drops of precious adrenaline ripping through me like two hundred-twenty volts of pure lightning.

"We've got to move fast, Keith. You have to get the van. I don't think I can walk that far. I'm feeling a little light-headed. You're going to have to save *me*, for a change. After all those times I bailed you out, now you can pay me back."

Bailed me out? What the fuck is he talking about?

"What about the ganja?" I ask.

"There isn't any pot, Keith... just coke: a hundred pounds of pure Colombian cocaine. It's inside the fuel tank; there's a special little door.... It's underneath the seats at the stern. You have to push a button on the console and the piece will slide back. First turn the ignition key to the left... counter-clockwise. It's the black button on the outside of the steering council. I think there's enough juice left in the battery... if not you'll have to grab a crowbar from the tool kit and..."

"Just a fucking minute, here, you told me this was a pot deal—fucking mari-ju-wana, for Christ sake, not fucking coke. Every time I touch cocaine, something bad happens. And believe me, I've got enough trouble as it is, without adding more.... Steve is dead, man... can't you see... it's happening already. A hundred pounds of coke can get you executed in this state. This is fucking insane. I should turn around and walk the hell out of here, leave you here for the cops...I do not want to fuck around with cocaine, goddamn it."

"T-t-take the damn cross off your shoulders, Keith, and get smart. Pot is for hippies; it's old w-w-world, now .The profits are less and the loads are larger—it's all yesterday's papers. You can cut this blow and keep cutting it, and you'll still be able to sell it for top buck. The p-p-profit margins are astronomical. You can put a hundred pounds in a backpack. You can't say that about weed."

He sits down on the sand, elbows resting on his knees, chin on his clasped hands. "Now go and get our nest egg so we can get the hell out of here, be-be-before I goddamn bleed to death."

"You seem like you're doing all right, Dan.... You've regained your gift for being an asshole."

"What do you mean by that? I haven't got much energy left in me.... What are you waiting for?"

I stare at him.

"Oh, I see..." he says. "So th-th-that's the way we're going to play it…. W-w-well then, ah… ah… I'll tell you what, I'll ah, ah, in-increase your share of the load—n-now that Schmidt is gone…."

"I want half," I say, looking him straight in the eyes.

"W-w-well… I w-w-was thinking a third—of Steve's share—but I guess half would be f-fair, if you insist."

"You misunderstand Mr. Bagley—I want half of the whole thing. The game has suddenly changed, you see. I never signed on for cocaine—and especially not death. I should think that those added problems warrant extra compensation."

"Huh, huh," he clucks, "You're not serious."

I turn away and walk down to the dinghy. Grab the rope and start to swing the bow around. A realization—no, more a question—comes to mind: If Dan and I leave in the van and Steve is no longer around, who is going to sail the boat around the horn? Yes sir that's the sixty-four dollar question. I pull the dinghy up farther on the beach then walk back to where Bagley sits, glumly, staring at me. In the bright yellow glow, the marks on his face look like scratches. He's dabbing at them with a wet cloth, the water jug at his feet.

He looks up at me, annoyed.

"What about the boat, Dan?" I ask. "We can't just leave the fucking thing here, can we?"

"You'll have to sink it."

"How in the fuck am I supposed to do that?"

"It's already leaking from where they rammed us."

"They fucking rammed you—and you're still alive?"

"Schmidt cut loose on'em with the twelve-gauge and they backed off, waited until dark."

"What the hell should I do?"

"Go out to the boat and put the coke in the dinghy. Then start the engine, set the rudder, lock it into a southwesterly direction, throw her in gear and get off."

"How do I lock the rudder? Is there some switch or something?"

"There's a rope that holds it in place. You'll see how it works."

"Will she sink fast enough?"

"Blow a hole with the shotgun, below the water line.There are a few slugs left. They're on the bed. You better take a lantern, I can't even see her from here."

"I'm not touching off a shotgun. Somebody'll hear that, and we'll be up shit crick without a paddle."

"Close the cabin door. In this rain, no one will hear anything. Or better yet, pull the drain plugs…but that will take you some time—and the shotgun won't. Yeah, blow some holes…that way it'll look like pirates, if anyone finds the boat."

"Yeah," I say and turn, like a zombie, toward my task.

Obvious signs of a struggle on the *Larson E*: blood on the deck, broken bottles and empty shotgun shells. But somehow the destruction doesn't live up to Bagley's story. The boat isn't rid-dled with bullet holes like I expected. I only see two holes, and they're directly to the right of the steering wheel, about head high. Two large clean holes and that's it.

Down below, two shotguns lay on the bed along with several live shells. The bed that Carole and I had slept in, not long ago. The Hawaiian shirt that Schmidt was wearing when we arrived in the Keys is hanging from a hook on the wall.

Tears well up behind my eyes and I fight them back down. I jam three slugs in the Browning semi-automatic and set it back down on the bed. Then I suck in deep breath after deep breath and go back topside.

Shakily, I push the button, tear off the seat cushions and stare, fascinated, as the panel slides back. A thin metal door on the "Emergency" tank is easily unlatched and lifted up to reveal a green North Face backpack lying high and dry on a mesh tray that's bolted to the sides of the tank. I crouch down and grab the two aluminum rods on the pack and lift. A hundred-plus pounds comes up as easy as squeezing a pimple.

I throw the pack on the deck and stare at it, my heart like a marching band. At my feet is a quarter million worth of coke, wholesale. By the time the last line has been snorted, smoked, or injected, well over a million dollars will have been generated.

Lordy mama, my ship has come in.

Suddenly I'm terrified and my body is doing the convulsion boogie.

I jump back to my feet and go down below deck, grab the shotgun, push off the safety and touch off a load by the side of the bed. Water rushes in and my ears ring. I go back up topside, a three-alarm fire in my head.

I heft the pack and start down the ladder towards the dark sea. My foot slips and I go crashing down, landing on my shoulder in the raft. The thing damn near tips over but somehow doesn't. I pull off the pack and laugh hysterically then climb back up the ladder, set the rudder on the *Larson E* and start the engine. Before pulling the anchor, I retrieve the Browning and throw it in the dinghy. There's already two inches of water in the cabin.

The engine murmurs softly. I put it in gear and quickly go down the ladder. I have to flop into the raft on my stomach but that's all right. I untie and she glides slowly into the darkness.

The grin is still on my face as I come ashore. I quickly turn grim at the prospect of facing Bagley.

He catches sight of the pack on my back and can't suppress a smile of his own and I hate him for it. Me, who, was balls out crazy a minute ago, laughing like a fool—and I hate him for smiling. These are strange times indeed.

There is a little bee starts buzzing around inside my head, telling me that something is not quite right. I can't shake the feeling. There's more to this situation than is meeting the eye or the ear but I don't know exactly what. Considering that I'm dealing with Dan Bagley, why should that come as any surprise?

I drop the pack down at Bagley's feet. "There's your guilt powder, Dan. You happy now?" I look up and down the beach and see nothing but blackness. The only sound the driving rain. "I suppose we should get going," I say, staring hard at Bagley as he struggles to his feet. Now I'm almost positive those marks on his face are scratches. Metallic sounding words begin to tumble out of my mouth: "Those look like scratches on your face, Dan? Were those woman pirates that attacked you?"

"W-w-what is that supposed to mean, Keith?" he says, grimacing.

"I was out to the boat, Dan; I saw the damage. I only saw two holes in the boat and they looked like shotgun slug holes. And, it also looks like they went out through the front of the cabin, which means they had to be from pretty close range. Those guys weren't very good shots, I guess."

"They were kids—teenagers—they had a double-barreled shotgun. They shot at Schmidt while he was at the wheel. He ran down to get our guns and I had to fend them off. My god—they rammed us—two of them were trying to get on board... Jamaicans... they were scratching at me trying to climb on. Schmidt comes back up with the twelve-gauge and blows one of the pricks away. Puts a hole in his chest. The other guy went scrambling into the water. Schmidt could have killed him, too— but he held back. He was standing there watching; letting the nigger escape; when a third one pops up from nowhere and lets go with both barrels. One of the slugs catches Schmidty in the chest and he goes down. He's down on the deck when he grabs the flare gun and shoots. Must have hit a gas can or something, because the whole thing went up.... It was gorgeous."

"That's heavy, man. Schmidt went down fighting, eh."

"He saved our bacon."

"At least your bacon. Those wounds don't look very deep.... What kind of knives did those guys have?"

"Christ, I don't know. Everything happened so fast."

"You gonna be okay?"

"I'm feeling weak. I need to rest."

"I thought you told me that they came back again, at night."

"I meant that they planned to come back at night. That is the usual modus operandi on the high seas. That's what they would've done, I meant, if Steve hadn't toasted them. I was shaken up from the ordeal—waiting the whole time for more of them to come along—but they never did. I ran without the lights until dawn. When the sun came up, there was nobody around. And thankfully for you and I, Keith, no Coast Guard or narc boats. Now don't you think it's time to get a move on? I think you need to focus."

"What happened to Steve, then, after he shot the flare?"

"He was dead a few hours later. I watched him die. There was nothing I could do to stop the bleeding."

"How did you know that he was dead?"

"You can tell, Keith," he said, a hint of superiority creeping into his voice, "when you see it firsthand. He had no heartbeat and he was bleeding all over, not breathing. Pretty good signs that the p-p-poor bastard was dead. What's with all the questions, Keith? Y-y-you're not letting your imagination run away with you now, are you?"

"Fuck you. What happened to Steve's body?"

"I had to bury him at sea."

"I'm sure you said some words."

"I did."

"I won't ask what; I don't know if I could take it. One thing, though, the only blood I saw on deck was by the helm, under the wheel…."

"We ran through a hard rain. Like now… tis the season."

"There was also blood by the rail, near the tiller—I wonder why that didn't wash off."

"Tiller, that's a good word. You're picking up on this nautical stuff, Keith… someday we can go for a sail, you and I. But now, don't you think we should get along down the road—as in highway?"

"Yeah, I suppose. But first I have to get something."

*   *   *

I go back into the darkness and come back with the Browning cradled in my arms. Bagley is sitting in the sand, tension creasing his forehead.

"You brought the twelve-gauge along?" he says, a confused look crossing his face. "Good thought... but I don't think it's a good idea to carry it in the van. Just one more thing for a cop to spot if we get stopped for anything."

"You're probably right, Dan, but I'm not bringing it to the van. It's for use here, right now." I push off the safety and point the big black barrel at Bagley's reddening face. He begins to resemble a jack-o-lantern, yellow glow and all. "First, Dan, we are going to sit here together and have a little chat, like the old buddies that we are."

"Very funny. Now cut the shit and let's get the hell out of here."

"Not before you answer some questions. And believe me, I'm serious. If I'm smirking, it's because it's funny to see you there on the ground—with a loaded shotgun in your face—and you're still giving orders like a fat, little general in some bullshit army. I guess you really can't help yourself.... But, first and foremost, I want one thing understood. If I'm going to assist you in this odious task of cocaine distribution—well, uh—let's just say that I'm not going to do it, if I don't feel comfortable—and right now, I don't feel comfortable."

"If you're too scared, Keith, drive me out to the road and you can walk away. Nobody has to know that you were ever here. I'll send you some scratch when I get back to civilization. Just help me get to the road, please."

"I'm afraid that won't work for me, Daniel—for many reasons. Not the least of which is that I don't trust you. Don't trust you now and never have. I mean, for Christ sakes, Dan, I haven't forgotten what a rip-off you are. Nobody that I know ever trusted you, whether it was with their girl or their money, or anything. I don't know how you manage to use everyone to the max like you do, all the while prancing around like some kind of fucking diva, but the real funny thing is that I always stood up for you, believe it or not. I'm probably the only guy in the world that ever had anything good to say about you, at all. And what did that get me? A load of fucking shit. Did you forget that we've done business together before, Dan? I know what an asshole you can be, remember? I've taken the brunt of your...your...condescending... and your... your arrogance. Arrogance and ignorance, your two strong points. I guess I'm the ultimate fucking sucker."

"Are you serious? That's what you're so upset about? If I promise to be a nice guy, will you point that shotgun away?"

"Shut the fuck up and listen to me. Something seems terribly wrong here. I can't accept this shit we've got going. Fucking bile is rising up in me; my gut won't accept this scene that we've got."

"I think you've finally gone off the deep end, Keith. Better give me that shotgun before somebody gets hurt."

"I went off the deep end a long time ago, Dan. That's why I wouldn't hesitate from pulling this trigger and ending your nasty fucking life. I'm sick of being shoved around by people like you."

"People like me... huh.... You mean someone who's made something of his life?"

"You fucking asshole. What does that exactly mean to you, 'made something of his life'? I've got a wife and kid, for Christ sake. Or at least I did before I signed on with you. But we're straying away from the heart of matters, here. I need to know more about this deal, and especially the pirate attack.... I remember you telling Steve, back in Key West, that this deal was going to be your people all the way. Some guy from Colorado, a high roller from Aspen or something.... This was going to be your deal, Dan; I do remember you saying that. How did infallible Bagley go so terribly wrong, I want to know."

He looks down at the sand, takes on a more humble tone: "There was trouble from the beginning—as soon as we landed. First thing we noticed was the narcs—they were everywhere. Dressed in three-piece suits hanging with the businessmen... wearing shorts and sailing...drinking in the pubs with the tourists.... All the hotels were booked up; there were so many narcs on the island. Uncle Sam is spending big bucks to winter these guys...I should've become a narc...."

"Get on with the fucking story." His eyes get wider as I shake the gun barrel in his face. "We haven't got all night," I say, backing up and sitting down at the edge of the light, resting the gun on my lap.

"Now you're catching on, Keith. You need to calm down a bit. Whattaya say we continue this discussion while we're driving out of here? Come on, you and I are old friends.... God, man, we go all the way back to high school...I'm not going to screw you around."

"Here will be fine, thank you. I've grown quite fond of this place; I'll have you know. I've been waiting here so long that it's beginning to seem like home, especially now that I don't have one anymore. ...You can talk now."

"Well... all right," he sighs. "Our connection never showed up, that's why we were late getting out of port. We waited days for him to show up. He never did; so we called his wife. She starts crying as soon as she hears my voice. Turns out that our man got popped about a week before he was supposed to leave to meet us. I guess, in some ways, we got lucky that the feds got him before he led them to us."

"No shit. So then what did you do?"

"Schmidt started hustling, talking to the natives, until he found somebody who could handle our requests."

"You did this in spite of all the narcs around?"

"I was against it, believe me. I was ready to turn around and come back to Florida and see what we could find—but Schmidty wouldn't have any of that. He was bound and determined to get us a good price. Sure enough, to my great surprise, one day he comes back with two Rastas in tow. Cow shit in their dreadlocks and the whole bit... stunk like pigs. But these guys had some of the highest quality blow that I've ever seen, at incredible prices."

"I thought Rastas were into weed."

"These guys had weed, too, but it was nothing special. Ordinary brown buds. Didn't even smell that good. That's why we did the coke. The price was so good we were able to get a lot more than we had initially planned. I wouldn't be surprised if they had ripped off the load from someone else. They had to be the ones that set us up."

"The guys who sold it to you were the ones that tried to rip you off? You sure it wasn't your rotten karma coming back at you?"

"They weren't the same guys—but they *were* Rasta punks. It just makes sense that it was them... how else would they know about us?"

"You'd think guys with that much money would have better weapons that just one double barrel shotgun. I'd think those dudes would have Uzis and shit like that."

"Well, maybe our pirates were just at the right place at the right time.... Maybe they patrol the area looking for lonely sailors, I don't know. All I know is that they attacked us and we fought them off and Schmidt is dead. Now, can we get the hell out of here?"

"I don't think so. I want you to hear my little theory. I have to have a theory because I don't believe there were any pirates. I..."

"What? What is this? You trying to rip me off?"

He starts toward me; I aim at his gut.

"Just sit the fuck down, Daniel, before this thing goes off. You'd like to get your hands on it, wouldn't you, so you could do me in like you did Steve. You see, I think you were the only one who shot at anybody on that boat. I think you got greedy and tried to blow Schmidt away while he was steering. That explains the holes and the blood by the wheel. Then you shot him again and he fell down on the deck. You thought it would be easy to throw a wounded man in the drink, but Schmidty fought you, scratched at your face as you tried to send him to the sharks. He got his hand on a Beck's bottle and broke it on your head and stabbed you around the neck a few times. That explains the broken beer bottle on the boat and the weird little wounds on your neck. You

struggled free and finished him off—that's what I think. I still
haven't figured out what the dent in the hull was caused by, but I
will. Just give me time."

"You have really looned out this time, Keith. All that acid has
come back to haunt you, I'm afraid. That's one of the biggest hal-
lucinations I've ever heard. Now let's act like men and stop the
fantasy. That was a good fable—until the part about the dent. The
dent in the boat proves my story is true. Now can we go?"

He stands up slowly, grinning—that condescending grin that I
hate so much. I point the shotgun up at the black sky and squeeze
the trigger. He jerks backward from the sound of the blast.

"Shit, man, you're nuts," he says, whining. "Ease off."

"Sit the fuck down, asshole. I'm going to do you a favor."

He sits down, shivering, a look of disbelief on his face.

"I'm going to save you from yourself, Dan Bagley. I'm going to
save you from a rude comeuppance in your old age. I'm going to
prevent you from having to discover the awful truth about yourself, when it's too fucking late. How do ya like that, asshole?"

He cocks his head up at me with a sniveling sneer feathering
across his lips.

I keep after him: "I can't help but get the distinct impression
that you think you can do anything you want, with impunity.
Karma means nothing to you. Nothing means anything to you.
All you care about is the gold, come whatever or whoever you
have to shit on. So fuck you. I almost feel bad that I'm going to
save you from growing old and all of a sudden realizing what a
greedy, useless piece of shit you are… but the fact is, I'm not at
all that sure about Karma, myself. I can't be sure that you'll suf-
fer enough to compensate for your trespasses. I'm going to end it
all for you, right here, right now."

I put the stock of the gun to my shoulder and point the barrel at
his head. He puts his hands in front of his face and rolls up in a ball.

"Don't shoot! Cut it out, please!"

I move closer to his fetal-positioned body, lowering the

weapon. He's crying: "Come on, Keith... you can't be serious. You'll never be able to sell all that coke without my help." Tears roll down his face and it smells like he shit his pants.

I tighten the pressure on the trigger.

"I'm going to throw that shit into the goddamn fucking ocean." I shout. "Gonna get some sharks wired so they can take out a few more goddamn tourists."

"You are insane, please give me a break...."

I point at his heart, squeeze the trigger.

CLICK. The metallic sound seems to echo through the deluge.

I turn and throw the shotgun to the sand, suppressing a chuckle.

"I'll go get the van," I say, heading up the beach, leaving shit boy and his backpack behind.

He is stammering something at me as he sits up in the sand in his soiled, khaki L.L. Bean deck pants. The rain drowns out the words.

I chug along. About fifty yards down the beach, a grin spreads over my face. It turns into a nervous laugh.

The rain has driven everyone out—no other cars around—but still, I'm nervous. Once the VW is running; I feel a little better. I no longer have a past, only a doubtful and terrifying future.

Slowly, I chug out to the highway, think about running. My headlights cut through the blackness; raindrops flash. Little silver stars float around in my vision like fireflies. Tires splash as I turn onto the access road. It's like I'm watching the whole scene from a distance and somebody else is driving.

The driver cuts the lights and bounces down the dirt that's turning slippery and muddy. Sometimes it's hard to see the road so he has to drive slowly. Has to flip the lights on a couple times for an instant, just to make out the direction. It seems brighter the closer we get to the water. We spot the lantern light and park. It's about a fifty-yard walk through the dunes. I'm thinking about gators and snakes the whole way. I step out on the beach and Bagley's holding the Browning. Standing there cradling it, a weird look in his eye.

I ignore him and walk over to the pack, squat down, heft it and stand up, not without some pain and effort. My bad leg is back to being bad. I look over at Dan; he's glaring at me, mouth all twisted up. Behind his glare, he seems weak and shaky.

"You coming along, Dan? You're not still hung up on my little joke, are you? Just kidding, man—right? Payback for jumping on my wife. Remember that time? I thought you deserved a little payback for a half a dozen other fucking things I could name, too. Turnabout is fair play, you know. We're old buddies, right? Can't hold a grudge, can we? It's you and me against the world, now."

His lip curls upward, his eyebrows tighten.

"You coming?" I ask again, starting to walk.

"Heh, heh. Shit, you joker... you had me going, you prick. Jesus... ha-ha... goddamn. I-I-I'll stay here and gather up the lanterns and things. We can't afford to leave anything around...."

"Yeah, I suppose."

I trudge back through the wiry underbrush; sand clings to my shoes like cement. The pack digs into my shoulders. I get to the van, slide open the door and throw it in back.

On the way back to the beach, I follow my path. My flashlight is barely needed. When I get to the beach, all the lanterns are out and Bagley is nowhere to be seen. I peer down at the water, thinking maybe that he's gone down, to get rid of the dinghy. I take a few steps in that direction. I hear something moving in the brush behind me. I turn in time to see Bagley running at me, Browning high above his head like a war club.

I freeze for a second, then charge. He swings the butt of the gun but I duck under and throw a cross-body block. He tries to avoid me but my hip slams into his knees. He tumbles back in the sand, losing his grip on the gun. He starts scrambling through the clinging sand, straining for the Browning. I struggle to my feet and jump on him, coming down with both knees on his back. I throw two punches to the back of his head and jump off, grab the shotgun by the barrel and sail it down the beach like a hammer thrower at the Killer's Olympics. Bagley lies there muttering, rubbing his head.

"You fucking asshole," I say. "I really should fucking kill you. You're so fucking pathetic, you deserve to die."

I spit at him and slump back toward the brush.

He's crawling after me, pleading: "Please don't leave me here, Keith, you've got to save me. You need me. Schmidt needed me...but he would never admit it. I showed him though, didn't I? He needed me there, in the end. I outlasted him... I won. Keith... Keith..." eyes begging like a whipped dog. "I'm sorry. *It is* you and me now. *We* can live the good life, like we used to dream about. Think of it.... You can have half.... I'm sorry.... Please help me. Please understand...."

I start to walk away and my foot hits something in the sand. I look down and see that it's my wooden weapon, from before. From before all this commotion came and ruined my nice quiet beach. Before this lying, fucking greed head came in and tried to fuck me over one more time.

I bend over and pick up the hunk of wood, squeezing it in my hands like Ted Williams at Fenway Park.

Bagley struggles to his feet then jerks an opened Swiss Army knife from his trouser pocket and lunges at me.

I bash his forearm with a downward swing and the knife falls to the sand.

He grabs his arm, falls to his knees and howls like a scalded cat. Breaks down crying again, a pleading, pitiful sound.

Horrified, I bash his fucking head in. Give him a right lot of whacks until his face resembles a rotting melon. The rain pours down and it seems a bit like old times. I'm back on the merry-go-round and it's still spinning.... *Na na, na na, hey....*

His head is pulp; I drag the body down the beach and put it into the dinghy. Pull his funeral boat out into the ocean until the water is chest high, loosening the air valve. The boat hisses softly at me as the burial at sea floats southward. I cross myself and I'm not even Catholic.

I'm thinking that now I might need religion.

Instead, I have cocaine—lots of it—and many miles to go before I sleep. Selah.

Chapter Twelve

Life's a Beach and Then You Die

In the type of situation I'm in, one can lose all humanity. You become a reaction, an instinct. Running just to keep from dying. Eating just to keep from shaking. Sleeping because you can't do anything else. Killing because it's your only choice....

I'm growing very tired of my continuous spiritual dilemma. It just doesn't relate to my reality anymore. Too much of the same old metaphysical crap: Sky Pilot or Jesus or Buddha or Gita or what-the-fuck-have-you? Stuff can be such a pain in the ass.

Seems like there should be something else to believe in that I haven't gotten around to yet. In the meantime, before I figure out what that is, I place Chance as the executor of my fate: pure random selection. From now on, like a spider in a web, I will take what comes along to me and thank the Fates for whatever it might be. Isn't that truly The Way?

The amazing thing is; I believe I can get away with all my crimes.

The boat is gone. If it is ever found it will more than likely be written off as another pirate attack—merely a statistic. The beaching of Bagley's bloated body will only confirm these suspicions. I find it hard to accept—but it seems like I'm home free. That is, if you consider being alone in a vehicle with enough cocaine to get you murdered, robbed, or sent to jail for the rest of your life, home free.

The weak VW heater is going full blast and my teeth are chattering along with the windshield wipers; sign says: Otter Creek—6.

Three miles later I swing off the road, crawl into the back of the van, towel off and put on dry clothes: white jeans and a blue polo shirt, (Bagley's) and a khaki windbreaker jacket (also Bagley's).

While searching for clothes, I come across a wallet in Bagley's duffel. A wallet stuffed with identification for one Elton Kirby. There's a Colorado driver's license, library card from Littleton, Colorado, social security card and three credit cards (Chevron, Texaco, Montgomery Ward).

I surmise that either Bagley found these, or had them made. It's the type of cheesy scam Dan was famous for. I can see it all now: after he murdered Schmidt and me, he would have had to disappear, become someone else.

People along the pipeline know of Bagley and Schmidt—but they don't know me from Adolph Monjou.... I can easily become Elton Kirby. The picture is badly blurred and the height, weight and hair color, are close enough. I might have a problem with the blue eyes....

I get nice and dry, stash the forty-five kilos in various places in the van, then, get back on the road and keep on rolling. On the edge of Yankeetown, I find a small motel with a parking lot that you can't see from the road. There's a diner a few yards away.

Elton Kirby gets himself a room at Friendly Haven with color TV and refrigeration. After showering and smoking, he wanders over to the diner for a bite; stomach growling.

The light is dim in Elly's Cafe and the paint is faded green, like pea soup. There is one plump woman behind the counter, with a wrinkled face and a hairnet. In the kitchen, I presume, is a cook. Only other person in here is a good looking, blonde girl, wearing blue jeans and a brown T-shirt, sitting at the end of the counter. She's drinking coffee and looking nervously out at the road, occasionally biting a fingernail.

If I wasn't so tired I might be interested in her. She's pretty, with a haunted look in her cloudy blue eyes and a sculpted nose and chin.

I look at the plastic-covered menu and order; I'm thinking about the girl. In what seems like no time at all, the waitress plops down a nice chicken fried steak with mashed potatoes and gravy. I temporarily lose interest in the girl as I dig in.

I wolf down the chow and then pay the bill and limp back to the room. All of a sudden, I'm burned out. I double lock the doors and flip on the tube. I pull back the green, chenille bedspread and plop down on the crisp white sheets. At least they're clean.

The TV picture is black and white, with some streaks of color on the edges of the screen. I find a rerun of Starsky and Hutch, where Huggy Bear goes undercover as a pimp, and let the drone put me to sleep.

I dream that I'm running in slow motion through a field of tall grass, like one of those television commercials where the man and the woman are moving towards each other, arms extended. You see the anticipation on their faces as they approach each other. Each stride carries them closer to true love and the intense joy they will soon feel.

My dream is a little different. Carole is gleefully bounding toward me in that pretty little flowery sundress that she wore when we got married. We get closer to each other and I'm trying to see into her eyes. The harder I try to focus; the more the face blurs. When we're almost together, I put out my arms and it's not Carole's face at all, but that of some unknown teenager with buckteeth and a pimpled chin.

I stop and stare at her and she changes into Mrs. Olson. Suddenly, I'm four years old and sitting on the little hill by the swing set in the backyard of my parent's home. It's a bright sunny day but it seems cold. My mother is hanging up wash. Some part of my brain tells me that I've been through this before, as Mrs. Olson stands on her back porch, calling to me.

"Keith, Keith honey... do you want to come in and play? There's quite a wind out here today. Come in and have something warm. I've baked some of those ginger cookies you like...." I look over to ask my mother if I can go but she is gone. Mrs. Olson and I walk up the flight of brown stairs holding hands. At the top of the stairs I stop and look back down for a second and wish it were warmer outside. Then I go inside and Mr. Olson is sitting at the white table in his undershirt, reading the paper. It's dark in there but still he's reading. Mrs. Olson takes my hand and we walk toward the bedroom and I feel a strange excitement.

The scene changes and suddenly I'm in the dinghy from the *Larson E*, in the middle of the ocean, and dying of thirst. The sun is beating down on me and I'm alone, with no food or fresh water. I rub my hand across my chest and feel a warm liquid. I look at my hand and it's covered with blood.

I've got a fucking bleeding heart.

My eyes jerk open and I sit up straight in the tiny motel bed. Gray light of dawn is creeping in above the curtains. I try to crawl out of the bed but my body is leaden.

I fall back down and sink into a deep dreamless sleep, like smoking good hash and lying in the sun with the radio on.

The green, plastic clock on the veneer bed table reads ten after ten when I finally put my feet to the worn, green carpet. I rub my eyes and the severity of my situation plunges down on me like a bucket of blood.

Dread and Fear push me into the shower, kick me in the ass when I get out. I dress, become resplendent in Bagley's khaki shorts and blue polo. Tan L.L. Bean boat shoes fill out the picture, like something from a catalog. My stomach is trying it's damnedest to eat itself.

I walk over to the diner and everything is eerily the same as the night before, same waitress and the same thin-faced blonde sitting at the end of the counter. I change the scene, this time, sitting down with only one faded, blue stool between me and the blonde. I smile at her, nice. Much to my surprise, she smiles back.

A true country beauty: shoulder-length blonde hair, milky complexion, blue eyes and a certain kind of softness about her. Daylight has pushed the haunted look out to the edge of her face, revealed only by a slight pinching of the skin. She's wearing a yellow sleeveless blouse that buttons up the front, faded blue jeans and open sandals with a low heel. Nice rounded ass. She's drinking coffee and smoking a Winston, the flattened pack lying next to her white coffee cup and saucer.

The waitress pours coffee in my cup and in a couple of minutes, I order. I can't help but notice two things: One, the girl isn't eating anything and two, she keeps looking over at me, the worried look back on her face.

I drink some of the coffee and get the urge for a cigarette. More coffee, coupled with the smell of the smoke from the girl's cig makes the craving grow stronger. I search my pockets, fidget on the stool for a moment, then turn to the blonde.

"Excuse me, miss," I say politely. "Could I bum a cigarette from you? I'm afraid I left mine in the room—and I'm afraid I'm dying for one. Pathetic, eh?" And then, as if someone else is doing the talking: "I tell you what, I'll buy you breakfast, in exchange for a cigarette...."

The sweet young thing gets up off her stool, moves next to me and shakes a Winston out of the pack.

I pick it up. "Thanks a lot." I smile.

"No problem," she says, her pursed lips rising slightly on the corners. "And you don't have to buy me breakfast, just for one cigarette."

"No, really, I'd love to. I just saw that you weren't eating and thought I'd offer. In case you ah... needed something to eat or something. You know, just trying to be friendly... I mean... I saw you in here last night and you didn't seem to be eating then, either, so I thought, well... you might be broke or something. God knows I've been in that situation myself, enough times.... I didn't mean to imply that—"

"Slow down, honey," she said, looking in my eyes and grinning narrowly, "You don't have to explain. You're a nice guy, aren't you?"

"I try to be—sometimes it's hard. But where I come from, that's the way we try to treat people."

"And where is that you're from?"

"Minnesota."

"You've got kind eyes,"she says, looking at her coffee cup and spinning it in the saucer with her long fingers. "For someone with eyes like that I can eat breakfast.... Mary Ellen, fix me up a steak and eggs with a tall OJ and a side of grits."

"You like those grits?" I ask, trying to grasp what it is about a soggy pile of white slop.

"Yeah. Used to eat'em with sugar when I was a kid."

I scratch a match to the Winston and inhale deeply. Blow out the smoke; the overhead fan spins it around.

"Whatya doin' in Florida, Mr. Kind Eyes?"

"I live down in Clearwater."

"No shit—excuse my French. Whattaya do there?"

"Not much. I used to be a tennis pro until I broke my leg."

"You must have made a lot of money, then...."

"No, not really. I was a teaching pro, not a guy like Jimmy Connors or Bjorn Borg."

"You make a habit of buying breakfast for strange women, Mr. Kind Eyes? What is your name, anyway?"

"Keith, er, Elton. Keith Elton. No, I usually only buy breakfast for those I've slept with the night before—just kidding."

I get a wrinkled up nose and a slurp as she directs her attention back to the coffee cup. "Well Keith Elton from Clearwater, by way of Minnesota, pleased to meet you." She sets down the thick cup and holds out a slender, long fingered hand, nails bitten down.

I shake it lightly.

"What is your name and where are you from?" I ask, finding myself drawn in.

"Dorie, uh… Lanigan… Dorie Lanigan from Tennessee, by way of Las Vegas."

"Now that's a tough one. I'll have to figure that one out. You were born in Vegas?"

"No, Knoxville."

"Oh, so you moved to Vegas after… ah hah…. So… what brings you to Florida?"

"A lot of bad trouble out in Vegas," she said, turning solemn. "My boyfriend was murdered, and my dog too."

"What? You're kidding me. Jesus! Who in the hell did that?"

"People I'd rather not talk about… some of my boyfriend's business associates. I found the bodies in the trunk of my car one day… couldn't stay in Vegas anymore after that, so I took off driving as far as my money would take me."

"Excuse me? …Then what did you do with the bodies?"

"Well I had already called the cops and everything…. It happened a couple months ago…. I had to get out of there…I knew those assholes wouldn't protect me. They had no leads and I wasn't going to say anything, so… I couldn't handle it… had to get outta Dodge."

"Some people killed your boyfriend and your dog? Fucking Christ. Must have been some bad people."

"My boyfriend was into some things..." She pauses, staring at the coffee cup. "Yes, these were some bad people.... How could anyone kill a nice, sweet dog?" She puts her hand to her eyes and sobs briefly, then snaps to as if nothing happened.

"Yeah. I mean... I don't know...." I stub out my cigarette in a black plastic ashtray on the counter. I feel a headache coming on.

The waitress comes out the little doorway from the kitchen with two steaming plates and sets them down on the counter in front of us. Dorie proceeds to tear into it like tomorrow is Judgment Day. Like cigarettes and coffee and sugar have been her staples for a while.

She wipes the thick white plate with the last hunk of toast, jams the soggy bread into her mouth and washes it down with orange juice and more coffee, making a slurping noise when she drinks.

I have the thought that the wise thing to do is to get out from under while I still can—but I just can't let her slip through my fingers that easy.

I finish my bacon, eggs and hash browns, pay the bill and have only a wrinkled twenty left.

"Do you need any money, Dorie?" I ask, my 'kind eyes' looking into her baby blues to see what I can find.

"I can't take your money, Keith, after you've been so nice to me. But if you could give me a ride down the road a-ways, it would help me out a lot. I'd feel safe with a man like you."

"Sure I'll give you a ride, where do you need to go?"

"About ten miles south of here, to Crystal River. My car is getting fixed at a gas station, there."

"No problem? Where you headed after that?"

I give her my soulful look.

"I don't really know for sure; I might even come back here to the motel. They been nice to me here. Old lady that owns it has been letting me crash in one of the rooms n'exchange for some cleaning. I guess she got sick of cleaning those lousy little rooms for a million years...."

"For sure. What's wrong with your car, then?"

"I think they said the timing belt... timing gear... something like that."

"Isn't that an expensive job?"

Her eyes fill with pathos and vulnerability; her thin lips curl down at the edges. "I don't know," she says. "They didn't say... seemed like nice boys, though...."

She's an attractive girl and I'm feeling needy. I can use some companionship. I've always been a sucker for a sad-eyed lady. There's something real nice about Dorie. There's also something else. I can't quite figure it out.

Sometimes she seems a little slow but that doesn't exactly explain it, either. Drifty. Maybe that better describes her. Sometimes I get the feeling that we aren't both walking on the same earth. But, come to think of it, I get that feeling around most women.

"You can certainly ride along with me as far as you want to go. I've got a Volkswagen bus; there's plenty of room. Why don't you get your stuff and meet me out front of the motel after breakfast. I've just got to get my stuff from the room. What do you think?"

"I think it's sweet. I really appreciate it."

I'm seriously wondering about my decision as I throw the bags into the van. But when I catch sight of Dorie standing by the motel office in a light blue, loose-fitting cotton dress that the breeze is pushing up against her bra-less nipples; I quickly shrug off my anxiety as something obviously not related to this lovely moment.

My heart is beating like a tom-tom as I reach over and unlatch the door. She steps gracefully in and looks at me, her eyebrows raised and her lips tight together, smiling thinly.

"Come on," I say. "Let's get down the road."

"Let's roll, cowboy."

She steps in and crosses her long, bare legs; the dress slides high up on her buttermilk thighs. All I can do is sigh. She lights up a cigarette and rolls down the window as we swing away from the motel onto the cracked asphalt.

The road stretches out ahead, shining in the hot Florida sun. Tires slap on spider webs of tar. I'm trying to decide what tape to put in, to set the mood just right.... Bagley's tapes are limited, but I finally find one that seems to fit the moment: Bob Dylan's Greatest Hits.

I jam it in the player. The raunchy, rolling notes come oozing out of the speakers and I know instinctively that I've chosen the right tape. Yes, Virginia, everybody must get stoned.

Dorie's head bounces softly to the rhythm; it's a pretty day. The sun is shining and a few large, cottony clouds are floating high in the searing blue sky. Dylan sings on. The wind blows. She's just like a woman.

It suddenly occurs to me that I have a million dollars worth of cocaine in the back of the van and I've taken a stranger into my midst, as it were. My dick shrinks; the skin on my nuts tightens up. Man, do I need a drink. And here it is coming on noon....

Who could blame a person in my situation for stopping to relax his jangled nerves? I mean, there's this sexy chick that god has sent my way....

We don't utter a word until we get to Crystal River, a small village soon to be overrun with development. Dorie spots a corner grocery store and asks if I could stop so she can grab a pack of smokes. I say why don't we wait until we find a bar somewhere and go in and have a beer and a smoke, just a little something to take the edge off. In the meantime, she can smoke one of the Kools that I had found in the glove compartment.

She screws up her face and looks at me, eyes narrowing. "You know they put saltpeter in those," she says. "Like they give to soldiers in the war.... You know, so they won't get horny."

"No way.... Where'd you hear that one?"

"It's true. How many of those do you smoke a day?"

"I don't know... not too many."

She studies me as I nervously light up a Kool with the dash-board lighter. I smoke about half of it before flipping it out the window with a snap of my finger.

"Did you hear if Marlboros have saltpeter in them?"

"Sure they do. Why do you think those guys in the commercials are always alone on the range?"

"I see what you mean…. So what cigarette do you recommend?"

"For me… right now… it would be any non-menthol I can get my hands on. Men shouldn't smoke at all. They should save their energies for other things." She flashes a knowing glance then blinks nervously and stares out the window. "Oh, all right," she says. "I'll have one of those Kools… if I can still have one?"

I'm turning into electrified Jello when I spot the all important tavern sign. Sandpiper Lounge: faded, blue box with a big air conditioner sticking out a side window.

"Shall we?" I say like the fly to the spider, "I'll buy you a beer…." I point at the fine establishment.

"Why not," she says.

Behind the leather-covered bar is a bartender, a few beer signs and a lot of bottles.

We have a couple beers each and get to talking. Then we get to laughing about things and teasing. I suppose, you know how it is…. Once in a while she puts her hand on my arm, real friendly and warm. I buy her a pack of Chesterfields (her "favorite" but they don't have them everyplace, so then she has to smoke Winstons).

I get the change and realize I'm down to my last five bucks and have no idea how I'm going to get any more. A pang hits my gut.

"We've got to go," I say, suddenly sober.

"You don't look so good," she says. "Is it me? You can leave me here if you want to."

"No, it's not you, Dorie. It's me. I'm down to my last five bucks, but you're welcome to share it with me."

"Cheer up, sweetie, things'll work out.... Hows about if I drive? I've never driven one of those hippie vans before."

"No... I'm all right. I can drive if I can do anything.... I'm just not sure where I should drive to...."

"Don't you have people? Didn't you say you were from Clearwater? Why aren't you going back there?"

"No place to go—well that's not totally right. There are a couple of options.... Say listen, five bucks isn't going to get us very far. What do you say we blow the rest on drinks and then hit the road and see what happens?"

"It's your party, cowboy. I'm only going a mile down."

"Then where are you going? You don't even know, do you? You're broke, just like me, aren't you? Can't you see? You and I have been thrown together by the Hands of Fate. And I think there's some meaning in that. I mean, what are the odds, for Christ sake? Two people find each other in the middle of Nowhere, Florida and get along famously like you and I do... what are the odds?"

"You are a dreamer, Keith Elton."

"But I'm not the only one."

I order us up two gin and tonics so at least we can enjoy our last few moments together in style. Five bucks turns to one and I leave it for the bartender. We finish the drinks in a hurry and walk outside into the bright sun and it's the best I've felt for days. I take a deep breath and a premonition that doom is right around the corner hits me and I don't even care. I have some food in the van and a million dollars worth of dope, why should I care?

I start thinking: what the hell, why not have a snort? Why not enjoy a little of the bounty that's been dropped into my lap by the powers that be? I can sneak back there and grab a little without the girl even knowing what I'm doing. She seems to be the type of girl that might enjoy a little toot, though... like a lot of people....

I wrestle with the idea as we get back onto the highway. I've got

a craving both for the drug and for the girl, or some twisted combination of the two. After five long minutes, with knots in my
stomach and bees in my head, I pull off the road, unable to fight
the urges any longer.

"What's the matter?" Dorie asks, nervously.

"I've got a little something in the back that you might enjoy,"
I say. "Well, at least I will. It'll only take a minute. We're out in
plane sight of the highway... nothing to worry about... I've got
to get something out of the back."

"I wasn't worried about getting hurt; I was afraid of getting
dumped."

"I wouldn't do something like that. I wanted to have a little toot
that's all. Thought, maybe you might want to join me. It'll take
the fuzz out of the booze high."

"Are you kidding? There's blow in this bus? Jesus, I don't
know...."

"Have you ever tried it before?"

She looks around nervously, fidgeting in the sheepskin seat.

"Oh yeah, I've tried it before. That stuff got my boyfriend
killed. This is just too unreal... I run into a dreamboat and he's
into coke, too. I mean, that's heavy... scares me a little...."

"Yeah, I guess... it is scary, I suppose. But there's coke around
everywhere these days, especially in this fucking state; it's hardly
rare. I've got a little bit... I just thought a toot would be a good
idea, help to bring out the sunshine... and ah... well, make it easier to drive, I'm kinda loaded."

"Well honey, so am I. Just high enough to say yes, against my
better judgment."

I smile and feel the adrenaline crawling up my spine.

I shut off the engine, get out and walk around to the other side
of the van, slide open the side door and get in. Dorie is craning
her neck around, looking at me. I smile up at her. She turns back
around, pushes her hair back with a snap of her wrist, lights up a
Chesterfield and watches the smoke disappear out the window.

"Could you hand me that mirror from off of that visor above your head, please, Dorie? And there's a pocketknife in the glove compartment. I need that too."

She slides the mirror off the visor and hands it to me. "You better watch out," she says playfully. "When I do coke, I get kind of crazy." Then she reaches in the glove box and brings out the knife.

"I think I can handle it," I say and crawl on my knees to where the duffel is lying and loosen the drawstring. I reach down until I feel the plastic wrap, pull a brick to the surface and squeeze the contents in my sweating fingers. There's a catch in my throat. I swallow hard and glance around at Dorie, who's staring out the window and twirling her hair with her middle finger.

I turn my back to her and make a small incision in the wrapping. My fingers tremble; my mouth is dry; my heart pounds. Somewhere in the back of my mind someone is screaming but I don't want to listen. All I crave is that feeling, that buzz. Now I have enough dope to make it last. This girl and me, together... life is a party....

I scoop a small pile onto the mirror and pulsate at the sight. Shining, glittering, soft rocks fall apart and sparkle in the sunlight. I carefully shove the brick deeper in the duffel, stuff some clothes over it. I crawl up and set the mirror down on the countertop behind Dorie's seatback.

"There you go," I say. "Just turn around and have at it."

"How am I supposed to do this? Where's the hundred dollar bill?"

"Ha, ha. You'll just have to scoop some up with the knife or... why don't you come around here so nobody can see from the road. We'll be two tourists stretching their legs."

"And packing their noses."

"You bet."

She comes around. We put the mirror on the carpet and lift little piles of powder to our noses with the knife blade. With this much coke—I'm thinking—not snorting it would be like going to Studio 54 without a dick.

So we're sitting next to each other, our feet dangling out the side of the bus, saying nothing and staring at the greenery. My lips and gums go numb and my brain is exploding like a bottle rocket in a fireplace. We are silent for a long moment, long enough for me to try and think up something to say and not succeed, several times. Finally, I turn to her nervously: "So, what do you thi—"

That's all I can say before she jumps at me like a sea bird snaring a dead shrimp, slams her lips against mind and begins probing deeply with her velvety tongue. I don't fight back when she puts her hand between my legs and feels the merchandise. In fact, I encourage it by demonstrating my growth as a human being, an upstanding citizen to be sure.

Just as she crawls on top of me and replaces her hand with her throbbing, hot crotch, a rush of paranoia rips through me like a blast of heat lightning. Jesus Christ, if I don't push her off me and climb out of the van. I mean, that's all I need: to get caught by some god-fearing cop for public fornication. These backwater cops have a way of taking everything so personally.

I've got enough coke in the van to keep the discos on Clearwater Beach going for a year or more and—I tell you—that suddenly becomes enough for me to handle.

She looks at me, flabbergasted, brushing down her dress, which is hiked up and revealing some of the creamiest thigh I've seen in a long time. It's enough to make you want to cry.

"I'm sorry," I say. "We're just too close to the road here… the drugs and all… you know what I mean… I just can't relax."

She stands up, walks up to me and grabs my shoulders, starts kissing me again, putting her hand back where I like it. I put my hands on her arms and slowly push her away.

"Maybe we can find a better place," I say. "Down the road. We can't stay here."

The back of my neck is burning as I slide the door closed and walk around to the driver's door. She climbs in the other side, looks over at me, throws her head back and laughs. I'm not quite sure what to think of that laugh; seems like a hint of mania riding its edge. I start the engine and pull out.

My blood is boiling and I'm worried that the moment has passed me by. Hot beads of sweat plaster my forehead as I shift into fourth gear and put the gas pedal to the floor. I'm thinking I have to find someplace in a hurry or everything is going to turn to shit; Cinderella's going to turn ugly and run home. Somewhere there's a place for us.

I'm bobbing with anxiety, searching the distance for a road that might lead to some privacy. There has to be a road, somewhere. I'm always reading in the papers about dead bodies being found on lonely, Florida roads; shit like that happens all the time....

I become so lost inside my head and its vainglorious struggles that I forget about my speed. My eyes are searching the distance so much that I forget what's right in front of me. I mean I know that VW vans don't go very fast—so it's not something you usually worry about....

The van is vibrating smoothly along when my ears pick up that horrible sound: A siren, closing fast.

I stare in the rearview mirror with disbelief as the white Chevy with the cherry on top comes up fast behind me. Everything turns to black and a sick feeling fills me up.

I tell myself that I'm okay if it's only a speeding bust. Then I remember the cocaine mirror is lying on the floor in back, uncovered, and look frantically for something to throw on it.

"Dorie," I say, my head throbbing, "Carefully reach in the glove compartment and get a map or something to throw over that mirror. We're getting pulled over, so try not to show any movement, if you can manage that."

Her shoulders rise up and her skin gets a few shades lighter but she manages to slide out the Florida road map and skillfully work it between the shifter and the bucket seat and drop it on the dope. As I come to a halt, I look back at the cop and notice a small corner of the mirror sticking out from under the map. It will have to do; the cop is out of his cruiser and striding toward us.

A big man, about six-four, with a small gut hanging over his belt and a toothpick in his mouth, he looks like a local but has the aviator shades, Mounty hat and jackboots like all the heat down here seem to wear. This one has an arrogant swagger like maybe he played football in college and misses the opportunity to hit people.

"May I see your driver's license, sir."

I reach above the visor where I put Bagley's alternative wallet.

"Take it out of the wallet, please."

He holds a clipboard with one hand while studying us. I hand him the license. He puts it on the clipboard and stares into my eyes.

"Are you aware that the speed limit is fifty on this here road, Mr. Kirby?"

"Yes."

Dorie shoots me a wicked glance.

"You were traveling over seventy, sir. Can I see your registration, Mr. Kirby."

"It's not my van, officer. It belongs to a friend of mine who's down in St. Pete. He just let me use it for a little sightseeing and camping trip. I don't know where the registration is."

The cop frowns: "Would you step back into the patrol car with me, Mr. Kirby."

I get out of the van and start to walk back along the highway toward the cruiser.

"Please step to the shoulder, sir. Around to the other side of the van."

"Dorie, look for that registration card, will you please," I say. "I'm sure it's in there somewhere. Dan always kept his things in order."

I go in front of the bus and the cop lumbers along behind me. I can feel him peering in the windows even though my back is to him.

He doesn't linger and I'm able to calm down enough to stop shaking.

I get into the cruiser; the cop slides behind the wheel. He leans back against the seat and the scent of garlic and onions and stale after-shave hit me like a damp cloud. He lifts up his shades, peers down at the license.

"What kind of name is Elton, boy? Some kind of limey moniker like that fruity Elton John? You a limey, son? They got all kinds of funny names over there...."

Yeah, like Billy Bob and Bubba. "No, I'm an American."

"And where in America do you reside there, Elton?"

"In Clearwater. That's where I'm headed."

"You need to get this driver's license changed then, this one here's from Colorado... you need a Florida license."

"Only been her for three months, officer."

"Then ya're only sixty days overdue, boy. But I 'magine you and the missus here, have plenty a things to keep ya busy?" He says, winking.

"Uh...well... ah, yeah. And here she comes now—the wife. She must have found the registration papers."

Dorie is walking toward us; red purse slung over her left shoulder and a white card in her right hand.

"Sure is a pretty one," the cop drawls. "You are a lucky guy, even with a name like Elton, and all," he laughs.

"Yes I am, Officer. I surely am. Sometimes I don't realize how much."

Dorie comes up to the driver's window and hands the card to the cop. "I found it, honey," she says, leaning in until her tits are damn near falling into the guy's mouth.

His eyes lock on the luscious mounds. Then he looks distractedly up at her face and then over at me and then back to the card. He stares blankly at it for a second, blinks, and looks back at me.

I'm smiling sheepishly when Dorie's hand darts into her purse like a cobra going for an egg.

Her pale, slender fingers pop out of the red bag and sunlight flashes off the shiny nickel-plated barrel of a small handgun.

Quick as a flash she sticks it at the cop's reddening face and squeezes the trigger.

I duck out of the way as brains and blood explode onto the cheap brown vinyl seats and the sound of the blast drifts away on the breeze.

"FUCK!" I scream; then jump out of the car onto the yellow, sun-baked dirt thinking she's gonna hit me next. Instead, she's reaching into the cruiser.

I scramble to my feet, run back to the VW and jump in, hoping that Dorie is lingering behind to admire her work but no such luck.

She climbs in, breathless, beside me, hands me the license and the registration card.

"I had to do it," she says, matter-of fact. "The fucking pig was going to bust us. Now let's get the hell out of here so we can screw. I'm dying to see you naked."

"What the hell is wrong with you? You killed a fuckin' cop. We'll fuckin' hang for this. Worse than that…."

"Did the pig call in your plates?"

"No. He never had time. He was too busy making fun of my name."

"Yeah, your name. We'll have to discuss that later. In the meantime, I think you should know that I saved you—and you and I both know from what. I was looking around for the registration form and I… ah… found a brick of cocaine inside one of the cabinets. I think the penalty in Florida is worse for that much coke than it is for murder, so I definitely did you a favor."

"Hey… in the future, ask me before you act on my behalf, will you please?"

Horrible vomit taste in my mouth; my heart is dead. I've gone beyond sadness to eternal despair. I'm looking out from inside of a damp, black cave and all I can see is the desert.

"Just one less pig around to hassle people, dude," she says.

What the hell is this younger generation coming to?

"Yeah, I guess. Maybe you're right. But a car went by that saw this van pulled over by a cop that is now blown all over his front seat. Somehow we have to get out of this van and into something else. And without any money, that might be a difficult thing to do. If we're lucky, we've got a few hours before they put it all together. Got any more bright ideas?"

"It's only a few miles to my car. If it's fixed, we take that. Dump this thing somewhere and be gone like the wind."

"And how are we going to pay for the repairs, offer to trade some coke for it?"

"You probably could, with these rednecks. I was going to offer them something else, if it came down to that. But now, I think we should just use one of those credit cards in your wallet. Or should I say Elton Kirby's wallet, ah, Keith? By the way, Dan Bagley, it says on the registration. Is that you?"

"No, that's my brother. I'm Keith Bagley. If you found the registration form why did you have to kill the fucking cop? Jesus fucking Christ."

"I can't take any chances; I already have two felony drug charges on my record.... I can't take another rap of any kind. Don't you see? But everything is going to be all right. We'll get in my car and ride off into the sunset, to the Honeymoon Hotel...."

The muscles in my chest tighten up and my soul cries out for release.

"There it is," she's saying, seems like her voice is miles away. Then: "There. There! Stop! There it is! What's the matter with you, you're going by it!"

I snap back from my trip down the tunnel of despair and slowly pull over to the side of the road. I look carefully in the rearview mirror and swing a u-turn. Some moments later I'm pulling into an old, dirty white service station that looks to be left over from the early days of Florida.

We park on the side by a pile of rusted springs and mufflers and various other parts. Dorie grabs her purse and jumps out of the van. I stay inside in a daze. I'd take off down the highway if I didn't need her car.

I need her and she knows it.

Five minutes go by before she comes prancing back like she's been playing Run around the Maypole. She's fucking skipping, again looking to all of the world like the damaged, frightened little buttercup that I discovered at the café. Deeply, I wish that I had known when to keep my mouth shut.

Running off at the mouth, whether an attempt at friendly conversation or nervous spewing, can get you in trouble. Trouble of any kind can be caused by something you say. The wrong words to the wrong person at the wrong time and BANG—you won't know what hit you.

She comes up to the window and I can't help but stare at the soft skin below her neck that leads to those luscious breasts. The sunshine on her hair and the glint in her pale blue eyes almost make me forget how fucked up everything is. For a brief moment, I'm starting to believe again that I might actually get away unscathed.

Everything's gonna be all right this morning, Oh yeah....

Dorie comes in real close, presses her hips against the door. She looks into my eyes and smiles broadly and for the first time, I get a look at her teeth.

Poor girl has what we Northerners call "hillbilly teeth": brown, decaying, uneven stumps, most likely the result of a one-hundred percent sugar diet and being too busy running away from her father to brush.

"Keith darlin'" she drawls. "If you'll come on in and bring along that Chevron Card and the rest of the wallet, we can pay the bill and get out of Dodge."

"I don't know if these cards are any good," I say. "And you better start calling me Elton. I don't know why they're in there or what they're for.... For all I know, they're on the Arrest Immediately list. They could be hot, I don't know."

"Ya think these boys have themselves all that fancy equipment? Shit, they can barely turn on the radio without help. All they can do is fix cars and jerk off. Don't worry so much. After I practically had to get down on my knees to get them to accept a credit card, we have to use it. I told them you were my fiance from Colorado, come to rescue me...."

"It's a fucking Chevron station for Christ sake," I say, stating the obvious, "They have to take the fucking thing."

"I don't know about that, but I 'magine these boys pretty much do what they please 'round here, ain't a heck of a lot of competition. Only station for miles."

"In five years it'll be a strip mall."

She crinkles up her eyes at me and pulls on the door handle. I climb reluctantly out of the VW. Dorie takes my hand in hers. My instinct is to pull it back but instead I swallow hard and keep walking. What the hell...

Marv's Chevron has two dirt-floor repair stalls, one of which contains a faded tan '69 Chevy Impala with a small dent on the driver's door. Off to one side of the building is an office with dull yellow paint and finger smears on the walls and a greasy window facing the road.

The flat, metal desktop is littered with dirty scraps of paper, nuts, bolts, pens and assorted pieces of wrapped candy. A turned-over hubcap in the middle of the desk is piled high with cigarette butts. A dark green wastebasket, half full of candy wrappers, cigarette packs and empty tins of Copenhagen, sits next to a tarnished spittoon with vile-looking stains congealing on the edges. A wooden chair on wheels contains Marvin, the station owner, as he peers over the repair bill.

I say hello and sit down at the side of the desk on a chromium-framed kitchen chair with a cracked, red plastic seat. I'm praying that Marvin won't call in the number on the credit card that I'm handing him. He squints at the card and then at me, tosses the card on the desk and returns his attention to the bill.

I lean over and try to decipher the scribbles: Timing chain, timing gear, shop supplies and labor. The easiest thing to read is the total: $177. 34.

The mechanic stands outside the office in gray coveralls and an oily, black skullcap, trying his damnedest to explain to Dorie—in a mostly incomprehensible mixture of Scandinavian flavored, Southern white trash English—what he has done to the Chevy. She's slightly inside the office door, staring up at his grease-smeared stubble, acting like she understands.

Marvin rummages around in the side drawer, looking for something.

My prayers are answered when he happily lifts out his credit card imprinter and a clean receipt.

"I gotta charge you fifteen bucks extra for using the credit card," he says gruffly. "It costs me money every time I get one of the goddamn things. Sposed to be ten percent, but I'm cuttin' ya some slack on account of the two of ya make such a fine couple."

"Thanks," I say, growing ever more restless and uneasy, sweat beginning to trickle down the back of my neck. "I understand… the big oil companies are always screwing you over."

His eyes get narrow. He tilts his head sideways, shrugs his shoulders and launches a brown stream in the direction of the spittoon. The goober hits the edge with a slippery clank and drips down into the soup. Marvin seems to be pleased. He writes up the charges on the slip and slides the knob across the plastic. He grins and pushes everything over to me, along with a cracked, and of course, greasy, ballpoint pen.

"There you go, Elton," he says. "You're all set."

Dude didn't know how right he was.

"Now we've got plenty of time to enjoy the sights before it gets dark, honey," Dorie says as my nose starts to run.

I sniff in and sign the slip. Marvin slides over a set of keys on a ring with a yellow card fastened to it. I take them and hand them to Dorie but she holds her hands up and shakes her head.

"You drive the Chevy so you can test out how it's running, darlin'," she says, looking at me with big, wide eyes. "I'll follow you in the bus. Maybe we can find a motel on the beach somewhere."

"I'm sure these guys fixed it quite well, Dorie. I'm sure it will be fine. I should drive the van and follow you."

"Oh come on Ke—Elton. Please let me drive the camper... please, please.... Can I please?"

Marvin smirks up at me. The mechanic says, "She be a runnin rel gooed. Y'all'll seeah."

I give up any thought of resistance and squeeze the Chevy keys in my palm. Dorie wiggles and giggles out of the office. I follow closely behind, waving, thanking Marvin and trying not to stimulate any more conversation. It feels like the devil is in my chest.

Dorie heads for the VW. I walk alongside her, smiling. We get to the bus and she climbs in the driver's side like there's no question about it.

I have to admit; she has me. I can't throw a big fuss at the gas station and besides that, she still has the gun in her purse.

The coke is wearing off and my stomach is making like a jumping frog. My head feels like a doormat at a wedding party. There is only one way to play it....

I hold the door open and slide my hand around her waist. Bring my head in close to her ear and whisper: "I think we need to recharge. We need to find someplace to dump this bus and get high. You and me got a lot of living to do. I sure want to get to know you better."

I put my hand behind her head and gently pull her to me. I kiss her full on the mouth and let my tongue explore. I close my eyes.

The muscles in her neck tighten up and she pulls away from me.

"What's the matter?" I ask, trying to keep from ripping her head off.

"Nothing, let's just get moving."

"And where is it that you think we're going with all the stuff in the van? You can't drive this thing out there in public for very long, anymore than I can."

"We go to the first beach road and leave it there like it's for camping," she says. "We throw the stuff in the car and go to a motel. Take care of business then go our separate ways…. I want half the stuff."

"Split the stuff in half? Are you fucking kidding me? Where did that idea come from, for Christ fucking sake?"

She blinks; her eyes glaze over and her face tightens up: "I saved your Yankee ass already today and don't forget it. And don't you be callin' me dumb. You smart-ass boys are always thinkin' yer so goddamn clever. Well you listen here; I'm the one that saved yer ass this time pretty boy… and now we are partners. Now I'd sure as hell go somewhere and party with you if that's what you want. But if it ain't, I'm still gonna get my share of the dope before I go. So you decide, smart boy."

"Hey, no problem, I'll just tell my Colombian financiers that I met a beautiful woman and decided to give her half of their dope. I'm sure they'll be real amenable to that. Then they can send somebody after you for payment. No fucking sweat. They'll just cut your pretty little head off and put it in a box…."

She blinks a few times, like she doesn't even hear me.

"Listen, Dorie, we'll have to discuss this later. Right now, we have to get our asses out of here. I'll follow you. But keep two things in mind: One, the Chevy is faster than the Volkswagen so I can always catch you. And two, if the cops do start chasing us they will be looking for the van, and not me in a Chevy. That of course means that you will go to jail and I will drive away. The lesson that I'm trying to get across here, is that we better get off the road real soon and do this thing real fast or we'll both be real fucked. *Comprende?"*

"Oooh, I love it when you talk like that."

"Fucking Christ…. Let's just go."

"Si, mi amoret. Via con Dios."

My throat seizes up.

As we leave Marvin's and head down the road, I have no idea what direction I should take or what I should do next. Basically, I have become a lap dog. It's the only thing I can do. And I'm wondering if this girl really thinks that I could still fuck her after she has pulled this power trip on me?

She doesn't really know what she is getting into, does she?

It isn't long before we come to a beach access road. I wave and point and Dorie obediently turns down. After a short distance, we roll out of the mangroves and discover a beautiful little bay.

It's a clear day with high, wispy clouds and a good wind from the northwest. Off in the distance, whitecaps roll, but inside the narrow bay there is a gentle lapping of soft, blue-green water. Three cars are parked on the side of the road.

We continue farther on the shell road, moving parallel to the water. I can't stop thinking that they've already found the dead constable and it's only a matter of time before they start looking for a white VW bus with two gun-crazy drug addicts inside. This, of course, will be enough to send every firearm-owning redneck in the area into a feeding frenzy—and who can blame them?

On the southern end of the bay, a long point stretches out. I can see only one car, near the tip. We drive on past the car and then around the point and find ourselves alone as the road jogs its way along a jagged and uninhabited shoreline. About a half a mile down, the vegetation begins to take over and the road narrows from the onslaught of gnarled, creeping vines and spiky foliage. The surf roars in my ears and I can't think straight.

The road straightens out for a hundred yards and I zip around, quickly pass the VW and make her ride my bumper for a while. We bounce along while I check her out in the rearview mirror.

Looks to me like she's getting uptight, constantly flipping her hair back with her free hand and gripping the wheel tightly with the other. The van bounces because she won't shift it out of second gear. Maybe she's Jonesing, needing another blast of coke before the roof falls in on her castle made of sand.

Up ahead, I see an opportunity: a small, offshoot trail going down to the sand. I veer onto it and Dorie follows. The VW's headlights bounce behind me like the eyes of an insane clown.

I come to a stop; the bus pulls up. The wind howls and whines; waves slam against the shore. The sound is fierce, like Neptune himself is roaring out his frustration with the state of the world.

I pull out a cigarette—a Kool—and punch in the lighter on the cheesy, maroon dashboard. I'm watching her in the mirror; she has a cigarette, too. She's puffing on it, looking around nervously. Then she climbs out of the driver's door and walks around to the front of the van, turning her head toward me as I'm putting the lighter back in.

I swing my right arm onto the seat back and face her. I smile my best fake smile.

She waves, turns her eyes back to the ocean and stretches her arms up to the sky. The red, vinyl purse is hanging from her shoulder.

I'm still facing her, smiling, when I slip the shifter into reverse with my left hand and floor the gas pedal.

Her eyes widen and she jumps upward.

The Chevy's rear bumper catches her below the knees; her body jackknifes and her head smashes down on the trunk. It's one hell of a thunk and she goes limp like a rag doll, her last gasps and gurgles signaling the end of another wasted life.

I shift into drive and pull forward until she rolls off onto the sand.

I get out and drag her body to the side door of the van.

Sometime soon, somebody will discover an abandoned hippie

van with links to three dead people. Traces of drugs and semen and god knows what all will be found among the carpet fibers of this four-wheeled wagon of sin.

SATANISTS INVADE FLORIDA! Could be the headline in the *Baptist Weekly*....

I stick poor Dorie inside Bagley's sleeping bag and clean out the van of important items. I throw a pair of Bagley's tennis shoes, shorts and a T-shirt, into the crashing surf. I leave behind Bagley's wallet and Elton Kirby's wallet, keep Keith Waverly's wallet. Then I stuff all forty-five kilos of coke and some clothes inside the two military duffels and throw them into the trunk of the Chevy.

Just before I drive away, I remember to go back and close the curtains on the van and say my farewells and regrets to Dorie.

I mean, what was I supposed to do? I really had to kill her. Could never have become partners with the heinous likes of that. And I couldn't have faced the responsibility of loosing her on an unsuspecting world, her in possession of massive quantities of cocaine and a loaded handgun....

Bagley and Dorie, I figure, were like two peas from the same pod, except Bagley had had the good fortune to be born rich while Dorie, on the other hand, had to learn to lie and cheat out of necessity.

They can both rot in hell as far as I'm concerned. I have deals to make and money to accumulate.

I'm beginning to see a new path. The seventies are fast approaching a horrible end and I can see an inkling of the new way....

It is time to be done with spiritual angst and uncertainty. The time is right for worshipping a new god, the god that the so-called successful people are already bowing and scraping to—Money. Mammon, if you feel the need to personify.

With cash as your guide, there is no guilt or agonizing soul searching. No one wails or gnashes his teeth (unless the stock market crashes). One simply accumulates—always going forward—come hell or federal investigation. After accumulating, you consume. And then you discard. It's as easy as one two three.

Feeling spiritual, I anoint my new Holy Trinity:

MONEY, SEX and DRUGS (not necessarily in that order).

These are things that you can feel and experience. Not pie in the sky and self-denial.

This time around, I'm not going to get caught short. I'll be riding high on the crest and running the shoot, hanging five on a golden surfboard.

First things first, though. I have to get back to Tampa without getting caught by the cops. Then I need some cash, a new mode of transportation and an outlet large enough to handle mucho kilos of Peruvian Marching Powder. Talk about your millstones.

If I think about it too much my head starts to spin. I have no choice but to take it one step at a time. I decide to wait on the beach for a while; in a couple of hours it will be dark.

After five minutes of vacant staring, my stomach is flopping so bad I have to leave.

I continue down the frontage road until it winds its way back to Highway 19. I turn right and head south through Homossa Springs. First road I come to going east, I turn, and #98 takes me through Brooksville and all the way to the freeway, where I head south.

It's a soft evening with no wind. Sun is falling, red as blood. As the night lights pop on, the sky turns gray and then black and I'm swallowed up in the swarm of traffic. Just another white trash evening for the guy in the maroon Chevy.

Now I'm strangely relaxed; emotion seems to have left me for the time being. The drive is surreal, like I'm floating on air and the only sound is the hiss of the tires. Like a homing pigeon, my instincts are bringing me back—or at least, to the general vicinity of my lousy apartment.

Why am I going home? I'm really not sure. I only know that I must get rid of the Chevy—find somewhere to dump it—and the only area that I know is near Twin Lakes. One thing in my favor: there are so many complexes and parking lots in the area and—correspondingly—so many cars—that one more decrepit sedan can disappear in the crowd without much trouble.

About a quarter-mile from Twin Lakes I turn into the parking lot at Palm Gardens: a vast, fern-surrounded, apartment complex that stretches across a full square block. I park and walk the remaining distance to Twin Lakes through the buildings. All logic has left me. I've become a hound following some long-departed scent. I walk on until I get to the laundry room behind my apartment. That's when something makes me stop.

Voices seep from the glow of the laundry room. I change direction, walk behind the laundry builng and then down to the next breezeway, which takes me to the far side of the pool area, directly across from the glass doors and living room window of our apartment.

I step out into the open and sit down in a poolside chair. I can see inside my former home; the curtains are open wide. Mike is on the couch watching television. I can't move, no matter how much I want to.

Envious of the seeming peace inside that warm light, I hope that they're at least a little worried about me. At least Mikey. But then again, what am I to them but an occasional interloper who always seems to run off when the going gets tough?

A slight breeze kicks up, carrying laughter from the second floor. Something wells up inside me. It isn't the same familiar pain. It doesn't really hurt; it's only a spasm from a memory. Not really longing but more a confusion that leaves me numb and wondering, more curious than hurt.

I sit in the chair until I see Carole come to the window and look out. Looking right at me but not knowing. She seems to search the darkness for something for a moment; then pulls the cord and the drape slides closed. I stare at the orange glow behind the curtains for a long minute and then get up and walk away.

Breathing deep and rhythmically, I try to concentrate on the task at hand. I have business to do. There is nothing left for me here and I need to get hold of Ted. He's the only one who can help me. The only one I know that might save my ass.

I move quickly down the dim sidewalks and into the dark space between complexes. As my feet hit the grass, burning tears and barely suppressed sobs come pushing out. They last until I get to the next complex; then abruptly stop.

That's the last time I will cry about anything.

I find a payphone bathed in the warm, red glow of a Coke machine. I drop a dime, punch out Ted's number and wait. It rings three times before a woman's voice comes on.

"Is Ted there," I ask, fatigue and fear creeping in.

"Ted doesn't live here anymore. Who is this calling, please?"

"This is Keith, Keith Waverly. Do you know where he can be reached, Ann? What happened, I mean, where did he go? I need to find him, it's really important. I'm sorry, I don't mean to be pushy, but this a matter of life or death, like they say...."

"I don't know where he's gone, you'll have to ask John Carino. Maybe he can help you, Keith. Ted's moved out... that's all I can say... goodbye."

She clicks off and I stare at the phone in disbelief. I pull out my last dime and dial up Carino. No one answers. I hang up and the dime returns. I start back toward the car and get about a half a block before I turn around and walk back. I'm way too paranoid to stay in that car, for fear of a security patrol.

I make another call to John. Saints preserve us, if he doesn't answer, fresh out of the shower and full of spit.

"Hey John, what's happening?"

"Man, man... where the hell are you? What is going down, Jack?"

"Same shit I told you about before, only now it's even more complicated. I need to find Ted, ASAP."

"Hey, hey... no need to get testy. There's been a cop hanging around Twin Lakes, looking for you, you know that?"

"I would imagine."

"What the hell does that mean? Carole knows you're in some trouble but she thinks you're taking care of it. Are you?"

"Not really... I fucked up. What can I say? Your suspicions about my white trash genetics have been validated...."

"Suspicions of your stupidity...."

"That's unfair, man. Watch it or I'll come over there and stuff that graphite racket of yours down your California-glory-boy throat. You'll be sorry you ever met me."

"I already am."

"Fuck you, John. Come on, man, you know we had some good times.... If it wasn't for your goddamn celebrity doubles match, I might still have a job and not be in this trouble I'm in."

"I doubt that very much."

"I do, too, but I thought it sounded good. Now come on and tell me how I can find Ted. I haven't got all fucking evening; I have to get out of town. I need you to tell Carole that you talked to me. Tell her I'm sorry it worked out this way, but me leaving, is probably the best thing for her and Mike. Got that straight?"

"Yeah, Keith, I do. It's a heavy burden. It's sad. First Ted's old lady finds out about his young honey on the side and kicks him out of the house—and now you and Carole are on the outs.... Now I know why I never got married."

"Probably because you're a fag.... Where the hell is Ted?"

"He spent the weekend on my couch, but now he's over in Tampa—I drove him over... some of his wrestling cronies' apartment, I think... on the edge of Ybor City. I've got the phone number; I'll get it for you."

"Just a minute, man. Do you have any idea what the cops were saying about me? I'm sure Carole must've told you something— fucking golden boy that you are... I'm sure you provided a shoulder to lean on, eh?"

"The golden boy who just got a job in New York City, my friend. I'm headed for the Big Apple."

"Congratu-fucking-lations. Now, tell me what you heard?"

"Cop was looking for you; that's all I know. Poor wife of yours was too embarrassed to say anything else. I got the distinct impression that she thinks she can wrap the cop around her finger, though... girl's got some spirit."

"That's it? Shit.... All right, John, thanks—I have to go. But just for the record, tell me what the deal is with the station and that whole ugly scene? Carole mentioned a few things: You're leaving, Chris O'Neill's leaving, people's paychecks are getting stopped—what's the deal? I'm worried about her job."

"Everyone's trying to cover their ass. It's a madhouse... people have been getting canned or quitting—left and right. Then they get to the bank and find out Paul has cancelled payment on their last paycheck.... Almost everybody is scrambling, trying to find another job. And that, my friend, was last week. This week, there's a rumor that Paul is under federal investigation for some kind of financial shenanigans.... Bill Terres split already, ran off with the station manager's wife... and now, Randy is in Paul's office, crying, every goddamn day. The whole place is falling apart. Pretty soon Ted's going to be the only one left."

"Chickens coming home to roost, eh?"

"Must be.... I'll get you Ted's number."

"Okay... ah... thanks, John buddy, for everything."

"No problem."

"We beat those rich pricks' asses, didn't we, Johnny...."

"Goddamn Beano, what a prick."

He gets me the number. I go back to the Chev and dig around in the seat until I find sixty-eight cents in change. Then I drive farther down Fourth Street to a 7-11 with an outside payphone.

I call the number John gives me; a guy, with a voice like a foghorn, answers. His annoyance at being disturbed is right there on top of his grating bellow. He's decent enough to tell me that Ted is no longer there and has "moved in with his bitch."

I dial "his bitch's" number and much to my relief, Ted answers.

To my surprise, he sounds genuinely glad to hear from me. He gives me directions to his new address.

I'm on edge the whole way over the Gandy Bridge, as usual. There's a feeling like somebody is watching me, or the car is going to break down, or something. After some paranoid times at red lights, with cops going by etc., I make it to a small apartment complex on a dark street in a shitty neighborhood. Seems like it's mixed, Cubans and whites, I don't see any blacks. Obviously the Colombians haven't moved in yet because there are no bodies or severed heads lying around.

Down here, the Cubans hate the blacks and the blacks hate the Cubans. They both hate the whites and the whites hate everyone who ain't white. The Colombians will kill anyone who fucks with them. Neighborhood like this one, you don't know who to be afraid of.

I go inside the small apartment and meet Ted's new girl: a cute little blonde whose chest size and IQ are roughly in the same ballpark. I'm being unfair. But hey, she can cook (we enjoy a nice little taco salad) and her tits are round and full, like grapefruit.

Goddamn Ted.... But what the hell, he doesn't have any kids and his old lady always seemed pissed off, anyway, so maybe he's better off. He doesn't seem like he's suffering anything more than a slight embarrassment, mostly about his living quarters.

He tells me he doesn't like getting kicked out of the house that he paid for. I don't have much time for small talk so I ask him if we can have some privacy. We move into the kitchen while Sonya watches television in the living room. Ted turns on the radio so she can't hear us.

There isn't much to hear: His goddamn old lady gave him the boot; Dracula has been missing for several days; the station is falling apart. He gives me two hundred bucks for some of the hash; says he's still getting stiffed on the rest. I tell him I'm delighted to put on a party for a bunch of steroid-stoked he-men and express my hopes that no harm will come to him. Then I ask him what I really want to know.

"Ted, my man, if you had to get to Orlando without getting seen by the cops, how would you do it? Bus? Rental car, what?"

"I'd hop a fucking freight, *muchacho*... jump on one at the main yard in Tampa and ride the rails to wherever you want to go. That's the way to travel, dude... ride the rails like a hobo. Nobody knows where you are."

"So the trains run right through Orlando?"

"Sure man, sure, all the time. All you gotta do is know what direction you're going in."

"How in the fuck am I supposed to know that?"

"The times are in the paper, man... the Tribune, I think.... You just find one that's leaving at the right time and hop on. It's easy, man."

"You ever done it?"

"No, but I got some buddies who do it all the time. They get on and ride up to Tallahassee... all over...."

"That would take more than I've got in me, tonight, I'm afraid. I'd need someplace to spend the night."

"You can stay here, man. Sonya won't mind. You can have the couch."

"Thanks, man, that's all right. I appreciate the offer but I don't want to drag you into this. I've become quite a popular guy with the pigs. I wouldn't want anything to rub off on you. You've got enough trouble."

"I hear ya, dude. I hear ya. But one night ain't gonna hurt anything. Hell, man, I owe you. You can have the couch, you'll be safe here."

"Thanks, man, that's cool. But first I've got to get rid of this car I'm driving. It's rather warm. Any suggestions?"

He laughs dryly. "I know some places in Tampa where the fucking niggers'll strip it down to the chassis if it's there for more than fifteen minutes. A junker, they burn it...cops won't even go there unless they can bring an army along. You want me to take you there; you get all your shit out of the car before we leave here because we won't have any time after it's parked. I be scared in that part of town. Those boys'll barbecue our ass if they snag us on the street."

"Let's do it," I say. "I'll go down and get my stuff ready; I think I want to be travelling light."

"Yo, Rinty…."

"Settle down, Ted, easy now."

I go outside to the Chevrolet and take one of the duffels from the trunk and leave the other. It's a hot night and I'm sweating. I wonder if the coke is hidden in the same trunk where Dorie's dog and boyfriend were found. I tell myself that her story was probably bullshit and reach for a cig.

Ted comes outside and I throw the duffel full of dope into the back of his green, Plymouth four-door. He jumps in the driver's seat, fires her up. I get in and we head.

Most of the way, our surroundings are relatively well lit; then all of a sudden it turns hazy and dirty. Buildings are boarded up and sometimes charred and nobody is walking on the sidewalks. Only people I see are standing around the random streetlights that actually work.

I feel eyes burning into my head like infrared sights on an Uzi and anxiety creeps up my spine like a big, black spider. I check in the rearview for Ted and hold my hand up, to say: What's up?

Ted holds up three fingers, waves them excitedly. His eyes are like saucers in a sandbox. We go by a liquor store on one side of the street and a bar on the other. Seems like that's where all the people are.

The stop light ahead of me turns to yellow and I floor it. Don't feel much like stopping at this particular time or place….

Ted follows suit and comes up alongside me in the outside lane. He's waving emphatically, yelling: "Three blocks… three blocks…."

He pulls in front of me and I slow to the speed limit.

Two blocks farther down, it's totally dark: no lights, no people and no cars. On one side of the street there's an empty lot filled with the rubble of several demolished buildings. On the other side there's a rusty iron-bar fence enclosing a three story brick building with no glass in the windows. Big black gaping holes staring out at you.

Ted pulls over at the far end of the block, head bouncing like a bobble doll. I roll in behind him, turn off the Chev, jump out and sprint toward the Plymouth. He pulls away from the curb and I have to scramble in while the car is rolling. My bad leg makes it difficult to do the footwork and I slam my shin on the doorframe. Ted hits the gas and we fly down the road towards the freeway entrance. Flop sweat clings to his forehead as he careens up the ramp. I can't help but laugh—if he only knew what was in his backseat.

Ted laughs, too and extends his hand, palm up. I slap it and we hoot like a couple of drunken owls.

"Hey *muchacho*, we did it. I told you old Teddy would save you, man. That's one for the cause, man. One for the people."

"That's right Ted, it is. One for us people, man—you and I."

I don't have the heart to tell him what I left behind in the trunk of the Chev. He'll never know that I saved his soul.

You see, it didn't make any sense for me to be carrying a hundred-pound duffel bag on a freight train. I had decided that I could do okay, financially, with only twenty kilos and that I needed to get rid of the extra weight. If the railroad bulls were to start chasing me with the full pack on my shoulder, I'd be up shit creek without a paddle. The expurgated version is heavy enough, for Christ sake.

At least with the fifty-pound sack, I can hit them with it, if I have to.

We roll toward Ted's apartment and I'm musing on the future, trying not to linger on the past, when he shoves a pipe full of hash over to me. He's all smiles and giggles now that we're "safe."

We toke up the hash and make a leisurely exit off the freeway. Ted weaves his way through side streets of small, well-kept houses and lush little yards. I relax and soak in the lushness. Then we pop out of the quiet onto a busy thoroughfare and I don't know where I am. Never did spend much time on this side of the bridge.

Ted stops at a liquor store and picks up a case of Bud. We get back to his place in good spirits. We spend the night smoking hash, drinking beer and playing Yahtze with Sonya.

I decide I've underestimated Sonya as she kicks our ass in Yahtze all night long. She's a lot of fun and very cute. We have a good time. About midnight, Sonya goes to bed. Ted sets me up on the couch before he joins her in the bedroom. I find myself wishing that I were back at home.

I turn the TV on to a cheesy, fifties-era sci-fi flick and settle in. Five minutes later, I have to turn up the volume to cover the sound of bouncing bedsprings and slapping flesh coming from the bedroom.

I fall asleep and dream that I'm a kid again, playing by the railroad tracks near my aunt's house in southern Minnesota. It's a beautiful summer day, with blue sky and bright sun and multicolored flowers waving in the breeze. My cousins and my brother and I put pennies on the tracks and watch as a train rolls through and flattens them. Then we go back to Aunt Lizzie's for red Koolaid and a jump in the river. Down at the cool dark water, I wade in too deep and my foot slips. The current grabs me. Suddenly I'm spinning down river toward the falls. My brother and my cousins stand blankly on the bank, doing or saying nothing as I drift helplessly by them.

I jerk awake, my hands flailing in the air. The ceiling is flooded with flashing red lights. My heart starts to pound as the guns start blasting.

Slowly, I realize there's a cop car on the television screen with its cherries rolling and uniformed officers crouched behind its open doors, guns firing away. I roll out and shut off the tube and then stumble back to the couch. Then I remember something I read in the paper once: Lying still and calm, even if you can't fall asleep, is eighty-five percent as effective as actual slumber.

The next morning, Ted and I go to McDonalds's for Egg McMuffins and coffee. Sonya stays in bed. My head feels gray and fuzzy. I grab a Tampa Tribune and check the paper for the railroad times but can't find anything of the kind. I decide to throw my life to the wind. Fate... God... Sky Pilot... Jesus...

After breakfast, Ted drives me around the train yard until we locate the freight trains and open boxcars. By looking through the fence, we attempt to determine which ones are heading where, according to which way the engine is facing. To the best of our limited ability, we determine that they all face to the East or the South.

The longer I think about it, I realize that Tampa is on the West coast of Florida, which means you have to go East to get just about anywhere of importance. All this figuring doesn't do me a lick of good, though, because I still have no way of knowing the trains' ultimate destinations.

I say fuck it and decide to trust my instincts. They've gotten me this far, haven't they?

Ted spots a cut in the chain link fence and pulls alongside. He looks at me, grins that great, wide smile that seems to reaffirm life. "Well, here you go, man. Your train is now loading."

"Fuck, man, I hope there's no railroad bulls or any shit like that...."

"Nah, man, don't worry. I heard it's easy nowadays, not like it is in those movies where they kick your ass and shit for ridin'... like that one Bronson movie, man... you remember that one?"

"Sure... great mountains scenes... I don't remember the title, though. I sure hope it's easy, like you say."

"You're going to be riding in style, *amigo*, a piece of cake. But just in case any trouble does come along, I have a departing gift

for you. In lieu of full payment of my bill, which I certainly will
take care of some day in the near future, I'd like to give you
something. Something I've had in my possession for a while;
something you might need if you're going to ride the rails."

He pops open the glove compartment and hauls out a set of
brass knuckles: a thick, heavy piece with a thick, metal plate fastened to the top that's rounded to conform to the back of your
hand. "Here compadre, these are for you," he says, sly smile on
his face.

"Thanks, man, Jesus... these babies look wicked. What's this
plate on them for, to protect your hand?"

His eyes have a wicked glint: "Put them on *pachuco*, put them
on, I'll show you something cool."

I slide the heavy loops over my fingers.

"See that little button on the side there, by your thumb," Ted
says.

"Yeah..."

"Slide it back and push it up."

I slide the little button back and a pointed, razor sharp, carbon
steel blade clicks out from under the plate.

"These are fucking cool, Ted, where did you get these babies?"

"In my travels, man, in my travels. Now it's your turn to travel
and you need them. I call them the Hammer of Truth."

"'Nuf said. Thanks a lot, buddy, you came through for me.
Now how do I get this blade back in?"

"You gotta push the button back, then force the blade in. Push
it against something hard, it'll catch and lock back in."

"Like what?"

"Like the heel of your shoe or something."

"I'm wearing tennis shoes, Ted. How about the floor of your car?"

"That'll put a hole in my carpet, man."

"Over here by the door, nobody will see the hole."

I press the blade against the floor of the car and it snaps nicely
back into place.

I get out of the car, grab my duffel, throw it over my shoulder, toss in the knucks and say one last *adios muchacho*. Ted reaches his hand out the car window and we do the clasped-hand handshake that hipsters use. The People's Handshake, Freak Power... Solidarity... or whatever the hell it means. Jailbirds call it the prison handshake....

He says *adios* and drives off, turning up the radio and bobbing his head to whatever song it is. I maneuver through the hole in the fence, walk quickly across several sets of tracks until I'm alongside the first train that's facing out of the yard—at least my impression of out.

I walk along until I find an open boxcar and crawl inside. Going anyplace seems better than hanging around.

I sit there for and hour, alone in the dark, sweaty box. We don't move. Then I spot another train, a few tracks over, moving slowly in the direction that I want to go—away. I jump out and run over towards a fading, orange, Southern Pacific boxcar. I hop on, bounce up and roll inside.

First thing that hits me is the diseased, gravelly laugh, then the smell.

Wino-looking dude in a dirty green cotton jacket and a pair of blue jeans is sitting in the dark corner of the car, cigarette dangling from his swollen lips.

Dude starts laughing so hard he has a coughing spasm. He's so skinny the wind could blow him over. He doesn't even arouse my fight or flight response, which is mighty close to the surface at this point.

He applauds as I right myself and then he takes a long pull from a bottle wrapped in a paper bag. As the alcohol runs through him, his eyes light up for a moment. Then they go dead again and he grins, a gap-toothed grin, hands the bottle over to me.

I thank him, wipe the top with my T-shirt and take a hit.

Shit tastes like anti-freeze. I like it.

My riding partner hasn't shaved in a while and the muscles in the bottom half of his face are damn near slack. When he swallows it looks like his Adam's apple is going to bounce into his mouth.

He shakes a Pall Mall half out of the pack and offers it over to me. I grab it, put it between my lips and he flips over a green military lighter.

"Here's fire," he says.

"Thanks," I say.

The wine and the tobacco drop down into my gut and send a warm poisonous rush to my legs.

"Have another swaller," he says, "looks like you could use it."

"You ain't said shit," I say and take another.

I pass the bottle back to him and stare out the car. We're bouncing slowly out of the yard picking up speed and making me feel better.

"Is this the train to Orlando?" I ask, trying not to sound too naive.

"Can't say fer sure," he says. "Won't know fer a while yet."

"When do you find out, there signs or something?"

"Ain't no signs, just tracks: Tracks and dinky ass towns. If we hang a left at the first set of tracks we come to, we're headed up to the Panhandle and then west. If'n we turn left at the second set of tracks we come to, we's headed up to Georgia and beyond, with a lot of stops. Third set heads north, also. We get by them three... and start winding our way through some real pretty country, lakes and rivers... well then, boy; we're on our way to see Mickey and Donald." He hacks up and swallows down a lunger. "Did ya know that Walt Disney was a goddamn pervert?"

"Ah, no... I never heard that one."

"Son of a bitch had opium all over his lungs when he died. Bastard used to smoke the stuff and then jerk off to cartoons of little nekkid kids that he made."

"No shit, eh? I never knew that. I s'pose that's why Donald never wore any pants, eh?"

"You goddamn right," he laughs and coughs.

Bob teaches me a valuable lesson: a steady diet of Mad Dog 20-20 will keep the demons at bay, make them easier to tolerate, anyway. The past gets fuzzy and the future hasn't arrived yet and that's a good place to be. It's kind of like the first month of summer vacation when you were a kid and the summer seemed to stretch out endlessly ahead of you....

School doesn't start until the buzz wears off.

We drink all the way down the line, clickety-clacking past the first and second set of northbound tracks without so much as a slowdown. Bob's got himself a good stash of bottles inside a worn leather satchel stuffed with blankets. A Korean War veteran on disability who likes to ride the rails; he says he has his checks forwarded to him wherever he wakes up after a long ride/binge.

We chug along through gently rolling, green hills. The sun feels warm and healing. Sometimes the smell of onions hangs sweetly in the air. There are farms and ranches and a peaceful, unhurried feeling. The rhythm of the rails the only sound. The horses, the cows—this is the kind of place where once I wanted to live.

After another hour of riding and drinking and bitching, the train starts to slow. I'm pretty shit-faced. Bob and I have become good buddies. Now, we both hate the Veteran's Administration and the Federal Government. Bob hates hippies, too, but not, clean-cut football-player-type guys like me, he says.

"Must be heading north, we're slowin' down for a switch." Bob says. "You can jump off here and wait for an eastbound or you can ride up to Coleman and jump there."

Indecision finds me a willing victim. Inertia wins over and I sit there, stuck to the wood plank floor, as the train switches and heads north.

"Better set back and have yerself another hit of juice, Jimmy. Be a while before we get to Coleman, hour at least." Bob cackles. "They'll have to switch us again there—and you can jump off. Orlando's about sixty miles down the road from Coleman. You gotta take 301 till you hit the turnpike, she'll take ya right there."

"Sixty goddamn miles? How the hell am I gonna get sixty miles fer chrissakes, Bobby, fuckin' walk?"

"If you wait 'til dark ya can jump on one a them 'gators they got up there, they's as big as horses... ride it all the way to Wonderland...."

"Seriously man, are there any cars on those roads?"

"A few, I 'magin. Whole lot of 'em on the turnpike... somebody might pick ya up, if ya get lucky. Shit boy, sixty miles ain't nuthin'."

"If you say so."

I grab the bottle and take another long pull.

What a wonderful world it can be....

By the time I get to Coleman I'm fading. I bid an emotional goodbye to my good buddy Bob and jump off the train. The pack feels like a dead body on my back. Milling railroad workers stare as I cross the tracks and make my way towards town, only fifty yards ahead. I can see a few small buildings and what appears to be a used car lot on opposite corners of a T-shaped intersection. Highway sign reads: North 301. There's an arrow pointing.

The air is soft and birds are chirping. The heat soaks into me and makes me sleepy but I still have a long way to go.

I walk parallel to the tracks until I come to the highway and a small, white general store. I go inside, buy a can of Coca-Cola and a pack of Kools. Then I give back the Kools and get a pack of Marlboros.

One can learn from anybody....

I ask directions and the balding gentleman behind the counter points me in the direction of the arrow on the road sign.

"Couple miles down the road to the turnpike," he says, "but it's a toll road... heck of a time thumbing on that one. Ya might wanna keep on goin' to Wildwood and head east from there on 441. It's about seventy miles to Orlando."

I start down the road in a daze, drunk as ten skunks and feeling nauseous. I hoof up past the used car lot. The up hill walk has me winded so I sit down on the shoulder and light up a Marly, worrying now about the effects of the heat on the contents of my pack. Be a hard time selling forty-five pounds of stuck together mess....

Cars whine by every so often and I stick out my thumb; not really thinking I have a chance in hell for a ride. I start to wonder if there's some deal I could strike with the car dealer back in Coleman, knowing how amenable to "good deals" those bastards can be.

Good sense comes to me from somewhere and I pick up the pack and start walking. I light another smoke as I walk. Every time a car comes by I turn and stick out my thumb.

After about fifteen minutes of sweaty, difficult movement, a brown Ford pick-up truck pulls off the road and stops. Farmer type guy is waving me in.

I shuffle up there, throw the duffel in the bed and jump in.

We ride along for a time and Roland tells me he's on his on his way to visit his kid and take him to Disney World. He tells me how his ex-wife stole the boy and moved to Orlando.

He says you gotta teach yer women "respect," teach 'em that they can't run off and do what they please and leave the one who loves them and knows what's best for them behind.

Next weekend, he says, he's gonna go back over and teach the ol' lady the proper respect. Gonna have his boy watch him and learn what he needs to know about women. See how a man handles things.

My gag reflex starts itching. Alcohol and formaldehyde ooze from my pores in the stifling cab.

Roland sniffs the air like a hound dog.

I put my arm on the window so it's catching air, then slide closer to the door so I can feel the wind on my face.

"I'm getting sick," I say. "I think I'm going to puke. You'll have to pull over."

"Hold on there, boy. Don't ya be ralphing in my truck, ya here? Yer looking mighty green between the gills, son."

He pulls off the road. It's quiet, just the birds and bees.

"Here ya are, now. This'll have ta do ya. Guess ya just can't hold yer liquor, boy."

"I guess you're right. But I appreciate all you've done. Let me give you some money for gas; I've got some in the back, in my pack."

"Y'all don't have to do that. I was glad to have the company till ya'll started turning green."

"No, I insist. Save it for your boy, when you go to Disney World, if you want. Please, I want to."

"Well okay then, as long as you think I got it coming to me...."

I walk to the bed of the truck and reach into the top of the duffel; feel the cool hard brass slide between my fingers.

My loaded fist hidden behind my leg, I walk around to the driver's window.

Roland is looking out at me in all his ignorant glory, oily brown hair falling down on the forehead of a wide, flat face resembling some ungodly cross between a pig and a dog.

He spits tobacco juice on the pavement.

In a trance, I punch him hard in the jaw with the knucks.

His eyes register pain and then go blank for a second but he snaps to faster than I can believe. Anger, pain and fear ripple across his face as his hand slowly moves toward the shifter, as if on a string.

I stare blankly as my thumb drags across the button and the shiny blade jumps out with a dull, metallic click.

I jab, like a cobra snake, at his head. The blade goes in his temple like a hot knife to butter, slurp and all. Warm blood spurts on my arm and everywhere and his body slumps forward into the steering wheel.

The "Hammer of Truth" has rung Roland's bell.

I shove him over and jump in, blood on the seat and my hands. I feel nothing but fear and anger.

"That's for your wife," I say to him, thinking that I did the world another favor, self-worth on the rise.

I drive a couple miles to Wildwood, turn right on 441 and don't stop until I find a dirt road going off between two pastures. I turn and go down about a quarter of a mile, park and roll the crumpled body into the high foliage along the side of the road. I strip off my bloody clothes and throw them on top of Roland. I wipe myself as best I can with one of Bagley's shirts and some water from the duffel. I use another polo shirt on the cab of the truck. Then I get a nice pair of shorts and a blue polo shirt from the pack and put them on. Three more shirts make a nice seat cover. Dude had a lot of shirts.

It gets dark about twenty minutes outside of Orlando. First strip mall I come to with a bar, I pull around back and park.

I go in, wash my hands in the men's room, order a Heineken and call Barry from the payphone. He picks me up in his 280Z.

He can't believe what he's seeing and keeps looking over at me, strangely, all the way to his place.

When I lift out a brick of blow and plop it down on his shiny black counter-top, his look changes to disbelief. Then to wonder and quickly, to paranoid.

We snort up some lines and his look changes to greedy.

Then I lay down the deal: Jack handles the selling out of his bar in Cocoa Beach. Barry will act as courier. Jack never sees me or finds out where the stuff is coming from. He's to think that it's from a bignuts from Colorado, a guy with guns and muscle.

Barry ponders for a moment and says no. Hears the price I'm asking and changes his mind. He can kick up the numbers; throw in some cut, and make a killing. He and I both know that Jack can move weight. The amount of powder the disco ducks put up their noses is truly phenomenal.

Chapter Thirteen

On to the Next

I hunker down with Barry and everything goes well until the third day I'm there. That's when I run across a story in the *Orlando Sentinel* about a van, registered to one Daniel Victor Bagley from Colorado, that's been found on the beach near Yankeetown, with a severely injured young woman inside. A woman, seemingly, in possession of a gun that authorities suspect was used in the shooting death of a local constable. Fingerprint evidence yet to return from state lab. Head trauma has evidently given Dorothy Lanigan Kinnison amnesia, as she claims no knowledge or memory of anything from the previous two weeks.

I'm glad that the poor girl is alive and even gladder that she can't remember anything. I cross myself, a new habit I'm picking up.

I spend the next two days destroying the newspapers and

turning off TV news to keep Barry from putting two and two together. I might enjoy bashing in Jack's skull and feeding his medulla oblongata to the sharks—if I had to—but taking Barry out would be tough.

After that, things go by pretty smoothly, the only hitch coming after I've socked away my first hundred grand.

Giddy with greed, Barry and I start partying and don't stop for forty-eight hours. Sunday morning, depression and loneliness hits me so bad that I'm suicidal. Wishing I could cry but unable to, I almost call Carole on the phone and ask her to join me. A voice in my head never stops harping that it's a big mistake and for some reason I listen.

I wait out the pain and vow to stop doing cocaine, altogether. It's a rotten, horrible drug—and far too expensive. Now that I have money, I have to learn to manage my funds wisely. It's just not good business to consume your own product.

Sixteen days go by and I have nearly three hundred thousand dollars and some new clothes packed inside an Italian leather suitcase. I also have a deep-seeded need to get far away from Florida and lay low for a while. Go someplace unobtrusive and not too crowded.

I bid Barry adieu and board a flight at the Orlando airport. Destination: my new life. A few hours later, we touch down and I realize that it's Halloween night—October 31, 1979—two months until the new decade arrives.

I take a cab from the airport into downtown Madison, Wisconsin and get a room at a Best Western. I have steak, shrimp and vodka gimlets in the dining room and then go back up to my room for a shower.

By the time I towel off, dress and look out the window at the street, it's full of revelers, revelers in costume.

There's somebody dressed as a stovepipe. There are two "Wild and Crazy Guys" ala Steve Martin and Dan Akroyd of Saturday

Night Live. Frankenstein, Dracula, the Wolfman... they're all there, along with just about every other creature one can imagine.

State Street is filled with party animals and I believe that I'll fit right in.

I go into the bathroom and admire *my* new costume in the steamy mirror.

The short-cropped, dyed-blonde hair looks good; my clean-shaven face the same. The gray Armani suit looks fantastic with the white, Van Heusen shirt and the hundred-dollar silk tie. The Cuban cigar, the rimless, tinted eyeglasses and the Rolex watch complete the picture quite nicely.

I'm ready to ring in the eighties...

Praise the Sky Pilot.

ALSO by Thomas Sparrow -

Northwoods Pulp -

Four Tales of Crime and Weirdness

Including the much-acclaimed volume one of the Northwoods Noir Trilogy, "Social Climbing."

"In the spirit of true pulp... an utter joy... downright good reading."
- Ripsaw News

... great hard-boiled writing..."
- Northland Reader

"Northwoods Pulp is like a peepshow curtain pulled back.
You don't want to look, but you can't help it."
- Jim O'Neill, The Paper, Grand Rapids, MI

"Four tales of the coldest North American states... crammed with hard
men, hard language, snow and speed... low bars, cheap diners,
empty motels, lonesome shacks, and the characters are tough
and quick with their firearms... Sparrow can <u>write</u>..."
- Russell James, SHOTS Magazine, UK

"Sparrow writes from the dark side well. His dialogue, in particular,
sparks with life... (his) pacing is immaculate..."
- Kyle Eller, Murphy McGinnis Newspapers

To order, call 218-724-5806

Northwoods Pulp is available at major online and offline bookstores. Or, order directly from Bluestone Press.

To order, send check or money order for $10, plus $2 postage and handling, to:

Bluestone Press
P.O. Box 3196
Duluth, MN 55803

To order the two-book set of Northwoods Pulp and Fatally Flawed, send $15.95, plus $3 postage and handling.

To order, call 218-724-5806